for Pig
and for Fiddly Mouse and the Leisure Dragon

CONTENTS

Introduction

When putting together this second anthology of *Doctor Who* fiction, I found myself questioning the very quintessence of the short story. '*Short*,' I thought to myself. '*Story*…' At last, it came to me. I finally had that elusive theme I had longed for to tie the collection together. *More Short Trips* would be full of *even more stories* of differing degrees of shortness. The marketing department was thrilled, and the concept was so ground-breaking, I was able to assemble a fantastic bunch of talent. Go on, look at the names on the back cover again. It's not a bad line up, is it?

Ho-hum. This introduction seems like I feel, somewhat tired and hysterical. Well, it's November 1998, and on the 23rd – that illustrious date – I pass on the baton of full-time *Doctor Who* editor not simply to a successor but to a relay team's worth of people working on different aspects of the whole. Somewhat vaingloriously, I'm reminded of Frazer Hines and Wendy Padbury recalling how they couldn't stop mucking around and being emotional during *The War Games*, once they knew the end was in sight. However, they, of course, were professionals doing a job (albeit one they clearly enjoyed), and I still feel like a child playing in a sweet shop from time to time, even after two years in the role of editor. This has always been more than just a job. It's been two or three jobs! No, no, no, as Ronnie Corbett might say. No, that's not what I really mean at all.

I've been asked a few times what I think the magic of *Doctor Who* to be. When I began in this job, I had a shiny, sparkling answer, carefully rehearsed (I'd probably cribbed it from Gary Gillatt, but it was still quite a good answer). As the months muddled by I lost track of it a bit – began to bluster more, had to grope around for my perspective on the programme. Sometimes I couldn't recall the answer at all, when things got very difficult, and only wise words from others over the years could soothe. '*Doctor Who* is the only prison where time is added on for good behaviour.' 'The BBC is just somewhere we go during the day.' 'Do the best you can, then go out and buy yourself something nice with the money'...

Eventually, I thought perhaps there *was* no magic of *Doctor Who*, only tricks. But just when I feared cynicism at last held me firmly in its languid grip, I realised: it's still a bloody good trick that continues to entertain and occupy such a large and passionate audience, that lingers in the memory for years after it was last performed. And in the end, who needs to understand how the trick works? It stops being magic at all, then, doesn't it?

Skip over this paragraph if you like, I'm going to have to say a few thank yous: to Lucy Campbell, first and foremost; to Mike Tucker for friendship and beers; to Gary Gillatt for being an acceptable face; to Dave Owen for his Jimmy Saville impersonation; to Paul Simpson for his helpful comments and input; to Gary Russell, Alan Barnes and Sue Cowley for their reassuring presence; to Peter, Jon, Justin and too many other authors to name here for their enthusiasm and support, especially those who gave up their time for *Attack of the Mongs*; to Terrance Dicks and Chris Boucher for getting me hooked in the first place; to Steve Roberts and the Restoration Team for a job well done and an ambition achieved; to Lesley Levene for unswerving loyalty and support and to Jac Rayner for invaluable assistance, and for helping me invade the planet Ronnos. Oh, and not really a thank you, but a single word to the swankily reinvented Rebecca Levene... *Zygon!*

By the time you're reading this I'll have been gone for months, sitting beneath different fluorescent lights in a different office, helping to orchestrate other fictional worlds and recalling my time on *Doctor Who* as the most ridiculous, frustrating and engaging period of my life.

Steve Cole
November 1998

MORE SHORT TRIPS

Totem

by Tara Samms

'Lovely eggs, Señora Panstedas, really, really lovely eggs!' He wolfed
down his breakfast, blue eyes shining at her. The morning was barely
breaking through the shutters on the windows by the time his meal
was finished, a rough hunk of bread mopping up any last remnants.
'*Beautiful* eggs.'

She half smiled at the compliment, although she'd heard the same
words every morning these last few months. John was a good man.
Quiet, strange, but undoubtedly good.

Señora Panstedas's husband had disappeared, believed dead, two
years ago; then her son had got sick and died. She'd spent six days
in darkness. The heat from the range in her rough stone farmhouse
kitchen barely lasted a day, and Señora Panstedas had sat motionless
in the cold silence. Until John arrived.

'I want to work,' he had said.

She'd stared at him, a tall handsome man who would have seemed
young and in the prime of life if not for the eyes – grey-blue, empty
eyes, sadder than her own. She had simply stared. He had been
knocking on her door for what seemed like a day.

'I want to work.' Silence. 'Someone in the village told me perhaps
you would be hiring.'

She had screamed at him, shouted abuse, pushed him off her
doorstep. She had cursed the village, cursed him, longing to curse
God but not quite finding the words. He had stood unflinching, eyes
looking into hers, at first blankly and then with some measure of
comprehension.

'I'll just wait over here, shall I?'

She'd shouted some more, then shut herself back into the darkness
of the kitchen. But it had nagged at her, kindled life from her despair,
this strange man on her doorstep.

His hair was long, brown and wavy, and his skin was pale – a
foreigner? His accent was unfamiliar, though each word was

1

carefully pronounced. Then, as now, he'd been wearing a coat of green velvet, a simple white shirt, grey trousers that looked to be of good quality, and brown leather shoes. She'd thought of him all day, until the sun had begun to set, thought of her husband, thought of God. She knew there was more than the dark in the shuttered room but she was fuming, reluctant to admit it to this strange young man who clearly already knew.

Could he still be there? Cautiously, she'd moved to the window and opened a creaking shutter, and gaped. There he was, talking to the chickens pecking around the yard, pulling wildly at weeds from the edge of her field, slinging them over his shoulder into an impossibly neat and ordered pile. Then she'd got angry. How dare he...

When she stormed to the door and flung it open, he'd been leaning on a rake, looking at her very seriously and speaking very fast. 'I know this is presumptuous of me but there's so much to do here and the sooner we start –'

The egg had hit him on the head. He'd stood in front of the bloodied fat orange of the setting sun, his gaze yo-yoing between her eyes and her hand. His finger had whipped up to his forehead and she'd flinched at the sudden movement. But all he did was push a straggling curl of hair away from the sticky trickle of yolk dripping past his eye.

'One egg a day, though preferably two if you can spare them, will suffice as payment for my services. I would prefer to take them orally, once you've cooked them in some way, but I can do that myself if it's a problem for you.'

She'd stared at him open-mouthed, struck by the quiet sincerity in his voice. But the man was smiling now, and so was she, and then she was laughing as much as he was as a warm night began to nestle over the crude stone farmhouse.

She thought of John now far more than she ever thought of her husband and son. It seemed to her that he had come, in some way, to play both roles now; she really felt that. During the days they worked; sometimes together, but usually he would go out alone, digging in the fields or reclaiming land lost to weeds and neglect. He would even go to the market in Funchal for her with sugar beet or some of their chickens, and come back laughing with a little money or some scabbard fish encrusted in salt. He would spin the coins on the table, having carefully opened the shutters just a little to let in a small shaft of sunshine, a tiny spotlight for their escudos to dance in. When the show was over she would take each coin and press it to her heart. He smiled to see her do this, a smile that shone brighter than the coins in their dance.

Five months now. John would often go for long walks when he'd finished work. He seemed to have boundless energy, and she admired him and envied him for it in equal measure. Some nights after dinner they would sit out in the yard and look at the moon.

'It's so bleak,' she had once said. 'It looks like a piece of old bone.' He had turned to her and smiled sadly. 'We must remember, Señora Panstedas, nothing is ever as bleak as first it seems.' And he had gently squeezed her hand.

Ever since she had always thought of John and the moon together.

She knew she must not covet him. He had arrived in her life when she felt that she was worth nothing at all and had made her remarkable. She no longer wore black. The first morning of colour she had been up all night, at first with excitement at what she might wear, then with fear at what John's reaction might be. Disgust, perhaps, that she could so soon abandon her mourning. Or perhaps he would see her in a new light. Could he think of her as woman and not just widow? Perhaps he would think her too old for the outfit, find her appearance improper.

No, never that. Somehow she knew that age had no meaning for John.

As she'd prepared breakfast that day she had trembled, fighting the desire to rush back to her room and revert to her simple, unflattering black smock. She was stupid, she'd insisted to herself, stupid and old and silly even to be wanting to do this. Then the door rattled open, creaking on its huge hinges. She'd dropped the eggs in surprise as John had barged in. He must have been up and out hours before.

'Look!' he'd said with a smile, making the word last for seconds as he held out his hand. Stunned, she'd found herself focusing on a small purple flower.

'First one of spring!' he'd beamed. 'I know its name, I think, but I can't remember since...' He frowned, then laughed. 'I don't *want* to remember!' He'd tucked the flower into her buttonhole, then spun around and slipped into his chair at the table. She'd waited for some reaction to her appearance, holding her breath, but John had remained silent until, suddenly, he'd bounded back up to his feet. 'I don't want to remember anything. Not even how hungry I am. No eggs today, please, Señora Panstedas!' And with that, he had vanished through the door, leaving her wincing as he'd slammed it shut behind him.

So she'd found herself mindlessly tidying the house, choking back tears as she moved from room to room. Ending up in his.

The sun had been low and orange in the sky through John's window. She'd sat on his bed and realised he must have slept on the floor, if anywhere at all, last night – the sheets were untouched. She'd noticed a chewed pencil on the bedside table and a piece of paper covered in sprawling handwriting. She'd traced a finger over the ornate swirls of the words as she'd read:

I feel now I am a totem pole, and my selves are dancing all around me. Or I am a maypole, and as they dance, the ribbons they hold stretch and twist and fray. One is tugging harder than most. Harder and harder.

There had been other pieces of writing on other pieces of paper, but she couldn't read them. She'd brooded over the words, suddenly feeling much calmer. 'My selves...' She'd thought of the people inside her – wife, widow, mother, worker, victim – all dancing round the woman she was. John had brought her into focus.

So she had continued to wear the brighter clothes, and one evening John had looked very hard at her after the day's work. When he'd spoken, his voice had been quiet and urgent.

'It seems to me sometimes that I have spent half my life living and the other half waiting, watching… Half hoping there'd be… resolution.'

She had looked at him the way she often did, with something between a bemused smile and a mildly disapproving frown on her face.

'Keep wearing colour, Señora Panstedas.'

And she had broken down in tears and smiles, and he'd looked uncertainly at her, concerned, and then rushed out to pick another purple flower for her. That night he had made her dinner.

Spring had become summer. Today the sun sat swollen in a sky that seemed more blue than any she could remember, the first blue sky for decades. She went outside into the yard, listened to the crickets and the birds, and wanted to walk. To Machico perhaps, or even to Funchal. Anywhere.

She soon tired of the dirt track leading to town and decided instead to wander through the fields. She paused to gaze at Pico de Facho, its greens and browns enriched in the gold of the sunlight, and then she heard voices.

Of course. John had told her he was clearing the levada of debris from a landslide brought on by the last storm, somewhere round here. Hard, exhausting work, and these last few days he had seemed quieter, withdrawn. She'd heard him pacing his room so many nights, had agonised again and again over whether or not to go into his room and see if he was all right. But at breakfast he had praised her eggs as ever, taken the splintering shovel and pickaxe from the yard and walked off determinedly. She had watched him vanish from sight and now had found him again. But who was he with? The outcrop she was standing on was directly above him. She could see nothing, but she could hear the voices – first John's plaintive tones and then a softer voice, low, dry, tinged with another accent she didn't recognise.

'…this is not an exile!'

'It's futile. A waste.'

'No labour is wasted if it enables progress to be made.' John's voice was punctuated by the scrape of the shovel against rock and mud, lifting, heaving, dropping again. His short gasps of exertion were steamrollered over by the commanding voice of the other man.

'Calluses won't hide the blood on your hands. Let others do the work for you.'

'Why? Why, when I should be doing it myself?'

'You are the champion of –'

'I am the *Doctor*.'

His voice carried strongly through the warm air. She imagined it could carry all the way to Funchal. Then the other man spoke again.

'You can't just –'

'I am the Doctor. No other.'

She lay flat on her front now, holding rough scrub in one hand, a clump of daisies in the other, tears sliding down her face and dropping to the fragrant grass below. She rocked her head with closed eyes, not understanding why the anger, the outrage, in John's voice hurt her so much. He was a doctor. So was she his charge? Was that what all this was about?

'You can't shirk your responsibilities.'

This other man's voice scared her, made her think of her son, her husband, the life she had trudged through.

'I will face them,' John said. 'On my terms.'

'You think you know best?'

'I think it's better not to know at all. Only to hope.'

She scrambled up and stumbled away. Hoping. More words, fiercer ones, floated up from below the ridge, but the sound of the shovel as it scraped into the ground began to cut them up.

'You can't mine me out!'

'But I can keep digging…'

She could hear the sound of the shovel long after the sound of the words had faded.

The moon had joined the sun in the late afternoon sky. When John returned, he was solemn, cowed even, but she felt a new vibrancy about him, an energy, almost like the tingle from the electric generators they were beginning to introduce to the island.

He sighed deeply and held out a clenched fist, slowly unfolding the fingers to reveal a tarnished silver ring in the middle of his palm.

She gasped and held her hand to her mouth. John's eyes were wide and his face grim, but his tone seemed almost light. 'Your husband's?'

She nodded, transfixed by the treasure in his hand.

'I found him out by the levada. Someone must've buried him in the hillside. His body was washed down when the earth crumbled in the storm.'

Now she stared at him. She met his eyes as his words continued to come, soft and measured.

'There's a crack in his skull. I think he was murdered.' He paused. 'I'm so very sorry.'

She moved a hand numbly to the red shawl around her black dress and pulled it away. She fingered the soft material. 'I should see him. For myself.'

He nodded. 'Yes. Yes, you should. And then I'll tell the police.'

She wanted to scream, shout, strike him. 'Why did you have to… How could you…?' she began, but he was distracted by the door creaking in the slight breeze.

'I'm sorry?' he asked, benign but distant, a sad sympathetic smile playing on his lips.

'You dug too deep.' She shook her head as if to stop tears from reaching her eyes. 'You dig too deep, you find secrets.' She almost spat the last words, she couldn't stop herself.

'Perhaps, Señora Panstedas,' John said quietly. 'I'll stop digging, for now. And we can bury our dead.'

He stayed for her husband's funeral but she knew he would soon be leaving. He wasn't the same; he seemed like a caged animal, a cooped-up bird. She felt uncomfortable now to be in the same room as him, it was as if his mind was fidgeting and his body unsure how to express it.

She pictured him as he'd been when the priest had intoned the last rites for her husband, eyes darting all around the tiny graveyard, lingering briefly here and there as if cataloguing every flower among the stones and crosses, filing the information, discarding it, looking for something else, something perhaps just out of view.

Now in the room, in the cool, rough kitchen in the early morning, she had closure and he had his two eggs as usual.

When she came back from visiting the priest, to thank him once again for the dignified service, there was a flower lying on the table in a chink of white sunlight and a pile of coins. There was a letter too, unsigned but full of warmth and charm; it touched her as their conversations had.

Señora Panstedas died a few years later, never learning the truth about her husband's last moments. The Doctor thought of her, sometimes.

Scientific Adviser

by Ian Atkins

The rising-falling noise groaned out across a London still half asleep.

It was the only noise.

Even the manhole cover, smashed into the air by a metal fist, went tumbling soundlessly down the nearby steps.

Something drew itself up from the opened tunnel, sliding into the daylight like an insect from rotten wood. A powerful silver body shone bright in the sun. Then a second figure clawed its way into the world.

Another manhole cover flew into the air. Then another.

Eight of the creatures took up position at the top of the steps. Their features were cast into metal masks, teardrop indentations denoting eyes, black slits functioning as mouths.

The eight moved as one, their metal legs striding forward with powerful momentum. Weapons were shifted into position. The leading figure reached the steps. A silver foot swung downwards –

– And missed the step, twisting.

'Whoahhhh – help!'

The giant overbalanced and bumped down on its rear. A handle detached from the side of its head. One of the figure's shining colleagues snorted with laughter, while others looked blindly around.

'Cut! Cut, you idiots!'

Lloyd Kingsley-Sayle hurried up to the fallen figure from where he'd been watching the monitors.

'Daniel! What is *wrong* with you?'

'I said these eye holes were useless!'

Lloyd turned on the cast and crew around him.

'Someone get this… this *idiot*… patched up. Quickly, people! You *know* we're behind schedule! And will someone stop the generator making that damned noise!'

Lloyd stomped back to his canvas-backed chair. He sat.

'Excuse me, are you the… "producer"… here?'

He looked at the stranger who stood fidgeting over him. 'What does it say on the chair, friend?'

The newcomer reached behind Lloyd. There was the sound of ripping and then Lloyd was given the paper that had been taped across the canvas. There was one word on it, crudely written.

Lloyd's eyes widened. He gestured around him, snapping his fingers.

'Julia! Julia! Find who wrote… who wrote *this* and sack them now!' A stressed-looking woman came reluctantly over and Lloyd pointed to a young girl who sat reading near them. 'For God's sake, there are children present!'

The child looked up and smiled, but Lloyd was already moving away. The smile passed through the space where he had been. The newcomer caught it instead and returned one of his own, with a green-eyed look that twinkled like a star. Then he, too, was gone, hurrying after Lloyd, short legs skipping in haste.

'So you *are* Mr Kingsley-Sayle? I'm delighted to meet you. My name's Smith. John Smith. How do you do?'

'Smith?'

'Your new scientific adviser, of course!'

'Smith?'

Lloyd could only look at the man's clothes in disbelief. This John Smith wore checked trousers, a loose, rumpled shirt with braces under a long frock coat, his hair a thatch of black in which grey was beginning to shine. The bow-tie at his throat was small and creased, giving the appearance of someone who had been out for days and had yet to change.

A wide smile dominated the man's face.

'That's right.'

'Scientific adviser?'

'Yes.'

'Not an actor, then?'

'No. Er, why?'

'Forget it.'

The new scientific adviser nodded towards the steps and the alien receiving first aid at the hands of the prop department. His hands knitted across his chest and a thoughtful frown accompanied his quiet question: 'Having problems with the invasion, then?'

Lloyd sighed. 'You could say that.'

'And, er, why are they coming out of the sewers?'

'Common knowledge: that's how the invasion started.'

'No, no, no. My dear fellow, that's a common *misconception*. After all, think about it. How *could* they? The sewers under London are Victorian – notoriously unstable, collapsing all the time. And it would be easy to put opposition in there. If they'd attacked through the sewers, that's where they'd have been fought.'

'Look, Mister, this film is being marketed as being more realistic than the *real* invasion.'

'Of course, that's why I'm here!'

'My reputation is on the line. I've got to deliver it straight, and people *remember* them coming up from under the ground, OK?'

John Smith nodded and lifted placating hands.

'Ah, yes, but memory's so unreliable, isn't it? What *really* happened was that they attacked through the main water-pipes. They didn't need air, so that wasn't a problem, and you couldn't fight them until they were out in the open.'

'Yeah...' Lloyd thought about it a moment, calmed down a little. 'Yeah, that makes sense.'

The newcomer shrugged and smiled.

Lloyd frowned. 'So how do you know this? You couldn't have been much more than a kid when it happened...'

'Ah yes. Well, let's just say that I'm older than I look.'

Lloyd believed him. Couldn't say why, or how, just...

'Julia! Change of plan! Get me the design team right now!'

In the darkness, tiny lights were glittering.

The noise of the chamber was barely more than the heartbeat of something dreaming. Power pulsed lazily through dormant systems.

And then there was a change.

A zero became a one. And then another, and another. Dividing and

11

spreading. Data fed into waking, hungry computers screaming for input. Strategy machines hummed into life.

'Schematic request: London water-supply systems.'

The pause was the time it took for a satellite to come into position; scan the city below; eliminate needless data; appraise what remained.

'Assess strategic value of city invasion based on infiltration through water-supply system.'

The answer came in an instant.

'Calculations improve on previous evaluations by 14.2 per cent. Insufficient improvement to commit resources.'

New data channels opened.

'Store water-supply strategy proposal for future action.'

'So there you are, Doctor.'

The Doctor had hurried into the restaurant, dodging chairs, tables and customers in a comical dance of avoidance.

'My dear Alistair, I'm *so* sorry to have kept you waiting. Do you know, I lost all track of time!'

'Is that supposed to be funny, Doctor?'

'I assure you, Brig–'

'Doctor, please!'

'Hmm?'

The Brigadier was glancing around pointedly, all eyebrows and steely looks, taking in the people near them.

'Oh, yes…' The Doctor tapped his nose and nodded with concentration. 'Yes, of course.' He leaned towards his companion. 'I say, isn't it exciting?'

'Quite…' The Brigadier coughed in resignation, thrusting a napkin into his collar. He ordered when a waiter came into earshot, then didn't speak again until the young man had moved away.

'So how's the movie business, Doctor?'

'Oh, *very* interesting. I'm enjoying myself.'

'Yes, well, don't forget it's not entirely about your enjoyment.'

'Brigadier, Brigadier…' The Doctor floundered. 'I haven't forgotten UNIT's interests for a moment!'

The Brigadier winced. 'Dashed annoying business,' he grumbled, reversing the cutlery setting, and then putting it straight. 'We should have been allowed to have the damned thing stopped outright.'

'And for how many days would that have gone unnoticed?' the Doctor asked carefully. 'The invasion happened. Nowadays no one remembers it exactly how *we* know it happened, but *enough* remember *something* to start getting suspicious if the film were stopped.'

'I've never trusted disinformation as a means of defence.'

'Well, of course,' the Doctor agreed. 'What better than a gun in your hand, a grenade in your pocket and more explosions than you can shake a swagger stick at, hmm?'

The Brigadier sighed. 'If we *could* keep to the matter at hand?'

'Eh? Oh. Oh, yes, well.' The Doctor leaned his head back to feel the breeze from the fans whirling like helicopter blades above their heads. 'I've already talked them out of any reference to the sewers. So a lot of our adventure is already part of a different history. And thank heavens they never got hold of the name of the Cy–'

'Careful, Doctor,' the Brigadier warned. 'Probably best not to use that word in public.'

'Oh, don't worry. Well... apparently, London was invaded back then by the Zexians.'

'The *Zexians*?'

'Well, I convinced them that no one knew what the invaders were really called. In lieu of that, they wanted a name with "z"s and "x"s in it. It's traditional in such matters, apparently.'

The Brigadier shook his head.

'And anyway, I should soon be finished. Apart from the sewers, there are only a few other matters that need to be –' The Doctor coughed theatrically. Heads turned. 'Diverted.'

'Doctor, please!'

The two friends looked at each other. A shadow of suspicion deepened across the old soldier's face. 'You aren't having any trouble with this, are you?' He watched a shifty expression ghost across the features before him. 'I've known you too long, Doctor... You may change your face without much more than a how-d'you-do, but you don't change what's inside. And you don't like this, do you?'

The Doctor innocently met the Brigadier's eyes. 'Telling lies to people who have a right to the truth? Now why should you think that?'

'I wonder…' the Brigadier commented drily.

The Doctor sighed. 'Well, I must confess that some things have left more pleasant tastes in the mouth, but that doesn't mean to say I don't understand what's at stake. If telling lies is what I have to do to keep UNIT a secret, then that's what I'll do.'

'I'm glad to hear it.'

'Besides,' the Doctor added, working hard to maintain the innocent expression on his face, 'there are all sorts of things here to keep me interested.'

London. Long ago. I am watching an air raid, the skies dark, propped up over the city by bright white beams. Flashes like lightning draw sharp-edged buildings across the skyline, there for a moment and then gone.

These are… These are *not* my memories.

This is not who I am.

'Ah,' the Doctor breathed. 'Hello again. Am I too early?'

The set was a mass of structural ghosts in the gloom. It made the Doctor uneasy as his footsteps echoed round the near-deserted room. He looked at the inactive cameras, their heads bowed unseeing towards the floor, and could not shake the feeling of being watched.

The little girl sat behind it all. She looked up, then turned a page in her book.

'Daddy's ordered a break while they get the smoke levels right.'

'I see.'

Two men wandered amongst a constructed control room – all flashing lights and elaborate displays – spreading clouds of fog from devices in their hands. The Doctor found himself thinking of another time in London, deep below the streets.

'Well, anyway,' he said, brighter than necessary as he tugged his mind back into the present, 'how do you do? I'm John, your father's scientific adviser.'

'I know.'

'Oh. And you are?'

'I'm Kate. But you might as well call me "brat", "missy" or "precious". Everyone else does. They think I don't hear them.'

'No, no, I'm sure "Kate" will do. How old are you, Kate?'

'I'm seven. How old are you?'

'Oh, er… Quite a lot older than that, I should think.'

Someone pushed through the double-doors at the back of the set, nodded to the Doctor, ignored Kate, and began changing the viewfinder on a camera.

'I expect this must all be very exciting for you?'

Someone on the set gave a derisive laugh, but the Doctor wasn't quick enough to see who it was. Kate sighed.

'It used to be. But I spend every holiday here and every weekend and I really think I've seen *all* there is to see.'

There was an echo across the set; the girl's words being mimicked. Again, the Doctor looked around to find the source. More people had returned to the set. It could have been anyone.

'What about you, John? Have *you* seen this before?'

'Oh, er, no. Not really.'

There was an appeal in the girl's eyes as she folded the book away and gestured to the space beside her. 'Well, you could stay here if you like and I could tell you all about it.'

'Thank you,' the Doctor said with a dignified bow. 'I'd be delighted.'

Kate giggled, and the Doctor found himself giggling too.

They announced a break after one of the Zexian invaders fainted with heat exhaustion.

As the Doctor left, he saw Lloyd crouched next to his daughter, deep in a whispered conversation.

Half-way to the exit, a voice called after him.

'Er… Mr Smith?'

Lloyd had to call again before the Doctor seemed to remember what name he answered to. He turned around with a questioning smile, to find Lloyd hurrying up to him.

'Mr Smith –'

'John, please,' he invited, getting back into character.

'John. I wonder if I might have a word?'

'Hmm?'

'It's about Kate. I gather you two have been getting on.'

'Well, yes, we have, rather.'

'It's just that it's not very easy for her... being here, I mean. But since her mother left, I'm all she's got.'

'Couldn't you... Isn't there someone who might help out?'

The Doctor received a strange look. 'You weren't in this country last year, were you?'

'You might be right there. Why?'

'The kidnapping... You didn't hear?'

'Ah... No.'

'She was gone almost a week. I blame myself: if I hadn't left her with the stupid school, then...' Lloyd shook himself out of his introspection. 'It's not happening again.'

'If you don't mind me asking, what did they want?'

'We never found out. Police found her wandering along a motorway in Shropshire, not remembering a thing. But it was money. Bound to be. Since they've started making big films in Britain, it happens more than you'd think. Most times the press don't hear a thing and it's resolved without publicity.'

'I take it there *was* publicity in this case?'

'Oh, yes.' Lloyd shuddered. 'Anyway, John, the thing is, you seem to be very good with Kate. I really wanted to thank you. Forgive me, I don't mean to insult you – but you seem to be on her level.'

'I think you'd be surprised at just what her level is.'

Lloyd avoided the Doctor's gaze to stare at the set and his daughter, tiny-big before it.

'I'd just be grateful if you could keep an eye on her for me. She likes you, and there's not many people I can say that about, believe me. I know you're being paid as the scientific adviser here, so I'm probably insulting you if I ask –'

'I quite understand. It would be an honour. And...'

'What is it?'

'Well, I don't suppose I could have one of those nice folding chairs, could I?'

* * *

16

As Joshua Sullivan lunged for the destruct switch, Tobias Vaughn stepped out from behind the control room's central display screen. There was a Zexian weapon in his hand. Sullivan stopped dead.

'The enterprising Joshua Sullivan. Well, well…'

'You're never going to get away with this, Vaughn.'

'Oh dear. I expected rather better than that from you.'

The huge shapes of the robotic Zexians entered, the lights of the control room reflecting in the blank masks of their faces. Emotionlessly, they stared at Joshua. Their weapons were raised, along with Vaughn's own. Everywhere Joshua looked, the muzzles of laser weapons covered him.

'You're betraying your own kind, Vaughn!'

Vaughn laughed, stroking at his chest, in which metallic fragments shone. 'Since the Zexians implanted their technology into me, I am more like them than like you!'

'You can't do this!'

'You are too late! In an hour, the Earth kinetic computer's car –' Vaughn stumbled over the words. 'The Earth computer's ko – No. Hold on. I can do this. The Earth's chronological controls. The Earth *computer's* kinetic chronological controls… Er.'

'Cut!' Lloyd Kingsley-Sayle sagged away from behind the cameras and swore to himself, before signalling to the crew. 'OK, start again. And Michael, get it right this time!'

As the display on the clapperboard changed take twenty-nine into thirty, the Doctor sat beside Kate, carefully braiding her hair for her. He knew the words off by heart now.

'Um. Er, Lloyd?' he called with reluctance.

The eyes that met his call were shot through with impatience. It seemed he was being watched from all over the set.

'Yes, John?'

'I was just wondering why it mattered so much if Michael here – I mean, Tobias – had to say "Earth computer's kinetic chronological controls". It not only sounds silly but it's woefully inaccurate.'

'You have a better suggestion? One you couldn't have made sooner?'

The hostile looks the Doctor was receiving brought a nervous

17

smile to his face. 'Well, sometimes it takes a little while for these things to filter through,' he said. 'It's just that the Zexians would have been a lot better off using a phased Tachyon technology in the first place... and maybe that's a little easier to say?'

'Phased Tecy... Phased Tachyon technology, oh yes, I can manage that, Lloyd.' Michael beamed at his director.

'All right, all right. Sarah, make the change in the script. OK, people, let's go again.'

New information crept into the strategy systems. Fingers of light stretched through displays and indicators, flexing with life.

'Schematic request: phased Tachyon technology research.'

The systems became dark.

'Schematic not present.'

'Evaluate implications of phased Tachyon technology, utilising previous references to subjects. Extrapolate schematic from implied and located data.'

'New schematic completed. Phased Tachyon technology evaluated.'

'Assess strategic value of city invasion based on infiltration through water-supply system for units equipped with phased Tachyon technology.'

'Calculations improve on previous evaluations by 41 per cent. Recent improvements calculated against time of improvements indicate potential of further data collection.'

'Store new schematics in priority channels. Continue collection.'

Human eyes have never seen this. Human bodies would not withstand being here. It is only through the metal of my skin and the protection of my systems that I survive.

The eight moons of Thera Secaul rise and fall over a ravaged, airless world, as if juggled by something just beyond the horizon. One of the moons has an atmosphere and is ghostly in the skies. Another is ice and slices sunlight across this world like a diamond. Two spin around themselves like twins unable to let each other go.

The dead Secaul sands are thrown by seismic rage into the skies, expanding into bouquets of colour.

They are beautiful.

Human eyes have never seen this.

These are not my memories. This is not who I am.

The set's huge lights came on as the Doctor arrived, making him blink uncomfortably as he approached his chair. Two of the crew were exchanging reminiscences and their words reached the Doctor as he passed.

'Don't you remember Winters doing that party trick – all the FA Cup players back to 1952?'

'I remember *Jordan* doing it. Mind like a steel trap.'

'Jordan? You sure?'

Kate was already there, staring unseeing across an open book, Lloyd's attempts at conversation going unheard beside her.

'Good morning, my dear!'

There was no response. The Doctor's smile faltered. He produced a paper bag from his pocket. 'Anyone for a gobstopper?'

Lloyd stood up, failed to meet the Doctor's eye. 'Maybe you could have a word,' he muttered, then moved away.

The Doctor heard him moments later, clapping his hands and shouting orders, and the noise seemed unwelcome in the brooding silence of the set.

'Are you all right, Kate?' the Doctor asked.

The girl nodded, still gazing across the book.

'Gobstopper?'

The girl shook her head.

The Doctor opened his mouth to speak, then closed it again. He fumbled through his coat pockets, but nothing he could find seemed appropriate. He gave a sad exhalation and edged his chair just a little closer.

'I'm sorry, but I just don't understand.'

'Oh, Michael, what is it now?'

The Doctor's head lifted as he focused on the latest argument. He shot a glance at Kate, but she was still staring into the middle distance.

The book had been on the same page ever since he had arrived.

'Well, Lloyd, this Tobias Vaughn. I don't understand why he would do this.'

'Do what?'

'Betray his world, be responsible for all this death and destruction. Why? I mean, what's my motivation here?'

Lloyd looked up the heavens, and then to the Doctor, who gave a nervous start as he realised that the rest of the crew were now staring at him too.

'Oh, er, yes?'

'John, maybe you can help?'

'Oh, I really don't –'

'I know, I know, science is your thing, but as the one man on this set who seems to give a damn about *quality* –'

The Doctor flushed and interrupted him hastily. 'Oh, motivation, yes… Well, I don't think anyone can be a lot of help there, you know. Tobias Vaughn was an unstable, sadistic megalomaniac, crazed with ambition. There's no real explanation for it.'

'That's it?' the actor reacted in outrage. 'No childhood bullying, no –'

The Doctor flapped out his hands in a calming gesture. 'Oh, perhaps, perhaps, but I really feel you're missing the point!' He became calmer, more confidential, as if inviting them to mull over his words. 'Vaughn's obsessions got in the way, if you think about it, didn't they? He was one of those "big picture" people, you see. Now, if he'd been more focused… Say, driven by a personal bereavement or personal sense of loss. Now that's a very different kettle of fish.'

'I see…' The actor nodded, realisation spreading across his face with increasing enthusiasm. 'Yes. That makes sense. I see. Bereavement. Yes, now if somehow my wife had been killed and my only way for revenge was to unite with these monsters… Hmm… I wonder, could we get some lines in to that effect, Lloyd?'

'Well…'

'I'd feel so much happier. Give you *real* quality.'

'Instead of real heartburn? It's got to be worth it,' said Lloyd. 'Julia! Make it happen!'

* * *

The lights were being shut down as the Doctor yawned and rose from his seat. He extended a hand towards Kate and waggled his fingers at her.

'Are you coming, my dear?' He frowned. 'Kate? You'll be left in the dark.'

'Don't mind the dark.'

'Well, if you're sure.' The Doctor stepped deliberately away, his footsteps resounding on the concrete.

'Have you ever had an operation?'

He stopped and turned at the words. 'Oh, is that what this is all about?' he asked. 'Oh, yes. All sorts.'

'What about a ton... a tonsil...?'

'A tonsillectomy? No, but I know lots of people who have. It's nothing to worry about, and when you wake up there's all the ice cream you can eat.'

'I'm scared.'

'Scared? Oh, but there's no need for that, no, no.' He took her hand and patted it. 'You mustn't be scared, really.'

Kate bit her lip and nodded. The Doctor could see tears, sparkling in her eyes.

'Come now, let's see a smile. Everything will be lovely.'

'I wish you could be there with me.'

The Doctor's face fell. He stumbled over words. His fingers stretched his collar as if he had become suddenly hot. 'Ah, well...' he began, and tailed off. Then he smiled. 'Here, you take this. Keep it with you during the operation and then I *will* be with you, won't I, sort of?'

Kate took the offered object, and a smile blossomed amongst tear tracks. Then she took the Doctor's hand and let him lead her away.

In her other hand she held a spotted bow-tie.

'Data file request: psychological assessment of all potential agents. Compare with master file 7243-8-28032-2-5 Vaughn. Reject all files where psychological assessment is below master file level of motivation.'

The systems scanned through thousands, people flashing into

existence for a moment, there and then forgotten.

Some were retained.

'Ninety-eight agents found with sufficient motivational factors. Eight agents exceed set psychological thresholds by factor greater than twelve.'

'Incorporate highest candidate in stored city invasion schematic. Reassess success probability.'

The person was plucked from data records and woven into new plans as a vital link. Numbers moved around them.

'Calculations improve on previous evaluations by 77.8 per cent. Store new schematics in priority channels. Continue collection.'

No!

Planet 14 explodes around me in the final seconds of my life. The power of the planet has been used against us and there will be no escape.

This *cannot* be who I am, for I am living and yet all I can remember is ending.

Our homeworld's power is drawn away from us. I can feel it leaving me, draining out of my memory cells so that nothing remains but a numb darkness.

I can experience a thousand remembered deaths. But none of them is mine. This *cannot* be.

I have been floating in space for nearly a hundred years. All that time I can perceive the gravitational fields drawing me towards this system's sun as if I were on an unbreakable thread. The end, when it comes, is of radiation merging flesh and metal into a fleeting comet of vapour.

These are *not* my memories. This is *not* who I am.

'Er, Mr Smith? John?'

'No…' Kate's face creased in an effort of patience. 'No, silly. Put your hands out like *this*.'

John Smith nodded enthusiastically. 'Ah, yes, now I see.' He beamed as he offered his hands and she bound them with thin wool. The red lines criss-crossed in a simple pattern.

'Now you –'

'Don't worry.' Smith winked. 'I think I'm with you.'

Kate was not sure what happened next. The hands before her moved several times and then the pattern had become something complex and fascinating. She tried to follow the threads with her fingers, but they never seemed to go where they should.

She stared up with new respect. 'How did you do that?'

'Oh, one picks these things up. Here, lift your hands.'

In a moment the pattern was transferred. Kate backed away as if she held a spider's web and a breath would destroy it. Only then did the adviser look up at the insistent calling of his name.

'Oh goodness, I'm so sorry. Did you mean me?'

'If you wouldn't mind?'

Lloyd stood surrounded by extras in militaristic uniforms brandishing weapons. The diminutive figure of the film's scientific adviser hurried over, coat-tails flapping behind him.

But Kate was too fascinated with the gossamer construction at her fingertips to pay much attention.

The sun was sinking behind the London skyline as the Doctor emerged from Leicester Square tube station. He hurried past some energetic buskers, barely pausing to throw away a handful of the 'spending money' he had been given.

He approached a public telephone with trepidation, frowning short-sightedly at the diagrams for use, then sighing as he scratched his head.

A few moments with the sonic screwdriver and he had a ringing tone.

'Lethbridge-Stewart.'

'Ah, Brigadier!'

'Is that you, Doctor? Everything all right?'

'Oh, yes. All sorts of fun today. We've been doing some crowd scenes.' He pronounced the last words with pride at his mastery of the jargon.

'I see.'

'Yes, I saw how UNIT might look battling the Zexians – terribly exciting. All sorts of bangs and flashes.'

'What? You sanctioned –'

'Oh, don't worry. I made sure that it wasn't *seen* to be UNIT.'

'I should hope so, Doctor. That *is* why you're there.'

'Quite. No, no, I explained how a specialised team like UNIT would have been neutralised well before an invasion attempt –'

'How very reassuring.'

'And they were happy to use the normal army in its place. Apparently the costumes are cheaper. Do you know, they were so delighted, I was even offered a part in the final battle –'

'What!'

'Oh, do calm down, Brigadier. The uniform didn't quite fit. Couldn't have a soldier tripping over his turn-ups, could they? Unthinkable…'

'Now, Doctor, let me make this quite clear. You are on a mission to misinform. That's hardly going to happen if you appear in the blessed footage!'

The Doctor looked mournfully at the silent receiver in his hand and then carefully replaced it. The expression stayed on his face as he turned towards Leicester Square.

And then changed completely as he slipped a recorder out of his pocket and advanced meaningfully on the buskers.

The systems awoke, considered the new data and then accessed long-dormant areas of storage with an electronic excitement.

'Load schematic of London invasion. Reassess probability of success if encountered Earth military are not familiar with invasion force.'

Power moved into computers not used since the installation began life. Numbers were formed, reduced, formed and reduced, tumbling through themselves in a cascade of information.

'Calculations improve on previous evaluations by 94.1 per cent. Improvement to evaluations require prioritising of new schematic. Data signal to fleet to be prepared for transmission when 100 per cent value achieved.'

The installation remained lit. Something almost like hope surged through systems in the form of a number growing ever closer to perfection.

* * *

The man's beret rolls down the alley like a hubcap even as the blast has thrown his body smoking into a brick wall.

These are not my memories. This is not who I am.

In a tunnel, the light of a weapon's discharge turns moisture into vapour, and the flesh in the way just disappears.

These are *not* my memories. This is not –

I extend my hand and the muzzle clamped to the back of it sends arcs of power across the space before me. The plastic walls of the corridor blister while the weak organisms before me practically explode.

More obstructions, screaming. Even as my hand slices down with fatal momentum, I can see the schematics directing the blow to its best placing. Bone and skin split and fracture.

Help me. This is not me. This is not who I am!

I walk through fire and brush away the intensity aimed at me. The people beyond the flames start to run but I have fire of my own. Their skins are not as mine, and I watch them peel. The people stumble and fall.

These are not my memories. This is not who I am.

These things are not me. I remember…

The figures stood huddled together, blinded by the glare of retros fired for the final descent, buffeted by the down-blast as dust swirled around them.

'It's the Zexian mothership!'

They exchanged terrified looks as a shadow began to fall across them.

'And… cut! Excellent, everyone.'

When the smoke machines were stopped, the only sound that Lloyd could hear was a gentle tut-tutting behind him.

'Is there a problem, John?'

The little man rocked on his heels and pressed his hands together before him, offering an apologetic smile.

'Well, I hardly dare mention it, but…'

'Yes?'

'I just don't understand why the Zexians would all land in one place. This landing-beacon thing, I mean… Well, it's not very likely, is it?'

Lloyd threw his arms up in the air in disbelief. 'Did our researchers get *nothing* right?'

'They really seem to have got the wrong side of the, er, story. I'm surprised. You see, London was only *one* of the main landing sites.'

'It was?'

'Oh, goodness, yes. The Zexian fleet made more-or-less simultaneous landings with sixty-four ships, evenly dispersed across the globe to enable reliability of communications and to divide resistance. It was a very elegant scheme.'

'So what defeated them?'

'A gold allergy. Yes, their systems are unable to process gold dust, you see. It causes massive short-circuiting.'

'Who found *that* out?' Lloyd protested.

'I really have no idea.'

'And couldn't you have told me sooner? I mean, you have *read* this script, haven't you?'

The Doctor sucked ponderously on a finger and seemed puzzled, as if trying to remember.

Lloyd sighed, and beckoned over an unfortunate script editor. He glared at his scientific adviser. 'Sixty-four ships? Are you sure?'

'Oh, absolutely. It's the minimum required to ensure a multi-rooting low-band-width communications system. Impossible to interrupt, capable of incredible resilience. A practically perfect plan.'

'Schematic request: recent developments on inhibitions to system functioning, reference gold.'

'Gold no longer inhibitive to function since systems refinement 542-4. All units pre-refinement 542 will not be deployed until upgrades can be actioned.'

The response satisfied the strategy machines.

'Update request: regenerate invasion schematic based upon previous data including sixty-four atmosphere-capable module landings including consequent multiple-node communications network.'

The computers began their work even as the first words of the new instructions were fed into them.

An answer finished the calculations; a single neat number.

'Calculations bring improvement on previous evaluations to 100 per cent. New schematic processed through simulation indicates total success of invasion. Prepare to transmit data signal to fleet.'

Power levels fluctuated as the data was passed into equipment that would send the message to the stars. A single warning raised in the strategy processors and action paused.

'Consult resources manager: request number of atmosphere-capable fleet-transport modules.'

The computers took a moment to return the answer.

'Four.'

'We don't have the budget for that many ships!' someone was telling Lloyd.

'Look, if that's how many it took the original Zexian invasion, then damn it, that's how many we're going to use!' he replied.

John Smith was behind him, watching the exchange with interest.

'Well exactly,' he added with a chuckle. 'Imagine having done all this work only to fall at the last fence.'

'Oh, come on,' Lloyd appealed. 'We can cut back on some of the opening effects shots, maybe double up on some of the later work. Surely we can stretch this?'

'Would you excuse me for a while?' Smith suddenly announced. 'There's something I have to do.'

'Projection required: time of resource growth sufficient to action new invasion plan at 100 per cent success rate.'

The response was fed back quickly from strategy units that had already asked the same question.

'At present resource-growth rate, date will not be within the operational life-span of this unit.'

The lighting in the installation dimmed.

'Request action.'

'Unit to become dormant until new data can be processed.'

The lights went out.

* * *

It is dark. It is the darkness of loneliness. There is nothing here.

Is this me?

It is silent. No voices in my head, no memories not my own that still sting my eyes and ears with remembrance.

There are no memories. Is this who I am?

All I have left in the darkness is a word, but it is so long since it has been used that it comes stranger to me than the things I have seen or heard.

The word is Kate.

This is not my name. This is not who I am.

In the darkness of the strategy installation, a hatch fell from the ceiling and clattered to the floor. Dank air from the cave system beyond condensed in the warmth of the small spaceship's interior.

A short figure dropped inside, even as lights and weapons powered up.

'Now, now, let's not do anything hasty,' the Doctor said slowly, raising his hands out before him. 'Yes… Yes, I thought I'd find you here.'

The room seemed to pause all around him. It knew who he was.

'A Cyber-infiltration unit…' he mused, as if viewing an exhibit at a museum. 'I've heard of them but never actually seen one before…'

The Doctor knitted his hands across his chest and peered curiously around him. A picture of Kate shone on one of the displays, and the Doctor's features darkened as he decoded the words 'SURGICAL HISTORY' beneath it. He gingerly reached past a wary sentinel auto-probe and touched a control. The room waited in silence, almost as if gloating, as the Doctor flicked through record after record: sports heroes, politicians, military personnel, more media people.

'My, my,' the Doctor murmured. 'You have been busy.'

'You must be destroyed.'

'Now, I wouldn't do that! I'm not the only person who knows where this place is, you know!'

'You must be destroyed.'

The Doctor relaxed. 'I'm amazed you didn't think anyone would find the implant in the girl's head. You can't see it if you look, I grant you, but if you feel her scalp it's just there under the surface.'

The systems waited on his next words.

'Now here's what we're going to do. When you put that thing into her head, you overwrote areas of her mind with control software and your own memory. You will give me the memories you overwrote and then you will leave Earth.'

'And if this unit does not leave?'

'I only stalled things this long so that I could triangulate the origins of your control signals. It's how I found you. The co-ordinates will be in UNIT's hands before the night is out. I got here in just a few hours – imagine how quickly all those helicopters and planes will arrive!' He looked sternly round at the room. 'You really won't want to be here tomorrow.'

The girl lay unconscious on the operating table. Monitor units displayed her status as staff finished the tonsillectomy.

Shift change.

A new team entered, ushering out the old. Different equipment was wheeled in and activated; sophisticated devices whose function would have baffled the previous team.

A member of the previous team returned: a short man, his eyes twinkling over the top of his mask.

'There's a little further surgery required,' he announced authoritatively.

'Are you the surgeon here?'

'Oh, I wouldn't say that,' he replied airily, checking the patient's hand. It held a strip of spotted material tightly. 'More a sort of doctor…'

Tiny flames leap into the air. Noise becomes *Happy Birthday* sung by the family's off-key choir in different tempos and pitches.

The cake is blue hiding chocolate. Yellow lettering spells *Kate* and *six*.

I remember this.

Mine.

Missing
One: Business as Usual

by Gary Russell

Sally's Café, Edward Street, Brighton, East Sussex
23 July 1991. 14.02.

Detective Inspector Bob Lines of Brighton CID pushed open the door of the tiny café, his well-trained eyes scanning the clientele in a moment. A couple of haulage drivers, at least one known crack dealer they couldn't pin anything on, a couple of tourists...

But his quarry was on her own, to the right of the café. Quite a few years older than when they'd last met, her red curls chopped to a short bob and wearing a set of smart clothes which might have come from a Knightsbridge store but could just as easily have been bought in another galaxy. Her eyes met Bob's and for a brief moment there was a flash of extreme sadness in them. But it passed. And it its place, just a hint of disappointment – not that he was there, but at something else. Being back in Brighton, probably.

'Miss Bush,' he said, sitting opposite her. 'Good to see you again. Must have been at least two years.' He knew damn well. Two years since they had met. Two years since they had been allied with his old friend, the Doctor (the version with the blond curls, the garish clothes and a propensity to shout a lot and look indignant whenever someone proved him wrong). Two years since they had put the affairs of SenéNet to rest.

'Almost to the day, Mr Lines... Although for me it's been – well, quite a few years longer. I only remembered it was my birthday yesterday, Dad's tomorrow. I'd forgotten the importance of birthdays. Time travel does that to you.' She looked up at him with a sudden desperation. 'How are they?'

Bob Lines smiled. He was glad that had been her first question.

31

'They're absolutely fine, both of them. Missing you terribly of course, but they've had a couple of cards, according to your dad. One from New York, I think, last Christmas. He said something about Stalagdons or something.'

'Stalagtrons,' said Mel absently. Then she added: 'They'll get a few more before the turn of the century as well. I was – or will be, or have been – very good at staying in touch whenever I could.' Mel smiled suddenly. 'Who's number one in the charts then?'

'Haven't a clue,' shrugged Lines. 'Thanks, Sal,' he added as two cups of tea were placed on their table. He looked at Mel. 'My shout.' She smiled, gratefully, and he nodded. 'I didn't think the Doctor would have thought to give you any Earth money.'

'I haven't seen him. Not for ages.' She looked down. 'I've no idea where he is. But I want to go home.' She looked up again, the desperation back. 'If you think it'll be all right with them?'

Bob grinned. 'All right? They'll be overjoyed. And so will that American lad who's been living there. He's been helping a couple of my lot out recently. Seems the Doctor was right about those mental powers of his… He's come in quite handy at spotting a liar or two.'

Mel smiled slightly at this. 'Good old Trey. You know, Mr Lines, I've been places and seen people where his powers would seem primitive. Or at the very least common-or-garden.' She sighed. 'I've seen people from all walks of life on Earth mirrored throughout the galaxy. The good, the bad and the downright ugly.' She drank her tea. 'It's the same all over, up there.' She nodded towards the ceiling, but Bob knew she was indicating much higher than that. 'People wanting to hurt each other. Or help each other. Making money, losing money. I thought going off into outer space would take me away from the mundanity of Earth. But the only real difference is that the guns make a louder bang, the clothes are a bit more exotic and some people look like lions or purple turnips.' She finished her tea with a final swig. 'It's a diversion, Mr Lines. That's all. Not an escape, not a new life, just a new twist on the norm. It got boring very quickly. And a lot of good people died.'

For a moment neither of them spoke, then Bob swallowed his tea in one gulp and reached out to touch her hand, to bring her back to reality. 'You want to go home now? I'll run you up there if you like.'

'Are you sure?'

Bob Lines smiled. 'Miss Bush – Melanie. You're a friend of a good friend of mine, and the much-loved and missed daughter of another. It's no bother at all. And I can fill you in on a couple of years' worth of planet Earth history if you want.'

'It's strange to be back.' She realised he was looking at her quizzically, and shrugged apologetically. 'Very strange.'

Bob stood up and so did Mel. 'Any regrets?'

Mel looked at him. Or rather, through him, in that way the Doctor used to. Something to do with time travel, he supposed.

'No, not really. But you know what? I wouldn't do it again. It was an experience, and I did meet a lot of wonderful people, but I'm glad to be home. It's where the heart is.' She crossed to the café door with him. 'Time for Melanie Bush to get back to business as usual.'

Moon Graffiti

by Dave Stone

Kimo Ani made his silent way through the white-walled tunnels – at least, he tried to make his way silently. The clammy soles of feet used to a life of air-sealed membrane made unpleasant sucking sounds and squeaks on the slick polypropylene floor. He was painfully aware of his breathing: a positive and conscious *effort* to haul air into the lungs, the strained and strangely painless thudding of the heart behind them. His extremities were red and grey: they ached and trembled and felt hot and strangely distant. He thought he was having some kind of heart failure.

These were, of course, just the symptoms of chronic hyper-ventilation – the cause of which, in turn, was a terror he had never experienced in his life. 'Terror' was merely one of any number of things Kimo Ani had never truly experienced. The cycles of the Line and its senseless and recursive routine did not allow for any emotional variation and its learned response. Stepping out of Line was akin to falling off some mental precipice and plunging, headlong, into a vertiginous chaos with which the mind could not yet cope.

As the white-walled tunnels seemed to pitch and yaw around him, turned alien and menacing not so much in themselves as in his new relationship to them, Kimo Ani wondered if his mind would *ever* learn to cope. He clutched the Talisman closer to his knotted, aching stomach, and forced himself to carry on. The terror of the Unknown lay before him, but if he gave up now and slunk back to the Line there would be nothing but a commonplace and endless living death.

The Talisman glowed more faintly now than when it had appeared. The light seemed to be retreating, slowly, from its edges and extremities. A kind of reddish, lazily swirling light like a viscous liquid thing in itself pulsed in the slits on its face from which it spoke. And now it spoke again:

'*Look, are we going to be hanging round here all night or* what?' it said in a high, shrill, polyphonic voice. '*This is getting right on my wick and no mistake. Let's just pick the* damn *feet up and have it away on our toes, OK?*'

A warm breeze drifted through the night: dry and chemical-tasting, not so much with an air of toxicity as with the smell of soot, potash and airborne gypsum from some builders' rubble yard. Through the dark tangle of wreckage – a landscape in itself, undulating to the skyline, geographical features built from petrified garbage – fires were burning with a kind of gentle constancy that suggested they had burnt for years, and would burn for years to come.

The wreckscape had a kind of desolate stillness about it – the remote sense one gets on walking through the ruins of some abbey sacked in bloody conflict, centuries ago. Death and destruction on ice.

Peri shivered, despite the warmth and softness of the wind. Seemingly of their own volition, her hands kept picking at her upper arms, nervously twitching and fingering the sleeves of her shirt. She *really* wished that the increasingly malfunctioning TARDIS had been able to supply her with something other than a shirt at least a size too small, obviously intended for an adolescent, made from nylon with a tacky iron-on decal of a heart that was already starting to peel. The lack of anything even remotely more suitable, she recalled bitterly, was only one of the more minor of the symptoms of the problems that had brought them here in the first place.

'You said this was Earth,' she said. 'This isn't Earth. How can this be Earth?'

'You're just subconsciously expecting it to be the world you remember,' the Doctor said, unconcerned. 'The "Earth", as such, doesn't enter into it, except in purely galactographic terms. This is just a place that used to have that name.'

He pulled the door of the TARDIS shut and locked it with a lozenge-like key on a ball-bead chain. He twirled the key a couple of times before letting go, so that it flipped in mid-air and dropped neatly into the pocket of his horrid coat. The gesture seemed a little reminiscent of the studied relaxation of a Frontier gunfighter: casually showing some upstart opponent a little trick he could do in his sleep. Quite whom this upstart opponent was seemed unclear – unless, perhaps, the universe in general.

'We're several tens of thousand years beyond your particular time-frame, Peri,' he continued. 'More than enough to make your own personal dating-system completely and utterly meaningless. Ages, aeons and entire civilisations have come and gone, and never given what you know of *your* world a second thought.'

Peri found herself irritated, not so much by what the Time Lord had said as by his tone, which contrived to suggest that everything she had ever been, or seen, or done had been completely and utterly insignificant and ineffectual, had not affected anything worthwhile for good, or ill, or at all. 'So what are *we* doing here, then?' she asked sourly.

'The old girl needs recalibration.' The Doctor patted the battered outer shell of the TARDIS affectionately, as one might pet some favourite but rather elderly and infirm maiden aunt. 'In the occasional lapses of my post-regenerative state I damaged her rather more than I'd thought, and acquiring a supply of zeiton 7 from Varos was only one of our problems. Several key control systems are still severely disrupted – I believe you've experienced some of the knock-on effects of that yourself of late.'

'If you mean not having had a proper meal in days,' said Peri, 'then you're right.'

Opening the wardrobe in her room to find completely unsuitable clothing had been the least of it. The corridors and chambers around the Console Room had acquired a sudden knack for shifting themselves around when your back was turned, so that you could wander about in them for hours without getting anywhere. The state-of-the-culinary-art utilities in the kitchens had transformed, overnight, into a… *thing* which, when activated, had belched blue smoke and churned its pistons, and had eventually produced a tray of tin-tack sandwiches, a lemon on a plate and a bowl of what had looked and smelled like puréed sprouts with a daffodil stuck in it.

And the less said about the current contents of the swimming pool the better. With that special kind of mild unease that occurs with the glimmerings of a nasty thought, it occurred to her that her irritation with these peripherally irritating things had prevented her from wondering what they meant to the *truly* vital things like interdimensional navigation and the mechanisms that supplied the air…

'Everything I do to fix her merely breaks something else,' the Doctor was saying, 'including her ability to tell if something actually *needs* to be repaired or not – we're stuck in a classic catastrophe of regression. What we need is an external factor that can serve as a benchmark.'

'And we're going to find that here?' Peri said dubiously, scanning the wreckscape around them for absolutely anything that might be of any use. Nothing seemed to fit the bill.

'This is one of the places where the… item I'm looking for has been known to occur. The easiest place to get to, all things considered. We can always remember where it is, no matter what else we might happen to forget.' He became pensive, and looked upwards. 'I just wish it had been a time in which the Earth was in better circumstances.'

Peri followed his gaze. Scudding cloud-cover was tearing itself apart like a sheet of calico caught on a nail; she looked up and saw the full, bright Moon and what had been done to it.

'What are you stopping for now?' snapped the voice from the Talisman, as Kimo Ani backed away from the ladder leading upwards to the Higher levels.

'I can hear a Monitor,' Kimo Ani told it in a hurried whisper – and indeed, from the hatchway above, there could be heard the clanking and whirring of caterpillar treads. The sound did not seem immediately threatening; the Monitor seemed to be merely on patrol – but any loud noise at this point would bring it down upon them.

'*Please* keep quiet,' Kimo Ani hissed urgently. 'Must not make a sound. I will try to find another way.'

'*Well just be quick about it,*' the voice from the Talisman grumbled.

'*Hurry it up. Chop-chop.*'

As Kimo Ani hurried back along the tunnel, looking for some other route upward, it occurred to him with a rush of some not entirely unpleasant feeling that he could not name that he had done something *else* that was new.

Even when the Talisman had appeared before him, with its offers of pleasure and power undreamt of if he did what the Talisman wanted, he had not understood what that meant – he had never dreamt of pleasure or power in the first place. Kimo Ani had quite simply waited until he could act without being seen by the Monitors, then peeled off his protective membranes, taken the Talisman away and headed up towards the Surface, simply because he had been *told* to. Even something so minor as *pleading* with something else – that minuscule and almost entirely ineffectual level of attempting to temper the will of something other than his own – was the most contentious thing he had ever done in his life.

Now, as he crept through the tunnels with the muttering and grumbling Talisman, looking for another way up and doing so simply because something other than himself had told him to, for the first time Kimo Ani found himself wondering precisely *why*…

Peri stared aghast at the markings scrawled across the face of the Moon like magic-marker slashes on a rest-room door. The very shape of them seemed hateful, dripping with an intent to insult and befoul. She had no idea what kind of alien processes or substance had been used in their making, but a nasty little voice in her mind had its suspicions.

'Is that supposed to be some kind of language?' she breathed. 'Is it supposed to *say* something?'

'Well, a reasonably literal translation might be *All-Hominid-Aboriginals-of-This-Place-are-Known-for-Attempting-to-Mate-with-Their-Own-Persons-and-All-Pararachnids-are-Very-Much-Better-than-Same*,' said the Doctor. 'I'll take it as read that you wouldn't be interested in an, as it were, more pithy translation.'

'Pararachnids?' Peri found that she had gone from shivering with unnamed trepidation to positively *shaking* with a hot and almost cripplingly atavistic rage. Defiling something so basic to her world as the Moon seemed like a physical assault, as though someone had actually slapped her. Later, when she was in a fit state to notice such things, she would find that she had clenched her fists hard enough to drive the nails some way into her palms. 'Who are the Pararachnids? Were they the things that did all this?'

The Doctor nodded. 'They're a variation of space-borne swarming organism – though with a difference from the swarming insects and pack-animals indigenous to the Earth. The swarm itself has cohesion and instinct, but no real cumulative intelligence. The individual components of it are self-aware and intelligent, tool-using and hat-wearing after a fashion – in the same way that some vicious human moron with a club and a pork-pie hat is intelligent, tool-using and hat-wearing as compared to a ring-tailed lemur.' His gesture took in the whole expanse of the gently smouldering wreckscape. 'The Pararachnids are basically vandals – they mark their territory by laying it to waste and dragging the wreckage into a big heap. That renders it uninhabitable, of course, even for Pararachnids, and so the swarm moves on.' He shrugged. 'I've always found it one of the more pointless biological processes.'

He regarded the devastation, evaluating the damage critically, as one might observe the particulars of a not particularly interesting new breed of moth under a microscope. 'The Earth was hit by a relatively minor swarm, I'd say. Seventy, eighty billion at the most. They'll be long gone by now, of course, leaving only their weak and their crippled behind.'

Peri tried to imagine the Pararachnid swarm as it fell out of the sky and tore the world to shreds. She failed – the magnitude of it was too much for the mind; it was quite literally unthinkable. 'What about the people?' she managed to ask. 'Are the people dead?'

'In their millions,' said the Doctor, 'if we're merely talking about *human* people as opposed to all other strains of indigenous biological life. Those who didn't die, or were evacuated in sufficient time, were forced underground – not so much of an undertaking as you might think, incidentally. This was one of those periods when the population of the Earth was a mere fraction of that of your time.

People were numbered in the millions rather than the billions.' He shrugged, seemingly completely unconcerned. 'Things could have been worse.'

Peri had to confess to being unsure how. 'This could be stopped. All of this. We could just go back in time to beat the monsters. That's what we *do*, isn't it?'

'No, it isn't,' the Doctor snapped. Then he sighed, as though preparing to explain, once again, to a particularly dense child, that it wasn't such a good idea to wear the underpants outside of the trousers. 'That isn't what we do, and we don't do it here, and we certainly can't do it now. This is one of the key points in the history of the planet – the razing of Earth was the catalyst for a massive rebuilding and expansion in centuries to come. From this mulch will grow a thousand new cities and nations, entire civilisations, some of them inexpressibly beautiful, some unspeakably and brutally draconian, some of them merely indifferent. If we attempt to interfere directly, to rewrite the wrongs of the world here and now, none of that would ever exist.' He stomped through crunching calcine debris that Peri could only hope was some kind of petrified timber or suchlike. 'We've come here looking for a single, specific item and that's all.'

'This "item" again,' Peri said. 'That's the second time you've talked about "an item". Are you ever going to get around to telling me what it actually *is*, or is something like that too big and complicated for my tiny human brain?'

The Time Lord looked at her face, and wisely decided not to answer in the way she fully expected. Instead, he took out a large brass fob watch and absently studied its complicated but strangely hazy and indecipherable face. 'I think we might have time before things make themselves evident. How much do you remember of the cosmology of Event One?'

Ever upwards, up inclines, ramps and shafts inset with cold-cast rungs, occasionally backtracking to avoid the sight and sound of Monitors on patrol. Up through the Higher Levels where nothing human had set foot for years, although perpetual light still burned.

Dust being a product of human habitation, the tunnels remained bare and pristine. Little robotic cleaning mechanisms the size and general shape of spiders, alerted by the presence of Kimo Ani, scuttled from their housings and fought each other viciously for the traces of contamination he left in his wake: the beads of sweat and shed skin cells. After centuries of inactivity they were ravenous to the point of cybernetic madness.

Ever onward, ever upward, ever closer to the final goal – until, at last, he came to the massive armoured butterfly-hatches that he had only ever seen in the historical edu-tapes streamed to him, as had been the nutrients through tubes, when he was small and waiting to be big enough for his induction to the Line itself. Kimo Ani was mentally unequipped to imagine what might lay beyond these shutters. If pressed, he would probably have guessed a network of the same kind of tunnels and shafts beyond as were behind – but the point was that they would be *other* shafts and tunnels, entirely different in a way that he could not define. The basic sense, in short, of some outside, other world.

The shutters were guarded by a pair of Monitors. Their mechanisms seemed different from those which, down below, had overseen the Line – and different from those Kimo Ani had glimpsed as they patrolled the Higher Levels. Their claws were massive and their eyes burned with a light that made the fear Kimo Ani had felt even thus far pale by comparison. Kimo Ani crept behind one of the ducts projecting from the tunnel wall and curled up, making himself as small and quiet as possible while he wondered what to do.

'*Here we go again,*' said the voice from the Talisman loudly. '*I've had just about enough of this. Are you a man or a mouse, boy?*'

Kimo Ani had no idea what a *mouse* was, but he was too busy with other concerns to wonder about it. He desperately clamped his mouth shut as it tried to gibber of its own accord and clutched the Talisman harder, trying to squeeze it into silence.

It responded by emitting an ear-piercing shriek. '*OI! YOU!*' it shouted, in a voice that seemed impossibly loud for one so small. '*YES, YOU! CHUNKY AND CLANKY OVER THERE! GOT SOMETHING NICE OVER HERE, JUST FOR YOU!*'

'Now you just wait until they get a leetle *bit closer…'* it said to Kimo Ani in softer, almost conversational tones. *'Wait until they're almost on us, wait until I tell you – and then you* run, *OK?'*

'So let me get this straight,' Peri said. 'Time Lords, World Meddlers, Eternal Guardians, spectres, ghoulies and a lot of the things that prehistoric people thought of as gods operate on or are merely the visible projections of entities that exist in other *continua* than the four-dimensional *continuum* of Minkowski space…'

'That's a gross oversimplification,' said the Doctor, 'but generally correct.'

'…but the so-called four-dimensional continuum of Minkowski space is actually comprised of *ten* dimensions…'

'At the very least.'

'…the extra six of them spitting off from the other four a fraction of a second after the Big Bang…'

'Spot on,' said the Doctor. 'I've always thought of them – if we take the cyclical view of Time – as the triggering mechanism of the universe as a whole. When the universe collapses back into the singularity of the Gnab Gib – or the Big Crunch, if you prefer – their reunification with space/time as we know it will trigger off a whole new cycle. Until then, basically they're just hanging around as an anomaly roughly one thousandth of the size of a proton. Could be anywhere. Now where was it? I'm sure I had it somewhere…'

To her growing horror, Peri realised that the Time Lord was absently patting his pockets.

'You're going to tell me that you've got it on you somewhere,' she said, 'aren't you?'

'What?' The Doctor, still searching through his patchwork coat, raised his eyebrows in surprise. 'Of course not. That would be completely and utterly ridiculous. If I'd had it *on* me somewhere then we wouldn't have had to come here and… aha!' He finally unearthed the object of his search: a small and battered-looking *livre de poche*, its brittle pages held together between leather-and-pasteboard covers by a selection of stringy rubber bands. 'A small *aide-mémoire*,' he explained, pulling off the bands and leafing gently through the fragile leaves. 'In every incarnation, I try to keep a note of the occasional important thing – little notes to myselves. It's not as if we're all exactly the same *persons*, after all. Hmm...' His voice became absent as he perused the salient information within. 'Street map of Ultima Thule... latitude and longitude of El Dorado... third door on the left past the midden and ask for Joseph of Arimathea... hello, what's this... the *Hand of Omega*?' He glared at the page incredulously. 'There? Really? What must I have been thinking? Oh well, *c'est la guerre*... the Seven Crested Spires of Praxos XIV... Sidcup... the Lost Constellations of the Cool Star Furies... and here, at last, we are. "*Cncrg addit sxth-dim amly ref Mkski Sp.*" I must have been feeling particularly terse and cursive when I wrote that.' He peered at the entry closely and then shut the little book with with a somewhat dusty snap. 'As I suspected, I didn't leave myself much more than a set of temporal and spatial co-ordinates. There's some indeterminate waffle concerning how the truth will eventually emerge, how things will be brought to light, but that, I'm afraid, is rather it. I must admit that other me was far more interested in making an utter fool of himself with his penny whistle than providing explanations.'

Peri quashed the slightly unworthy thought that started with the word *if* and continued with the word *only*. 'So how are we going to find it? Do we just wander around and look for it or what?'

'Not a good idea,' the Doctor said. 'My eyes might be somewhat unique, in a number of respects, but I seriously doubt their ability to distinguish between subatomic particles unassisted. And besides – the problem of the Pararachnids remains. There are several colonies of them still around.'

'I thought you said they'd left only their weak and crippled behind.' Peri had been slightly lulled by the preceding lapse into Doctorial inconsequentiality, but was starting to feel worried again.

'Weak and crippled are relative terms. Those that remained would be quite capable of tearing you limb from limb as soon as look at you.' The Doctor strode towards the remains of a toppled, fluted stone column and, mindless of the liberal coating of ash, sat down on it. 'Our best bet, I think, is simply to wait and see what happens.

Something always does.'

Peri sighed to herself and sat down beside him. It occurred to her that lately their lives had been too hectic simply to stop and look around; to take things in and just generally chat about them. Seen in that light, this could be taken as a small respite, a chance to relax and get to know the man again; to try to find something of the man who, before he'd changed, had been so charming in his boyish way and had inspired trust enough to whisk her out of her existing life and into dangers she had never imagined.

The problem was, in this oven-warm wasteland with the baleful moon graffiti looking down upon her, she simply couldn't think of anything to say…

'*Hat*-wearing?' she said, eventually.

'I beg your pardon?' said the Doctor.

'Hat-wearing. When you were talking about the Pararachnids, you said something about animals who were intelligent, tool-using and hat-wearing…'

'Ah, yes.' The Time Lord settled back, in a physically improbable way that suggested he was lounging in an invisible armchair, and began to expound: 'The wearing of hats is one of the quintessential, landmark factors denoting abstract thought, and an intelligent adaptation to one's environment. Any animal can take shelter from the elements operating purely on instinct – it takes a greater, and quite specific degree of mental sophistication and concept-ualisation to hit upon the idea of carrying said shelter *around*. Additionally, a good hat provides a vast repository of additional information from which one can infer – anything from the wearer's place in the social pecking order to the state of his or her entire culture.'

The Doctor smiled to himself. 'It's no accident that those from a decadent culture or a culture in decline can be spotted by their increasingly ludicrous and complicated hats. I may prepare a small monograph upon the subject for the Royal Society, for the next time we're passing through a timeframe where the Royal Society actually exists…'

Further details of the hypothetical monograph, however, were never known, because it was at this point that the Doctor was cut off in mid-flow by a loud and polyphonic crash. Various items of ruined masonry had fallen in upon themselves to produce a kind of makeshift ramp – or at least, if they hadn't, then the figure clawing his desperate way out of the hole must have been levitating on a slant.

The figure was human, but so ectomorphic that for a moment Peri completely failed to recognise him as such. He was naked, bald and pale to the point of albinoism. As he emerged, Peri saw that he was clutching something to his chest. It glowed through his fingers with a kind of reddish shifting light.

The new arrival ran from the hole, looking back over his shoulder, obviously far more concerned with what might be following him than where he was going. This proved to be rather a mistake; his foot tangled in something and he pitched forward, still clutching the item he held and smashing face first into the rubble. He rose, weak and groaning, to his knees – and caught sight of Peri and the Doctor. He shot to his feet as though galvanised and, with a little squeak of pure terror, ran from them into the ruins.

'Now I have no idea what that was about,' the Doctor said, bounding to his feet in a sudden burst of energy, 'but I'd say it merits further investigation.' He set off in a kind of deceptively rapid dog-trot after the pale man, not bothering to see whether or not Peri was following.

For a moment Peri hesitated, mindful of what the Time Lord had said about the remaining Pararachnids in the wreckage. Then she heard the sound of the things in the hole from which the pale man had come. Mechanical, menacing and above all *approaching* things. Never mind what might be lurking above ground, she really didn't want to face this alone. She set off after the rapidly diminishing Doctorial form.

The general and the specific, Peri thought. The abstract and the concrete. The difference between the two is always waiting there to trip you up. Ruins so extensive that they became a generic landscape were bad in themselves, but having to deal with them up close, in all their particulars, as you clambered over them and under them, was even worse. Shards of broken glass sliced at her bare shins, tangles of wire tore at her arms. Scattered, broken personal items – crockery, the shreds of clothing, things that might or might not have been toys for some long-vanished child – sank hooks into her human heart and scored it.

There were bones, here and there, and the desiccated remains of other, softer things. Nothing moved but to flap and rattle in the wind – but all the while there was the unconscious, unglimpsed impression of spindly things scuttling through the debris, waiting in the dark places to catch you with a claw and pull you down, but always just out of sight…

The Doctor was ahead of her – she despaired of catching him up but never quite lost sight of him and even made up some ground. How much of that was intentional, for all that the fact of her existence seemed to have gone from his head, she couldn't say. Abruptly, he stopped, and completely misjudging the distance between them, Peri almost ran straight into him.

They were on the lip of a shallow incline of loose shale that dipped into what was more or less the wreckscape equivalent of a clearing. At its bottom, the pale man had weakly half-collapsed. He seemed little more than a boy, his skin withered and puckered by chronic malnutrition. Peri saw a collection of ulcerated wounds on his arms, reminiscent of hypodermic track marks but more severe. The boy had obviously been on some kind of multiple, heavy-bore intravenous drip, she thought, for quite some time – maybe even for all his life.

This close, it was possible to make out the object the boy clutched so protectively to him in more detail: a convex disc slightly bigger than a human palm, made of some mirror-bright and faintly golden metal. From it, though it was impossible to be sure, there seemed to project a series of slim and swept-back lateral fins, as though a three-dimensional representation of a child's drawing of the sun had been given a spin.

'Not a particularly prepossessing sort of chap, is he?' said the Doctor. 'Decidedly on the peaky side, I'd say.' He began to slither down the scree. 'You there!' he called to the boy, in the kind of condescending tone that had in the past – and in the future, for that matter – had heavily armed representatives of any local authority wanting to shoot him on sight. 'Stay where you are. I want to talk to you.'

The boy backed away from him with a fear that, Peri thought, was probably innate: almost anything approaching would have provoked it. With a look of desperation, he hurled the object he was carrying directly at the Doctor's head. The Doctor ducked, and the disc continued under its own momentum to land by Peri's feet.

'*Ow*,' it said.

Peri bent and picked it up. It was strangely warm to the touch – or rather, it did not feel quite as cold as the cold metal she had been expecting. It pulsed very gently in a way that seemed almost organic.

'Are you alive?' she said, vaguely unsure if she were actually speaking to the thing or musing to herself.

'*Of course we're alive,*' it snapped. '*Though probably not in the way you seem to think. We're a ship full of several hundred thousand of what you might call a race of intelligent bacteria. We, on the other hand, call ourselves the* Wibliwee.'

'Um…' Peri's astonishment was such that, even years later, she would recall what she said next as probably the dumbest and most stupid thing she had ever said. 'You speak, uh, human very well.'

'*There's several hundred thousand of us,*' said the voice of the Wibliwee. '*We're incredibly advanced and as effectively immortal as amoebas. Mastering the common apostrophe – go on, have a guess, what do you reckon to the odds?*'

The Doctor, meanwhile, reached the pale boy, had helped him up and was dusting him off in a friendly manner. The boy seemed slightly mollified, now it was clear that the Time Lord didn't actively mean to attack him, but he remained cautious. Peri, with the muttering Wibliwee ship in her hand, was about to head down into the hollow when something reared up from the other side. Three somethings, each with entirely too many legs, antennae and the ragged flaps of atrophied wings for comfort.

'Doctor!' she cried as the shadows of the Pararachnids fell over him and the boy – but he had already shot into action, pushing the boy behind him and glaring up at the advancing insectoid monsters as if his gaze might form a barrier in itself.

'Get away from here, Peri,' he called over his shoulder. 'Get back to the TARDIS and wait for me there.'

Peri stood rooted to the spot, torn between concern and panic.

'What are you waiting for?' the Doctor snapped. 'I'll have quite enough to do looking out for this chap here – and the last thing I need is to have to worry about you as well. Now get a move on!'

Kimo Ani looked up at the… things looming over himself and the impossibly big, healthy-looking and brightly coloured man, reaching for them with snapping, jagged claws – and a long-suppressed memory flared inside him. It was a real thing, not an image from some subliminally imposed edu-stream. It was a memory of being very, very small. A memory from before he had been sent into the tunnels to take his place on the Line. A memory of these… *things* tearing through a world he had thought of as being utterly safe, inviolate, because it was the only world he knew.

He finally realised, then, that this was one of the monsters of which he had *truly* been afraid, afraid of all his waking life – and that he had somehow, in some complicated way he could not fully work out, confused them with the Monitors in the tunnels down below. The fear that had so debilitated him, ever since the voice inside his head had woken him up and turned into the glowing Talisman, had been directed at almost completely the wrong thing.

'Steady up, young chap,' said the big bright man. Kimo Ani was aware that the actual noises coming out of his mouth were nonsense, but he could understand them all the same. 'I'll get you out of this, never fear.'

Another memory surfaced. Kimo Ani remembered how some of the grown-up people had acted when the monsters came. Vaguely, he expected the big bright man to pull out his gun and start shouting at and shooting the monsters any moment now.

He was therefore a little taken aback when the big bright man stuck his hands up in the air and said to the monsters, 'I surrender abjectly, and so does my young friend. Take us to your, if you'll pardon the unconscionable lapse into the profoundly trite, leader or nearest applicable equivalent.'

Peri headed back the way they had come, maintaining a kind of fearful and precarious balance between speed of escape from the things behind her and an awareness that her surroundings themselves were potentially lethal. It would just be stupid if, in getting away from ten-foot-tall, ten-legged quasi-spiders, she tripped in the dark and drove a rusty nail or something into her head.

'Where do you think you're going?' the voice of the Wibliwee said. *'Take us back* right *this instant!'*

The voice had her glancing at her hand at the faintly glowing thing. What with other things on her mind, she'd forgotten that she still had it. The voice also wrenched her mind away from something else that was vaguely worrying her – something she couldn't quite pin down. It wasn't worry for the Doctor – he'd said that he was capable of looking out for himself and for the pale boy, and she implicitly believed him. It was something to do with the boy himself, something about the fact that, when they had first seen him, emerging from the hole, he had been obviously running *from* something…

Lights came on with a crash. They were like headlamps, the beam they cast designed to be viewed from behind their source. From the other side they dazzled rather than illuminated; Peri blinked and shook her head as purple flares detonated and swirled across her vision.

Two bulky objects were waiting for her. One of them moved forward with the clunk and hiss of hydraulics, and Peri squinted to make out the form behind its blazing lights. She more or less instantly wished that she hadn't.

It was clearly robotic, though some of the masses attached to its metal frame seemed to have been sculpted from a fungus-like material – some kind of semi-organic artificial flesh? It had a pair of massive, blocky-looking arms, giving it the overall impression of a hand-built gorilla – but no gorilla ever born had a head like this one. It was like some sort of claw hammer, from which the headlights ran on lateral struts. The front, flat end that in a hammer hits the nails was of wire mesh. It was just possible to see the indications of complex machinery within, though whether this was its sensors or robotic brain it was impossible to say.

'*Oh, damn,*' said the voice of the Wibliwee, with a kind of resigned anger at something it was patently not going to be able to change. '*Here we go again.*'

The robotic thing advanced across the wreckage on cantilevered caterpillar treads faster than Peri could back off. When it was within an inch of grasping her with its mechanical claws, or smacking at her with its claw-hammer head, it stopped. Peri had the impression that, so far as a robotic mechanism can be imbued with human impulse and response, it was peering at her dubiously.

'You are Biological Unit One Seven Nine Zero Seven Four One,' it said, in a voice that seemed surprisingly well-modulated and not at all mechanical – save that it was quite obviously generated and pieced together from sound-samples of discrete and complete words. 'Biological Unit One Seven Nine Zero Seven Four One Shall Come With These Monitor Units Immediately.'

Hurtful little Doctorial jibes about the American usage of the English language had taken their toll, and Peri noticed the 'Shall'. The machine was not making a request or even, precisely, giving an order. It was simply stating how things were, and how they were going to be.

'I'm not your Biological Unit,' Peri said, with a bravado she didn't quite feel in the face of this overwhelming mechanical certainty. So far as she knew, she *might* have been this Biological Unit One Seven Nine Zero Seven Four One for years and never known it.

The machine appeared to consider this – calculating and compiling a response by way of complex but quite specific algorithms that had it pausing for a moment. Any attempt to characterise its state as puzzlement or the like would have been complete and utter anthropomorphic nonsense.

'This Is An Impossible Statement,' it said at last. 'All Other Biological Units Are Accounted For. You Are Biological. You Are Biological Unit One Seven Nine Zero Seven Four One.'

'No, I'm not,' said Peri.

'If Biological Unit Is Not Biological Unit One Seven Nine Zero Seven Four One Then It Is Hostile Biological Unit.' A series of notched and ancient, but still lethally sharp, blades extended from their housings in the machine's claws with a concussive and multiple electromagnetic *clunk*.

'I mean I am,' said Peri hurriedly. 'Biological Unit One Seven Nine whatever it is. That's me. How could I be anybody else?'

The blades retracted – although, Peri thought, they didn't retract quite as swiftly as they had extended. The machine raised its claw – and fired something directly at her head. It lashed aside before she could even begin to react and wrapped itself around her throat: a thin tentacle of tensile steel, restraining her like a leash restrains a dog.

'Biological Unit One Seven Nine Zero Seven Four One Shall Come With These Monitor Units Immediately,' the machine repeated.

In the relatively short time since the Talisman had woken Kimo Ani up he had, if not exactly learned new things, experienced things which had left their mark. This had made him strangely bigger inside, able to put things together and compare them. It made him feel – he groped for words to define it – it made him feel more like a Real Person. He was able to make himself move through the world, and effect it, and be affected by it.

That was before the present circumstances, naturally.

After the fat man had surrendered (and the Real Person in Kimo Ani was starting to wonder if the fat man was *really* fat, or just fatter than him) the pair of them had been marched off through the wreckage by the monsters (who, Kimo Ani remembered, were called Pararachnids, without quite knowing how he knew the name) to a place where there were more of them. More than as many as his fingers plus his toes, which was thus far as many as

Kimo Ani could count (although he had the vague but steadily growing idea that things didn't necessarily *have* to be the same number as other things to which one could physically point).

The Pararachnids lived in makeshift shelters seemingly constructed of things from the surrounding ruins – sheets of thin stuff piled against and on top of other things stuck in the ground. Kimo Ani remembered the tunnels that held the Line and the other things in them and felt an obscure sense of pride. His senses of proportion and self were still stunted, but he could see that those things had been in some sense made *better* than the things made by the Pararachnids.

In this cobbled-together Pararachnid village, he and the big man – he and the *Doctor* – had been brought before a creature larger than the others, its limbs so huge and bulky that it was unable to walk. The Breeder Male, the Doctor had told Kimo Ani out of the corner of his mouth. You could tell the Breeder Male, apparently, because it was only good for hitting things and grunting.

The Breeder Male had looked Kimo Ani and the Doctor over with horrible segmented eyes on extensible stalks, then had uttered a sound similar to a belch but as loud as a bellow and lashed out at a swarm of smaller creatures, who had crawled all over Kimo Ani and the Doctor, leaving behind them strands of a kind of sticky substance which had solidified to cocoon them from their knees to their shoulders. Kimo Ani and the Doctor had then been taken away to a large hut and left to hang from one of the mismatched joists that after a fashion supported its roof.

Strewn across the floor were items that Kimo Ani failed to recognise. The Doctor had explained that they were canisters containing various condiments used for the seasoning of food, scavenged from the ruins. The Pararachnids, so he said, were noted for adopting certain of their victims' customs and pleasures, just so long as it didn't involve any creative effort on their part. If he was any judge, he had said, reading from the visible labels, they were just going to sprinkle Kimo Ani and himself with pepper and salt and eat them raw.

They had been here for some while now. Kimo Ani's sense of the passage of time had been stunted, as his other senses, by his years spent on the Line, but he was aware that his crippling fear had subsided into a kind of feeling that itched inside his head and stomach for something, almost anything, to happen.

Hanging beside him, the Doctor seemed to know what he was feeling. 'Won't be long now,' he said, with a cheerfulness that even Kimo Ani could see was utterly wrong for their situation. 'We're only waiting until I'm quite sure Peri's perfectly safe and back at the TARDIS.'

Kimo Ani hazarded a guess that a Peri was the female who had been with the Doctor when he had caught him. 'What's a TARDIS?' he asked. It only occurred to him later that this was the first thing he had said to the Doctor – the first thing he had said to anyone – since awakening. The first thing that hadn't been just a fearful squeak to the Talisman, anyway.

The Doctor appeared to consider this deeply, nodding thoughtfully to himself. Then he shook his head. 'It can take years to convey the old girl even in her smallest aspect. Years we don't have to spare. In fact, I rather think it's time to make our dramatic escape.' He became conspiratorial. 'Now there's a trick I learned from a man named Houdini. When someone ties you up or something like that, you tense your muscles to make them bigger…' He began to wriggle around inside his Pararachnid silk half-cocoon, and then his face fell and he stopped. 'Of course, it does help if you're occupying a body that could *then* dislocate its own shoulder. Oh, dear. It appears that we're really stuck. Sorry.'

This was Kimo Ani's day for new emotions. He couldn't put a name to the one he now felt, but he sighed and found himself wanting to say the word 'typical'.

It was then that a medium-sized Pararachnid entered the hut. 'Medium-sized' in this case meant that it was merely twice the size of both Kimo Ani and the Doctor combined. It seemed quite elderly: Kimo Ani could see that a number of its limbs had gone over the years. It scuttled about, picking up the occasional canister and tossing it aside, as tough looking for something the use of which it did not quite understand.

The Doctor stared at it slyly for a moment and then said, sharply,

'No, no, no! That's not the way to go about it at all.'

The Pararachnid turned to face him and chittered belligerently.

'You might very well say that,' said the Doctor, 'but I happen to know your Breeder Male very well, and I can tell you for a fact that he's extremely particular about what he'll pop into his mouth. If you put some of those things down there on us, he wouldn't like it at all. No doubt kill you on the spot.'

Despite itself, the Pararachnid seemed to consider this. It turned back to the partially cocooned Doctor and chittered suspiciously.

'Of course I know what I'm talking about,' said the Doctor with a slightly affronted air. 'It can do no harm at this point to reveal that I myself have worn a chef's hat in my time and know exactly what I'm talking about. Tell you what, why don't you just let me down and I could lend you a hand? I'm sure that a Pararachnid of your obvious quality and experience could stop me escaping and doing anything dangerous. Nice occipital markings, by the way. Very fetching.'

More chittering from the Pararachnid party.

'What do you mean, what's in it for me?' said the Doctor. 'As you can plainly see, I am a stupid bipedal hominid and well known for doing stupid things. This is one of the stupid things us stupid bipedal hominids do. Don't you even know that? I'm sorry, what was I thinking, of course you know that...

'My word, it's the secretions of that particular gland that dissolve the webbing, is it? We learn something new every day, some of us. Except, of course, for those of us who don't. Now, if you could free my legs and hands completely, it would make things easier for all concerned. Thank you. Now, let's see what you have here. Rosemary's nice with lamb, but on a stupid bipedal hominid it can be rather tart. Salt, pepper, all good stuff, but we're looking for something a little more piquant and out of the ordinary. Turmeric, quite possibly, but I'd advise you to go easy with it. Saffron, to be perfectly frank, does nothing worth the effort of having to clean the stains off your mandibles afterwards. Aha! An industrial-sized can of Extra Strong Cayenne Pepper. Just the chap we're looking for. Now, if you'll just come over here and have a look, I'll show you precisely what I mean...'

* * *

Little metallic things scuttled out of their way as the robotic Monitors led Peri down through white-walled tunnels. The tensile steel around her neck was not painfully tight, but held her with a firm pressure that made her constantly want to gag. They travelled at what would, in other circumstances, possibly be called a comfortable walking pace. Peri was almost completely sure that, if she were to stumble, the machines would stop and allow her to recover, rather than simply moving on and dragging her. Almost certainly.

'We lost our reaction core by accident,' said the voice of the Wibliwee. Peri found herself listening to it carefully – not so much out of interest but because concentrating on it helped to take her mind from her situation. *'The actual details of the accident aren't important, but suffice to say that there is now a small colony of Wibliwee mutineers on one of the smaller asteroids of your solar system. The processes that drive our ship are unique, and the loss of the core severely crippled us...*

A nasty thought occurred to Peri. 'This drive core,' she said, intensely aware of the queasy not-quite-pain the act of speaking caused to her constricted throat, 'it wouldn't involve some kind of six-dimensional anomaly, would it?'

The voice of the Wibliwee snorted. *'What do you take us for? How could you power an entire ship with a space/time event less than a thousandth of a proton across? That would be totally stupid. We use* that *as the basis for our navigation device.'*

'Silly me,' said Peri. 'I should have guessed.'

'It operates upon entirely different terms, demonstrates entirely different properties, from the "up", "down", "strange", "charmed" and so on that are demonstrated by common subatomic particles. On its own terms, the universe is, in an absolutely literal sense, Everywhere Else, and we're able to extract meaningful positional data from its reactions. Our navigation unit quantifies the balance of its elements of jumpiness, fishiness, chubbiness and flutiness, and extrapolates them to a macrocosmic model. The end result is an absolutely solid space/time fix in terms of the galactic spin.'

The voice of the Wibliwee stopped smugly, no doubt waiting for Peri's reaction to the complete idiocy of a large part of its explanation. Long exposure to similar explanations by the Doctor of the inner workings of the TARDIS, however, meant that she was made of sterner stuff than that.

'So you lost your drive core,' she said. 'What happened then? How did you end up here?'

We managed to limp to this planet on emergency power,' the voice of the Wibliwee said with a tinge of disappointment. 'We needed several trace elements in their refined state – chromium, tellurium, molybdenum and the like – and the Earth was the nearest post-industrial society. Just our luck that we hit it in the middle of the evacuation. We didn't have the power left for sustained flight, and in the confusion, due to a set of circumstances only really interesting to us because we were involved in them, we ended up down here. In the Line. And we've been stuck here ever since.'

'Couldn't you have smashed you way out or something?' Peri asked.

'Force to mass ratio,' said the voice of the Wibliwee. 'With a fully functional drive and enough velocity to go irrational, such things don't matter – but with the sort of run-up we'd get on the tungsten doors they have here, we'd merely splatter ourselves over them. Besides, we've barely got enough power left to keep our communications going. We're actually using inductive resonance to fire off the synaptic signals ordinarily caused by your eardrums vibrating. With a few minor modifications, that's what we used to wake up that boy from the Line and get him to find us and pick us up – after about seven of your decades, we might add.'

'The Line…' Peri said. 'You keep mentioning this Line. What is it?'

'You don't want to know,' said the voice of the Wibliwee gloomily. 'Believe us, you don't want to know. Problem is, you're going to find out right about now.'

The automata had reached the bottom of a spiral incline, and now took Peri and her new-found friends through a dark portal. The difference in light-levels from the access corridors to the caverns leading off was so marked that, for a moment, is was like stepping into the dark. It took some moments for her eyes to adjust.

And then they did.

Only later, much later, when her mind did not simply and instantly shy away in terror and revulsion, did Peri recall the details of the Line – the membranous, supportive coverings, the servo-mechanisms, the nutrient tubes, the hordes of robotic units of various designs that ministered to the semi-living livestock. You could hardly call the things that the livestock had become *human*, after all…

At the time, in that instant when she first saw it and felt the full impact of what it meant, all she could take in was the vast switchbacking layout of the conveyor belts, the faceless, vaguely human figures that hung above them from hooks, trudging slowly and in unison – a halting, slow-motion parade without beginning or end and leading nowhere.

Peri thought she had experienced terror before – at the knife point of a mugger outside the college dorm, under the lambent psycho-transforming rays on a medical bench in the Varos prison complex, at the claws and jaws and slimy tentacles of any number of hideous and villainous monsters as she was hurled erratically from one end of space and time to another. Now she knew she had been wrong – in the same way that one might imagine what a broken bone feels like, before one feels the smack of impact hard enough to break bone and the shattered pain that fills the world. That was when she panicked, tried to fight in vain against the steel that held her.

'Ah, well,' she was peripherally aware of the voice of the Wibliwee saying. '*Here we go again. If the power holds out we'll see you in seventy-odd of your years.*'

The predawn sun was spreading its nimbus across the skyline of the ruins when a gasping and utterly exhausted Kimo Ani reached a tall and bluish box, recognised it as one of the first things he'd seen when emerging from the tunnels of the Line and let out a kind of hysterical cross between a sob and a groan. After everything that had happened, he was merely back where he had started.

The Doctor, on the other hand, did not seem out of breath in the slightest, for all he had spent their flight from the Pararachnid camp running ahead, looking back and exhorting Kimo Ani to hurry up. The Doctor was, however, peering up at the box worriedly.

'Peri doesn't seem to be around,' he said. 'The TARDIS beacon would be on if she were occupied. Where could she have got to? It's not as if there's an actual plethora of places she can go…'

Kimo Ani gestured in the direction of the tunnels. 'Down there. In the Line. I think the Monitors have her now.'

The Doctor nodded to himself, as though certain things previously obfuscated had at last become clear. 'Why don't you tell me all about it?' He glanced back the way they had come. 'But not here. The Pararachnids are slow to anger and react, but the momentum they can build up when they do is quite astonishing.'

He produced a small, bright sliver of metal and stuck it in the side of the box. A door swung open and lights blazed from within. 'Come inside,' said the Doctor, 'and prepare yourself for a bit of a surprise.'

As it turned out, the Doctor's warning was unnecessary. Kimo Ani was quite at home with the idea of small holes leading into vast and complex spaces. The fact that this particular one was vertical, with nothing around it to *contain* those spaces, was just an incidental detail.

And a few minutes later, when almost a thousand enraged (and in some cases still slightly peppery) Pararachnids reached the place where the TARDIS had once stood, all that remained were the vestigial traces of its outer plasmic shell, dissipated during dematerialisation and wafting gently in the breeze.

A Pararachnid's primary sense is that of smell – indeed, this had been the main factor in the success of Kimo Ani and the Doctor in their flight from the Pararachnid camp. It had also been the main factor in the Pararachnids, once alerted to the escape, being able to follow. Now the thread of scent had been snapped.

However, as they cast around in angry confusion, they caught the fainter, older scent of one of those they had been pursuing.

They followed it back.

And they found from where it had come.

Without an overall, overriding control, the robotic mechanisms that Kimo Ani had known as Monitors were forced to rely upon their own inbuilt programming – and this programming contained an inbuilt, fundamental flaw. Quite simply, they had been built to protect human beings from Pararachnids, and the default state of that was to prevent human beings leaving the caverns of the Line and going where it might be dangerous. Preventing Pararachnids from coming *in* required the secondary control systems that were no longer operational. They were quite simply, in the literal and figurative senses, looking entirely the other way.

Thus it was that, as almost a thousand Pararachnids piled in through the gate and boiled down through the tunnels, coming across supposedly protective robotic devices in their thousands, they were met with not even the slightest resistance.

The TARDIS rematerialised, and Kimo Ani and the Doctor stepped out. The Doctor looked about him in the light from the TARDIS door at the hanging bodies, the conveyor belts, the endless introverted mechanism of the Line.

'It's just a variation upon the theme of suspended animation,' he mused sadly. 'The metabolism is slowed, the bodies are kept minimally active to prevent such deterioration as is possible. What is it about the human mind that thinks the only way to extend life is to attenuate it, to chill it and extrude it?' He seemed to remember that Kimo Ani existed. 'Are you perfectly all right?'

The fear was back with a vengeance in Kimo Ani; so big that he couldn't feel it properly. He could sense the razor-edges of it around him, and somehow thought that if he could only hold himself in and keep very still, his skin would do no more than brush it.

'The monsters came,' he managed to say at last. 'They came very fast. Other people went and there were no more ships, so we had to come down here.'

'There is that, I suppose,' said the Doctor. 'And the main problem was that all of this had to be done on short notice. All it took was for a couple of key systems to fail, and these people just kept marching on, long after the main body of the Pararachnid swarm had gone. Marching on for centuries.'

Abruptly he turned and took Kimo Ani by the shoulders. Kimo Ani felt that his body might shatter like glass from the shock, and was surprised in a remote kind of way when it didn't.

'I know you don't like being here,' the Doctor told him. 'And I'm sorry that it's going to get worse. If my friend Peri's been taken into the Line, then there's only one place she can possibly be. I want you to take me there. Can you do that?'

Possibly it was the simple prospect of doing *something*, of moving through the world again, even if the direction in which one moved was back to the last place one ever wanted to go, but Kimo Ani felt the fear move from him. He nodded. 'I can take you there.'

They moved through the Line. The bodies and the belts were almost entirely similar, but Kimo Ani found that, in a way he could not express, certain areas and directions were familiar and others not. Even so, it took them quite some time to find the place he had once occupied on the Line.

The woman hung there, wrapped in a pristine polymerised sac which had not had the time to build up stains from within like those around her. You could see the tubes in her arm, the eyes rolled up in the head and the loosely yawning mouth from which saliva had been pumping before a slowed metabolism had shut down the glands.

Lying on the floor beside the belt she trod, dropped from her hand and subsequently overlooked by the mechanisms that had installed her here, was the Talisman. It was speaking to itself – although speaking might not be the proper word. It was arguing amongst itself in a thousand tinny little voices.

'All right!' a louder, more authoritative voice cut through the hubbub. *'I know we've done it all before, and we're all of us sick to death of it, but we're gonna have to do it all again. You know why? 'Cause if we don't we're gonna be stuck here for all eternity and then some.'*

The hubbub from the Talisman trailed off into a high-pitched muttering and then ceased.

'OK,' said the single voice. *'All together, count of three and follow*

my lead. One. Two. Three...'

'Excuse me,' said the Doctor, picking the Talisman up. 'I'm the Doctor, and these are my friends Kimo Ani and a slightly but, in all hope, temporarily inconvenienced Peri. I wonder if you can help us.'

'What?' the Talisman said, in full chorus. It was as though all the other voices, once ordered to follow their leader's, as it were, lead, would continue to do so until further notice.

'Do try to keep up,' said the Doctor a little tetchily. 'We're never going to get anywhere if you keep failing to pick up on what's already been said. Now, I gather from what Kimo Ani has said that you've been down here as long as he was, if not longer, and that you've been aware of things for all of that time. Is there a control nexus in this place? Is there some way we can help our friend?'

The Talisman was silent for a moment. *'There might be a place,'* it said at last. *'We saw it on our scanners just before the drive-power finally went and we hit the ground...'*

'Splendid!' the Doctor said happily. 'Now if you'll just tell us the way then we can –'

There was an explosion of steel from one end of the cavern as an access door ruptured. Through it, scrabbling and clawing at each other in their rush through this bottleneck and then fanning out, came the Pararachnids.

The Pararachnids, by way of their alien metabolic processes, could subsist perfectly well for centuries between meals, but even so there was little to beat walking into a room to find the most sumptuous banquet imaginable. The hierarchical processes of Pararachnid society should have had them carefully selecting the choicest victims, and taking them back for the Breeder Male to feed upon before even thinking abut their own modest requirements.

The hierarchical processes of Pararachnid society, however, with all this bounty spread before them, could quite frankly stuff it – and the invading Pararachnids now proceeded to stuff themselves in nothing short of a feeding frenzy.

For the rest of his life, Kimo Ani would never forget the sounds he heard behind him. He tried to pull away from the Doctor's grip. 'I must help them. I must…'

'And that's precisely what we're going to do,' said the Doctor, half-dragging him down the transom of the Line, heading off and at an angle from the gustatory chaos. 'If you went back there and tried to fight them you would simply die – and that wouldn't help anybody. This is the only intelligent course of action we can follow – and the occasional flash of abstract intelligence, harnessed to the greater good, is one of the few reasons for having human beings in the galaxy at all.' He glanced down at the Talisman in his hand. 'How far now?'

Just up here, then to the left, then right and up and to the left again…'

At last they came to a point where mechanisms, conduits and cabling converged: a large console in the shape of a metallic doughnut, in the centre of which, a circlet of electrodes attached to his scalp, sat a partially mummified dead man.

'The conditions here prevented decay to a certain extent,' said the Doctor, examining the body. 'He must have been left as a controller, ready to shut things down when the danger had passed, and then died of heart failure or something similar – not as unlikely an occurrence as it might at first seem. Positions like that are by their very nature incredibly stressful and debilitating. The number of times I've had to deal with dead men falling on the dead man's handle, or stopping the people in charge of The Button from actually pushing it…' He seemed to recall that this was not the right time for wandering off in reminiscence. 'Well, be that as it may, I think it's time we took control of this whole show and brought it to an end.' He reached over the console to pull the electrodes from the dead man's head.

'No.'

The Doctor turned. 'I beg your pardon?'

'No,' Kimo Ani said again. The conflicting impulses, thoughts and emotions in his head seemed to have forced themselves together into a single lump – a lump that was, in some sense, bigger than his head and bigger than the entire world. It was everything out there and everything inside him, looking out at everything from behind his eyes. It was too big to ever possibly comprehend. All you could do was live it.

'These are my people,' Kimo Ani told the Doctor, taking the circlet of electrodes from his hands. 'This is my place. I have to do this thing.'

And the Line stopped.

The first thing that the invading Pararachnids knew of it was when the conveyor belts, every single one of them, juddered to a halt, and the nutrients fed to the livestock via tubes were replaced by stimulants. So far as the Pararachnids were concerned, the only real difference was in the colour of the liquids gushing from the broken tubes of the already eaten, and the fact that those they were about to eat moved a little differently, were just that little bit warmer and tasted of slightly different things.

That was, of course, before several crash-hatches racked themselves back around an entire quadrant of the cavern wall, and from them shot more than a thousand Monitor units, each fully armed, their programming switched to deal with Pararachnids actually in their midst.

It was later.

Peri stood in the doorway of the TARDIS watching the stream of pale, dazed figures shuffling by – part of a line that now wound up through the tunnels and emerged into the wreckage, there to spread out and populate it, to put things right – or to try, anyway. There were still Pararachnids and other dangers out there, the Doctor had said, and many would die. But at least, before they died, they would have a chance to live their lives on their own terms.

Peri fingered the marks on her arm where the nutrient mechanisms of the line had been plugged in. Now that the TARDIS seemed to be operating normally again – whatever *that* ultimately meant – she was going to have to check in to its medical facilities and see if they couldn't remove the scars.

The Wibliwee had already departed, taking with them a collection of rare elements in total roughly the size of a pinhead from a storage room the size of a warehouse. Before leaving, they had spent twenty minutes by the TARDIS console, hooked to it by archaic-looking coiled wires and crocodile clips. They and the Doctor had then pronounced the TARDIS recalibrated – although Peri herself could see no actual change in its workings at all. It occurred to her that for far too long now she had been taking people's word for things rather than finding out for herself. There again, though, she supposed she'd find out for herself soon enough, when she tried to get the TARDIS to do something and it didn't all blow up in her face.

What it came down to in the end, she decided, was finding out whose word you could actually trust.

Peri turned from the door and heard it shut smoothly behind her. The console room was a mess from the recent tinkering. She picked up the arcane tools and dropped them in their bag, which she then took to one of the nearby storerooms. Incredibly, it was exactly where she had thought it would be.

Leaving the storeroom, she felt a familiar crawl and wrench in the pit of her stomach that denoted a dematerialisation. On her way back to the console, she stuck her head into the kitchens just to be sure. They had been completely restored, with no trace anywhere of a steam-and-clockwork-operated, smoke-belching *thing*.

She returned to the console room to find the Doctor in his shirtsleeves, wiping his hands with an oily rag (the console room was spotless; whatever technology the TARDIS operated upon, Peri very much doubted engine oil was needed). He was gazing happily at the healthily rotating time rotor with the general and slightly smug air of a job well done.

'Sound as a pig-iron guinea,' he said, 'to quote some remarkably famous human personage, the name of whom I shall recall in a moment. Always assuming I actually met him in the first place. My memory could be playing tricks on me or I could, not to put too fine a point upon it, be lying like a four-poster bed.'

'Well, *you* seem to be back on form at any rate,' said Peri.

'These little breaks do us all a world of good, and leave us ready and renewed for the fray,' said the Doctor, beaming.

'A little break?' said Peri sharply. 'It was hardly relaxing, and I can't help thinking that we really didn't do any good. Shouldn't we have at least stayed to help that Kimo Ani guy? He's the only one with the pencils in his case sharpened, and now he's got to look after a million-odd reawakened people.'

'We've already done more than we should,' the Doctor told her. 'I don't *think* we did any ultimate harm – but I know for a fact that any more and we would. Sometimes you have to touch things lightly and move on, and hope that there are enough people alive at the end of it all to clean up the mess.' For a moment he seemed pensive – and then, suddenly and sunnily, he smiled. He gestured to the console. 'At least with the old girl working properly again, from now on things can hardly go wrong.'

And later still, in the terms of the predominantly four-dimensional space the TARDIS had just left, as their six-dimensionally navigated ship passed the orbit of Pluto, building up enough momentum to go irrational, Captain XiiXwiiB of the Wibliwee lounged thoughtfully in what, for the sake of argument, we will call his chair.

He was feeling a little out of sorts. An intangible sense of responsibility nagged at his mind. As he understood it, something the Wibliwee were going to do or say in the future – or had done and said in the past – would end up in the Doctor's little pocket book and thus lead him and his companion to the right place at the right time. It was a discrete causal event, the Time Lord had explained, a singularity in the temporal flow, and as such it was an absolute certainty that it did or would happen. The Wibliwee wouldn't have to actually *do* anything about it either way. It was the uncertainty of it, the fact that one had no idea what this thing *was*, that preyed on the mind.

But it wasn't important. What *was* important was the fact that the Wibliwee now had power for a thousand years, in return for nothing more than supplying the corrections for the computers in those people's time machine. It had been rather odd. Quite apart from all the other errors, there had been such a fundamental flaw in the thing that Captain XiiXwiiB had wondered how it could ever have operated in the first place. Of course, the Wibliwee had corrected it, but all the same Captain XiiXwiiB wondered how any otherwise seemingly intelligent life form could think that thirteen divided by itself resulted in an integer...

One Bad Apple

by Simon Forward

'Try it, Doctor. The fruit is good.'

'Hmm?'

The Doctor, minus his coat, was busy beating the thick air with his hat as he searched around for signs of special interest or danger.

Leela had detected few of either since their arrival. It was a mystery to her why the Doctor had stalked so far through this dense jungle only to stop at a place that none among her tribe would have called a clearing. Overhead was a canopy of low branches and oddly leaning trees, with light falling everywhere in dappled shafts – like golden rain, she thought. Yes, the shadows of this land whispered of finer magics than her home forest boasted. There was much to like here: the winding routes between the richly laden trees; a knitted carpet of vegetation to cushion every footfall; a host of different animals seen scurrying aloft or burrowing away, scarcely visible, along channels deep beneath the undergrowth; and sometimes the trickle of streams and watercourses, both managing a faint sparkle even this far from the brilliant sunshine. Everything was speckled with vibrant colour, on steady branches or fluttering wings, and in her ears were the musical whirrs and screeches of a flourishing jungle. The air was like warm breath on her skin and the sweet scent of life was everywhere. The hunting would be good and the cover was excellent. And biting into the sweet, plump yellow fruit she had picked – Leela gave a start and shifted uncomfortably as the Doctor suddenly registered her, his eyes gaping with what she well knew was a guardian's anger. 'What?' she moaned. 'What have I done?'

The Doctor grabbed the fruit from her hands.

'Haven't I told you before about eating things off strange trees?'

he snapped at her severely. 'You know, I really can't be expected to –'

'No,' Leela defied him faintly.

'Hmm?' demanded the Doctor, stopped in mid-flow.

'No, you have not told me before about –'

'Ah, yes, well.' The Doctor shrugged moodily and turned away. Before long he was idly tossing the fruit from hand to hand, then lifting it to his nose for an experimental sniff. Plonking his hat on his mop of curls, he turned with a conciliatory grin to Leela and threw her the apple for an easy catch.

'Don't let me find you've been scrumping again,' he warned mischievously.

Leela smiled, then frowned in quick succession. 'Doctor, what is scrumping?' No answer. 'And why are we here?'

'Ghosts, shadows… probably nothing, but you never know. This planet's sitting on the frontier of a major war.'

Suddenly, Leela hurled the fruit aside and tensed, the cryptic answer forgotten. Crouching, she wiped the juice from her lips and listened. The Doctor, trusting her instincts, squatted down beside her, his gaze probing deep into the jungle.

They could both hear it now, the crash and tramp of something huge and heavy marching along their route.

'I rather had the feeling we weren't alone here,' said the Doctor.

'Why did you not say so before?' hissed Leela, and she craned her neck for the first glimpse of the approaching threat. Her fingers teased the knife smoothly and silently from its sheath. Then she froze as the Doctor clamped her arms.

'Quick thinking, Leela! You'll need that to cut us a path clear of here.' The Doctor must have anticipated Leela's protest, because, frustratingly, he planted a hand over her mouth. Muttering in her ear, he added, 'These tracks we've been following had to have been beaten down by something, don't you think?'

Leela gasped. She could see it clearly now. They were like the small game, moving through larger burrows under the jungle canopy. Burrows tunnelled by something big.

She nodded once to signal understanding, then, with no time to be annoyed with herself, she scrambled quickly to the nearest wall of grass and vines, starting to slash at it with her knife. Pulling with her free arm, she worked to prise an opening in the curtain. The stamping, crunching and thrashing were closing on her to her right.

Blocking them out, she yanked the opening wider and hauled herself through on her belly. The Doctor ploughed in behind her and they hastily beat their hideout into a sort of nest. Finally, Leela squirmed around for a better view of the 'clearing' they had abandoned.

By the time Leela remembered the half-eaten fruit lying so obviously outside, it was too late. She and the Doctor waited tensely for the giant to make its entrance.

Long before the spaceship *Acolyte* had touched down, its sensors had built a model of Paradise in one half of Colonel Joshua's brain. Stepping on to the surface, he turned the model over, studied it from every angle, wondering if his panocular visor had painted it in appropriate colours.

Still, he didn't much care – any view was preferable to that of the ship: those hard lines were all too deeply etched in his mind…

Calling upon his troops to kneel, he directed them in the dedication. All the while, he dreamed of pressing an eye to the spy hole in the gateway to Paradise, of getting the barest glimpse of Heaven. There, he knew, lay those vital memories, the sum of his past before his conversion; murky images tantalisingly close under refracting waters.

Beneath the murmur of his prayer, he reviewed the bricks of data that had constructed so complete a model of this latest world his Fusiliers had claimed:

Ocean: H_2O: 96.25% Surface Area // Terrain: Archipelagos (single cluster): 3.75% Surface Area // Précis: Dense tropical rain forest separated by wide rivers or channels, max height 0.5m above waterline, outer trees curve down to meet ocean, forming natural domes with edges max distance 0.2km beyond island coasts.

Plant Life: Dense, varied. Animal Life: Dense, varied. Sentient Population: Unknown.

No, he decided. This place could not be Paradise. The computer model's colours were a shade too bland. Heaven described could never have sounded so cold.

Something special lay hidden here, though. The ragged hulk of a Cyberfrigate in orbit was testimony to that, a whole force wiped out by *something* here. Naturally, he had set the wreck to pitch into the vast ocean. Left in place, it was too bright a beacon to unwelcome eyes. The discovery of this new power *had* to be his.

Standing, Colonel Joshua straightened the uniform cap on his head and sealed the collar of his coat. The suit's cooling systems were already at work. Inhaling, he crossed himself and saluted to the ranks of his men. If prayer was the discipline of his meditations, then discipline was the focus of his actions.

There were two targets for their immediate attention. First, a brief signal dispatched Lieutenant Cain with a squad to investigate the as yet colourless large rectangular box nestled under the umbrella of the adjacent archipelago. Then he was ready himself to lead the rest of his men to the ruins of the Cyberbase.

The shambling animal was neither as large nor as menacing as the image its noise had conjured. Leela could see instantly that it was not born for stealth.

The Doctor still took pains to shush her as he craned forward in fascination. 'Something between a pangolin and an ankylosaurus,' he murmured.

Whatever the named creatures were, Leela's own view was of a lumbering barrel-shaped body, spiked and plated, a long flexible nose low to the ground, four great clawed pads for feet and a casually flexing tail tipped with its own clump of bony daggers. Sniffing as it meandered along, it detoured slightly to pass over the fruit, but gave it no apparent pause or acknowledgement. Not even a snort of disdain. Clearly, the offence of scrumping was not rated highly.

'Doctor, these creatures are –'

'Shush!' the Doctor silenced her again. To her utter astonishment, the Time Lord jammed his hat down firmly and plunged into view. As if his steps and his bright scarf were not enough, he announced his presence with a theatrical cough. 'Excuse me! Hello there! My friend and I are lost and we were –'

The Doctor was set to continue rambling, but the creature, which had scarcely turned its conical head, tramped away on its set course.

Leela smiled as she too emerged from their crude hideout, taking some satisfaction in the Doctor's disgruntled expression.

'How terribly rude,' he complained.

'Doctor, it is a beast.'

'Well, I wouldn't have put it that strongly. Probably has a lot on his mind – things to do, places to visit, that sort of thing. Come on.'

The Doctor led her off at a run to catch up with the strange creature and even Leela found herself drawn by its unnatural lack of curiosity. The inadequacies of her hideout had been a source of faint shame until now. She hurried after the Doctor, feeling the extra gravitational pull of the planet like a heavy overcoat. She was soon confused to see him overtake their prey and doff his hat in his gentlemanly manner.

'Hello there. As I was saying, I'm the Doctor and this is my savage friend, Leela –'

Leela stopped running, forced to double over at the sight of the Doctor barged aside by this single-minded creature. He scrabbled around in comic disarray, before rising and indignantly dusting down his rumpled coat.

'Huh! Beast!' he called after his assailant.

Leela stifled her laughter as the Doctor glanced her way, and she trotted up beside him. 'Why do you wish to talk to the animal?'

'It's a thing with us Doctors,' he replied vaguely as he set off in pursuit once again. 'Ah, look – it's stopped.'

They joined the mysterious animal at the base of an especially broad-trunked tree. The bark was delicately rippled, with a mottled sand colouring similar to the creature's armour. Lifting itself close to the Doctor's height on its hind legs, the creature produced a pair of tools from a pouch below its stomach.

Leela stared as it began drilling into the bark. The Doctor, meanwhile, cleared his throat and tapped the animal on its shoulder. When that failed to provoke a reaction, he leaned in and waved a hand in front of its eyes.

That did the trick. The animal aimed its nose at them both and uttered a stream of hard consonants, tongue clicks and hisses, all of which drew a blank from the Doctor. But Leela understood every word perfectly.

Cain, formerly Lieutenant Warner Bruch of the Imperial Marines, summoned his squad to line up behind him, backing the transmitted command with the habitual wave of his arm.

Abel settled down close to his shoulder, prompting a stab of remembrance.

Cain was used to that and he had any number of methods to shake off the feeling: a rapid count to ten, a physical shrug, a short prayer... But only after he had taken the time to swill it around in the glass of his mind, stirring up what remained of a fragrant bouquet. Friendship. Memories of a sergeant who had shown him how to be an officer. He had chosen their paired names when they had been ordained together. Cain and Abel, because Warner had enjoyed irony, and because who knew how the biblical Cain might have turned out if he too had been granted a second chance.

Batting Abel's stout arm, he sent the view from his own target-scope, highlighting the different figures. 'The Colonel will want some prisoners, but let's take no chances.'

'Yes, sir.' Abel trained his impassive mask on the scene ahead.

Cain studied the targets, the computer supplying his mind's eye with the details: decking the man in bizarre costume, clothing the woman in animal hides and delivering a compositional analysis of the tools in the native's paws. Cain noted it all dully and replayed the deep notes of his friend's voice.

Cain preferred to break with Fusilier tradition and issue verbal orders to Abel. It always prompted a verbal response and it hardly mattered to Colonel Joshua, as long as they got the job done. And Cain was a far better soldier than Warner Bruch.

* * *

The short interview so far was as much of a trial to Leela, brimming with so many questions of her own, as it was to the Doctor, impatiently waiting on Leela's translation with each exchange. The words, she told him sulkily, were not easy to produce and the Doctor seized on this as the reason the TARDIS's telepathic circuits were not translating for him in their usual way.

Leela felt drained by the effort of concentrating, but the Doctor gave her an encouraging pat on the back. At the same time, he seemed more distant than ever.

For her part, she had not seen the reason for the Doctor's sudden air of gloom in their discussion with Trok'larr, as he had named himself. His people were the P'tarr and they lived in a city a half-day's walk back along the Tail, which they had established was a string of islands stretching out from the main group. That much was simple. Trok'larr had ventured here to drink the sap of the thu'loth tree because it was his time to mate. The connection was lost on Leela, until the Doctor explained that the sap probably triggered the necessary changes in his body chemistry.

'Like carrots to help you see in the dark,' she murmured, repeating the Doctor's example to herself.

When the Doctor had her (reluctantly) inquire about the fruit she had stolen, Trok'larr had regarded her dubiously with black-bead eyes she was beginning to see as highly intelligent. She retreated a pace as he briefly snuffed the air closer to her mouth.

'I did not mean to,' she pleaded defensively.

Trok'larr bowed his head and brushed her arm with one claw, the image of a sympathetic village elder. Leela was surprised and touched by his gentleness. 'All trees bear fruit. All fruit is knowledge. But some knowledge is poison.'

Leela, puzzled and perturbed, translated Trok'larr's lesson for the Doctor. His silence worried her further, before he shrugged unconvincingly. 'Oh, absolutely. A little knowledge is a dangerous thing. We'd better get both you and your apple under the microscope! The next time you're hungry, you have only to ask for a jelly baby.' A distant resolution glazed his eyes and Leela guessed he was seeing dangers again. 'Meanwhile, there are people a lot greedier we should be worrying about.'

Trok'larr traded looks between herself and the Doctor, but the Doctor's gaze was elsewhere. A blur of motion upset the corner of her eye, a splash of light colour bursting through the forest.

'Doctor, look out!'

The Doctor had spotted the six attackers some moments ago and dodged to their left flank. She heard him shout in anger as she ducked under the first one's charge and skewered her knife up between his ribs.

A blank visor obscured the features, but the facial muscles sagged and red blood oozed from the grille at his mouth. The man's weight dropped dead against her, so she dipped aside and yanked her blade free, letting him fall and wheeling around to pick out where the fight needed her most. Too many places.

The Doctor threw one of the guards over his shoulder, slamming him into a tree. Another two soldiers were standing off, bringing rifles to bear. Trok'larr was on all fours again, ambling back the way he had come. The fifth man made the Doctor's mistake, dashing ahead to bar the creature's path; he was flat on his back before he had time to aim his rifle. The sixth, just on her right, raised his gun and fired.

A singing bolt of white flame exploded over Trok'larr's rump, leaving a smoking patch of charred armour-plate. Trok'larr merely notched up his pace a little, his crashing bulk encouraging the fallen trooper to roll swiftly clear. But the firer drew a bead on the weakened armour before Trok'larr could disappear.

Leela hurled herself at the man, grabbing for his rifle. She yanked hard on the barrel, but he stubbornly held fast. However, her efforts were such that the bolt sizzled harmlessly down into the undergrowth. The soldier roared at her; Leela dug her elbow into his stomach.

As he was buckling over, the Doctor's shout came a second time: 'Leela, run!'

She would never have obeyed if it hadn't been for the glimpse she got of him raising his hands, and the fact that she knew he would have some sort of plan. Wasting no time, she scooped one of the rifles from the forest floor and sped along the trail, vaulting over the attacker Trok'larr had almost trampled.

The planet dragged at her and her lungs ached and she worried about the Doctor. Still, as she overtook Trok'larr, she knew exactly where to head.

The angry volley of shots behind her and a bestial cry of pain warned her not to wait for Trok'larr.

Now the Doctor was very unhappy.

He observed the movements of his captors around him, while pretending half-heartedly to be concerned with the sluggish behaviour of his yo-yo. Ridiculously overdressed in sky-blue parade-ground greatcoats with polished silver buttons, forage caps and sturdy boots, it was difficult to see where the men ended and the cybernetics began. Those visored face-masks were embedded into the front of the skull, he could tell that much from the men on either side of him. Only the mouthpieces were detachable, and they seemed to be fairly standard respirators, quite unnecessary for humans on this world. He assumed that the uniforms were, imperialist fashion statements aside, sealed combat suits.

The biggest fellow, massive as he was, needed another's help in dragging Trok'larr's corpse back to the tree that would have made him fertile. The officer shook his head at the sight and gradually became aware of the Doctor's shadowy scowl.

'I ordered them to take prisoners.' He paused, then shifted angrily away to stab a gloved finger at the burliest figure. 'I gave a direct command, Abel! You could have wrestled this thing to the ground. Why in the name of God did you have to shoot it?'

The Doctor studied Abel. The distorted bass of the voice was not without its telling note of remorse. 'It was too big, Cain. It took four bursts from the cannon.'

The Doctor found himself appraising the slain Trok'larr anew. He had been a formidable, beautiful creature. Remarkable in so many respects...

The officer sighed and clutched the big man's shoulder, where the serious bulk of the blaster cannon was suspended. For a leader, this

Cain spent too long searching for the right words. In the end, all he managed was, 'Don't worry about it, Abel.'

'Huh! Letting off a murderer rather lightly, aren't you?' The Doctor jerked his yo-yo hard into his hand, ready to stare straight into the officer's visor as the man rounded on him. 'Yes?'

The struggle for the right words was shorter this time. Cain prodded the Doctor in the chest. 'Abel is worth ten of you, you miserable tramp! Ten!'

'Really?' The Doctor affected a misty disappointment. 'Pity – there's only four of me so far and I've no idea when we'll be getting together again.' Angrily, he then caught the man's finger before it was withdrawn. 'Now, are you taking me to your leader or not?'

Snatching his finger free, Cain retreated. 'You're right. There's no sense in delaying.' He waved at the two guards to march the Doctor off. The mighty Abel bent low to hoist their dead comrade over his shoulder.

The Doctor shrugged. Whoever these soldiers were, at least he would get to meet their commanding officer. He hated being bullied by mere subordinates.

'Did you do all this by yourselves? Can't say I'm impressed.'

The Doctor's contradictory tone was designed to provoke. When Colonel Joshua struck him, the blow was hard enough to wind him and knock him to his knees. Recovering gradually, he regarded his surroundings again from this fresh angle.

The Cyberbase was a scrap yard, a shattered skeleton straddling the island. Heaps of shredded steel, ripped from the foundations; walls and bulkheads battered into twisted sheets; communication towers and sensor rigs lying broken like scattered cocktail sticks; perimeter guns, shield projectors, Cyberman helmets and chest units littered like so many crumpled tin cans around the ruins. In the midst of it all a handful of standing structures, punctured, bruised and blasted until just a vestige of their original design remained. In fact, he noticed, the only area that looked relatively intact was an enormous pit, ringed by a sort of vented gunmetal cone.

The Doctor had his own disturbing ideas about that structure, but he was suddenly distracted by Joshua looming over him against the clear night sky.

'Let me see, all this would make you either very efficient soldiers – or very poor archaeologists.'

Joshua hauled the Doctor up by the lapels. 'I have razed a city or two, Doctor, rest assured, in the quest for Paradise,' he seethed, his soulless visor boring into the Doctor's eyes. 'But something else wrecked all this some time ago – wiped the Cybermen clean off this planet and used that –' he thrust an arm out in the direction of the pit – 'particle battery to do much the same to their frigate in orbit. Perhaps you'd care to apply your obvious intelligence to that puzzle.'

The Doctor hazarded a guess. 'It's possible they didn't have planning permission.'

Joshua shook him violently by the shoulders, demonstrating in the process the power of something more than human muscle. The Doctor endured until he could safely bite his tongue.

'Don't provoke me again.' The finality of the warning secured the Doctor's attention. 'It's this simple: if we learn nothing from you, we hunt down your woman friend and torture her. Then we torch the forest and see if the natives feel like talking.'

The Doctor considered. His mood hadn't improved since meeting Colonel Joshua, but maybe now was not the time to antagonise the fellow any further. Grudgingly, he said, 'Well, if you must know, I've been trying to learn the truth myself. Of course my interest is of the more detached scientific variety.' He lent his voice a more conspiratorial quality. 'I'm sure it's nothing that can't be figured out if we put our heads together. You seem like a logical sort of chap.'

Cain stepped into the lengthy pause. 'He has been fairly co-operative since we picked him up, Colonel Joshua, sir. Full of questions, but otherwise reasonable.'

Joshua nodded once, curtly, his mind made up. He kept his visor trained on the Doctor. 'What sort of questions?'

'Oh, just curious about this and that. Who you chaps are, where you're from, the significance of those interesting uniforms you're wearing, that kind of thing.'

Joshua actually laughed, if a little grimly, seeming to measure every pore and line of the Doctor's face. One of his gauntlets squeezed the Time Lord's shoulder.

'Have you ever played othello, Doctor?'

The Doctor looked surprised. 'Alas no,' he sighed. 'Hamlet. Oh, and –' he struck a heroic pose – 'Henry V, of course! "There is some soul of goodness in things evil, would men observingly distil it out." Such an optimist, the Bard.'

'You're babbling, Doctor,' Joshua cautioned dangerously. Even so, he drifted off a pace or two in thought before facing his prisoner again. 'What *are* good and evil? The Cyberwars are a game of strategy. If the enemy captures one of your pieces, fences it in, they convert it to their colour so it works for them.' He paused, satisfied to have the Doctor's full attention. 'You see where the comparison falls down? Mankind never gets to convert its pieces back. They are lost souls, numbered among the dead so they might be destroyed with a clear conscience.'

'Ah, but then, I always say a little *gilt* comes in handy for destroying Cybermen.'

Joshua's fingers clamped around the Doctor's throat and tightened ever so subtly. 'Try a drop of blacker humour, Doctor. What am I, exactly, would you say? I'm sure a man of your intelligence can see how it might happen: another victory, and the Imperial Marines sweep in to rescue all the poor unfortunates reserved for the Cybermen's operating table – there are always some who aren't quite finished. And then the Imperial High Command has to do some sweeping of its own, under the nearest available carpet.'

'Which is where you come in?'

'No. We've been abandoned. But we've grown stronger, gained our own identity. The Mithran Fusiliers are a mercenary organisation, dedicated to gaining more might, more security – in fact, power of our own. We answer to neither Cybermen nor humans, and we welcome any man or woman fortunate enough to have survived the surgical knife of the Cybermen. Our church is a home for the thousands of lost souls.'

'So, as victims you turn to religion for salvation?'

To his annoyance, the Doctor's probing went largely ignored. Joshua pounced instead on the semantics. 'No, no! None of us is a victim. That's the difference. That's the dividing line between the lost souls and the ones who embrace our Order.'

The Doctor listened patiently, some warning light bracing him for a stream of religious rhetoric. His instincts were not mistaken.

'Mondas was torn from the arms of her sister, Earth,' Joshua continued, as if preaching, 'and the Cybermen were hurled across an abyss from their human brethren. Do you see? If you know the history, the whole purpose of the Cyberwars falls apart. These sides were never meant to be in conflict. We are all meant to cross that abyss, to stand on the bridge and look into the clearer waters below.'

The Doctor kept his face as blank as possible, but it wasn't laughter he was masking.

'There is a point between states, as you put it, Doctor, a singularity between the Cybermen and humanity, where a perfect balance is achieved. The souls of Mondas and Earth reunited. Paradise, if you will. Once a… *victim* has seen that the Cybermen's surgery has merely set them on that bridge, they can see themselves as chosen. Then they can serve the Order, dedicate their lives to following that path –'

'Out into the middle of the abyss.' The Doctor nodded his dubious understanding. And, predictably, the fist punched him to his knees again.

The sun had fallen suddenly in an ocean of night, splashing darkness all over the islands. Leela moved with confidence, familiar now with most of the animal sounds and the shapes that scuttled in the shadows. Sure of her path, she was comforted too by a foggy understanding of some of the forces that worked the rifle she clutched at her hip. It was a good weapon.

The secret of its magic did nothing to lessen her appreciation of its power.

There was an expanse of shining water ahead, visible only in fragments through the leaves and branches. Edging closer, Leela was soon standing on the shoreline, the lapping waters enclosed under a magical cavern of trees.

The P'tarr city was a community of bulbous nests, clinging at dizzying heights to tall trunks or floating on enormous raft-like leaves strewn over the surface of the channel. Hundreds of P'tarr were clambering up to their homes, claws digging deep into the bark, or paddling fairly clumsily to and from their giant lily-pad tents. Some harvested plants from the shore or higher branches, stuffing the crop into their pouches; others were plodding about and young could be seen rolling and grappling on land or playing in the water.

Shouldering the rifle, Leela slipped down the low bank into her own more graceful swim. The sea and air were still warm from the recently departed daylight.

A few strokes took her to the nearest of the pads and the chief work was in hauling herself on to its waxy surface. Her weight scarcely tilted the leaf, but by the time she was on board a long snout could be seen poking from the opening in the tent. The black eyes shone curiously for a second, then prepared to duck back inside.

'No, wait, please,' appealed Leela urgently. 'My name is Leela. I am a friend of Trok'larr. We were attacked by blue soldiers and I fear he may have been captured.'

The P'tarr hovered in his doorway. 'You have eaten of the kess'tak.'

Leela hung her head. 'Yes,' she said humbly, 'I did not mean to scrump. Trok'larr and my friend, the Doctor, have said I might be poisoned.'

The P'tarr shuffled about and dipped its own head. Emerging from its home, it shambled towards Leela. On hind legs, it perched a claw on Leela's knee, snuffing the air before her as Trok'larr had done. Finally, it tipped its head to examine her features.

'I am Kan'rath,' he declared chirpily, 'and you are welcome, Leela, friend of Trok'larr. What is it you wish of the P'tarr?'

'I wish nothing,' Leela explained earnestly, 'except your help to rescue Trok'larr and the Doctor. We must quickly mount a counter-attack.'

'You must tell me everything that happened. Then we will decide.'

In the P'tarr language, it was said pleasantly enough. Leela had just been hoping for a touch more enthusiasm.

* * *

82

The Doctor was preparing to play the serpent. The temptation would be simplicity itself; avoiding suspicion would be the tricky part. Seated on a small heap of debris, he was biding time with his yo-yo while the overzealous Colonel Joshua organised the sifting and analysis of the wreckage for clues. Abel, his guard, was not the best of company.

Even so, he couldn't disguise a sniff of disappointment when Joshua's moonlit shadow eventually fell over him. Whipping the toy neatly into his pocket, he brushed a hand back through his curls and looked up. 'You know what I think?'

'What, Doctor?' Joshua inhaled, tensing himself apparently for a smart quip.

'Coded RNA programmes in the local vegetation, passed on through the digestive system.'

Joshua squatted in front of the Doctor, hooked but wary. 'You're serious?'

'Well, I've seen stranger things.' The Doctor kept his tone speculative, objective. 'One of the locals gave me a few pointers before your man shot him. Now I've had a chance to think, it makes a certain sense. Throws up a whole range of questions in the bargain, but that's science all over. You never get to the end –'

'And you never get to the point, Doctor!'

The Doctor idly played his hat for a concertina as he scanned the forest, already encroaching on the ruined base. 'Think about it. The natives are a primitive lot, content with the status quo. Why shouldn't they be? More than enough to go round, no need for squabbles. They don't even react to much, unless you're in their way.'

'Or until an outside threat appears, yes, I'm beginning to see. Go on.'

'Well, use of electronics, shield technology, nuclear physics… It's all here in one form or another, I expect. They just munch on whatever they need in a time of crisis. Food for thought. Not much different to you chaps plugging in another chip – except, of course, they get a square meal thrown in. I don't know quite what my friend ate, but it certainly helped to break the language barrier. Yes, pick a few bananas and you'd soon be able to reproduce the works of Shakespeare with – oh – a fraction of the monkeys and typewriters.'

'Yes, I think I get the picture. And spare me the quotations.' Joshua stroked his chin around the respirator. Ugly greed lurked behind his visor. 'But the ability to programme like that –'

'Exclusive to the P'tarr, I'd imagine. They must be one of the truly ancient races. Old enough to have forgotten more than they know. There's no telling what secrets might be locked away in those trees. You haven't seen any fruit flies, have you? A few nibbles of a peach and who knows what they –'

'Shut up, Doctor.' Joshua stood, determination in his stance. 'You'll have plenty of time to play court jester as soon as my men have done some foraging. I think it's time I staged a banquet in celebration of the Order's new claim.'

'I was rather afraid you might,' the Doctor murmured under his breath. He watched the figure of Joshua stride across the wreckage of the base. Bound for Eden.

The P'tarr decision process consisted of Kan'rath paddling off to carry the news to his fellows, whereupon the other P'tarr would drop what they were doing and bustle away to inform their neighbours. The activity looked set to continue for ages.

So Leela lay down and curled herself into a sleeping position on the floating pad. She was just about to dip into a dream when a nudge against her upper arm disturbed her. Waking, she opened her eyes to a close-up of, she supposed, Kan'rath's muzzle.

'It is agreed,' he told her as she shook herself alert. 'These soldiers are not the first to hunt near the thu'loth farm. I and nine others will accompany you to battle them. But first we must relearn the arts of war.'

The latter took a moment to register. Leela grabbed at her host's forelimb. 'Your people have no warriors! But we do not have the time to train you.'

'We will harvest berries from the tik'ssotar trees along our route.'

'And you will tip your blades with their poison?' Leela frowned. And then she remembered: like carrots to help you see in the dark.

* * *

84

The Doctor stretched back, the night shut out by the hat over his face, deliberating on the unnatural silence with which the Fusiliers went about their business. It offered a keyhole into their reverent observance of artificial traditions, their literally religious dependence on cybernetics. Misguided, no matter how fervently Joshua insisted otherwise, these Mithran Fusiliers were still victims – and of more than just the Cybermen. The Doctor was hoping that it was the key to the situation here.

His every sense was alert for the signal sound of Joshua's voice.

Instead, a lighter approach over the debris revealed an unexpected visitor. Tapping up the brim of his hat, he recognised the figure of Cain standing over him. The Doctor's guard, Abel, moved around next to his comrade.

'Doctor,' Cain's voice addressed him. His arm jerked and a soft, round object plopped on to the Doctor's stomach. The Doctor trapped it in his hand. 'The fruit checks out toxin-free and the Colonel has sampled the produce.'

The pale colour and furry texture were certainly reminiscent of a peach. 'Ah, no thanks,' the Doctor muttered, tossing the fruit aside and patting his belly. 'I've already eaten the plums. Taught me everything I know about thermodynamics. Go on, test me.'

Cain started picking his way to where the fruit had landed. His fingers worked to unclasp the respirator at his mouth. 'If you've no use for it, I'll eat it my –'

In a flash, the Doctor was rolling to his feet and diving for the fruit like a baseball player for the plate. He heard Abel chasing after him and felt the boot hammer down on his arm, fixing it in place. Inches from his goal.

Cain regarded the Doctor carefully, looking more human with his thin smile exposed. His right hand snaked out to reach for the fruit.

'I wouldn't if I were you,' warned the Doctor, grimacing.

'And why's that exactly?'

The Doctor lowered his eyes, fighting more than the pressure on his arm. He had been caught cheating at cards and now he had to own up and trust in his judgement of human character. Meeting Cain's blank gaze, he added, 'What if I simply said, there's no reason why one bad apple should make the whole barrel rotten?'

Cain couldn't avoid an involuntary glance across the ruins. 'You mean the Colonel?'

The Doctor prepared to explain, but Leela's sudden shout, breaking over the forest like a war cry, robbed him of his chance.

'Doctor! Look out!' she called, as the first tremors began in what seemed like a monstrous earthquake.

As soon as he saw her, the Doctor regretted telling her that story about Hannibal when she had asked if any warriors were counted among the great men of history. He should have just stuck with old Boney. It was the former she emulated, leading her small band of P'tarr stampeding out on to the open field of debris.

They had chosen their moment well, with the enemy preoccupied, himself off to one side with only two guards. A solitary shout of alarm went up from Colonel Joshua.

Leela herself was sighting along the barrel at Abel and the Doctor was a fraction too late in waving his spare arm. The blue-white bolt sang out and Abel keeled over, a smoking gouge in his flank. Freed, the Doctor leapt to his feet and waved at his companion with great urgency.

'Leela, no! Call them off! Call them off now!'

It was a vain request: Leela's ten P'tarr were as unstoppable as Hannibal's elephants. Charging from several directions over the scrap piles, they ignored the first wild hail of blaster shots and fell on the Fusiliers like living siege engines. Some balled themselves into spiked boulders, practically catapulting themselves at their foes with a powerful spring of the tail. Others wielded their tails as maces, digging deep and shattering bone. From the downed men, the P'tarr seized rifles and found new targets with quick, deadly accuracy. In a few frenetic seconds, the Fusiliers were totally outmanoeuvred.

The Doctor sought out Joshua, who was throwing off a P'tarr corpse, pulling a bloody sword from its underside. Dumping his dead foe, he staggered clear, his uniform darkened by a spreading stain.

Nearby, another P'tarr charged. Cain's rifle fired, but he was pinned flat, the P'tarr claw stabbing for his open collar. The Doctor shouted a protest and Leela, scampering over, echoed him at last.

'Kan'rath! Spare that one!' Her cry hinted that she thought she might just possibly have acted a little rashly.

Kan'rath hesitated. 'You are the better judge in warfare,' he said eventually, and shrugged.

'I can't disagree, unfortunately.' The Doctor was glowering. He snatched the rifle from Leela and flung it with sufficient force to genuinely startle her.

'I am sorry, Doctor. I was only thinking to rescue you and Trok'larr.'

Her mention of Trok'larr helped spare her the rest of the Doctor's wrath. That and the fact that there were other more pressing concerns. 'Trok'larr is dead. And there'll be plenty of time for apologies later.' He knelt to examine Abel, whose breaths were rasping loudly. To Cain, he said, 'He'll need proper treatment – but he'll live.'

'Thank you, Doctor. For sparing us.' Cain regarded the P'tarr above him, an uncertain flicker crossing his lips. 'Am I free to go?'

'Yes, I should think so,' the Doctor said. 'But we have to find the Colonel. He's in a fragile state of mind right now and there's no telling what your little escapade might have provoked. Probably the opposite of what I'd hoped. Come on, Leela, don't dawdle!'

The Doctor was already striding off and Leela had to trot to keep up. Kan'rath shuffled aside to release Cain, taking care not to plant a foot down on any part of him. Cain lifted himself on to his knees, watching the Doctor and Leela go.

After a moment's thought and a full analysis of his comrade's status, he followed the strangers. 'I won't be long, old friend,' he said to Abel, almost mechanically.

So this was Paradise.

Those refracted waters had been slowly crystallising into a clear image even as the native life forms had commenced their crude assault. Heaven's majesty unveiled.

Then a lucky thrust of his sword had saved his life, but stained the blurred image in blood, resolving it, as he fought clear of the creature's armoured bulk, as a landscape drowned in red. Colonel Joshua could scarcely contain his screams.

Because Paradise, that absolute clarity of vision, was a panorama of death, surrounding his senses and suffocating him with the faces and souls of every single man, woman and child he had killed, their bodies lying charred and bleeding in the streets of the cities he had destroyed. Where once cold memory had noted the statistics, a heart struggled helplessly to come to terms with them.

The Doctor had been right: the world he had plundered was really Paradise, after all. This vision, he realised with terrible certainty, was Hell. The weight of conscience broke the fragile bridge on which he stood and plunged him into the abyss.

The only choice left to him there was the manner of his death.

They found him on the bare, functional floor of the *Acolyte*'s grey bridge, curled like an infant in death's womb, a bloody spike jutting through his back – a warrior's sword embraced with superhuman strength. Over this dismal scene, the flickering console lights were like a hundred tiny candles. The Doctor knelt beside the fallen soldier and spoke in suitably hushed tones.

'He took his own life. He must have distilled out what little good there was.'

'Doctor, that is another of your riddles.' Leela enjoyed a chance to challenge the Doctor.

'The fruit from the trees, Leela. Knowledge biochemically stored had to be accessed intuitively, as the P'tarr do. It would have supplanted the logical interface with the cybernetic half of his brain. Reinforced the human and cut him off from the Cyberman. Separated the man from the machine.'

Leela preferred the warrior's perspective. 'And he came here to seek an honourable death?'

The Doctor stood and shrugged expansively. 'Well – that, or to atone for his sins – a whole career of bloody deeds confronted for the first time.'

'Memories restored?' hazarded a voice from just inside the bridge bulkhead. It was Cain, who had stolen silently in to listen some moments before.

Leela whirled around. The Doctor turned at a more leisurely rate.

Cain's visor was fixed on his dead commander as he spoke. 'Doctor, I'd like to believe you were right. We aren't all the same. I still have a soul in me and I think this place should be protected. Inviolate. I'm offering to... well, to guard its secret.'

The Doctor seemed unsure. 'That's a very generous offer, but the salary's poor.'

'I thought I might manage on an apple a day.' He waited for the Doctor's smile to match his own. 'I think – I'm hoping – the effects on myself and my friends will be quite different. The ship can be scuttled, our records of this world erased, and there are weapons at the base, force-field projectors that can be repaired –'

'Then why do we not adjust them?' suggested Leela, the light of insight firing her eyes. She had some small measure of guilt for which she wished to atone. 'A refractive field could be made to reflect back a view of empty ocean, could it not, Doctor?'

The Doctor stood like a statue, his expression set to mimic the Venus de Milo's immediately after her arms had fallen off. Eventually, his features furrowed into an irritable frown.

'Have you been scrumping again? I'm warning you, the effects of those apples had better fade fast, young lady, or else – or else –' He faltered.

Leela prompted him, only slightly worried. 'Or else what?'

The Doctor ignored her and looked to where Cain had been standing. 'You wouldn't happen to have any vacancies for an Eve, I suppose?'

His hopeful inquiry was left unanswered. Cain had already stepped out into the garden.

64 Carlysle Street

by Gary Russell

Statement by Thomas Greene, Footman to Lord Greystone

Mr Golightly had been in service all of his life. Born into it, he always said. Literal like. His Da had been butler to old Lady Bostwich in her Harlech estate and Golightly had been born there. Brought up to be footman and assumed the mantle of butler on his Da's early passing. Almost immediately the Bostwiches had come to a sticky end out in the Crimea and Golightly had moved to London with one of the nephews in about '56. Now, fifty or so years on, he was due to retire.

Of course, there was no way of knowing for sure that I was going to take over, but Mr Golightly seemed to like me and I got on with the master – well, as much as any of the servants could say they got on with the gentry – so I just kept my fingers crossed and hoped.

Mind you, this meant I had to be on my best behaviour at all times – no larking around downstairs with Matilda or Emily; up at the crack of dawn to oversee the parlour maid cleaning out the fireplaces and to help Mrs Doyle fetch and carry from the butcher's. She was a good'un, our Mrs Doyle. Not really a missus at all – I remember Mr Golightly telling me once that it was customary for cooks in big houses to be called missus even if they weren't. Oh, she shouted and scorned and cursed us at times, but underneath it all, she had a heart of pure gold.

I tell you, it all started to go wrong that morning last week when I answered the door. Whoever it was had an impatient air about them – they were using the end of their cane to tap repeatedly on the front door – you recognise the noises like that, you see. Well, Mr Golightly, he couldn't get to the front door so fast these days, and it had sort of become my job to answer it.

So I did. The man standing there was a bit... well, unusual I suppose you could say. I mean, not common or nothing, just a bit... well, he didn't carry himself like most of the master's acquaintances, if you get my drift. Oh, he was class all right, no two ways about that. But he reminded me of those types you see who've been out in the Congo or India. Colonial types. Though he weren't no military man, of that I was sure. Of course, with the master's visitors, he might've been an explorer, one of them lot from out in Egypt or Greece.

Anyway, I opened the door to him and he came in, giving me his cane. Nice cane it was too, pure silver top, good mahogany shaft. Not cheap or nothing. He was old and moved slow, but his eyes seemed very… young. That's what I mean by strange, really. Here was an old man, but he didn't act old. Just irritable.

What was really strange was that his chauffeur was outside on the step with his bag. Blow me down if he didn't start to follow the man in, casual as you like. Of course, I took the bag and pointed out the way down to the servants' entrance – and he actually looked put out by this! As if going in through the front door was an everyday occurrence for him.

Anyway, this old gentleman looks around the hallway and then tells me to announce him to the master. What could I say? I mean, I didn't know who he was and he'd not given me his card so… Well, I had to ask him, didn't I? I could feel Mr Golightly watching me from the top of the stairs, but what else could I do?

'Name?' he said to me. 'Well, let me see now. Yes, yes, kindly tell your master that the Doctor is here to see him, hmm?' So I nodded, placed his cane in the basket and crossed to the morning room, where the master was… working.

I announced this Doctor, and the master seemed very pleased to see him.

He said, 'Doctor, my dear friend, do come in. How delightful to see you.' Then he asked me to get some tea sent up, so I hurried out.

I asked Mr Golightly if there was anything else I could have done, and he assured me I'd done it right. So we went downstairs and Emily started boiling a kettle.

Alice, the parlour maid, was already dressed in her afternoon clothes by now, and offered to take the tea up, as Mr Golightly was tired and I needed to ask the young mistress what her plans for the day might be. She was up on the first floor by now, you see, entertaining some of her friends in the drawing room. Mrs Doyle didn't like that, I can tell you, but the master didn't seem to mind. Since her ladyship passed on from the flu three years gone, the master's been very keen to allow the young mistress to have her way on things. She's a fiery one, she is, going to do well one day. Wouldn't be surprised if she doesn't make it right through the door into Parliament House. Ever since they jailed Christy Pankhurst, the young mistress has got more and more involved with all that. I mean, that's how we all came to meet… to get involved with the Marquis of Rostock. They had met at some political meeting and she brought him to the house to meet the master. And that was when it all went wrong, really…

Statement by Alice Fittle, Parlour Maid to Lord Greystone

I don't remember the exact date that she turned up, but I do remember the fuss she caused. She was soaking wet from the rain, looking a right state with her hair all over the place. Gawd, she was a right old mess. Mrs Doyle took to her immediately, though, which made her all right in my book.

She let her in and we all led her to the fireplace to keep warm. Mr Golightly gave her a nip of brandy, which Matilda thought was very funny – but she's easily amused, not all there if you get my drift. Anyway, this poor wretch said she'd come looking for a job. She'd heard from a friend of a friend that, as we'd lost Doris up to the Bellamys in Chelsea, we were looking for a new under-parlour maid. Mr Golightly and Mrs Doyle seemed keen on the girl, but since I'd be responsible for her, they offered me the choice of trying her out or telling her to go. Well, although the girl looked like she'd never done a day's work in her life, quite frankly, I said yes, and sent her to tidy herself up.

About an hour later, after she was dry and in a clean uniform, we took her up to meet the master. He saw her in the drawing room and they seemed to get on well.

'What's your name?' he asked.

'Dorothea Chaplet,' she said, a bit smug-like, if you ask me.

'That's a big name for such a little servant,' the master replied, and that's when I knew we had trouble on our hands.

'Well, I like it,' this Dorothea snapped at him. I fair thought he'd have a heart attack, but no, he just laughed and said he'd call her Dottie.

'You won't, you know,' she retorted. 'If you must, call me Dodo. That's what my friends used to call me.'

So Dodo it was, and I still don't know how she got away with speaking to him so rudely.

Later that night, Dodo and I were talking about her duties. Despite her claims of service experience and her references, she was very ignorant of what was expected of her. She said it had been some months since she had last worked and I chose not to inquire further. That was Mr Golightly's task, if anyone's.

Over the next few days, Dodo fitted in quite well. She was a bit lippy, for certain, but she quickly got used to quietening down when His Lordship or Miss Annabel was around, which was a blessing! She was good at her job, very thorough, very efficient, but clearly didn't like the work and I often found myself wondering what made her go into service. Despite her voice and her common looks, she clearly knew far more educated things than the rest of us, except Mr Golightly, of course. I was really warming to her.

And then the Marquis of Rostock appeared one afternoon, and nothing was ever the same again.

Tommy had come downstairs to tell us that the marquis – a friend of Miss Annabel's – had arrived.

I was a bit intrigued, which I know is wrong, but you can't always help yourself, if you know what I mean. I made sure Tommy was too busy to take up afternoon tea so as I could do it myself.

When I walked into the room, I should have known something was wrong. The air was… well, it was cold. Like a window was wide open. Although it couldn't've been cold really, because Dodo's fire was blazing away – she done a good job, there. Can't fault her on that.

The marquis, well, he looked at me, strange-like. But he smiled and took the tea and a fancy, and kept on making small talk with Miss Annabel.

Then Dodo walked in, completely unexpected. Of course, I tried to make her go, but it was as if she wanted to be there, to break the rules and spoil the afternoon. She ignored my shooing, and just stared at the marquis.

He stared back at her. 'Good afternoon,' he said, and smiled. 'Do I know you?' She kept staring at him. 'Perhaps you feel you know me?'

I didn't understand none of this, mind. I just knew that Dodo shouldn't have been there, and the marquis shouldn't have spoken to her so informally.

I had to drag Dodo away, and I led her straight down to Mr Golightly, to tell him what had happened.

Statement by Lord Geoffrey Greystone

First, for the record, I feel I must point out that my title is honorary. I am not a lord by birth but by marriage. My late wife, Lady Edith Greystone, née Howarth, and I were married in 1883. My background is in finance and engineering management. Amongst my major dealings have been overseas plantations, European exports, and, most recently, I have been involved with the creation of the train system being expanded beneath the streets of London.

I met Edith at a banquet and we become betrothed after her father, the late Lord Howarth of Lanarkshire, gave his blessing. Many of my... detractors – and as a man of wealth and importance in society, I have many – have claimed I married into money. Whilst that may be literally the truth, figuratively it is not. I married the most beautiful, intelligent and joyful woman it has ever been my privilege to meet. Her death in 1906 was a great sorrow to me. I proceeded to bring up my dear daughter, Annabel, as best I could, although I fear that without a mother she may have been more easily influenced by those outside the walls of 64 Carlysle Street.

But, to the business at hand.

I met the Doctor while dining with some old business partners at the Bentinck Hotel in Duke Street. He was staying there, aided by his confidant and chauffeur, Taylor.

Like me, the Doctor seemed to be enamoured of the fictions of Verne and Twain, two authors less similar you cannot imagine. We spoke amiably about their work, the Doctor offering new insights into the minds of both men; although as Verne has been dead nigh on four years and Mr Clemens is reportedly very ill, quite how the Doctor can claim to have spent many years working alongside them at the start of their careers and during their respective twilights somewhat confounds me. Still, he is very aged and, I suspect, rather given to fanciful stories to brighten up what must be a desperately lonely dotage.

The Doctor asked me if I had ever heard of the Marquis of Rostock during our second or third dinner at the Bentinck (you must understand that the lady owner of the hotel is one of society's most famous cooks as well – one suspects that to eat there is the closest one may get to eating as royalty do. It has been suggested that she and the King himself are more than just close friends, if you get my drift).

But I digress once more. The Doctor... Yes, he seemed very interested in the marquis. I had never heard of him, which he thought was strange as he seemed to believe my daughter knew the man.

That evening, I asked Annabel about this and she claimed she did indeed know 'Ross' as she called him. I suggested a meeting between this 'Ross' and the Doctor, and she agreed immediately.

The Doctor duly arrived on the evening arranged and I asked Thomas – although he was our footman, he was acting as butler at the time – where was I? Oh, yes, I asked Thomas to fetch the marquis and Annabel from the drawing room, to join the Doctor and myself.

A few moments later, he did so, and I knew instantly that he and my new friend the Doctor had met before.

And that there was nothing but hostility between them.

'So, you've got here then, hmm?' the Doctor said to him. He was holding his head up imperiously, as if daring the marquis to reply.

'You know I cannot let you do what it is you are planning. No, I cannot. And I shall stop you, sir.'

The marquis just laughed and said, 'My dear Doctor, must you be so... so alarmist in front of our hosts. I recall last time we met, you deeply upset the local government. Indeed, they were so upset with you that they confiscated your – ·your rather intriguing mode of transport.'

The Doctor clasped his lapels and gave a haughty sneer. I was rather perturbed now – surely these two would cease their verbal brawling, especially as Annabel and the servants could see or hear them. But I was wrong.

'You do not belong here, young man,' he said. 'I detected your presence, and I've been tracking your movements for many months now. Oh, yes, I have.'

And that was when my world turned upside down.

This Marquis of Rostock held open his hand.

'A gift for you, Lord Greystone,' he said. 'A gift I trust your kind will help me employ wisely.'

In his palm was a strange silver... thing. At first I thought it was a giant ball-bearing, but then I realised it was soft, pliable. Indeed, it appeared to be moving of its own accord, gently rocking in the palm of his hand.

The Doctor breathed in noisily. 'No,' I recall he said. 'Surely you haven't brought that with you as well! It could do incalculable damage –' But he stopped.

And so did I as the silver thing leapt off Rostock's hand and, under its own momentum, shot across the room and hit my darling daughter Annabel in the chest.

What happened next remains just a blur to me... I cannot claim to understand it...

Statement by Emily Trott, Kitchen Maid to Lord Greystone

Working down here in the kitchen I never got to go upstairs, where they says all the goings-on started. I mean I ain't *never* been up there. I seen it through the front door once, when I got sent on a holiday to the seaside by her ladyship a few years ago.

It looked lovely inside. I mean, it had plants and I could see the big staircase and the black and white tiled floor and the big painting of an animal above the morning room.

I have to use them small stairs behind the pantry to get up to the room what I shares with Matilda. We don't get to see much of anything that way. It's a nice room, mind, can't say anything but that. Not too big, but all right for us two.

Anyway, I was downstairs cleaning out Mrs Doyle's big pheasant pots when there was a tapping on the servants' door.

The new girl, Dodo, ran to open it. She knew the man there, I'm sure of it. She began to speak to him, but he ignored her, hoping I wouldn't notice nothing.

But I did.

I saw the look what he give her. Telling her to shut up, I say.

'Hello,' he said to me. 'My name is Taylor. Can I get a drink?'

He was very handsome. Tall, broad man, looking a treat in that green uniform. He had a lovely smile and when he took his cap off, he had short hair all smoothed back.

I offered to make him a cup of tea, just as Mrs Doyle come in.

'Who're you then?' she said, not unkind-like, just a bit short. Like when she talks to me or Matilda.

'I'm with the Doctor. That gentleman what's come to see Lord Greystone,' he said. Well, I expect he said it better than that because he was quite cultured, he was. Didn't seem the service type really.

Did I say he had lovely eyes? Really brown and smiley, they was.

'Well, get our guest some tea, Emily,' Mrs Doyle said to me, so I started to boil a kettle.

Dodo sat him down. Mr Golightly was sleeping in the corner, snoring ever so loud he was, but no one said nothing about it. Alice was coming down the stairs, Matilda behind her and I guessed that Tommy was upstairs if a gentleman had come to see the master because he was having to be butler, what with Mr Golightly's illness and everything.

This Taylor, he was chatting away to Dodo, and I knew I was right.

They talked about the weather and the house, but I'm not as stupid as some people think, you know. They were talking in some sort of secret code, I think. But it didn't matter none, because he was really nice and I didn't think he was the type to cause no trouble or nothing. Of course, I was wrong.

After a few moments, I brought him a tea, and one for Mrs Doyle. 'Oh, thanks. Where's mine?' said Dodo.

I ask you – a servant wanting tea in the afternoon. Well, you can imagine the look on Mrs Doyle's face at that…

'Where are you from, Mr Taylor?' she asked.

'Oh, around and about. The Doctor travels a lot,' says he.

So Mrs Doyle says, 'Been anywhere exciting?'

'Oh, a few places. Nowhere you'd have heard of.' He glanced at Dodo again, and she was smiling.

She knew something, I tell you.

Mrs Doyle shrugged. 'I've heard of lots of places, Mr Taylor,' she said. 'Try me.'

'Tombstone in America,' he says. 'And Paris in France.'

'Well, of course I've heard of Paris,' Mrs Doyle snapped. 'I ain't been there, but I know where it is.'

Mr Golightly woke up for a minute and said as how he'd been to Paris when he was a boy. Then he dropped off again.

At least, that's what we thought.

I think it was Alice that said it first. She reached out and took Mrs Doyle's hand and spoke to her quiet-like. I didn't hear nothing she said, but I could see Mr Golightly weren't sleeping no more.

Mrs Doyle gasped and Taylor moved beside Mr Golightly, touching his neck, then his wrist. He moved back slightly and took Mrs Doyle's other hand, but she'd started crying and wailing and everything.

I heard Matilda start up too and realised that, if no one stopped her, she'd make a terrible row, so I tried to calm her while Alice looked after Mrs Doyle.

Dodo said she'd go get the Doctor, and although it weren't really her place to do so, I don't think none of us thought about that at the time.

And that's when everything went really strange.

The door at the top of the stairs to the hall were flung open and… and then she come downstairs. All silver she was, with things like fireflies buzzing around her.

'Miss Annabel,' said Alice, and it was her and all… Except, like I said, she was all silver. Her face, her clothes, her beautiful hair, like… like a statue brought to life.

I remember Taylor pulling Dodo aside, trying to protect her.

'Why is this creature making this noise?' Miss Annabel says – I can still remember it – them words sent shivers up my spine. That weren't really Miss Annabel talking. It looked like her, but it weren't her. Not no way.

And Mrs Doyle, who was still wailing, looked up at her and started screaming.

That's when Miss Annabel did the pointing thing and Mrs Doyle stopped her noise. She just sat back in her chair, her mouth open and staring forward. It were like one of them electrical lights being switched off. Mrs Doyle were just switched off.

Then Taylor and Dodo rushed up the steps, past Miss Annabel and out into the hall.

Statement by Miss Annabel Greystone, daughter to Lord Greystone

It was as if I was not really there any more. As if I was inside my body, but actually not inside it. I could feel someone else beside me. Rather like going for a walk in the park with Mama, like I used to.

I heard it speak to me. I have no idea now whether it was male or female. It reminded me, I suppose, of Ross, but at the same time it was different.

But I know what it said to me. Every time I think about it, I remember. It is rather like a recording on a wax cylinder. It is inside my head now. Always.

'I am not here to hurt you,' it said. 'I just wish to explore. That is my purpose. To adapt. To create. To begin anew.'

I had no idea what it was talking about, of course. I turned to look at Papa and his guest, but they seemed to be not quite… well, not entirely there. I can only think I was either unwell or seeing things through the eyes of the voice in my body.

My father's guest was pointing angrily at Ross and then me. He said, 'Look what you've done, you meddlesome fool. Is this your gift to this planet and this time? This universe, hmm? The absorption of this delightful young lady?'

And then the noise started from below. I remember thinking something was happening to the servants – it sounded like dear sweet Mrs Doyle – and before I knew what was happening, I was on the steps to the kitchen.

Mrs Doyle was crying loudly and all I could think was how I wished she would stop.

And then she did.

I was aware of two people pushing past me – one I recognised as that new under-parlour maid with the silly name; the other a man I did not know. We... I followed them back upstairs and into the hall.

They were standing with the Doctor, arguing and pointing at me.

'This wasn't supposed to happen, Doctor,' said the man.

'I know, my boy, I know. I miscalculated the depths this young fool would sink to.' The Doctor said, then looked straight at my father. I wanted to tell them that it would be all right, that I was enjoying this experience, but I could not speak.

'We have travelled far,' the voice said to me, and I realised the others could hear it as well. 'I ordered Roztoq to bring me here as a result of your meddling on our planet, Doctor. When we learned what else was out there, when we learned there were other universes beyond our own, our home seemed microscopic and unimportant.'

The man I didn't know seemed to agree. 'I can understand your desire to explore. I'm guilty of it too. But I'm careful. I have the Doctor as a guide. How did you get here?'

Ross – or Roztoq, as he had been revealed to be – answered, and I knew the voice that spoke through him was also the voice inside me. 'Because, to use the vernacular of these primitives, we "rode the coat-tails" of the Doctor's TARDIS. He brought us here, to this planet. I... we... "let go" shortly before you landed. Once we learned of this planet through his… heritage, we knew it was what we needed.'

'Heritage?' That was that silly Dodo girl.

'Oh, ignore his babbling, my child,' said the Doctor. 'He knows nothing of my heritage. But I know of his. Of theirs.' He addressed Roztoq once more. 'You poor, pitiful, lost creatures. Don't you realise that you have no part in this Universe? Every second you spend here is destroying the nexus of all realities? Well, does that mean anything to you, hmm? Just by leaving Quinnis, by leaving the Fourth Universe and entering this one, you have damaged a reality that isn't your own.'

'So? You do it all the time,' Roztoq said.

'My ship is protected, it re-seals the breaches it makes in the Vortex, whether through time or space or other dimensions. You broke through, you and your symbiont here, and the damage needs repairing. The longer you stay in a universe not your own, you risk tearing at the very fabric of their reality. Do you understand me?'

'Then repair it yourself, Traveller,' said the voice inside me. 'We want to live here. To escape the state of Ronnos.'

The Doctor tossed his head back, giving Roztoq and then me – or whatever possessed me – his most unsympathetic gaze. 'So, you are criminals, are you, hmm? On the run from the prison moon. Well, if I brought you here, I see it as my duty to take you home. Willingly or unwillingly.'

My father was confused, I could see it written on his face. 'Who are these… people, Doctor?'

The Doctor gave Roztoq a contemptuous snort. 'This? This is nothing. Cattle. The equivalent of a mindless beast of burden on your planet. Like an ox. Or a faithful dog. His thoughts, his words and his actions are animated by the symbiont controlling your daughter. By creating the personality of this "marquis", they were more easily able to blend into your society.'

He turned back to look at me. Us.

And then something extraordinary happened. The Doctor walked towards me. Us. And reached out for my face.

And I heard him speak, but so softly it was like… like the wind on autumn leaves, gently brushing my ears.

'Fight it, dear child,' he whispered. 'This power that has enveloped you is misguided, dangerous. It has no place here. Now it's left its original host, it needs you to keep it awake. To keep it sentient. It does not belong here on this planet, in this place. If you shut it out now, before it can absorb you wholly, it cannot function. It is nearing the end of its energy, and will soon take yours. Fight it, my dear, you must fight it. Remember who you are.'

And I saw Mama. And Grandpapa. And Aunt Morag. And other people I knew to be dead and gone.

They were all asking me to fight the voice. And there, amidst them, I could see the imperious face of the Doctor, smiling at me. Encouraging me.

And I knew that however pleasant the voice inside me was, I could trust this Doctor more.

And so I told the voice to leave me.

And it did.

Statement by Matilda Jenkins, Scullery Maid to Lord Greystone

We was watching from the top of the stairs. Me and Emily was frightened but we still watched as the silver angel flew away from Miss Annabel, and she fell down and weren't silver no more. Then the angel seemed to vanish and the old gentleman what was His Lordship's visitor reached down and picked something up, and His Lordship took poor Miss Annabel into the morning room, helped by Thomas.

Oh, and then the driver what had had tea with us hit the young marquis on the chin, just like this – *wallop!* – and he fell down, and the old man told him to carry him out to their car. And he said that he knew where the 'entry point' was or something, that his 'TARDIS had traced it' and that now they'd 'found them' they would take them back and 'seal up the breach'. But I didn't know what none of it meant. I just held Emily's hand and prayed Miss Annabel would be all right again.

And Dodo went with them and we never saw her again. Never.

Nor the driver, Taylor weren't it? Nor the old gentleman or the marquis.

And that's really where it went funny, because the next thing I knew was that the policemen came and the ambulance took away poor Mr Golightly and Mrs Doyle, who never spoke another word, never.

And… and now I'm sitting here talking to you and I'm really a bit afraid because I've not seen Emily or Alice or Mrs Doyle or his Lordship since and I don't like it up here much. I don't fit in with all them fancy pictures and chairs and things.

I just want to go downstairs again. Back to my life in the kitchens of 64 Carlysle Street.

Where I belong.

'What do you think, Sergeant?'

Sergeant Dunston shrugged as they walked down the long pathway. 'I really don't know, sir. It all seems a bit odd to me. And I don't think we'll be getting much out of Mrs Doyle.'

Inspector Brown agreed. 'At first I was tempted to think that someone had assaulted Miss Greystone, possibly this Rostock fellow, and they were covering up to save her honour. But the death of the old butler and this, this… what did the quack call it?'

'A "catatonic state",' said Dunston, consulting his notebook.

Brown nodded. 'Right, well, whatever Mrs Doyle is in makes me think it's some sort of delayed shock to the old man's death. I mean, he'd been a pretty permanent fixture in the household for donkey's years.'

'The lads checked up on this Doctor Whoever-he-was and this Dorothea Chaplet and Steven Taylor. None of them were registered at the Bentinck Hotel and Mrs Trotter there doesn't recognise their descriptions at all. And there's no Marquis of Rostock either. Never has been as far as we can tell.'

'Guess we'll not get to the bottom of all this in a hurry, Sergeant.'

Sergeant Dunston flipped his notebook shut and pointed to the sign next to the tall iron gates as they passed through.

'I reckon the whole lot of them should be in there with Mrs Doyle, sir.'

'If they stick to this mad fiction, Sergeant,' said Inspector Brown, shaking his head, 'I've a feeling they'll be joining her. Masters and servants all waited on together.'

As the Inspector trudged off down the road, smiling at his little joke, Dunston shut the gates of the Little Sisters of Marcham Common's Home for the Mentally Unstable behind them.

The Eternity Contract

by Steve Lyons

Patricia Hopkins died today. It came as something of a surprise.

As she lay on dirty tarmac, life ebbing from her broken body, her fading thoughts were of the things that she had still to do. Who would chase up those creditors? Deal with the coffee account? Voyeurs crowded around her. She wanted to stand, send them scuttling away with a few well-chosen words and resume her daily bustle. Patricia had always lived at top speed. She had not become one of London's most successful advertising executives by standing still.

She hadn't seen the car coming. Too busy juggling too many things. Hurrying to a meeting; checking her organiser to see if she could fit in a lunch date; scolding her PA into action over the mobile, while considering a replacement.

Too many things. Now she could do none of them. The spark of life abandoned her, before she could even accept what was happening.

Patricia Hopkins died today.

And found herself in the drawing room of an old house, the sympathetic faces of an elderly couple looming over her.

'Awake at last, dear,' said the woman; a voice and a smile like melted sugar. 'Would you like a cup of tea?'

'Take it easy,' said the man. 'It is a bit confusing at first, I know – but welcome to our humble home, all the same.'

'What home?' Patricia stammered, brain feeling like a sponge. She tried to sit up, remembered too late that her bones had been shattered, then realised they had mended. She didn't know whether to feel relieved or apprehensive. 'What happened to me? How did I get here?'

'You died, of course,' said the woman. 'You died and came here.'

'To the next stage of being,' said the man, with a reassuring smile. 'I'm Richard Ferris, and this is my wife, Jean. So pleased to meet you.'

* * *

The beast cannoned into the Doctor's side. He was floored, caught off-guard by the speed and ferocity of the attack. Nyssa screamed. The Doctor was on his back, struggling to keep jaws from clamping about his throat. Saliva cascaded over jagged teeth.

Nyssa felt as if she was moving at half-speed, too slow to save her friend. It took seconds to find a hefty enough stick; more to wrench it from the sodden undergrowth.

The Doctor caught hold of the beast's neck. It pulled free. Its head swooped again. He batted it away with an elbow. Unhurt, it resumed its attack.

With a whimper, Nyssa drove the stick down, over and over, into the monster's hide. Droplets of water erupted from matted fur. The beast cast its head about, snapping for the stick until it caught it and yanked it from Nyssa's hands. The Doctor seized his opportunity to send it sliding into the mud, claws scrabbling to gain purchase. It was wary of them now, torn between their soft meat scent and the safety of retreat. The Doctor ushered Nyssa behind him, and they backed away together. His blond hair was plastered down, the pastel colours of his cricketing outfit lost beneath the greens and browns of the forest. His expression was intense and unsure. For long seconds, the only sound was that of rain. Despite the shelter of leaves, Nyssa felt cold water dribbling into her velvet suit. She suppressed a shudder, until the beast was out of sight behind the trees.

When at last it was, the Doctor turned to her and whispered: 'Back to the TARDIS?'

'The TARDIS,' she agreed with feeling.

They turned – and froze, at the sound of a feral cry from in front of them. Another beast. Nearby.

The Doctor's haunted eyes belied his casual tone. 'Or we could see what lies *this* way.'

Lightning bleached the world for an instant. A peal of thunder followed, too loud, too close, for Nyssa's liking. The rain bore down with increased intensity. She was glad to see that the forest was beginning to thin out at last, although it meant losing its protection from the downpour.

They had discussed the wolf-thing in subdued tones; had agreed that neither of them had encountered its species before. 'It seems the TARDIS has brought us somewhere new,' the Doctor had mused. 'Now, if only the old girl could tell me where – and why.'

They stepped beyond the tree line, and a wonderful sight caused Nyssa to forget her weariness. A building. Shelter.

'Doctor, look!'

He had seen it too – or, at least, its shadow against the overcast evening sky. It was a hulking structure: an imposing, asymmetrical conglomeration of turrets and wings. As they gazed upon it, another fork of lightning filled in the silhouette for them.

Nyssa was struck by the building's sad condition. In its prime, she could imagine it had once served as a country mansion, a home to the rich. Time had taken its toll, eroding stonework and causing walls to crumble. Vegetation grew in ever-widening cracks and deepening holes. It evoked an unwelcome sense of regret. She was reminded that the march of time was inexorable; that years gone by could never be reclaimed. She thought of her home world, Traken.

Soon, they were standing before a pitted wooden door, to which decades of neglect clung fiercely. Conversely, the brass doorknocker with its lion's head motif gleamed proudly. Nyssa could see her own bedraggled reflection, warped by its camber.

'Well, it looks as if somebody lives here, at least.' The Doctor lifted the knocker, but paused and frowned.

'What is it?'

'Just a thought. A rather worrying one. We assumed those beasts in the forest were trying to herd us away from their territory.'

'But?'

'What if their intention was to do the opposite?'

Nyssa had been uncomfortable enough even without the shard of fear that the Doctor words sent slithering down her back.

His eyes remained distant for a moment. Then, shaking off his foreboding as if he could just box it away for future reference, he faced their situation with renewed confidence.

'Let's see if we can wake somebody up, shall we?'

* * *

Three great cracks snapped Patricia out of her doze. She had dreamed of home and, for a second, did not know where she was. Then her mind sorted memory from fiction, and a familiar weight settled upon her heart.

She was cold, although she had been sleeping in the long, red dress that she had dug out of an old chest. She sat on her bed, stared up at the wooden timbers, and resumed her furious attempts to think of a way to escape from this damnable house.

The knocking came again, and merged with thunder from without. Somebody was at the door.

The police, come to find her? A concerned neighbour? Hope surged through Patricia like electricity, jolting her into action. She hurried out of her room, along the corridor and on to the balcony from which she could peer down into the great hall, three floors below. She held her breath as the door opened. She had never seen that door open before. She thought about dashing down the stairs; hurtling through it before anyone could stop her. But fear froze her. Fear and logic. How far could she get?

'You see, Nyssa?' said the Doctor with deliberate cheer. 'The door was unlocked all along.' He strode into the hallway. '"Knock, knock, knock and it shall be opened unto you." Now, I wonder if anyone's home?' He glanced around, taking in the threadbare carpet on the grand staircase, the faded paintings and the chandelier glinting in the flames of newly lit candles. Despite its musty odour, the house had had recent occupants. He cupped his hands to his mouth and yelled: 'Hello?'

A crash punctuated the echoes of his call. He and Nyssa whirled around to see that the door behind them had slammed shut. A freak air current, perhaps. They exchanged brief, worried glances. The temperature seemed to drop.

'Doctor?'

'Nothing to worry about, Nyssa, it's only an old house.' He didn't meet her eyes. He had to take her mind off the cold, the dark, the air of gloom. His own mind too. He was reminded of an uncomfortable part of his past. On Gallifrey.

In search of distraction, his eyes alighted upon a painting by the door. 'Oh, I say, that's rather interesting.'

Nyssa frowned as they moved to inspect it. 'A picture of a skull?'

'Ah, but do you see those lumps on its temples?'

'Horns?'

'Precisely. And yet, it appears otherwise human.'

'It's only an old painting,' Nyssa pointed out.

'I wonder.' The Doctor pulled at his lower lip and tried to focus on insubstantial thoughts. He stared into a pair of blank eye sockets and, for a second, was drifting alone in a void.

He heard Nyssa's gasp of surprise, as if from the end of a long tunnel.

He tore himself away from the bleak image, and felt a wrench as he returned to a world that had seemed momentarily distant and unreal.

He blinked. He followed Nyssa's startled gaze. He saw the elderly couple.

The couple smiled in unison.

A clock ticked softly in the drawing room. Plush velvet curtains shielded the room from the storm raging outside.

Jean Ferris offered to make tea, and the Doctor accepted gratefully. Nyssa dried herself by the fire in the open grate. As Jean collected a soot-black kettle from atop the sideboard, her husband Richard drew her to one side.

'Two new arrivals?' he whispered urgently. 'Two?'

Jean looked at him with dead eyes and an impenetrable expression. Then, seeing the Doctor's inquisitive look, she forced a smile. She hung the kettle over the fire, and asked the new arrivals what had brought them here.

'Oh, just exploring really,' the Doctor lied breezily. 'We got caught in the storm.'

Jean shook her head and tutted softly. 'Exposure to the elements. I see. You should have taken an umbrella, young man.'

'Well, it wasn't raining when we came out,' he said defensively.

'Where are we exactly?' asked Nyssa.

'This is Carnon Manor, dear,' said Jean.

'But where is that?'

Richard and Jean Ferris glanced at each other, but didn't answer. The Doctor studied their body language. They were nervous, but not overly so. Tired, perhaps. Or weary. They posed no immediate threat. But there was something sinister about the couple.

'May we stay here,' he asked, 'until the storm passes?'

That look again.

'We'd be no trouble,' he continued, as if he hadn't seen it. He stuffed his hands into his pockets and gave them his appealing, little-boy-lost routine. 'We'll leave as soon as it's light.'

'There is no light here,' said Richard. 'The storm doesn't pass.'

His words were underscored by a fierce thunderclap. A china ornament on the mantelpiece rattled in sympathy. Candles flickered as cold tendrils of wind crept around the window frame.

Jean's face fell. 'Oh dear, you really don't understand, do you? How do you think you arrived at this house?'

'Well, I rather thought through the front door.'

'That's not possible!' snapped Richard, with a sudden and unexpected severity.

'There is only one way to reach Carnon Manor, dear,' said Jean. 'I am very much afraid you both died in this forest of yours.'

Steam whistled from the spout of the kettle, and she moved to fetch it. 'Now, does anyone take sugar?'

China rattled and flames flickered again. This time, there was no doubting that the building had trembled, just slightly.

They sat and sipped tea from dainty cups. The Doctor chatted casually, about the weather and all manner of nothing. Nyssa could not settle. It was something about this place. The decor, the candlelight, the storm. Its occupants too. She imagined creatures pouncing from the shadows in the corners of the room. She glimpsed a leather-winged monstrosity, swooping for her neck. She turned sharply, but it was a flapping curtain.

She was not one to surrender so to unscientific fears.

Even so, she jumped, spilling tea into her lap, as the door flew open.

A wide-eyed, wild-haired teenaged boy hurtled through it, and stopped short. For a moment, his chin trembled too much for him to speak. 'What is it, Douglas dear?' asked Jean.

'M-Melissa was right. She said… the creature. It's started. There are two of them. Two. My God, my God…'

The Doctor gave him a friendly smile. 'Hello.'

The boy's face crumpled. He turned and fled from the room.

'Oh dear,' said the Doctor, 'it seems we haven't made a very good first impression.'

'Young Douglas is somewhat distraught,' said Jean. 'It's just his way, I'm afraid.'

'Who else lives here?' the Doctor asked.

'Well, there's Dr Morton. We don't see much of him; he hides himself away in his lab. There's Melissa – she'll find you soon enough, you'll get used to her – and that smart young woman, Patricia. Always in a rush. She's new here, she'll learn.'

'And Lord Carnon, of course,' said Richard. 'He owns the house.'

'Hmm. Does he now?'

Nyssa could restrain herself no longer. 'What did the boy mean,' she blurted out, 'about a creature? About something starting?'

The Doctor glared at her disapprovingly and the Ferrises clammed up.

'What was he so scared of?' cried Nyssa.

'I've been on edge since we arrived here,' she explained later, in the generously proportioned bedroom to which the Ferrises had directed her. 'I don't know why.' She sighed, and sat on her impressive four-poster bed. She sank into its mattress, feeling weary.

'It's understandable.' The Doctor stood at the window, and observed the patterns of the storm. 'Thunder and lightning. A young couple in search of shelter. A Gothic mansion with strange occupants. How many times have you seen this scenario in old horror movies?'

'We didn't have "horror movies" on Traken.' Nyssa's best friend, Tegan, had explained the genre to her once. She had been repelled. Such glorification of evil and violence was alien to her culture.

A frown crossed the Doctor's face as he turned to her. 'No, you didn't, did you? The iconography is Earth-specific, then.'

'You're saying that all this – this building, this environment – has been engineered by someone, to trigger primitive fear responses?'

'Perhaps.'

'Do you feel it too?'

'I can feel that there are… forces at work here, yes,' muttered the Doctor. He could be every bit as evasive as the Ferrises when quizzed about his feelings, or his past.

Nyssa was sure that he would not answer her next question, but she had to ask it. 'What frightens you, Doctor?'

The lights of Traken grew dim.

Nyssa clung to her mother's skirts as the protective dome dwindled around them. There were Melkurs in the night beyond; evil spirits that lived only to vanquish the Union's goodness. Though she could not see them, she knew that each bore the face of the man who had slain her father and destroyed her world. Many Trakenites had fallen from the shelter of the dome already. The Doctor was there, providing comfort, but he was so vulnerable himself.

The lights went out.

Nyssa screamed as she jerked upright in the bed in Carnon Manor. Her scream turned into a stifled gasp as she realised that somebody else was present. A woman, thirty-something, hair tied back into a neat bun. The woman leapt back, startled. Then, composing herself, she spread out her hands in a placatory gesture.

'I'm not here to hurt you.'

'Who are you?'

'Patricia. Patricia Hopkins. I've been held here for three days.'

'You're a captive?'

'Please say you can help me. I must get out of this madhouse, before I'm driven as insane as all the others!'

If the rest of Carnon Manor was patterned after a generic horror movie, then Dr Morton's laboratory came off the set of *Frankenstein*.

Coloured liquids boiled in glass beakers, connected by copper pipes. A sulphurous odour pervaded the air.

The Doctor inspected the equipment with casual interest. Morton hadn't heard his approach. A middle-aged man whose remaining hair had prematurely greyed, he perched on a stool in a stained lab coat, mumbling to himself as he scribbled on a pad. Discarded balls of paper were strewn about the floor, a few spent biros amongst them.

The Doctor cleared his throat politely.

'Yes, yes, what is it? Can't you see I'm busy?'

The Doctor peered over Morton's shoulder and spotted a small error in his equations. 'Six,' he corrected, pointing it out. Morton stopped his frantic writing, glared at the offending number and, with bad grace, tore the sheet from the pad and flung it across the room.

'Well, there was no need to go quite that far.'

'It was useless,' said Morton sulkily. 'Always useless. So close to making a breakthrough – so close – can't afford to make such basic mistakes!' He banged a fist into his bench.

'Then perhaps you should get some rest. It is nearly five o'clock, you know.'

Morton looked at the Doctor for the first time. His eyes were red-rimmed, but the fervour in them blazed just as red. 'No time to rest. Don't know how long I've got. Been given a second chance, you know. Can't squander it.'

From somewhere in the bowels of the house, a clock struck the hour. Morton levered himself to his feet and moved, as if sleepwalking, to where a Bunsen burner heated a clear solution in a beaker atop a tripod. He turned off the flame, peered myopically at the liquid and sighed. Deflated, he sank onto another stool and rubbed his eyes

'What are you trying to do?' the Doctor asked. 'I might be able to help, you know.'

'Cancer,' Morton answered, almost voicelessly.

'Ah.'

'I'm trying to find a cure.'

The Doctor clapped him on the back; a hopeless gesture of support.

'Very worthy.'

'Not really,' said Morton. 'It's for my own benefit.'

'I see.' The Doctor pursed his lips, thinking long and hard before he asked his next question. 'How long do you have?'

The bewildered look on Morton's face confirmed his suspicion, before the man even spoke.

'I died two months ago,' he said woodenly.

The clock stood at half-past eight, but the darkness hadn't lifted. Rain still lashed the windows. Clouds painted the sky black. Patricia assured her new friends that the thunderstorm never ended.

They had searched the house – Patricia, Nyssa and the Doctor – familiarising themselves with its tortuous layout before coming to rest in a small, out-of-the-way study, where they talked.

Patricia was surprised when the Doctor asked her from which world and time she hailed. She told him, because she had begun to believe that he was her only hope. He didn't seem much, but his contemplative manner gave the impression that he secreted all the knowledge in the world.

'I expected as much,' he muttered. 'It seems that all the residents are from Earth, 1999.'

'Is that significant?' asked Nyssa.

'Perhaps.' The Doctor turned to Patricia. 'Has anybody said anything to you? Any clues about where we might be?'

She shook her head quickly, shutting her mind to the unnerving claims of Richard and Jean. 'The old couple talk in riddles. I think they enjoy scaring people. So does Melissa Hamilton: a spiteful, horrible child. The boy, Doug Williams, hasn't said anything coherent at all.'

'Hmm. I spoke to the other resident, Doctor Morton, earlier. A sad man, driven by a futile cause. He supported the Ferrises' claim, by the way.' The Doctor looked directly at Patricia as he said this. She shivered. 'He says he died too. It seems that Nyssa and I are the only people here who didn't.'

'I won't accept that we are in some sort of afterlife,' insisted Patricia.

She couldn't accept it. There would be no escape, in that case.

'No, nor will I,' said the Doctor. 'Not yet.' He sprung to his feet, newly charged with energy. 'Time to leave, I think.'

He breezed out of the room, and Nyssa followed without complaint as if she was used to so doing. Patricia felt hopeful, but she dispelled the cruel sensation with reason. She had tried to leave Carnon Manor before, without success. She had told the Doctor as much, but he could not have listened.

He couldn't lead them out of here so easily. Could he?

As they approached the front door, the Doctor motioned to the women to stay back. He stepped forward, tentatively at first and then with more confidence. His hand tingled as he reached for the knob, as if the air around it was charged. An illusion. The effect of a low-grade telepathic force field, simple for a Time Lord to resist. He smiled.

And felt a dreadful pressure in his mind.

His attention was dragged to the source of the assault. He stared into the skull painting, reeling beneath the energies that radiated from its hollow eyes. His soul was turned inside out.

He didn't remember falling, and yet he was on the floor. He massaged his temples, blinking as a cloud of pain dispersed in his head. Nyssa asked how he felt. Instead of answering, he put a question of his own to Patricia. 'Did this happen to you?'

'Not exactly. I just couldn't reach the knob. I did tell you that.'

He nodded. 'Windows?'

'Unbreakable glass.'

'I doubt it – but impervious, all the same.'

'Then we are trapped in here?' asked Nyssa.

'For now.'

They found the topmost room of the house and, from there, emerged on to a narrow outside parapet. Though assaulted by the elements, they were grateful for the fresh air. Nyssa peered over the edge, but could not see the ground, through darkness and mist.

'We couldn't climb down there,' she concluded. 'Could we?'

She wanted, against all logic, to believe that they could. She wanted the Doctor to find a way.

'I'd be surprised,' he said. 'Somebody's gone to an awful lot of trouble to keep us in this house. If the weather itself is under their control – and I suspect it is – we can expect it to work against us. The attempt could be fatal. That's even if we could find a long enough rope.'

It seemed too much for Patricia. 'What are they trying to do to us?' she cried. 'They've just left this open as a torment, to… to show us what they're keeping from us!'

'I think you're right,' said the Doctor.

'There are three of us. Why can't we confront those people, Richard and Jean, force them to tell us the way out of here?'

'I shouldn't imagine they actually know.'

Patricia gave a moan of anger and frustration, turned, and pushed her way back inside.

'I had that impression too,' said Nyssa, raising her voice to be heard over the wind and the rain. 'I don't think the Ferrises understand this place any more than we do. I think they're prisoners here like everybody else.'

She expected the Doctor to respond, but he was silent. She looked, and saw that he was staring into the distance.

'Evil,' he said, his voice little more than a murmur but carrying clearly. 'Evil, festering in the cracks of the universe, while those who could challenge it sit idly by, not caring. Not seeing it in time. Not being strong enough to hold back the black tide.' He turned to her, as lost and uncertain as she had ever seen him.

Nyssa had survived many perils with the Doctor. She had confidence in him, believed in him, or she couldn't have gone on. But sometimes, her faith was shaken. Sometimes, when he didn't believe in himself.

'You asked what frightens me,' he said hollowly.

The building gave its most protracted and violent tremor yet.

Patricia did not recognise her surroundings; could not remember how she had come to them. The corridors of this godforsaken house seemed to shift each time she walked them.

She had to think clearly; take control. This frightened, weeping, dependent girl was not her. Not the tough-hearted executive who had won success through determination. She composed herself, wiped tears from her face and marched around the next corner.

She screamed as Doug Williams barrelled into her, knocking her against the far wall and onto the floor.

Fear turned to embarrassment, and then anger. 'You should learn to watch –' she began, glowering up at him. Her throat was stopped by the terror in his eyes.

'It's coming,' he whispered hoarsely. 'I can feel it!'

The springs of the rocking chair creaked as Jean Ferris swayed to and fro. She stared at the ceiling and sipped her tea. Richard hovered by the door, occasionally crossing the room to move something on the mantelpiece or to straighten a picture.

'Carnon Manor,' said Jean, 'is a brief respite on the voyage to oblivion. That's how Nicholas refers to it.'

The Doctor cocked an eyebrow. 'Nicholas?'

'Lord Carnon.'

'We haven't met him yet,' said Nyssa.

'He comes and goes as he pleases,' Richard put in gruffly.

Nyssa and the Doctor exchanged a hopeful look.

'A half-way house to the other side,' said Jean. She was almost talking to herself, and Nyssa had to strain to hear her. 'We are brought here when we die. Eventually, we shall leave. For whatever else awaits us. The creature will take us there.'

'The creature?' prompted the Doctor, leaning forward, making no attempt to hide his eagerness.

'In the cellar,' said Richard.

'It is stirring,' said Jean, in the same quiet, haunted voice. 'The house feels it. The creature always stirs when we are too many. Carnon Manor will hold only six guests. There are eight of us now.'

'So this creature will manifest itself in the house?' said the Doctor. 'It will take two people? It will… kill them?'

'We don't see it,' said Richard, a hint of resentment filtering into his voice. 'We can't stop it.'

The couple seemed resigned to their fates. So placid. Nyssa couldn't understand them. 'We could at least try!'

Jean chuckled softly. 'I don't think it will take us, dear. You are too new here. And Richard and I, well, we are too old. We have lived here for decades now.'

'The creature favours us.'

But Jean's knuckles were white on the arms of her chair. Richard made to move an ornament, and knocked it into the hearth instead. Nyssa watched them both through narrowed eyes, and knew that they did not believe their own assurances.

'We have to get out of here,' Doug insisted. 'We have to get out before it's too late!'

'That's hardly news to me,' said Patricia drily.

'We have to get *out*,' Doug cried, more earnestly.

'And you know a way, do you?'

'Just one way. Just one.'

Doug turned and fled. Patricia scrambled to her feet. The boy was deranged with fear, she told herself. He couldn't even know what he was saying. She ran after him anyway, saddened by the thought that false hope was better than none. She was desperate. So too was Doug.

She realised too late what he had planned. She called after him in vain as he mounted the stairs to the tower room, gaining ground on her with every step.

A curtain billowed in the wind. Patricia rushed out through the open door, recoiling from the rain's stinging greeting. Shielding her eyes, she made out Doug's form, a silhouette against the stormy sky. He stood precariously on the balcony rail, shaking.

Patricia had always imagined herself staying cool in such a crisis; able to use common sense, to talk the boy down. Instead, she shouted something ill-judged about his cowardice. It was blown back to her on the wind.

She reached out to him, but it was too late.

Doug Williams leapt into the storm.

* * *

120

The Doctor tried to provoke Dr Morton into action. 'Your work will mean nothing,' he insisted, 'if you can't take it to where it is needed.'

'There will be a way. Fate has provided thus far.'

'We have to learn the secret of this house. We have to find out why some mysterious creature is killing its occupants.'

'We are dead already, Doctor. I only know that I have been given a chance beyond death.'

'And don't you want to know why? Aren't you curious?'

Morton had eyes only for his test tubes.

'What if the creature takes you next?'

Morton shook his head. 'It would not be logical. I have been given this chance to complete my work and I am close to so doing. Why should it be snatched from me?'

'Fate can be capricious,' the Doctor warned. 'And some of us,' he added as a parting shot, 'aren't dead yet.'

Nyssa had been resting, hoping to ease the dull pain in her head. Something about Carnon Manor seemed to sap her reserves. But she could not sleep.

She found herself wandering, in a semi-daze, around the house. She was looking for the Doctor, Patricia, anyone. She found only distorted shadows, leering in the deceptive candlelight.

She descended a flight of stairs to the ground floor. Although she had explored before, she did not recognise this hallway.

The house shook again and she almost fell. Jerked into alertness, she watched as, in seeming slow motion, a dislodged candle pirouetted to the floor. Improbably, its flame survived and caught in the dry carpet. Nyssa half wanted to see this building burn, but feared she would be trapped inside as it did. She looked for something with which to smother the fire, and ripped a dusty tapestry from the wall. She threw it down and jumped on it, until smoke no longer seeped from its edges.

Turning, she saw for the first time that she had uncovered a door beneath the stairs. Richard Ferris's words came back to her, and she knew that she had found the entrance to the cellar. The cellar in which the creature lurked.

Nyssa stared at the door for what seemed like an age. She was curious about what lay beyond. No, more than that, she wanted to overcome her fears, to pull open the door, to reveal the rational, scientific explanation for all this that was being kept from her.

The fear was too strong. She could not make herself move.

'Still fighting against it, girlie?'

Nyssa whirled, surprised that somebody could have crept up on her. She saw a young woman, dressed in black, white make-up plastered over her face, an ankh design tattooed on her left cheek. She sneered, and light glinted off gold rings in her lip. 'They all fight it at first. They look for ways out of the house, explanations for what goes on inside. They don't find them. After a few years, they accept it: those who aren't driven mad.'

Nyssa swallowed and tried to sound in control. 'You must be Melissa. I was told about you.'

The woman scowled. 'Oh, were you, girlie? I suppose they told you to beware of poor Melissa; too common for your upper-class clothes and speech and pretty-pretty little face. You won't last a week here, girlie. You'll crack, like all the spoilt ones do.'

'At least I'm trying to do something constructive. I won't just accept being trapped here!'

Melissa threw back her head and laughed: a hard, spiteful cackle which stoked a resentful anger in Nyssa. She was almost grateful for it. It overcame the fear. She let it carry her forward. 'Laugh all you like. I'll find a way out of this house, without your help!' She turned the handle and yanked the door open.

To Melissa's delight, she revealed only a brick wall.

Patricia was in the drawing room, with the Doctor and the Ferrises, nursing one of Jean's cups of tea and trying to appear strong. It irked her that Richard and Jean seemed not to be upset by Doug's suicide. A part of her wanted to be so emotionless, so centred. She had been, once.

'My dear,' said Jean, 'young Douglas didn't die today.'

'Because he was dead already?' snapped Patricia. 'Don't give me that afterlife crap!'

The woman laughed. 'You misunderstand, dear. Douglas could not have left here. The decision is not ours to take.'

'Well, he took it all right. He couldn't have survived that fall.'

The Doctor leaned forward, staring at Jean intently. 'What are you saying? That Doug Williams is alive?'

Richard barked a short, cruel laugh. 'Not alive, exactly.'

They found him in the spacious kitchen, where the Doctor had promised to fix a long overdue meal for Nyssa and Patricia, and for anybody else who was interested. Patricia took two breaths, then turned and fled. The Doctor understood her reaction. Most of what they had seen could be explained somehow. The claims of the residents did not have to be believed. But Doug Williams had died – and yet, here he was, seated upon a stool, pale and quiet but most definitely alive. How could science explain that?

'Is something wrong with Patricia?' asked Doug, and the Doctor was struck by his calmness. He could almost have been sedated.

He buried his hands in his pockets. 'I think there has been a slight misunderstanding. She rather had the impression that you died.'

Doug shrugged indifferently. 'We all did, didn't we?'

The creature came for Dr Donald Morton in the small hours of the next morning. It was heralded by an almighty tremor, and by an awful sense of loss. Nyssa knew that Morton had gone, and grieved although she had never met him. She found herself slipping on her shoes and wandering to the top of the main staircase, where she discovered the Doctor, Patricia and Jean.

'I take it we all felt the same thing?' said the Doctor.

'Everybody felt it,' said Jean, in a dulled voice. 'Morton has been taken. You responded because you are still new. In time, you will react as they all do. You will turn over in your sleep, and you will rest more easily through relief that the creature did not take you. I alone maintain a vigil for those who have passed beyond.'

The Doctor stared at her, and seemed lost for words. At last, without speaking, he turned and hared down the stairs. Nyssa called to him, but he ignored her. She followed him instinctively.

When the next tremor came, she was caught unprepared. She missed her footing and pitched headlong, screaming.

Somehow the Doctor was beneath her, breaking her fall. She held on to him gratefully. Glancing up, she saw that Patricia had taken a few tentative steps towards them, drawn by her plight. She had stopped now, uncertain again. Jean had not moved.

'There is no rest for the creature today,' she intoned. 'Lord Carnon allows only six guests to reside in his house. One more must leave.'

The Doctor scowled and, pushing Nyssa aside, hurried on. She dogged his heels determinedly as he darted along passages and tore open doors, sometimes bobbing into a room and back out again, sometimes hurtling through one. They came to the drawing room, finally, though it was not where Nyssa remembered it as being.

There, the Doctor halted at last, though his head jerked from side to side, eyes searching, body restless but deprived of purpose.

'What is it, Doctor?' Nyssa asked, when she had recovered breath to speak. 'What are you looking for?'

'Dr Morton's laboratory. It's gone. I had hoped to examine it, to find some clue to the nature of this creature, but it's gone.'

'The configuration of the house keeps changing.' Nyssa spoke the words absently, more concerned with watching the Doctor. She knew he was much older than he appeared, but this was the first time she had believed it of this particular incarnation. He rubbed his eyes with the fingers of one hand, and gritted his teeth with the effort of thought.

'There's no logic to this place. Events occurring at random, things making no sense. I can't operate without logic.'

'You need to rest.' Nyssa's voice trembled with the fear that rest might not be enough. 'You haven't slept at all yet.'

The Doctor seemed almost outraged by the suggestion. As if to disprove her words, he jerked into motion, although he could only pace the room impotently. 'Time could be of the essence. We're dealing with an unknown foe. Why does he want us here? What are his plans?' He pivoted to face Nyssa, his eyes alight. His words came in staccato bursts, through a barely contained panic that robbed him of breath. 'What – what terrible evils are being let loose upon the universe now, as we stand here talking about sleep?'

'Doctor…'

'What if I can't escape? What if I'm not strong enough?'

Nyssa burst into tears. 'You're scaring me, Doctor. I trust you, and you've given up!'

The Doctor fell silent and suddenly Nyssa was aware of what she had done. She felt stupid and immature. She had not cried since… since Traken and the Master. She controlled herself and looked up at him, expecting to see disappointment in his expression. Instead, he was just surprised, as if her outburst had shocked him out of his own uncharacteristic behaviour. He produced a handkerchief and dabbed the tears from her cheeks, the kindly gentleman again.

'This house manipulates our emotions,' he deduced, his voice calm but strained. 'It's more than the obvious trappings. It's the secrets, the disparate characters with whom we're confined, the whole "land beyond death" scenario, the creature. And perhaps more. It began with the beast in the forest. Whoever is behind this, they don't just want us imprisoned. They want us scared.'

'They're doing a good job,' said Nyssa, forcing a laugh through her embarrassment.

'I think, perhaps, we both need to sleep.'

'I wish I could! This place gives me nightmares. I feel like I'm being watched all the time.'

The Doctor said nothing, but Nyssa could tell that she had launched a train of thought.

Another day ground by in Carnon Manor.

The Doctor spent most of it in silent contemplation, punctuated by manic bursts of energy in which he sought out other residents and questioned them, often about their absent landlord.

Doug remained subdued and amnesiac. He knew nothing of his suicide bid, so could not explain his resurrection. Patricia kept away from him. She maintained that she was coping, while her capable façade continued to peel.

The normally placid Ferrises erupted into a flaming row and crockery was thrown. So far as anyone could tell, there was no reason for it. Melissa laughed and assured Nyssa that such incidents were commonplace. The strain, she said, told on everybody, in one way or another. She hinted that, were it not for the couple's tempers, they would not have survived so long.

Nyssa clung on to her faith in the Doctor. He was acting more like his old self, but everything about Carnon Manor conspired to challenge her confidence. In him. In everything.

There was still no sign of Lord Carnon, but the creature in the cellar continued to make its presence felt. The house shook at ever more frequent intervals. Richard opined that it would not be long before it came for its next victim.

The Doctor began to form a theory.

He slept, at last.

His dreams presented him with a bus terminal. A woman's voice droned from a broken loudspeaker, corrupted by an electrical buzz. Fumes swathed the Doctor's feet in a blue haze. Wind blew and scattered refuse. Human refuse drifted through, or waited in queues. Though he never saw their faces, he knew they were watching him.

He confronted one woman, but she tightened her headscarf and hurried on by. A harried driver called over his shoulder that he was running too late to deal with passengers. A drunk, sprawled across a bench with two slats missing, swore and rolled on to his side.

The Doctor found a window marked 'Information' and rapped on the glass. The attendant didn't look up. He was shuffling papers, his features obscured by a peaked cap and poor lighting. 'What do you want?' he asked rudely.

'Well – information, please.'

'The 68 goes in forty minutes. Bedfordshire, calling at REM State. You want a ticket?'

'I was thinking of something rather more profound than a bus timetable.'

'Oh yeah? Like what, for instance?'

'Like, what are you doing in my dream?'

The man ceased his work and was still, for a moment. Then he raised his head. His skin was chalky, his face angular and pinched. His eyes were a penetrating green, and a cruel smile twisted his lips.

'Your mind is a fascinating place to visit, Doctor.'

'But you wouldn't want to live here, I know.' The Doctor met the attendant's stare evenly. He had expected this, to find a man known by all, apparently seen by no one. 'Lord Nicholas Carnon, I presume?'

The house shook again, and Patricia knew.

She was in the library, ostensibly to check for references to Carnon Manor. Instead, she had quizzed Nyssa about the Doctor. Despite his promises, he had failed to help them thus far. She wanted some reassurance that he was not wasting her time.

But now she knew.

She looked at her colleague and saw that she too had had the dreadful premonition. There was fear in Nyssa's eyes. Patricia felt a pang of sympathetic horror.

The creature wanted Nyssa.

They ran. It crossed Patricia's mind that she needn't have done so. She was in no danger. A week ago, perhaps, she would have left the girl to her fate. Not her business. But then, a week ago she would have known the futility of running too.

The final quake knocked them off their feet, before they had gone a dozen paces. The creature burst into the corridor, oozing through its walls. A great amorphous blob, in the depths of which Patricia could see a vast panorama of stars. No living organism, this. She didn't know how, but she knew that she was looking at a vast spatial distortion; a hole punched through reality's surface.

Patricia's throat constricted as the distortion surged over her, but she felt only a static tingle. She was not its target.

Nyssa was engulfed, and her helpless screams seemed to echo through the fabric of time.

Then the corridor was empty, but for Patricia Hopkins, and she screamed too.

The passengers all bore Carnon's face, as did the drivers, the conductors and the woman in the ticket office.

'A life in eternity can be so empty, you see,' explained a man in a business suit as the Doctor strolled alongside him. 'You dwellers in time have such vivid imaginations. Your emotions, your interactions, your sense of your own mortality; it all makes for very entertaining thoughts.'

'You're talking about living beings!' the Doctor protested, but the businessman walked on and ignored him.

He was answered by a youth who sat on a bench, his eyes closed as a tinny beat issued from his headphones. 'I'm talking about those who have died already.'

'I've made a deal, you see.' This from a bearded inspector, who counted the queues and wrote on his clipboard as he spoke. 'A deal with an entity more powerful than even my kind.'

'Oh?'

'I am allowed to borrow six souls,' said a young woman as she bustled by, late for her bus. The Doctor jogged after her. She spoke in Carnon's voice, without any sign that her exertions were telling. 'I bring them here, to where I can stimulate their emotional responses. When they cease to entertain me, I replace them.'

'As you did Dr Morton?'

'A poignant case, I thought,' said Carnon, with regret, 'but he failed to interact with the other characters. He was useless to me.'

The woman caught her bus, and the Doctor turned to find the next vessel for Carnon's intelligence. A small boy with a red balloon grinned up at him.

The Doctor crouched beside him. 'And where do I fit in?'

'Entertainment has its price, Doctor,' said the boy, 'and I have something in my grasp that my, ah, business partner has been denied many times.'

'I... see.'

The Doctor stood and turned to find the inspector again. 'As payment for her loan to me,' said the latest aspect of Nicholas Carnon, 'Death wants you!'

Drawn by inexplicable urges, the residents had gathered in the drawing room to meet the owner of the house. Lord Carnon was splendid in top hat and black robes, and Patricia felt that she already knew him, though it was not possible. She did know that, mere days ago, she would have challenged him, lambasted him, demanded release from this hellish prison. Instead, she sat and listened with the rest. She felt numb, and wondered if the others had been right. She was becoming inured to Carnon Manor; beginning to accept it.

'The Doctor has cheated Death many times,' pronounced Carnon. 'She insists that he take his rightful place with her. In return, she is prepared to grant a considerable boon.'

He explained, and Patricia felt new hope blossoming in her heart. New hope, and something else: disgust with herself, for feeling it.

These, then, were the details.

The Ferrises, Douglas Williams, Melissa Hamilton, Patricia Hopkins – Death was prepared to renounce her claim on them all. She would do this in return for one prized soul; one that she could not take while its owner still clung on to existence.

Lord Carnon had gone now, though Patricia had not seen him leave. She looked at the others, saw their hope, their greed, their malice, and knew that they had made the logical choice.

If only the Doctor died, then everybody else could live.

The bus station grew like an organic thing, until the Doctor was trapped in a maze of shifting passages. He ran, and tried to ignore the battered posters on which a grinning skeleton extended a finger above the slogan *Death Wants You!*.

He denied his fear, suppressing the chemical reaction in his brain that caused it. He concentrated, knowing that his fate lay in his ability to wake.

He wrenched his eyes open, felt the pressure of hands on his throat, looked up into Doug Williams' fanatical eyes and knew that he was being choked to death.

He reacted quickly, putting his respiratory bypass system on standby and pushing up hard. The boy had little strength, and he was easily flung off the couch. The Doctor swung himself into a standing position, alert for his next move.

Doug whimpered in frustration, and tackled the Doctor around the legs. They crashed into the carpet together and rolled. The Doctor was gasping out words, wanting to know what had precipitated this attack. Tears streamed from Doug's eyes, and he couldn't answer.

Ending it was harder than the Doctor had anticipated. The boy was thin and lithe, and he twisted and wriggled until at last the Doctor managed to find the nerve cluster at the base of his neck. His eyes slid into their sockets and his head lolled. The Doctor lowered him gently, his mind distracted by the suspicion that Carnon was responsible for this. His nature uncovered, he had taken his twisted game to the next level.

Nyssa!

The Doctor raced out of the reception room in which he had chosen to dream. He was back in the main hallway, and drawn to the malevolent glare of the skull painting. Did he only imagine that its lipless mouth had twisted into a sneer?

Melissa Hamilton was draped over the stair banister. 'Nowhere to run to, Doctor,' she taunted. 'Nowhere to hide.'

'Where's Nyssa?' he snapped.

'Gone. The creature came for Miss High-and-Mighty. On your own now, Doctor. Left to die.'

He fought down a surging dread at the thought of Nyssa's fate. He didn't know what the creature was; couldn't guess what it had done to her. She was intelligent. She might still be alive. Might.

'Lord Carnon's turned you all against me, hasn't he?'

'A bargain. Your life for ours. Five against one, Doctor.'

'Four,' he corrected.

'Doesn't matter. Be ready to die, Doctor. When you least expect.'

Melissa slipped away into the shadows.

Patricia walked down a wood-panelled corridor, hugging herself and trying to deny that this was happening. The residents had split up to find the Doctor. What if she found him first? The others might be capable of murder, might have been here long enough to do even that to escape, but she was not. She didn't have to be. Even without her, it was four against one. She didn't have to dirty her hands; didn't have to do anything but wait. Just wait. Then, when the Doctor was dead, she would wake up on a

London street and it would all have been a sick nightmare.

Patricia hated herself.

The Doctor found the Ferrises in the drawing room. He had hoped to take them by surprise, pre-empting their plans for him. But they had not been hunting like the others. They had simply waited.

Richard closed the door behind the Doctor. Jean brandished the boiling kettle, protected by an oven glove.

'We are frightfully sorry about this, dear,' she twittered, although her expression said otherwise. 'We don't want to kill you. It just has to be.'

The Doctor backed away, trying to keep an eye on Richard, behind him. 'You have a choice,' he insisted. 'You could say no.'

'The prize is too sweet for that.'

'And what makes you think Carnon won't betray you?'

'Does it matter? We have nothing to lose.'

Jean threw the kettle. The Doctor was prepared. He snatched an embroidered cushion and flung it to intercept the missile. Hot water erupted, creating spots of pain on the Doctor's skin. His defence had cost him. The Ferrises pressed their attack in earnest. Richard was on him, strangling him with a belt. Jean closed in with knitting needles, stabbing, stabbing for his hearts, as he squirmed and tried to bat her away with one hand, the other straining to break her husband's hold. Desperate purpose had lent strength to Richard's aged muscles.

It could have ended then. It crossed the Doctor's mind that this would be an ignominious way to die: having defeated Daleks and Cybermen, to be murdered by two senior citizens in a haunted house. Then something hit Richard from behind, and he dropped the belt. Emitting a keening wail of pain and loss, he fell to his knees and scrabbled after the makeshift weapon.

The Doctor had already recovered. Disarming Jean was simple.

And then he saw his rescuer for the first time. Patricia Hopkins.

'Thank you,' he murmured, breathing deeply as he loosened his collar. She didn't meet his gaze. He wondered what dark thoughts she had had to defeat before coming to her decision. In saving his life, he realised, she had thrown away her own. His words of gratitude hung between them, and seemed inadequate.

Jean Ferris sank to the floor by Richard's side. The couple were drained, their faces grey and dead. Richard's hands ceased their fumbling quest for the belt, and held Jean's tightly. Their chance had passed. It didn't even seem worth the effort to bind them.

A deep-throated cackle alerted the Doctor to the fact that somebody else was in the doorway. Melissa Hamilton.

He faced her, and locked eyes with her, ready for another fight. Melissa shook her head and kept on laughing. And turned. And walked away, the echoes of that laugh lingering long after mortal eyes saw her for the final time.

'Of all of them...' the Doctor muttered, in surprised admiration. He was beginning to remember why he held such affection for the people of Earth.

'So,' Patricia said with a sigh, 'what happens now?'

'We wait, I think.'

The Doctor was in a sunlit meadow where birds sang a haunting melody and a soft breeze wafted lush grass. The TARDIS stood at the foot of a gentle slope and, to the Doctor's joy, Nyssa emerged from within. She ran towards him happily and they embraced. No words were needed yet.

The Doctor's memories of the house were fading. He could not be sure what had happened there, especially at the end. There was an image of Nicholas Carnon in his mind, screaming as his construct tumbled; as a skeletal hand tore its way out of a dimension most vile and seized him in a frigid grasp. He had failed to honour his bargain and payment was due.

Or had the Doctor imagined it? A half-remembered scene from an old movie, jumbled with the eerie images and ancient fears that Carnon Manor had deliberately excavated?

'I understand that Death couldn't just take us while we were alive,' Nyssa said later, upon hearing what the Doctor recalled of his experiences. 'That's why the creature – the distortion or whatever – could only send me back to where I belonged. But aren't you worried that she's after you now? That she might try something else?'

'Oh Nyssa!' said the Doctor with a grin. 'A mythical personification of Death? I thought you didn't have such things on Traken. You're starting to believe too many of Carnon's lies.'

'Well, I know it doesn't sound very scientific, but there are so many things I don't know yet.'

'And there are some things,' said the Doctor reflectively, 'that we aren't meant to know. Still, I would be surprised if Carnon's story was anything more than a corrupted version of the truth. He thrived on provoking emotional responses, after all.'

'Then why would he have wanted you?'

'To test the dreams of a Time Lord? To provide a psychic battery for his experiment? Who knows? He was obviously a highly advanced telepath. He was powerful enough to snatch human minds at the point of death; to influence the TARDIS, even. I can't pretend to fully understand the abilities of his kind.'

'But by fighting back,' said Nyssa, 'you made it too much of a strain for Carnon to hold his imaginary world together?'

'I hope so, yes.'

'What about the others? Patricia? Richard and Jean? Doug?'

The Doctor just shook his head sadly.

Patricia shook her head in disbelief. 'Two weeks? Two weeks?' It wasn't possible. How could a stupid accident have wiped fourteen days from her life?

An urgent thought occurred to her. 'What about the coffee account?'

'It's in hand, don't worry. The ads ran three days ago.'

She frowned and stared at Andrew, her personal assistant, surprised that she believed him. He was quite efficient really. She had been planning to fire him, but she could not recall why now. Overreacting to some minor misdemeanour, she supposed. What was the point? You only had one life.

She settled back into her pillow.

'The doctors say you've made a miraculous recovery,' said Andrew.

'They say you only survived at all because you fought death so hard. That sounds like you!'

Patricia smiled, but the smile froze at a fleeting image of Carnon Manor and the Doctor and her own stark terror. It was dissipating now, a dream exposed to the daylight. Of course, it could have been no more. So why did it leave her with a sense of well-being; of pride, even?

'I fought Death all right,' Patricia Hopkins mumbled happily. 'I fought her and won!'

The Sow in Rut

by Robert Perry and Mike Tucker

Sarah stood up and stretched, rubbing the back of her neck wearily. She reached down and unplugged her keyboard from the socket on K9's back panel. With a whirr he made a quick circuit of the coffee table. Sarah got the impression he was stretching his... legs?

She crossed to the little window set deep in the thick stone wall, and stared out across the lake, taking a deep breath. This holiday had definitely been a good idea. She had spent too long writing for other people. Ever since she had placed that ad in *Time Out* and met some of the Doctor's other companions she had been itching to get on with her new novel. The cottage was perfect – ancient, remote and spooky. Cornflower Cottage – a delightfully inappropriate name. Apparently it had been an inn once, ages ago. Back then it had been more suitably called the Sow in Rut. Sarah smiled grimly; no wonder it had closed down. The tall beam which had once held the pub sign still stood outside the door. It put Sarah in mind of a disused gallows.

The inside of the cottage was ancient and gloomy. Low wooden beams crossed the ceiling and the shelves on the walls housed an eclectic mixture of trinkets, pictures and old books. One wall of the living room was dominated by a huge fireplace – a basket of cut logs had been waiting for her when she arrived. She got the fire going every night, regardless of whether she needed the heat or not. It was all about atmosphere.

She peered at the heavy mantelpiece. There were letters carved into the dark wood, two inscriptions vying for space. They had intrigued Sarah for days. She brushed at the carvings, running her fingers over the letters. *And all the devils besought him, saying, Send us to the swine, that we might enter into them.*

The inscription was carved in a delicate script, but had been partly obscured by the other quote. Here the letters were harsher, less refined, gouged into the timber. *My name is Legion: for we are many.*

Wonderful.

She turned back to the window. The Lake District – away from London, away from Morton Harwood. Away from Brendon – at least for a day or two. He had understood, of course, when she told him she needed peace and quiet to write, but the lure of a remote Lake District cottage at this bleak time of year was just too much – he said he'd join her in a couple of days.

She smiled. For all his irritating habits Brendon had been invaluable in getting her up to speed on some of K9's operating procedures. He had installed her word processor and transferred most of her CD collection into the little robot's memory.

Rachmaninov's 'Isle of the Dead' was currently drifting through the dark stone cottage. Sarah found that sombre classical music helped her mood when writing, but now that she had stopped she found it a little too depressing. 'Oi, K9!'

'Mistress?'

K9 stopped, spinning around to face her.

'Change the soundtrack. Something a little more lively.'

'Affirmative.'

Sombre violins changed to the thumping drums of the Spice Girls. Sarah winced. Not quite what she had had in mind. She turned back to the lake. Obscured by grey clouds, the sun was sinking behind the hills. She frowned.

'Hey, what time is it?'

'Nineteen thirty-seven and twenty-two seconds, Mistress.'

'Damn! I wanted to get to the shop. Why didn't you tell me it was so late?'

'You left no such instruction, Mistress.'

K9's tail drooped. It never ceased to amaze Sarah that a tin box could arouse so much sympathy.

'No, it's my fault. I got too caught up in things.' She crossed to the small kitchenette and hauled open the fridge. 'We're not exactly brimming over with food either.'

K9 trundled across to her, his ears whirling furiously. 'Sensors indicate that cultures currently forming in bovine lactic fluid are liable to be harmful to humanoid life forms, Mistress.'

Sarah glared at him. 'If you mean the milk's off, just say so.'

She straightened, closing the fridge. 'Right, that settles it. I'm going down the pub for dinner tonight. You're on guard duty, K9.'

She breezed into the small bedroom and pulled her tweed jacket out of the wardrobe. Her nose wrinkled. There was an overwhelming smell of damp. The cottage was on the edge of Grasmere and it had been raining for days, but even so…

'K9…'

The robot dog glided into the bedroom.

'Be a good boy and see if you can find out where this damp is getting in. I'm beginning to smell like a swamp! Oh, and spell check the last few chapters for me will you – in English, this time! You may have a multi-species dictionary but I doubt many other people have! See you later.'

Patting him on the head, Sarah shrugged her jacket on and pulled open the door.

The pub was in the village – only a five-minute walk, but the roads were narrow and the pavement was practically non-existent. Not that there was much traffic. It was September, and the Lakes were hardly overrun with tourists. Sarah took a deep breath. There was nowhere else in Britain that smelt as fresh as this. Then she grimaced as she got a waft of brackish air drifting up from her jacket. She was sure that the cottage hadn't been that damp when she had moved in two days ago.

A gust of wind made her shiver and she pulled her jacket tighter around her. Fat spots of rain were beginning to fall. She ducked under a tree, struggling to pull her old woolly hat from her pocket.

'Cold tonight, innit?'

Sarah stifled a scream. What looked like a bundle of leaves struggled to its feet, coughing. Sarah could see a middle-aged woman under the grimy rags.

'You nearly scared the life out of me!'

'I'm sorry, m'dear. I just wanted to give you something.'

The woman fumbled inside her coat and thrust forward a bundle of heather. Sarah smiled and shook her head. 'I'm sorry, I haven't got any change.'

The woman looked affronted. 'I don't want money! Nah, you'll pay if you *don't* take it!'

Sarah looked at her, puzzled. 'I'm sorry?'

'Pay with your soul!' She stepped forward. 'Keep you safe, it will. Lucky heather.'

She reached for the collar of Sarah's jacket. Sarah stepped back, laughing.

'Honestly,' she said, 'you'll have to try someone less gullible. I don't believe in all that black magic stuff. I had a friend who used to say that magic was only the bits which science had yet to explain.'

'That's as maybe,' said the old woman, 'but it can still harm you. You southern city types... you don't know what goes on.' She spat into the gutter. 'Well, I've said my piece. My conscience is clear.' Gathering her rags about her, she shambled off into the rain.

Sarah watched her vanish into the dark, then pulled her hat down over her ears and resumed her trek towards the pub.

Back in the cottage, K9 was scanning along the edges of the walls for damp, whirring contentedly. He rounded the door to the kitchen and stopped. Peat-stained, malodorous water was beginning to creep under the white wooden door. K9 trundled forward, probe extended. The water reared up and slithered to one side, like a living thing. K9's sensors fluctuated wildly, and he began to back away from the writhing water. Something flickered through his positronic brain. If K9 Mark III had been built with fear circuits, he might have recognised it.

The Red Lion Hotel was warm and full of hikers. Sarah shouldered her way over to the bar. The barman saw her eyes running over the wine list.

'Now then, miss. What would you be wanting with Australian wines when you could be drinking one of the finest ales in the Lakes.' He tapped a pump handle. 'Sullivan's Original. You won't find a better pint in the district.'

Sarah smiled. 'All right. I'll have a pint, but make it a shandy.'

Leaving the scandalised barman to cope with the lively head that the lemonade was creating, Sarah craned her neck to see round the pub. It was large and old-fashioned; a real fire burned in one corner, groups of climbers steaming quietly in front of it.

'There you are, miss.'

The barman placed the pint in front of her and Sarah took a long gulp. The meeting on the path had rattled her, despite herself.

'Thanks. I needed that.'

'Will there be anything else?'

Sarah put on her best little-girl-lost look. 'I don't suppose you're still doing food?'

A couple of hours later Sarah was content, well fed and ever so slightly tipsy. The pub had managed to rustle her up a chicken and ham pie, and best of all she'd got chatting to one or two of the locals. Beer, pie and ghost stories – the perfect evening, even if it had got off to a shaky start. The raggedy old woman – the heather-seller – had shuffled into the bar with murmurs of disapproval. The landlord had moved to intercept her. 'Now, Aggie,' he had said in a voice friendly but firm, 'you know you're not allowed in here. Off you go.'

'Ye're a hard man, Jack Tatum,' she had whined, 'sendin' me out on a night like this.'

'Aggie…' The landlord's face had grown stern.

'Ah, I'll not be stayin' long in your precious pub,' she had snarled. 'It's her I've business with.' She had swung around, her long arm extended, one bony figure sweeping the pub and coming to rest on Sarah. 'Her soul's in danger,' the old woman had cried. 'She's stayin' in Cornflower Cottage.'

The landlord had begun to laugh. 'Cornflower Cottage again, is it? That old chestnut.' He had turned to Sarah. 'I should buy some of her wretched heather, if I were you. Then she'll be happy.'

'I don't want her money!' Aggie had snapped. 'There's some of us thinks of things other than our wallets, Jack Tatum.' She had held out her ancient, clawed hand. 'Take the heather, miss,' she had pleaded. 'I don't want no money for it. Take it. Wear it all the time ye're in that place.'

A tingle of superstitious fear had unexpectedly run down Sarah's spine. Convincing herself she just felt sorry for the old woman, she had allowed her to weave a sprig of heather into her button-hole. She had fumbled inside her pocket and handed the old dear a couple of pounds. 'Much obliged to you, dearie,' the old woman had said, and begun to shuffle towards the door. 'Ye're kind. Remember what I said.'

'Aggie…' The landlord's voice had acquired a warning edge.

'All right, I'm goin', aren't I?' the old woman had grumbled, and pushed her way through the door and out into the night.

'I'm sorry about that,' the landlord had said to Sarah when the door had swung shut. 'She drinks… Thinks she's a witch. Got some fixation with Cornflower Cottage too. She's bothered customers before… frightened one or two…'

'Well, I'm not frightened,' Sarah had replied, sipping at her pint. 'Cheers.'

She had drunk in silence for a while, listening to the formless ebb and flow of pub chatter. She had eaten her food and had another pint.

A quiet voice had tickled at her ear. 'She's right you know…'

An old man who she had noticed sitting alone in the corner was now sitting next to her.

'I beg your –'

'Old Aggie. She was right. About Cornflower Cottage.' He had practically spat the name. 'Bad name. Bad place.'

Sarah had had to suppress a grin – this was pure Hammer Horror. 'Why?' she had asked, all innocence.

'Ah,' the old man had replied, and had said nothing more for a good five minutes.

Finally he had begun his tale. 'The cottage used to be a coachin' inn,' he had said.

'I know,' Sarah had interrupted. 'The Sow in Rut.'

The old man's scowl had silenced her. 'The landlord there, 'e allus used to keep a herd o' pigs. It were a tradition. Now, you knows what the Bible says about pigs. Unclean beasts. The good Lord 'isself cast the demon out o' the madman an' into a herd o' swine. You look into the eyes of a pig – there's summat there. Summat that's almost 'uman.' He leaned close to her. She could smell flat beer and rolling tobacco on his breath. 'They says pig-meat's the closest thing to man-meat you'll ever taste. Now, ol' 'Enery Cunniforth, what was the last landlord o' that pub – eighty year ago, this'd be – 'e started up the ol' tradition again. Kept pigs, 'e did, like in the old days. Used to serve up the best cuts o' pork in these parts. Cutlets, bacon – 'is wife used to cure 'er own ham and make 'er own sausages, an' the inn came to be a bit of an attraction, on account o' their table.'

The old man had taken a long, slow pull on his pint before continuing. The pub had fallen silent, everyone listening closely.

'Then, one day, a stranger come to the inn. Started pokin' round. Said 'is brother'd gone missin'… las' place 'e wrote from was the inn. 'E started pokin' round… an' what 'e foun' –' the old man shuddered – 'it'd 'ave chilled the blood of Lucifer 'isself. Them pigs wasn't bein' killed to eat… the people was. Travellers, on their own – 'Enery Cunniforth an' 'is missis, they was cuttin' 'em up an' cookin' 'em… servin' 'em up at table. Tastes jus' like pig-meat, see. An the rest o' the carcasses they was feedin' to the pigs thesselves.'

The pub erupted in laughter. Only Sarah, contemplating the night ahead, was silent.

The old man spoke to her alone now, his voice a rasping whisper. 'An' you know what they said in court when it come to trial, 'Enery an' Martha Cunniforth? They said it was the pigs as told 'em to do it.'

The pub didn't close until well after midnight. It was blowing a gale when the landlord had finally called time, and the rain was heavier than ever. Sarah stumbled back to the bleak old cottage, past the gallows post that had once held the pub sign, to the low front door. Sullivan's ale was obviously not as innocuous as it looked. She fumbled with her key, trying to get it into the lock.

A great gash of forked lightning ripped across the sky, sending shadows dancing. Sarah started: a great sheaf of heather was tied to the door knocker and hung there, swaying in the wind. She laughed to herself. Aggie and the old man had got to her a bit. She took the heather down from the door – it would help mask the slight smell of damp inside – plunged her key into the lock and pushed.

The door swung inwards and Sarah stepped into the gloom of the cottage. Something squelched underfoot. Sarah looked down, puzzled. The floor was sopping wet. She flicked at the light switch but there was a crack and a shower of sparks. Sarah snatched her hand back, suddenly sober.

'K9? Where are you?'

There was a mechanical whirr from the darkness. She strained to see. The red glow from the robot's eyes was visible on the far side of the room.

'K9, what's going on?'

She took another step forward, feeling water lapping around her ankles. The floor was awash and there was a harsh smell of rotting.

'At last…'

K9's mechanical voice was low and grating. Not the familiar chirp Sarah was used to.

She stopped. 'K9?'

'At last we are complete. Water, Energy, Flesh. Soon the three will be one.'

Sarah could see blue sparks crackling around K9's casing. She began to back away, reaching for the door. Her hand had just closed on the handle when the door was wrenched from her grip, slamming shut. Outside in the rain she could hear things shuffling, snuffling. She could hear harsh hide and sharp bristles scraping on the doorframe, squeaking on the glass of the windows. Gruff animal snorting echoed through the walls. Lightning flashed again, and thunder boomed.

K9 began to move forward, a shallow wake glistening in the moonlight.

Sarah edged around the walls of the room, trying to shut out the noise of the things slithering around outside.

'What are you? What have you done to K9?'

'Trapped is what we are! Trapped and isolated in this vile filth! Trapped in the bodies that you rear for slaughter! Life after life spent breeding and eating and dying!'

The mechanical voice was horrible now, a swinish snorting underlying every syllable. The smell was getting stronger. Sarah had to cover her nose to stop gagging. The voice became calmer.

'We have waited, trapped in the ooze, for summer and winter, again and again, waiting. Deliverance now! Now! Now!

'Well, what do you want me for?' Sarah could hear her voice cracking.

The snuffling became a vile machine cackle, burbling with malevolence. 'You have used our bodies for so long, now we will use yours.'

The noise from outside became a crescendo. The walls of the little cottage shook and the doors bulged. Sarah screamed. She could see K9 advancing on her, his probe extended, the energy crackling through his casing.

She hauled one of the armchairs into his path and clambered over it to the other side of the room. K9 spun and Sarah could hear the whine of the laser in his nose powering up.

'Awake or asleep we can still use you.'

There was a sudden burst of ruby light. Sarah threw herself to one side and something shattered in the dark. Broken glass showered down on her.

Sarah looked up at the broken mirror. All around her, shards of silvered glass threw crazy reflections across the room. She rummaged in her pocket for her keys. Her car was just outside, she'd need only a few seconds. They slipped from her fingers on to the slimy carpet. She scrabbled for them desperately. God, she wished she hadn't had those beers.

She could hear K9 approaching, the light from his eyes casting a dull red glow, the animal rasping of the creature that had possessed him getting closer. She struggled out of her jacket, crouching behind the sofa. As K9 appeared she lunged forward, draping the jacket over his head. He gave a squeal of protest. The jacket was now smouldering as the beam from his gun began to burn through it. Sarah bounded for the window, struggling with the clasp. She hauled herself up on to the window-sill.

There was another flash of lightning. Sarah screamed and fell back from the sill, hitting the sopping floor hard. Distorted by the rain, a bony face was leering in at her through the rain-soaked window. It was the old witch, Aggie, she was sure; old skin stretched tight over bone, wild fronds of grey hair floating in the gale. She could hear the old woman screeching and cackling above the wind.

There was a horrible mechanical shriek from the room. She spun. Her jacket, now in two smouldering halves, dropped from the metal dog to the floor. With a snort of triumph K9 raised his head, the red of his eyes blazing.

'Now!'

Sarah closed her eyes, but the blast never came. There was an anguished mechanical squawk from below her. She stared back into the room, puzzled. The bundle of heather she had removed from the front door lay on the floor, half covered by K9's casing. Strange, she thought – she had left the heather on a chair on the other side of the room. Now the little robot seemed fixed to the spot by it, and there were weird whirrings coming from inside his casing.

She turned back to the window. The old woman – if she had been there – was gone. K9 remained motionless. She looked frantically around the room... the old fire iron next to the grate! She picked it up and swung it at the window. The ancient glass broke. She punched the last shards of glass from the window and began to haul herself through. The window was small, too small. She struggled wildly. Her foot caught the lamp standing nearby and it crashed to the floor. The bulb broke and bare terminals sparked on the wet carpet. There was a crackle of electricity and an anguished squawk from K9, then there was a sudden silence, broken only by the quiet hissing of rain through the trees.

Sarah stepped back into the room. K9 was motionless in the dark. She crouched before him. The heather was caught up in his traction system; tentatively, she began to haul it free.

There was a creak as K9's head slowly rose, the light from his eyescreen soft and low.

'Mistress...?' The voice was weak and faltering. Sarah patted his nose gingerly.

'It's all right, K9. I think it's all over.'

The little Metro sped away from the cottage in a shower of fine spray.

K9 was wedged in the back seat, silent and motionless. Sarah drove through the blinding rain for an hour, putting more and more distance between herself and Cornflower Cottage. Only when she was out on the motorway did she allow herself to relax. She realised she had to be well over the limit, and kept a careful eye on the speedometer.

Finally a Little Chef loomed from the dark, bright and garish and inviting. Sarah pulled into the car park and, pulling a blanket over K9, splashed her way over to the restaurant.

She sat for a long while with her coffee, just glad to be somewhere bright and full of people. She clutched the heather from her lapel, mulling over and over the events of the evening.

Finally she crossed to the pay phone and dialled Morton Harwood. After a few moments a sleepy voice answered.

'Hello?'

Relief flooded through Sarah. 'Hi, Brendon, it's me.'

'Sarah? It's… it's a bit late, isn't it? No… it's *very* late. Sarah, it's three in the morning!' His tone suddenly became concerned.

'Are you OK? Is everything OK with the holiday?'

'Holiday's over, Brendon, I'm on my way back.'

She began to explain about what happened. The old woman, the ghost stories, the Sow in Rut. 'There was something awful there, Brendon,' she said. 'I don't know… it used K9. It seemed to take him over… it used him to attack me. It seemed to want to –'

She stopped in mid-sentence. Brendon was laughing at the other end of the phone. A deep, booming, honking laugh.

'It's no joke, Brendon!' Sarah snapped. 'He could have killed me.'

'I'm sorry… But I think I know what's going on. I've been using K9 to run some games.' Brendon began honking again.

'Games? Brendon, will you please tell me what the hell you're talking about.'

'Hang on a minute.'

Sarah heard the phone being put down and muffled scrabblings from Brendon.

The phone began to bleep at her and she struggled to press more coins into the slot.

'Brendon? Are you there. Look, I'm running out of cash.'

'I'm here.' He was on the line again. 'Just listen for a minute. "In the vile swamps of Olchfa, the robots of the third battalion must battle against the brutish animal instincts of the Boralth, hideous hog-like creatures of the night…"'

Sarah interrupted him. 'Brendon…'

'It's a computer game! I got it off one of the guys. I've been running it through K9's processor. He's faster than my game console. Something must have corrupted his memory. A virus, I suppose. Um… Sorry.'

Sarah's mind was in a whirl. A game? One part of her wanted to scream at Brendon, another just felt relief. Was that all it was? Too much beer and an overactive imagination? She suddenly felt both incredibly stupid and ridiculously tired.

'Sarah? Sarah, are you still there?'

There was a series of beeps from the phone. 'I'm out of cash, Brendon. I'm going to see if I can get some sleep. I'll see you tomorrow.'

She hung up and crossed the car park back to her car. She pulled the blanket off K9 and stared at him for a moment. A game. A misunderstanding. A technical error.

She looked at the sprig of heather, then, stifling a yawn, tossed it to one side and settled down in the car, pulling the blanket over her.

In the pool of rainwater under the car, the heather suddenly shrivelled, blackening like old leaves. There was a quick flurry of wind and it was gone.

Dawn came up over the Lakes brilliant and fresh, the night's rain drying slowly under the rising sun. Cornflower Cottage was empty and damp, the only noise that of the local builder chipping broken glass from the window-frame. Strange girl, he thought, cutting her stay short like that, all because of a burst pipe. He slurped his coffee noisily and took a bite from his bacon sandwich.

In the mud around the edge of the lake something bubbled angrily, its swinish instinct raging against humanity. Its chance at resurrection was gone, but it had infinite lives, infinite patience. It had probed the memory of the machine and it knew that its wait was not for ever. It would bide its time. One day, it would be free.

Special Weapons

by Paul Leonard

I

'This is bad,' said the Doctor.

It was dark outside. Mel stared at the viewscreen, the blackness there, and then at the Doctor's face again. His eyes watched the viewscreen with a smouldering anger, the kind that looked as if it could ignite at any moment. For a second, Mel was actually afraid of him.

But there was nothing visible. The scanner might as well have been broken.

'They shouldn't have done this,' the Doctor concluded. 'We have to stop it.'

'Stop what?'

But the Doctor thumbed the door control, opening the roundelled doors on to a draught of icy air.

Mel wrinkled her nose at the stink of it. 'What's that, Doctor?'

'Burned rubber.' The Doctor was already standing in the doorway, twirling his umbrella, and yes, he was sniffing the air. 'Burned rubber and death. Come on, Mel, there's work to do.'

Mel looked down at herself: cornflower-blue dress with yellow polka dots, white socks, black buckle-on shoes. 'Do I need to change?' she asked.

Outside, it was no less dark. Mel's eyes didn't adjust. There was nothing for them to adjust to. The Doctor had a torch: it was like an usherette's, a red glow in his hand, a vague pool of light at the end of the beam. She saw splashes of tarmac, ashen grass.

A sound. Chrr-rr-rr. Mechanical, repetitive. Starter motor? Yes – there was the soft roar of an engine starting up. And light – two dim pools of yellow, with the faint shine of metal between them. A car, old-fashioned with huge headlamps, ghosting its way up the road, engine rumbling.

Yes. A road – a street. Buildings on either side, grey brick. Mel saw a market cross in the transient light, very English, and the words PAX LUCIS.

The car was passing them, the interior dark except for a coal-red point that Mel realised was a cigarette, and a glint from – eyes? Glasses? Then it was gone, leaving a smell of unburned petrol.

'Now, Mel –' whispered the Doctor.

Then the searchlights came on, closely followed by gunfire.

Oliver didn't want to think about the blood. He could still feel it on his hands and face, sticky, congealing.

Stay with me, she'd said, and he'd stayed, listening to her hideous breathing, his own body burning with shock, his hand on hers. He had felt her death as it stole her.

Had she realised she was dying? Probably.

Ellen had been nineteen, two years older than Oliver. He'd liked her face, broad and pretty, framed by hair the colour of copper beech leaves. Her eyes dark, browny-green like woodland shadows, her cheeks roseate, the colour reminding him of the pale sheen of sea shells. She'd let him kiss her, out there in the dry stubble in the shadow of the green branches, even though he was shorter than her and younger. She'd tasted of tobacco, but he'd still wanted to kiss her again, and go on kissing, like in the song on the radio, me for you and you for me…

They'd been kissing when the planes went over.

Oliver had known the shapes, yelled, 'They're German!' They'd pounded down across the field to the stile that overlooked the village, watching the planes in the air, high, tiny crosses, their movements strangely slow. They cast precise shadows, like spiders crawling over the small, sunlit buildings. Still Oliver and Ellen had thought themselves safe, still they'd been holding hands – because no one ever bombed Pax Lucis. There was nothing to bomb.

They'd seen the parachutes, dawning white flowers under the bellies of the planes, the beetle shapes of armoured cars suspended from them, and tiny men, dolls with machine guns. Ellen had gasped, pointed a broad arm at the village where Oliver saw a huge shadow, spreading far too fast, a tar-black fluid. They looked at each other, afraid and confused.

'What –' began Ellen.

Then the sunlight had died, as if someone had switched it off. The ground heaved like a rowing boat in a storm, and Ellen's body was falling away from Oliver's. He heard her scream over the cracking of the earth.

A bomb? He'd said it aloud into the ringing silence: 'Was that a bomb?'

He couldn't hear the planes any more, couldn't see anything. Was he blind?

But there had been no answers, there had only been the silence, and the warm sticky blood on his face and hands.

'Ellen?'

'Stay with me.' Her voice wounded, trembling, each word forced, choked. And then there had only been her breathing, her hideous breathing, and the darkness.

After the breathing stopped, Oliver ran. But he was blind, he was still blind and the Germans had landed, and he didn't know where he was going, or whether there was anywhere to go.

Bullets shredded the air, leaving trails of sound, pressure waves. Mel flinched at each crack, each shiver in the air. Somewhere, glass shattered. Were people dying?

The Doctor was crawling along the pavement, waving his umbrella like a flag of truce, shouting something. No one was taking any notice. Mel pressed herself flat against the wall of a post office, cold stone against her back.

Cold. It was terribly cold. She was shivering. A man was screaming horribly. And – there, with the guns, the black uniforms moving out of the shadows – were those Nazis?

'Doctor!' she shouted. 'Doctor!'

But he didn't hear her. And he didn't fight when the two black-uniformed men grabbed him and dragged him away. Mel wanted to run after him, but her body just hid of its own accord, slipping into a doorway, fear moving her limbs as if she were a puppet.

151

Dark soldiers ran up the road, their boots crunching on the gravel, their faces shadowed. They didn't look at her.

A final burst of gunfire, and a ringing of metal – had they hit the car? Then silence. The lights died, leaving a dim, low illumination that cast long, weak shadows. After a while, the soldiers returned, carrying something. Dark fluid dripped on to the road from the burden.

When they were gone Mel ran back, back towards the TARDIS, back out of here.

But there was a soldier standing guard outside the TARDIS, his eyes shadowy. He shouted, and Mel just ran, and ran, and ran, the hard asphalt jarring her ankles, the cold air tearing at her lungs.

II

Killing had the quality of a dream for Luther. Dead people were like straw dummies, empty of the load they had carried in life. He envied their waxen faces, their hardened eyes. He dreamed of the dead – every night he dreamed of them. They drifted through dark clouds, wreathed with solemn music. They smiled at him.

So easy to be dead. So difficult to be alive. The living had responsibilities.

'This is the last chance, Franz,' he said to the tall, pale-faced man standing beside him. 'It will all be over after this.'

Franz nodded, his eyes moving nervously as if he were looking for enemies hiding in the walls. The English room was strange around them: the puffed chairs and sofas pushed back against the wall were dark, like corpses swollen by water. A stout, wooden table was like an oversized coffin. The windows were tall, church-like, the warped glass reflecting the bright field lamps in amoebic shapes that resembled screaming faces. Behind them, outside, trucks hunkered in the near-blackness.

The Englishman's corpse was lashed to the hatstand, the skin of his face taut, distorted, the holes in his body dark. Luther smiled at him, snatches of *Gotterdämmerung* moving through his mind.

It had been a meeting room for the English villagers: posters on the wall proclaimed the virtues of Land Girls, and advised that 'Careless Talk Costs Lives'. They were different from German posters, softer, more homely, the gentle pastel colours flowing into one another as if they had been painted by children anxious to please Mamma. German designs were by contrast sharp-edged, declarative and frightening: statements of the supremacy of the Aryan race. How could these pastel poseurs – these Mamma's boys – be winning the war?

Luther answered his own question aloud. 'It's the Russians, Franz. This lot couldn't win a fencing match against Germans. But the Russians – they're crazy.'

Like us. But he didn't say that. Even to think it was almost treason.

Franz just nodded again. He was tall, blond, blue-eyed: a good child of Germany. And he was a child. He believed it. Superior men, true men, cleaning the world of all falsity and darkness. Ruling it according to the principles of justice and light. Luther had chosen Franz for that, for the dream, for the belief, for the cleanness in his heart. It was refreshing.

There was a knock at the door. Franz moved his hands to the holster at his waist.

'Enter,' snapped Luther.

The door opened on Lieutenant Herz. Intelligent, thin-faced, reliable, a good killer.

'The man we captured, sir. We found – devices. He is not an ordinary man. He says he's a doctor, but –' He reached forward, showed a metal device too small for a gun. 'A "sonic screwdriver". He says it's harmless. But he has other things – some are toys, he calls one a "yo-yo". He's strange.'

Luther knew what the question was: it didn't need to be asked. Should he be killed?

'Bring him here,' he ordered. 'I'll talk to him.'

He could sense Franz's quickened breathing.

When Herz had left, he whispered, 'Maybe, Franz. Maybe. But I need to talk to him first.'

He went to the posters and read the small print. He wanted to know everything he could about the country he was about to destroy.

The collision knocked the breath out of Oliver's body, and he fell, the stone of the road scraping his cheek. The woman screamed, one short, sharp call. There was a moment's silence, both of them breathing hard.

Then she asked: 'Doctor?'

'No,' said Oliver. 'I was looking for a doctor too.' His voice sounded rough, broken. Almost like Ellen's. He hadn't known he was looking for a doctor. He'd just been running. But it seemed as good an idea as any.

'A doctor?'

'I can't see,' he explained. 'I'm blind.'

'No, you're not.' The woman's voice was brisk, practical, all trace of fear and confusion gone. He heard her getting up, stamping shoes on the road. 'There just isn't any light, that's all.'

'There was a bomb –'

'A bomb?'

Oliver realised he didn't recognise the woman's voice. There was a hint of a posh accent, a distinctive high pitch. 'Who are you?'

'Melanie Bush.'

Oliver introduced himself in return. It felt strange, in the darkness, with blood on his hands, exchanging introductions as if they were at a tea party. She must be another Land Girl, he decided.

'Ellen's dead.' He blurted out the story, his tongue falling over the words: the planes, the shadows, the bomb, her death. When he'd finished, there was a silence. Belatedly, he thought to add, 'I'm sorry, was she a friend of yours?'

But Mel ignored this. 'Are you sure you haven't been unconscious?' she asked.

Oliver hesitated. 'I'm – almost sure. Not for long. I mean, if I was, it wasn't for long.'

'So it was the middle of the afternoon – bright sunlight – and now it's midnight. Hmm. Time travel? No wonder the Doctor said it was bad. What year is this?'

'What?'

'Sorry. Something peculiar's happened here and the Doctor - I mean, we're both here to help.'

Oliver felt his body begin to tremble. 'No,' he said, though he wasn't quite sure what he was saying no to. 'You're Germans, you must be Germans. You're a spy.'

A loud sigh. 'Why does everyone think that?'

The wind rustled trees nearby. Oliver saw a glimmer of light, the faint line of a horizon. So Melanie was right: he wasn't blind.

'Look, we're British,' the woman said. 'At least I am and the Doctor's - well, he's not German, anyway.'

Oliver realised then. The woman wasn't a spy: she was mad. She didn't know what year it was, she had an invisible companion with no nationality. It was obvious that the bomb, and the sudden darkness or blindness or whatever it was, had all been too much. She thought she could help, but she couldn't. He had to think of something, to plan something.

'Listen,' he said quietly. 'We've got to get to the village. My dad's in the Home Guard. Him and Mr Faraday will be organising them to resist - you know, clear up. They'll telephone - there's a procedure -' He stopped. 'What have you seen?'

'German soldiers. Someone in a car was killed. And they took the Doctor away.'

'Dr Allen?'

'No. The Doctor. He's my friend. Weren't you listening?' A moment's silence. Oliver heard a single chirrup from a bird. It sounded lost, afraid. 'The Germans have got the Doctor,' Mel went on. 'Unless he's escaped. He usually escapes.'

'We have to get to the village,' said Oliver again. 'I know the road, even in the dark.'

But he didn't. At night, maybe, but not in this darkness. And Mel said they had shot someone in a car. And Ellen was dead, her blood caked on his skin.

He felt cold. 'What happens if we run into the Germans?' he asked Mel.

'I don't know.'

* * *

'Who is this man?'

The prisoner sounded angry. His face was torn into an ape-like scowl. He paced the room, twirling his strange umbrella, his two-coloured shoes clicking on the bare boards. The corpse on the hatstand smiled.

'Why have you killed him? You can see he's a civilian –'

'Was a civilian, Herr Doktor,' interrupted Luther gently. 'His status is no longer important. Think of him as a scarecrow, a straw man. His function now is to instil fear.'

'In me?' The Doctor raised his umbrella. Franz moved beside Luther; Luther held up a hand. 'You're trying to frighten me?' He took a step closer. 'You're mad.'

'Very probably,' said Luther. 'But I have the gun.'

The Doctor didn't reply, just turned away in theatrical disgust.

'I need some information before I kill you,' observed Luther.

'Well, you're not going to get it, so you might as well kill me now.' The Doctor was examining a small canvas bag, rummaging inside like a child looking for the best sweet. Franz was watching, his body tense.

Metal clattered, then the Doctor gave a satisfied 'Ah!' and raised a hand. A light flickered on his palm, brilliant, like a tiny piece of magic caught for an instant inside mundane reality.

'He put something in his pocket,' said Franz.

The Doctor glanced up, nodded. 'You have splendid powers of observation. It's such a shame that you've chosen to use them in the cause of evil.' He strode up to Luther again. Franz pulled his gun, but again Luther waved him back. 'It's part of a living thing,' hissed the Doctor. 'A lightwanderer, in its crystalline phase. I suppose it must have crashed here, and you have found it.' His scowl broke open again. 'You!'

Luther had heard enough. He didn't know where the weapon had come from. He hadn't needed to know. This man was either insane or he knew too much. Either way, there was a solution.

He turned to Franz. The young man was standing relaxed, the buttons on his uniform gleaming against the black. 'Prepare him for questioning. Ten minutes.'

Franz's eyes widened with anticipation. Luther smiled. He counted Franz as a friend, and Luther liked to give his friends the things they needed.

III

Mel wasn't going to let Oliver die. Not after Pex – it would be too horrible. She could hear the young man's shoes behind her on the road, hear his breath – rapid, still in shock after that girl's death. She was the responsible one, she told herself. She had to get them both out of this alive.

And rescue the Doctor. Yes. That too.

The road was still dark, but a faint electric brightness glimmered somewhere ahead. Possibly headlights, though Mel couldn't hear any engines. She felt very exposed walking like this, her heels clicking on the asphalt, but crossing fields and hedgerows in total darkness was likely to be worse, if not impossible. And staying still was no use.

'There!' said Oliver suddenly, in a stage whisper.

Mel saw lights, tall windows. Faint boxy shapes that might be army trucks. No insignia were visible.

'That's the vicarage,' Oliver told her. 'That's where the Home Guard will be.'

'Or the Germans,' said Mel.

They stopped, silent for a moment.

'Perhaps we should –' muttered Oliver.

'Take a look,' said Mel, cursing herself. 'We'll have to.' Briskly she added: 'Stay with me, move as quietly as you can, and don't say a word.'

Grüber was touching the machinery as usual, his long thin fingers balanced on the fine wires that suspended the Exclusion Generator. He looked up when Luther came in, his metal-rimmed spectacles glinting in the light from the device. The same light shone, more faintly, on the stone pillars of the church, and was captured by the silver cross of the altar.

'It's ready,' Grüber said. 'More than ready.' He indicated an instrument, a heavy metal needle pointing at the figure 12. It meant nothing to Luther. 'It's just a matter of checking the field extent.' Grüber explained. 'An error of just 2 per cent in the voltage –' he indicated the instrument again – 'would be an error of 100 per cent in the field extent. We could destroy Berlin. Moscow, even.' Refracted light moved under his spectacles, and his thin lips twitched. Perhaps he thought that he'd made a joke. Luther didn't think it was funny.

'The English know we have a special weapon,' Luther told Grüber. 'Herz captured a scientist. They must have known we were coming. They may have a counter-weapon. Watch for any abnormal activity.' He glanced at the crystal, the green-blue light moving and shaping in the depths. Like wings, he thought, a thousand wings captured in unison. And the Doctor had said it was alive.

He shook his head. What nonsense. It was a machine. A special weapon. That was all.

'When will the squad return?' Grüber's obsessive fingers stroked the support wires. His lips twitched again and he glanced at the altar, his expression nervous.

'Soon,' said Luther. 'I told them one hour.'

Three men had been sent out into the fractured countryside to make measurements, to calibrate the effect, so that Grüber could adjust whatever needed to be adjusted. It should have been done in Germany, but the Führer had refused to risk so much as a single handful of German soil. And why should they? The English had made this war; the English should suffer.

'The ultimate penalty,' Luther muttered.

Grüber glanced up.

'And us,' he said. 'We, too, will not survive this.'

Luther shrugged. 'For the good of the Fatherland,' he said, saluting. 'Heil Hitler!'

Grüber returned the salute, reluctant, his eyes on the machine as if hypnotised. The light danced on his face, a dim reflection of the unknown truth inside the machine. 'No one will survive,' he said. 'Anywhere.'

'I don't agree,' said Luther.

* * *

The church and vicarage were surrounded by a low wall. He knew that wall, he knew the trees inside it; but in the non-light it was only rough dry stone under the tips of his fingers, a smell of brick, an oppression of unseen branches. Mel had been a pale shape ahead of him but now there were no shapes, only a ghosting of light to his left. A warmth behind him, a breathing – that was Mel, or might be Mel. Or might be his imagination. Perhaps she was ahead of him. Could he risk talking?

He took a step along the wall towards the light leaking from what must be the gateway. He remembered the stone arch, the cool space underneath it, the worn wooden bench, the brown and gold notice board that gave the times of the services. Would the gate be guarded? Oliver stopped, his hand still touching the wall, and tried to listen.

A stick snapped, and something crackled and shuffled in the loose leaves beyond the wall, under the trees.

A voice, ahead. Low, a man's voice, and strange.

German. It must be a German.

There was a blaze of light, sharp long double shadows reaching towards Oliver like hands. He saw the archway, the notice board. Twenty yards away: further than he'd thought. A man was standing with his back to Oliver, shadowed against the light – but that was a helmet, that was a gun.

A German. A sentry. What was he going to do?

'*Ein Fuchs!*'

Oliver felt Mel touch his arm, sensed the message: keep still. But he didn't want to keep still; he wanted to move, move now when the enemy's back was turned. While he had a chance. He took a step towards the man, heard Mel's faint gasp, saw the man turning, saw his face –

And then the lights went out.

A harsh crack. A gunshot? Mel's voice, 'Run!'

He ran, straight towards the sentry.

'Run away!' Mel was almost screaming. But Oliver couldn't stop. Ellen was dead, she was dead and this was a German –

Impact. The man's uniformed body was curiously cold, almost as if the alien cloth were wet. The man gave a grunt, then a shout, so loud that Oliver recoiled. A thing like a wooden beam thudded into his back and he was falling, the rough stone a cold shock against his face, the air gone from his lungs.

I've been shot, he thought.

Breath on the back of his neck. 'Who? Who are you, boy?' Almost no accent. But German, yes, surely German. 'You are being a hero? Why? I should kill you. Klaus!'

Light returned, showing grainy stone, the bevelled gap between two grey flags, fragments of soil.

'Please –' Mel's voice. 'Please, we were just coming to the church. It's so dark… we didn't know what was happening…'

She sounded young, weak, frightened, confused. Not like she had in the road. An act? It must be. At least she wasn't a German. At least he'd been right to trust her.

The wooden beam was removed from his back, and Oliver realised it was the German soldier's arm.

'Stand up.'

He stood, trembling. A glance at his body showed no blood: he hadn't been shot, then. The man must have knocked him over, that was all. But his legs felt weak, distant, as if blood was gushing out of him.

A hand turned his face, cold, clay fingers pressing into his flesh.

'Look at me!' The shadows on the young German's face were long. Eyes met his, shadowy, glinting. 'Go to your home, English boy. We are in control. There is a curfew. You will know when it is over.'

There was something in his voice that frightened Oliver more than the words: pity. You will know when it is over. Was the war over, or nearly over? Had the Germans won? But how? Surely they couldn't have invaded the whole of England. Their armies were in Russia and in Italy, mostly, everyone knew that. And they were losing. If he and Mel could get out of Pax Lucis – get a message out…

But to where? What had happened to the world? Why was it dark?

He looked into the German's eyes, tried to frame the question in a way that would bring an answer, or at least a clue.

Before he could speak, a shot sounded from the vicarage. A voice shouted in pain or anger – Oliver couldn't make out any words.

Mel whispered something, a single, strangled word.

Oliver couldn't move. He could see the vicarage lawn, pale and shadow-streaked in the light, which he could see came from the headlamps of an armoured car.

'We must save the Doctor!' This time Mel's hoarse whisper carried to Oliver and his captor.

'You can't save anyone,' said the German. The quietness, the terrifying pity, had returned to his voice. 'Go home. Both of you. Now!'

'We'll go home,' said Oliver, half to Mel, half to the German soldier. 'It's just round the corner.' The little row of cottages stretching up from the crossroads, the flowers bobbing in the garden – or had that been bombed too? Was there rubble, torn earth, where home had been?

There was another shot from inside the vicarage, and a thud like a sack being thrown to the floor.

Mel screamed. 'Doctor!'

'Silence!' snapped the soldier. 'Silence or I will kill you!'

Oliver turned towards Mel, ran to her. In the light from the car he could see his hands, the skin patchy with darkness. Blood. Blood on his hands.

He grabbed Mel's arm. 'We can't do anything. Follow me.'

As they walked away into the false night, Mel made a faint snuffling sound. Oliver realised she was crying.

'Was that your friend in the vicarage?' he asked.

She didn't reply.

IV

Oliver's mother was a small woman, her black hair peppered with silver and cut quite short. A white hand rested on Oliver's shoulder, as if the woman was reassuring herself that he was real. The room around her was filled with dark, clumsy furniture: chairs, a sofa, a wooden cabinet with a glass front and a glimmer of silver inside. An oil lamp had been placed on a low table, and it cast huge, distorted shadows. They seemed to move, just a little: monsters, growling on faded wallpaper patterned with leaves, waiting to pounce.

Nonsense, Mel told herself. But the image wouldn't go away.

Oliver's mother kept talking, as if to fill the silence creeping in from the street. 'Mr Faraday was going for help, dear. But we haven't heard anything. And there were gunshots. Oh, surely it can't be an invasion. Not now. It's so nearly over!'

Oliver glanced at Mel, his expression serious and more than a little afraid. She remembered that she'd told him about the car, and the gunshots she'd heard. She wondered who Mr Faraday had been, before he'd been a corpse in the arms of soldiers. The vicar? A farmer? Had he left a wife? Children? Would they die too?

'What is it, dear?' Oliver's mother was looking at Mel, her eyes bright with attention.

Mel realised she was crying. 'My friend's dead,' she said. 'He came to help you and they've killed him. We heard him die.'

'I don't think he's dead,' said Oliver.

Mel stared at him.

'Your friend knows what the Germans are doing, doesn't he?'

'Maybe,' said Mel.

'So they won't kill him. They'll try and find out what he knows. They probably fired the gun to frighten him.'

Mel nodded. It was possible. It had happened before. And the Doctor had let himself be captured – hadn't he? He must have known what he was doing. He usually did – in the end – even if he never seemed to. And if they were questioning him…

'We have to save him,' she said, without thinking.

'No, my dear.' Oliver's mother. She was looking at the ground, her face shadowed with anxiety. 'We have to wait. The army will arrive soon – they're certain to find out what has happened. If we try to do anything in the meantime…' She stopped. 'What can have happened to Mr Faraday?'

Mel made a decision.

'He didn't get out of the village,' she said briskly. 'They killed him.'

Oliver's mother sat down on the arm of a chair, clenched her fists in her lap. She said nothing.

Mel looked at Oliver. He wasn't just strong: he was competent, and fairly sensible. Not like Pex at all. And anyway, he was all she had. There was no time, in the dark, with enemy guns all around, to organise anything better. 'C'mon,' she said. 'We're going to have to do it.'

Oliver's mother looked up at him, then at Mel. 'Please. We should wait.'

'No,' said Mel.

Oliver said, 'I know a way we could get out. We can go by the stream. They won't have guarded that.'

After a long moment, his mother nodded.

Mel thought to herself, If he dies, then what will you say to her?

The Doctor's face was pale, and covered with red welts, but Luther knew that he was still strong. His eyes were implacable, and his grimace was one of anger, not pain. There was light in his eyes, too much light.

The lamp, he thought. It's the lamp. It's very bright, almost a point source. And the Doctor's eyes will be full of tears from the pain, which will make them more reflective. That's all it is.

He glanced at the corpse, as if for reassurance. It grinned darkly.

'But if I'm dead I won't be able to help you, will I?'

The Doctor's voice was quiet, entirely without panic, but oddly persuasive. He didn't want to die, that much was clear. And yet...

Luther often wished he could read minds, and he wished for that gift now most of all. The Doctor didn't seem to be afraid of death, as young people were, but he didn't seem ready to welcome it either. Why not? Surely once you had ceased to fear death, you could only desire it? It was a riddle. Finding out what the Doctor knew about the Exclusion Generator was secondary, incidental. As in music, where the melody should arise from the deeper harmony, so the trivial truth of the Doctor's mission as an English spy would arise from the depths of his character.

Luther became aware of Franz, still standing to attention in his starched and perfect uniform, the buttons gleaming. He felt a pang of irritation, like an itchy eye. He turned to the young man, snapped,

'Leave this to me. Go and watch Grüber. Report on his progress.'

Franz nodded, saluted, left. No surprise showed on his face. Luther found himself thinking that perhaps Franz was not, after all, so worthy. Perhaps he was an automaton, a golem, in his perfect love of cleanness and truth. He turned to the Doctor, asked softly, 'Why do you cling to life? You know what happens in the world. You know that nothing can be made clean, nothing can be made perfect, nothing can even be made good. I can see it in your eyes. So why live?'

'Because it's better than death,' growled the Doctor.

'Is that the only reason?' asked Luther.

'I can fight people like you.'

Luther felt strangely disappointed, and realised that this was because he had allowed himself to hope. Why had he felt that this spy could give his life a meaning? It must be an illusion, a hypnosis.

'Life is better,' the Doctor reaffirmed. 'Give me a day, and I'll prove it to you.'

Luther looked out of the window at the English village slowly freezing into the darkness. 'There may not be time for that,' he said.

They had found a flashlight, but it wasn't like the Doctor's. It was big and unwieldy, a metal box, cold under Mel's fingers. The beam was bright, too bright.

Oliver led the way, and they kept to darkness, following side paths, tracks across fields. Finally they came to a narrow road that he said went to a place called Wyecombe Maltravers, three miles away. Mel wondered what would be happening there, whether they even knew about the invasion. If the Germans had warped time...

This might even be a time before the war, or after it. The air was cold, cold as a winter's night. The birds, the trees, were silent. Yet Oliver had said that it was summer – July. That it had been a warm day. What if they found themselves in the Middle Ages? Or the Bronze Age? Were the Germans trying to save the Reich by moving it back in time?

No wonder the Doctor had been so worried.

Ahead of her, Oliver stopped.

'There's something in the road,' he whispered. 'I think it's a bomb crater.'

Mel manoeuvred the chunky switch on the flashlight. The beam showed crumpled asphalt under Oliver's feet. Oliver's breath, frosting the air. Nothing beyond.

Mel tried it again, directing the flashlight beam across the slanting surface of the road. Broken rock glinted inside the cracks – or was it ice? Above that, there was no reflection at all. She swung the beam to left and right: fallen hedges reached like ghosts, leaves shining, then sheared off into splinters.

'Should we try to get closer?'

Mel shook her head, but Oliver was already taking a step across the broken ground, reaching out –

'Ow!' His fingers were touching something, a dark invisibility above the broken road. Mel saw him try to pull away, saw the ends of his fingers whiten. She felt a surge of cold panic and grabbed hold of him around the chest, pulling backwards as hard as she could. They both fell, tumbling on the hard ground.

She stood up slowly, winced at a pain in her elbow. The flashlight was on its back, shining into the air.

'What is it?' asked Oliver, his voice edgy, afraid.

'I don't know,' said Mel.

His fingers were bleeding – skin had been torn away. Mel picked up the flashlight. Its beam wavered: perhaps the battery was dying. She saw a reflection, a white blob cemented to the wall of nothing. She frowned, looked more closely.

It was a fragment of Oliver's skin, and a few drops of his blood.

The blood was frozen.

'What do you see in this room?' The Doctor was sitting, propped against one of the English stuffed sofas. The marks on his face seemed to be fading. Healing. Why?

'What do you see?' he repeated.

'An English room,' said Luther, playing the game, waiting for the Doctor to reveal himself. 'Furniture. Posters.'

The Doctor's expression was expectant, calm.

'You. Me. A corpse.' Luther looked around for more. 'Windows. A door.'

'No no no no. What do you *see*?'

Luther had no reply.

'Vicarage tea parties,' said the Doctor suddenly.

Luther stared at him. He was pointing at the table, on which Herz had spread a map.

'Look! Here! I see the people who live in this place, sitting at that table, or on these sofas with plates on their laps. Cups of tea, pieces of jam sponge cake. People talking about the things that humans talk about – each other, the things they do, their small friendships and their petty squabbles. Their children, their futures, all the possibilities. That's what they'd be doing now if your Führer hadn't insisted on fighting this war.'

'They're happier now, Doctor.' Luther allowed the anger to show in his voice. This was too easy: the Doctor's arguments were facile, stupid even. He turned to face the windows and gestured at the silent village. 'They're much happier than they've ever been. They have something to fight. A cause. An adventure.'

A pause. 'That's possible, in some cases. The struggle for survival is important to humans.' He seemed suddenly lost in his own thoughts. 'I sometimes think that's why Mel and the others –'

'Others?' Luther whirled to face the Doctor, wondering if this was the revelation he'd been waiting for. 'So there are others? Where are they? In the village?'

But the Doctor only smiled, an absurd, amiable, smile that made Luther want to kill him. 'Oh, I don't think any of my friends will be in Pax Lucis,' he said.

There was a knock at the door, and Herz came in, his eyes dark. He glanced at the Doctor.

'Go on,' said Luther.

'The survey team have come back. Grüber is making the calculations.' Another glance at the Doctor. 'It will be ready in thirty minutes.'

Luther nodded. 'I want the prisoner to see this,' he said. 'Get Franz. When the time comes we will carry him down.'

Herz stared.

'I want him to see that he has failed,' said Luther.

Herz still stared. His uniform was dark, coal-black, the buttons and badges like diamonds. His eyes, quick, intelligent, searched the room.

'There's no danger,' said Luther. 'But handcuff him, just in case.'

Herz nodded at last.

'He may reveal something,' said Luther. 'Something that I need to know.'

'Very well, Herr Oberleutnant.' But Herz still wasn't happy. Luther wondered whether he had been listening at the door.

Vicarage tea parties. Happiness. No doubt Herz would think these were treasonable subjects. Luther felt an unfamiliar tension in his face and throat, and realised that he was suppressing a smile.

He glanced at Herz, saw no flicker of life, only the perfect, aquiline, killer's face.

'The method of interrogation is my responsibility,' he said. 'It is not necessary to be direct.'

Herz nodded, once, like an automaton on a chiming clock.

When he had gone, Luther knelt down by the Doctor and whispered, 'We're going to destroy England. All of England. As an example.'

'Using this "device" of yours? Do you know what it does?'

'It makes a barrier. Nothing can pass through. No people, no air, no sunlight. Everything inside the barrier will die.'

The Doctor stared at him.

V

'There has to be a way through.'

Oliver was determined, Mel could give him that. But he wasn't being sensible, not this time. She said, 'If the Germans put the barrier there, they won't have left any holes. If there were holes, we'd see the light coming through them. There isn't any light.' There was none at all: she'd switched the torch off, to conserve its wavering

167

power supply. 'We ought to go back to the village. Perhaps the Doctor –' She broke off.

'If he's alive,' said Oliver. There was an edge of cruelty, of certainty, in his voice that Mel didn't like.

'I thought you said he would be. That they wouldn't kill –'

'I just said that to get you going again,' snapped Oliver. 'I need your help, because you seem to know more about what's happening here than I do.'

'I don't know anything,' protested Mel. Her heart was sinking inside her. Had the Germans killed the Doctor? Surely that wasn't possible. But that had been his voice. There had been a gunshot.

'You do know,' Oliver was saying. 'You must.' He was close to her in the darkness. She could hear his breathing, feel a slight radiated heat. 'You said you came here to help. Who sent you? The War Ministry?'

'The Doctor brought me.'

'How did you get here? In an aeroplane? Can it go through the barrier?'

The questions were fast, bewildering. 'I don't know,' said Mel miserably. 'And even if it could I can't steer it and I don't know where we'd end up. It could be anywhere. Any when. We might never get back.'

An intake of breath. 'Very well. We'll have to try and find a way through, as I said.'

'Or go back and rescue the Doctor.'

'Without weapons we've got about as much chance of rescuing him as of walking to Wyecombe along this road. How much do you know about this barrier thing?'

'I told you. Nothing.'

'Weren't you told about it before coming on the mission?'

'The Doctor doesn't work like that. He doesn't have missions, he doesn't have plans. He just does things.'

An intake of breath. 'I thought that the Ministry would be organised.'

'Life isn't always like that, Oliver,' said Mel softly. She'd almost forgotten she was talking to a teenager. Since she'd started travelling with the Doctor she felt so much older.

'What if we went underground? Do you think the barrier would still be there?

'I don't know.' Mel was feeling impatient. They had to help the Doctor, somehow. This speculation was aimless. 'We can't get underground,' she said.

'We can. There's a quarry, about a mile from here. Across the field where Ellen and I were – where Ellen –' He broke off. 'Well, across the field.'

Silently, Mel reached out and found his hand in the darkness.

'I hope your friend's still alive,' he said after a moment.

'Thank you,' said Mel.

There was no light in the quarry, and no sign of movement. Oliver said it hadn't been used for a couple of months: the workers had been directed elsewhere, to something more urgent. The quarry owner had made a fuss about it, demanding compensation.

The flashlight revealed little: heaps of mud-coloured stone, dim parallels that might be railway tracks. Nearer, there were wooden crates abandoned on the lip of the workings. Tall grass was growing through them. The grass was coated with frost.

Mel remembered that it was supposed to be summer, and shivered.

'There's a way down,' said Oliver. His voice echoed: ow-ow-ow-n.

'Shh! There might be guards!' whispered Mel.

Oliver dropped his voice to a whisper, but said, 'Don't think so. They'd have shot us by now.'

Mel had the impression that he was smiling. When had he started to think that danger was funny?

As they walked and slithered down the crumbling path, she could hear only the scrape of shoes on the rough rock, the occasional faint rattle of a displaced fragment jittering down the slope.

At the bottom it was oddly warm. It gave Mel hope. She thought she could smell summer through the quarry dust, the summer evening that it should be, according to Oliver's wristwatch. Perhaps there was an escape, a relief from the cold weight of the barrier that surrounded them, crossing the sky, shutting out the sun.

'Here,' said Oliver. 'In here.'

He had the flashlight. The beam picked out more of the sallow rock, angled chunks of it like small mountains. Then a ragged mouth, a hole in the quarry wall.

'Railway tunnel,' whispered Oliver. 'It comes out south of Wyecombe, near the Summerworks.'

'I'm going in first,' said Mel. 'You hold the light.'

'No,' said Oliver. 'I should –'

Mel just started walking. The flashlight was wavering again. She wondered if the batteries would last long enough. Not that it would matter if the barrier continued underground. She sniffed at the air again, wondered if the summer she could smell was just the accretion of scents trapped in the quarry. The tunnel looked entirely dark.

There were some crates stacked up against the entrance, half-blocking it. Red crosses of paint were splashed on the wood. Mel picked her way to the left of the crates, walking on the sleepers between the rust-coloured railway tracks. Her shadow bobbed in front of her.

The walls of the tunnel were bare rock. Mel couldn't see more than a hundred yards: she guessed the barrier would be at least half a mile away, if it was there.

The light behind her dimmed abruptly, leaving her in a brownish twilight. Oliver shook the flashlight, switched it off and on again, but it had little effect.

'We can't do this,' said Mel. 'The batteries won't last.'

'We can run,' said Oliver.

'We don't even know if –' Mel stopped speaking. Her head was making connections. Electricity – sparks – detonators –

Now she knew why the Germans ought to have had guards here. Boxes with red crosses on them.

Explosives.

'Oliver,' she asked. 'How much do you know about blowing things up?'

* * *

170

In the church, Luther watched the Doctor. He watched that face, turning to the strange light of the device that Grüber called an Exclusion Generator but might in fact be anything, might as well be magic. He watched the Doctor's eyes light up in sympathy with it, watched the curt nod of understanding.

'The crystalline lightwanderer survives on traces of solar energy in deep space. It's a cold, cold creature. Running energy through it as you are doing will make it a killer. It will disrupt the matter around it, and the more power you put through it, the more disruption you'll get. On the scale you're planning the stress on the Earth's crust alone will send out a shock wave that will flatten the rest of the planet. And you'll leave a hole a hundred miles deep. Magma will pour out – dust and ash will fill the atmosphere – everything will die. Everything. And it will kill the lightwanderer too.'

The Doctor was all but shouting, his face contorted. His words echoed from the stone recesses of the church. Herz and Franz stood silent, their eyes averted. Franz had a hand on the pistol at his hip. Crouched by the machine, a pad of scribbled calculations in his hand, Grüber was nodding in time with the Doctor's words, like a bulky puppet. The blue crystalline light etched lines into his face and neck. He spoke, his jaw moving crudely, as if it were wooden. 'You see? It is as I said.' But he only seemed excited, amazed at the great possibilities offered by his device. As if it were truly his. Did he care what it did? His eyes were turned to the light from the central crystal, but where the Doctor's face had been illuminated with sympathy, Grüber's burned with the cold flame of obsession.

I have to do something here, thought Luther. His mouth was dry, as if he were about to go into battle. I am the officer in charge.

But what should he do?

Without warning, Herz kicked the Doctor. It was fast, fierce, like a snake striking. It connected with the abdomen. The Doctor winced, and his breath whistled from his throat, but he made no sound.

'Stop that!' snapped Luther.

Herz looked at him. 'The prisoner made an attempt to undermine our morale,' he said. 'We cannot allow him to tell these lies.'

'It's the truth!' wheezed the Doctor.

Herz kicked him again.

'That's enough, Lieutenant!' Luther walked up to Herz, whispered, 'We may need this man.'

'For what?' The Doctor's voice was choked and glottal. 'What do you need me for, if you're going to destroy the world?'

'That isn't going to happen!' snapped Luther. 'Herr Grüber, recalibrate the Exclusion Generator for a radius of twenty-five kilometres. That will be demonstration enough.'

Silence, except for the Doctor's ragged breathing.

Then Herz spoke quietly. 'Herr Oberleutnant, you have disobeyed the direct orders of the Führer. I am removing you from command of this expedition.'

Luther stared at him, saw the cold reason in his eyes. A good officer. It would not occur to Herz to disobey orders, even if it meant the end of the world.

'Can't you see –?' he began, but realised his mistake. The words died, frozen in the wilderness of the Lieutenant's face. Persuasion was wasted. It was a sign of weakness. He should know that. He should use force.

He turned to Franz, who had already drawn his gun. He opened his mouth to speak, then, too late, saw the swift glance from Herz to the tall man, the glint of ice.

Of course. Franz believes in fairy tales. He has spoken to Herz –

But Luther was not ready for the shot, even so. The impact of the bullet knocked him sideways. He almost fell, recovered his balance.

He was tired. Very suddenly tired. Was he dying?

Echoes of the shot chased themselves around the church. Grüber was standing up, his obsession broken at last. The light from the device seemed brighter – had he switched it on?

Luther knelt, just because he was so tired. He heard Herz speaking again, but the words were mere sounds. They trembled in the light. Franz was walking, his body outlined in deep blue, the black-blueness of coal in sunlight. He looked oddly like a priest, the pistol in his hand a benediction.

He pointed it at the Doctor.

No, said Luther in his mind, but no words came out. The light was crawling in rivers across the floor now, sparking along the cables that suspended the crystal, and Grüber was smiling.

Were there angels?

VI

Oliver heard the shot as Mel was climbing the side of the road bridge below the vicarage. They hadn't gone back by the road. They hadn't dared. Instead they had followed the Otty, the tiny stream that ran under the railway bridge. There was a path beside it, brambly and wet, but unguarded. The stream had made a gentle popping sound next to Oliver as he walked, the dynamite in his arms like an awkward Christmas parcel. He had kept wondering whether the explosive would work, how many people it would kill.

He'd handed it to Mel so that he could climb the bridge, his hands finding the gaps left by missing bricks, a familiar route from schoolboy dares. Then she'd passed it up to him before starting the climb herself. He'd almost dropped it at the echoing sound from the church, the flicker of light.

'Get down!' he hissed at Mel. He thought he could see the pale shape of her face, half way up the wall. She was carrying the fuses – two, just in case one didn't work. They'd had to smash their way into a padlocked box to get them. Oliver hoped she knew what she was doing, that they had everything they needed. Not that it would matter if the Germans caught them.

A rattle of stone, a breath. Mel was at the top, scrambling over the parapet. 'You could've given me a hand!' she whispered.

'Shh!'

But Mel was already running towards the church, her footsteps noisy. Oliver reluctantly followed, thinking about sentries, guns. The dynamite in its paper wrapping felt heavier now. Drops of sweat were running down the inside of his shirt. He wanted to wipe them away, but dared not shift the burden in his hands. Ahead, he could see the dim lights of the German trucks seeping around the church and the vicarage. Where was Mel? What was she doing?

He almost bumped into her, crouching by the wall. 'Now!' she hissed. She held a stubby fuse in her hand, slowly uncoiled it. 'We've got to set it off now!'

There was another shot, frighteningly loud. A cry of pain.

Mel lit the fuse. Oliver handed her the dynamite, sure that this was dangerous, but what could he do?

'Run!' she snapped.

But Oliver felt the cold metal snout of a gun at the back of his neck.

'Get up,' said a cold voice, heavily accented. 'Get up now.'

Luther watched Herz shouting at the Doctor, wondering why he wasn't dead yet. Hadn't Franz shot him?

Perhaps he was dead and this was his first punishment: to see the consequences of his actions.

Herz fired the gun into the Doctor's leg at close range, then resumed his barrage of questions. The words meant nothing to Luther: they were only little demons, sharp-edged, jumping around the light from the miracle (and yes, it was a miracle: how could he have thought of it as a machine?). Luther tried to call out, but he couldn't. He shuffled forward, trying to reach Herz, trying to stop him from hurting the Doctor any more. But he could only move towards the light.

There was a clatter of sound from outside. After a moment, Luther recognised gunfire. The Russians are here, he thought. This is our end, our *Gotterdämmerung*.

Except that we were never gods.

Oliver watched, startled, as Mel punched and kicked the fallen soldier. How had she overpowered him?

Then he saw the burned-out fuse, stuffed into the man's right eye. He was howling in pain, rolling like an animal.

'The gun!' shouted Mel, as if Oliver were an idiot.

He scrambled for the fallen weapon, picked it up. He heard boots thudding on soil, a metallic click, an explosion of sound –

– gunfire –

– and light flickering across the wall, the stone breaking. He dropped to a crouch, looked round and saw Mel behind him standing up, struggling with the fuse and the dynamite.

'Get down!' he bawled, his words echoing in a sudden silence.

But Mel was lighting a match, and then the fuse. No one fired at her. There was shouting – shouting in German. Oliver realised he was still holding the gun, half-crouched. He struggled upright, saw Mel throwing the bundled explosive.

He thought, That won't work, and sure enough the bundle landed in the vicarage garden and just lay there, useless. A faint trail of smoke came from it.

Lights came on, and Oliver saw how many soldiers there were. Four at least. Two more emerged from the church.

Oliver dropped the gun and raised his hands, but he didn't think that surrendering would save him.

VII

'Herr Grüber,' said the Doctor. 'You must disconnect the crystal now.'

Luther watched him speak from his vantage against the cold tiles of the floor. Grüber said something, but the words were blurred grunts. He looked like a bear, a heavy, dark animal hanging over the crystal. The light was like fire.

'Do you realise it's a living creature?' urged the Doctor. 'Do you know what you've done to it by imprisoning it in that machine?'

More grunts. Luther's head was heavy, cold, a brass and iron machine, but by a tremendous effort he lifted it so that he could see the Doctor. He was lying against one of the huge stone pillars. His hands were still cuffed together. His face was tortured into a scowl, perhaps of pain, perhaps of anger.

'If you do this, Herr Grüber, it will be the end of the world. The end of your "Thousand Year Reich", the end of –'

Grüber barked, like an angry dog.

The Doctor looked down at Luther and their eyes met. The Doctor gave a slight nod.

Life is worth living, thought Luther.

It was a conscious effort to reach out to the clotted machinery of his arms and legs, to begin to shuffle across the floor. Zigzags of pain bit through his chest. The light dimmed, brightened, dimmed again.

The Doctor's voice was a constant: '– won't be any second chances, won't be any chance at all. You should break it now, now before Herz comes back –'

The bear, distracted, danced in front of the Doctor. Words settled in Luther's brain: 'duty', 'loyalty', 'superiority'.

Yes. Once I believed in those things, thought Luther. But now I am dying, and so I believe in life.

A crash behind him, and echoing shouts. Herz was back; Luther could feel the coldness.

'Oh, yes, kill everyone. That always makes sense.' The Doctor's voice was heavy with sarcasm, but Luther knew the words were for his benefit, a translation. He had to get to the light –

Had to get closer, to free the light –

Before –

Oliver stared at the scene in the church, the bizarre machine like a many-legged insect with the brilliant light in the middle, the wounded man slumped against a pillar, shouting, the German officer crawling towards the machine.

'Doctor!' shouted Mel, her voice lighting up. The wounded man glanced at her once, and seemed to smile. The crawling German officer was almost at the machine now. What was he doing? Had the Doctor shot him?

The Lieutenant was running across the church towards him, a revolver in his hand.

'No!' shouted the wounded man, who must be Mel's friend, the Doctor. He seemed to be trying to get to his feet, but his legs wouldn't hold him and he fell to the floor, wincing with pain. The officer glanced across, but went on and put his gun against the wounded soldier's head.

There was a flash, a thunderclap sound. The floor shook. A window exploded inwards, showering the stone floor with shards of coloured glass.

'Yes!'

Mel's ecstatic shout made Oliver realise what had happened: the dynamite had gone off at last.

When the floor shook, Luther knew he had won. He heard the glass falling, and wondered if the Doctor too would die. Probably, but it didn't matter. What mattered was the light, freeing the light. Consequences were irrelevant.

The Doctor would understand.

With his last strength, Luther stood. He felt his body starting to shake, felt the terrible pain as his heart tripped and stopped.

Then he fell.

It wasn't spectacular. No one except Oliver and the Doctor noticed, at first. The German soldiers were still staring at the broken window. The Lieutenant and three others were running for the door, presumably looking for attackers, leaving only one to guard Oliver and Mel.

The wounded officer stood, then fell heavily into the delicate complex of wires around the crystal. They broke, the crystal fell, and the light went out. There was a delicate tinkling, which might have been glass from the window settling.

Then light blazed in from the windows: the true light of a blue sky, the real light of a summer's evening.

Everyone stopped then, even the soldiers in the doorway, and stared around them. But the Doctor was still watching the crystal, and Oliver watched too. Was that a faint blue light, seeping skywards? Or an illusion, a dazzle from the newly lit windows?

From outside, he heard the sound of aeroplane engines. He turned, saw the daylight streaming in through the door, the Germans silhouetted there. A fierce wind started to blow, stirring air inside the church, moving the trees outside. The German officer pushed past him, the cloth of his uniform creaking.

'No!' shouted the Doctor, at the same time as the officer shouted a single word.

Oliver, confused, watched as the officer sank to his knees, his face darkening. He saw Mel step forward, then back, her hands going to her face. Her hair was long, he noticed, and red-gold. She looked young.

The officer collapsed sideways, convulsing. Oliver rushed forward, just in time to see the light fade from his eyes.

Outside, the others were dying, thrashing like broken machines, their faces darkening in the evening light.

An hour later there was still a deep grey-blue twilight, enough to see mist creeping over the chilled fields and choking the valley of the stream. Mel and Oliver stood in the road above the village, almost where they'd first met. The army hadn't arrived, but the Lancaster had flown over again and flashed lights down at them. Somebody, Oliver supposed, would get here soon.

'Will the Doctor be better soon?' Oliver asked. 'He looked badly hurt.'

Mel shrugged. 'The Doctor? I expect so. He's got all kinds of amazing things in the TARDIS.'

Oliver looked over his shoulder at the curiously English-looking blue police box. A disguise, Mel had said. Oliver wondered what it really looked like. He remembered the light in the crystal, remembered it leaking away into the evening. He knew that Mel and the Doctor weren't from the Ministry now, at least not any Ministry he knew.

'What's inside the TARDIS?' he asked.

Mel shook her head. 'It's not as exciting as you'd think,' she said. 'All plastic and bits and pieces. Once you've got over the fact of how big it is –' She seemed to catch herself. 'I suppose it's fun. Until people get killed.'

Oliver looked at her. She was beautiful, he thought, beautiful and sad. 'People get killed all the time,' he said. 'And the Germans deserved to die.'

She looked at him, frowning. 'No one deserves to die.'

'They killed Ellen. They killed Mr Faraday. They were going to kill us. They've killed thousands of people, Mel. They deserved poison.'

But Mel just turned and started down the road towards the misty blue machine.

'I'm going to join the army next year,' he shouted. 'I'm going to kill Germans!'

There was no reply, just the gentle shutting of a door.

After a while, light strobed from the Doctor's strange, disguised miracle and it vanished, leaving darkness.

Honest Living

by Jason Loborik

The service had gone on for far too long.

Ashes to ashes. Dust to dust.

Kate Forbes couldn't take much more. She surveyed the gathering of relatives, blank faces, pale and grey, staring at a gaping hole in the ground which glistened with frost in the bitter December morning. Some of them had already dissolved into tears, unable to comprehend the finality of the moment, but Kate just felt numb; she couldn't cry, not yet. But what if they thought she should be sobbing her heart out too, that her composure meant she didn't really care? She glanced at her mother. Her face was a mask, tired and drawn, white with the cold, her eyes, unblinking, fixed firmly on the hole in the ground.

Kate couldn't stand it. She turned away and scanned the churchyard for a distraction. Anything. It offered all you'd expect: ranks of weathered, mildewed headstones, a solitary, leafless tree, patches of muddy turf, a hunched old gardener…

Her eyes flicked back to the tree. There was a man standing there, dressed in black. He hadn't been there a moment ago and couldn't have got there without her seeing. He was spindly and old, much like the bare, blackened tree he was standing beneath. He looked like he belonged there, as if it were perfectly natural for him to spectate at funerals.

The service had ended and the relatives were dispersing now, some embracing, some clasping each other for support. Her Aunt Claudia caught hold of her, eyes brimming with tears and sympathy, and when she finally shuffled off, Kate turned back to the tree. Her mother was there, standing next to the stranger, talking to him, her hands clasping her head. She turned away from him, but he grabbed her arm and twisted her back to face him. What the hell was he doing to her? Kate was already running towards them, gripped by sudden nausea, her heart thumping.

'What's going on?' she yelled. Her mother turned to look at her, but as she tried to move away from the man, her legs buckled beneath her and she fell. Kate caught her as she collapsed, sobbing hysterically.

'What is it, what did he say to you?'

'He's… he's…' choked her mother, tears streaking down her lined face.

Kate looked up at the gnarled tree. The man was gone. She shook her mother. 'Tell me what he said. Who was he?'

As a group of mourners detached itself and hurried over, Annie Forbes recovered enough to finish her words. 'Your father's not dead,' she gasped. 'The man said he's going to live again.'

The mission was a joke, Tuala knew that, but she knew she couldn't disobey orders. She held up the night visor and scrutinised the building perimeter, noting the positions of the sentries and surveillance systems: two guards and three antiquated video cameras. Maybe the odds weren't so bad after all.

Steeling herself, she broke cover and sprinted for the main gate, gun in one hand, immobiliser in the other. She sped past the cameras and their red lights blinked then went out. The sentries had barely registered her presence when they were vaporised by two perfectly aimed laser bolts.

First stage complete – and it had been child's play; a fact which nagged at Tuala as she pulled out the tracker and made for the main building. She made short work of the other CCTVs – at least that's what she thought they were, she could swear one of them looked like an ancient stills camera she'd once seen in a history book. She came to the door of the main building. It was unlocked. Tuala's eyes darted about the compound, a sickening sensation building in her gut. It was as if they were helping her. Should she abort, go back? She thought of how she'd explain that to her uncle, what he would do if she returned empty-handed. It wasn't an option. She slipped into the building and, following the tracker, ran up numerous flights of stairs and along interminable corridors until she finally reached the lab. It was unlit, but she could make out a tall box in the corner and pieces of scientific apparatus and circuitry littering the benches. Greedily, she began piling components into her kitbag.

'Can I help you, my dear?'

She spun round. The lights came on, revealing a man at the entrance to the lab: tall, with a mass of wavy, white hair crowning a beaky-nosed, lined face. This had to be the Doctor, as Intelligence had suggested. A pretty blonde in a miniskirt was standing in the doorway of the large box, rubbing the sleep out of her eyes.

The Doctor was eying her kitbag. 'Perhaps I should say help yourself.'

Tuala had the gun on him in an instant. For some reason, she couldn't seem to hold it steady and she realised she was still panting from her journey to the lab. The illness must be worse than she thought. 'What are you doing here?' she demanded. 'My uncle said only guards patrol this installation at night.'

'Well, your uncle is mistaken. My assistant, Jo, and I occasionally work into the small hours, if we're busy,' the Doctor explained, as the blonde girl stifled a yawn. His expression hardened. 'Now, perhaps you'll explain why you're so interested in my work... and why you had to kill two innocent people.'

'Quiet!' Tuala snapped.

Jo was desperately trying to take in what was happening. She'd been up all night helping the Doctor, who, in a flash of inspiration, had been convinced he could repair the TARDIS console. But as his own enthusiasm had waned as yet another dead end was reached, the desire to sleep had finally overcome her. She'd dozed soundly until the Doctor had wakened her abruptly, warning her about the intruder.

Suddenly, Jo felt the cold metal of a gun against her temple and she cried out as her arm was twisted viciously behind her back.

'Don't follow me,' hissed the girl in her ear, 'if you want your friend to live.'

'Wait,' said the Doctor. 'If you're in trouble, perhaps I can help you.'

The girl seemed to consider this for a moment, then shook her head. 'We don't need your help. Only these.' She waved the bag of circuits in the air and dragged Jo out down the corridor.

'Where are you taking me?' gasped Jo.

The girl held the gun up to her face and Jo could see the wild fear in her eyes. 'I said be quiet.'

Jo looked at her closely. She sounded little more than fifteen, but her coarse, blistered skin made her appear twice as old. Her teeth were yellow and broken, her eyes tired and bloodshot, but they burned with determination.

'Now get moving,' snarled the girl. 'Or you die here.'

The Doctor was already on the radio. 'Brigadier? Are you there, over?'

'I've just arrived at the main gate. It's unguarded. Over.' Even through the static, the Doctor could detect concern and more than a little irritation in the Brigadier's voice. 'What the blazes does the intruder want, Doctor?'

'I'm not sure exactly. Sorry for getting you up at this hour, old chap.'

'I just want to know what's going on, Doctor. Why didn't you let the patrols intercept her?'

'She's too dangerous, Brigadier. She's killed two people already. I thought I might be able to reason with her.'

The Brigadier sighed. 'And now she's taken Miss Grant hostage.'

'Yes. Any sign of a getaway car?'

'There's a brand-new Mercedes parked further down the lane. We've already taken care of it.'

'Good, keep out of sight. I'll follow them in Bessie.'

'But, Doctor –'

'Please, Brigadier, do as I say. The girl is scared out her wits. I don't want to put Jo in any more danger.'

'Roger. Out.'

Seconds later, the Brigadier watched Jo and her kidnapper exit the main gate and pelt down the lane. There was a roar of a revved engine and as the noise receded into the night, he saw the glare of headlights as the Doctor's Edwardian jalopy sped out of the gate in pursuit. The Brigadier shook his head. 'That's fine, Doctor. I'll just go back to bed, shall I?'

Jo's head slammed against the window as the girl swung the car round another tight bend. She finally stopped under a broken streetlamp in a deserted street of derelict Victorian houses, many of which were boarded up. She pulled off her headband and used it to blindfold Jo.

'Out of the car and walk next to me,' she ordered. 'I will have the gun on you at all times.'

Jo didn't dare argue. She was led down the street and up a short flight of steps to a door which the girl opened. The smells within hit her immediately: a pungent mixture of paint, ozone and fruit. The door slammed behind her.

'Move forwards,' said the girl.

Jo took a few faltering steps, then stopped dead. Iridescent colours began to flash and pulse before her eyes. She tried to tear off the blindfold, but her arms were useless, dead things hanging limply at her sides. She twisted round, but a fierce heat scorched her skin. She felt her flesh begin to burn.

'Come on... come on...'

The voice echoed faintly in the distance, but there were other sounds now: a cacophony of wails and screeches piercing her eardrums, almost blotting out the voice so far away: 'Move, or it will destroy you...' But she had no energy, no will to move. Consciousness ebbed away as she sank slowly to the floor.

'Jo... Jo!'

She felt a sharp slap across her face as the blindfold was ripped away. Her eyes snapped open and she saw the girl, sitting next to her on the stairs. 'What was that?' breathed Jo.

The girl was gasping for air. 'Something you could never understand. Come on, we'd better get out of here.'

Leaning on each other, they limped slowly upstairs. On the landing, a collection of tables and chairs was blocking their path. The girl turned to Jo, eyes flashing. 'Someone's been here,' she said accusingly.

Jo said nothing, praying that the Doctor had somehow got there first.

The girl shoved the obstacles aside and pushed at a door which appeared jammed. Eventually it gave way and she bundled Jo into the bedroom beyond. The girl tied her up, then collapsed on the bed, seemingly exhausted.

Jo looked round the room. It was like a five-star hotel: four-poster bed, lavish furnishings and decor. How come this girl lived here? 'What was all that downstairs?' asked Jo, nursing her scorched arms.

'Like I said, you wouldn't understand,' said the girl wearily.

Jo had had enough. 'Look, you kidnap me and bring me to this... this madhouse. I want some answers. At least tell me your name.'

'Tuala,' the girl said dully. Then she sprang back to life, scrambling over to Jo and pressing a knife to her cheek. Jo could see the sweat on her forehead; was she ill, or something? She caught some of Tuala's rank breath and turned away, the knife glinting in her peripheral vision as Tuala twisted it against her skin. She closed her eyes, petrified, but the next thing she knew, her bonds had been severed and Tuala was holding up a plastic bag.

'What's in there?' asked Jo, suspiciously.

'Oranges. Real ones,' said Tuala, as she began to peel one. She offered it to Jo. 'Eat it,' she encouraged. 'It's good.'

Jo gingerly bit into a segment, while Tuala scoffed one whole. Even by the Doctor's standards, this was weird.

Standing at the end of the street, the Doctor was tinkering with a sophisticated, albeit ancient-looking, tracking device. Satisfied, he flicked a switch and set off down the street, the tracker humming faintly. Seconds later, it started emitting a high-pitched bleep, and the Doctor hurriedly muffled it under his jacket for fear of waking the neighbours – and alerting Jo's captor. He turned it off and looked at the house – No. 33: a handsome Victorian residence. But why should it look so well maintained in a street full of dilapidated houses? And why was the front door wide open?

As he moved to the steps, his foot caught on something. Crouching down, he saw a power cable, partially hidden by fallen leaves. He lifted it up and saw that it led over the side of the steps and into a basement window. He climbed the steps and looked cautiously inside the house.

It was an Aladdin's cave. Dozens of oil paintings lined the oak-panelled walls, gold and silver ornaments glinted in the opulently decorated rooms beyond, and period furniture and priceless antiques vied for prominence in the hallway. The paintwork gleamed like new, and as he looked up he saw an intricate crystal chandelier glittering above the treasure trove. Quite a collection, he mused. He tried a door off the hallway and flicked a switch on the wall, but no light came on. As his eyes adjusted, he made out a staircase leading down to the cellar. He produced a torch from his pocket and descended into the gloom.

'Anyone there?' His voice echoed in the darkness.

Reaching the foot of the stairs, his foot caught on the cable again. He stroked his chin, lost in thought, and followed it to a rusting, metallic box sitting in the middle of the room, the torchlight picking out a dial on its surface. It was a safe.

'My turn for a spot of pilfering,' he muttered, setting his sonic screwdriver to work on the lock. Seconds later, the door opened and painful brightness spilled into the dingy room. Peering through his fingers, the Doctor could see a newspaper and a sports bag. He reached into the safe, but pulled his hand away sharply as a crackle of energy bit at his fingers. Some kind of force-field, no doubt. He tried again, and this time was able to grab the bag before his fingers were too badly burned. He unzipped it gingerly and pulled out a wad of ten-pound notes, then tossed them aside. He snatched up the local newspaper and scanned the lead story, blowing fiercely on his singed fingers:

Business Tycoon in Death Crash.
Relatives and staff were last night mourning the sudden death of Bernard Forbes, who was killed yesterday afternoon in a head-on collision with a lorry. Police on the scene commented –

A scream echoed from upstairs.

'Jo!' The Doctor dropped the newspaper and leapt up the cellar stairs into the hallway. He looked around. Where had the scream come from? He heard a scuffle somewhere on the first floor and hared upstairs, taking three steps at a time. When he got to the bedroom, the girl from the lab was standing with her arm around Jo's throat, gun pressed to her head.

The Doctor sighed. 'Surely you must be a little tired of this kidnapping business by now, my dear.'

She glared at him, balefully. 'I warned you not to follow me. Don't you care if I kill your friend?'

'You know, you don't look like the kind of person who kills for the fun of it, but I imagine your boss expects you to follow his orders to the letter. You don't agree with them, but there's nothing you can do. Am I right?'

The Doctor took a step forward, but sensing the movement the girl pulled Jo back, her finger tightening on the trigger.

'Doctor!' Jo squeaked, helplessly.

The Doctor's foot connected sharply with the gun and it clattered against the wall. At the same time Jo shoved the girl backwards into the wall and ran over to the Doctor, embracing him.

'You all right, Jo?'

Jo nodded, still clinging on to him.

'Now then, young lady,' said the Doctor, gently extricating himself from Jo's arms. 'Perhaps we can talk in a more civilised fashion. What's your name?'

The girl said nothing, still rubbing her bruised wrists.

'It's Tuala,' offered Jo.

'How did you find me?' demanded Tuala.

'Well, I've upgraded UNIT's surveillance systems, you see,' replied the Doctor, with no hint of smugness. 'They can't be immobilised quite as easily as you imagine. The Brigadier attached a homing device to your car, then I traced my components with this.' He brandished the small box-like device, which bleeped loudly as he held it up to the bag.

'Please, Doctor, you must let me go,' Tuala whimpered. 'Krashen will kill me for my failure.'

'Your uncle?'

Tuala nodded.

'He has a curious set of family values,' said the Doctor. He considered her. When he'd first seen her in the lab she had acted like a ruthless guerrilla, now she was behaving like a helpless child.

'You don't belong to this time, do you? Why are you here? Why did you want to steal my equipment?'

'I'm sorry, Doctor,' said Tuala, 'I wish I could trust you, but I can't.'

Before the Doctor could react, she grabbed hold of Jo once more, pulled out a black box and flicked a switch.

'No, wait!' yelled the Doctor, but the two girls had already been engulfed by a vortex of strobing colours. Seconds later they faded away. The Doctor looked down at his tracker – the readings were going haywire. He sighed and switched it off. He had a pretty good idea who the girl was, but there was nothing he could do for Jo here; his only lead was the newspaper.

Lost in thought, he made his way back down to the cellar. The light spilling out from the safe was still cold and harsh. The Doctor looked for the bag of money but it had disappeared. Uneasy, he picked up the newspaper and was about to start reading when it began to blur before his eyes. Then it simply winked out of existence.

'Where's the Doctor? What have you done to him?' demanded Jo.

Tuala was leaning against a wall, studying a screen on the side of the box. She seemed feverish, finding it difficult to draw breath.

Jo studied her, trying to remember who the girl reminded her of. Someone she'd met recently... Yes, that was it, those guerrillas from the future who had returned to the present in order to kill Sir Reginald Styles. He was chairing a world peace conference, but they believed he was responsible for the terrible war which would pave the way for a Dalek invasion. Despite the guerrillas' efforts, they had only managed to trigger the war themselves. What had the Doctor called it? A temporal paradox...

This girl wore the same clothes as the guerrillas, carried a similar gun... and that box had to be a time machine like the one that had taken her to the twenty-second century. But how far forward or back through time had they travelled now?

'My uncle's signalled me his co-ordinates,' said Tuala, looking up from the screen. 'We must meet him at the rendezvous. Now.'

Jo helped her downstairs, but as they passed the entrance to the cellar, they froze. Someone was unlocking the front door.

'Quick, in here,' hissed Tuala, bundling Jo down the cellar steps and closing the door behind her – just as the front door opened.

'Who is it?' whispered Jo.

'You'll find out any second.'

'*Move forwards.*'

The voice was unmistakable: it was Tuala's.

As suddenly as before, the same blinding incandescence filled Jo's vision, searing the backs of her eyes and the same intense heat seared her skin, making her scream out in agony as she scrambled down the stairs to escape the attack.

Then it was over.

'We were lucky,' gasped Tuala weakly. 'We didn't get too close, so the energy release wasn't fatal. When you travel back in time and meet your earlier self, time attempts to short out the differential and resolve the anomaly.'

'So that's what happened before,' Jo murmured.

'I should have realised then.' Tuala managed to heave herself into a standing position. 'We must reach my uncle. Our machines are too unstable to use safely any more.'

Jo glared at her. 'So that's why you wanted the Doctor's circuits. You want to use them for your machine.'

Tuala shrugged. 'That was the original plan, but I need to convince my uncle that the Doctor is our best hope.'

Jo snorted. 'Why should he help you? All you've done is kill people, kidnap me, threaten –'

'True,' said Tuala. 'But you don't belong in the past. Imagine if you met your previous self again. The energy release is never predictable.'

Jo stared at her. 'It could kill me?'

Tuala looked grim. 'You need us to return to your own time.'

Jo's mind reeled at the possibilities: what would it be like to live a few minutes in the past, trying to avoid her previous self? She decided to help Tuala, for the time being at least, creeping up to the cellar door and opening it a little. 'All clear,' she said. 'We went upstairs, remember?' Quickly, she yanked open the front door and the pair hurried down the street, not daring to look back.

Minutes later, when the Doctor arrived, the front door was wide open.

'Good afternoon. Mrs Forbes?'

'Yes, but I'm afraid I don't –'

'Oh, I do beg your pardon.' The Brigadier produced his security pass. 'I'm Brigadier Lethbridge-Stewart of an investigative organisation called UNIT. This is our scientific adviser, the Doctor. We need to speak to you about your husband.'

Annie Forbes looked a little baffled. 'Oh. Well, you'd better come in.'

She led her visitors into the sitting room. 'Please sit down,' she said, uncertainly, waving in the direction of a sofa. A tray of tea and flapjacks was already perched on the Queen Anne coffee table, and the Doctor wondered absently if Mrs Forbes had refreshments on permanent stand-by in case an unexpected visitor should drop by.

'I must apologise for the intrusion,' continued the Brigadier, rather embarrassed. 'We appreciate how difficult things must be for you right now.'

Annie Forbes looked curiously at them, then began pouring the tea. 'I still don't understand what it is you want.'

The Doctor glanced uncertainly at the Brigadier. 'It's about your husband,' he said. 'It's very important.'

Annie Forbes paused, teacup at her lips, brows furrowed. 'What about him?'

'I just need to know about the circumstances surrounding his accident.'

'Accident? What do you know about him?' she said, alarm in her voice.

On cue, Bernard Forbes shuffled in, a stooped middle-aged man in a brown cardigan, flannels and slippers. He was carrying a fluffy toy bird of indeterminate species.

The Brigadier stared at him in surprise, then at the Doctor. 'I thought you told me this man was dead?' he whispered.

'Do you know my friend?' Bernard asked the Doctor, his words slurred and indistinct.

The Doctor's eyes narrowed as he studied the man before him. Surely this couldn't be the same Bernard Forbes the newspaper had described – a supposedly shrewd businessman and entrepreneur?

'Do you know my friend?' Bernard repeated, gesturing to the white bird.

The Doctor hazarded a guess. 'Know it? Is it a goose…?'

Bernard's face fell and he stared at the toy, turning it round and round in his trembling hands.

'What's your name, old chap?' asked the Brigadier.

'Bernard.'

'Bernard who?'

The man glanced at his wife nervously. 'Don't know.' He shuffled stiffly out of the room without another word.

'He seems to get a little worse every day.' Annie's eyes filled with tears. 'He's been like that for three weeks now.'

'Do you know why this has happened?' asked the Doctor, gently.

She shook her head. 'The doctors did all sorts of tests on him. At first they thought it might be a stroke, but they can't find anything at all. But *you* must know.'

'I'm sorry?'

'You mentioned an accident. Do you know what's happened to him?'

The Brigadier fidgeted uneasily in his chair and the Doctor swallowed, patting the woman's hand. 'I'm very sorry, Mrs Forbes. I don't have any answers. But I'll be back as soon as I discover anything.' He stood up, nodding at the Brigadier. 'Please excuse us.'

Outside the house, the Brigadier was bursting with questions, but the Doctor strode ahead, his face grave with concentration. 'Doctor, how on earth can that man be alive? You told me the newspaper reported his death in some car accident.'

The Doctor didn't slow his pace. 'No time for questions, Brigadier,' he snapped. 'We've a potential catastrophe on our hands.'

The Brigadier bristled. 'In which case, you'll need my help, Doctor,' he retorted. 'And if I'm to help, I'll need some answers.'

The Doctor halted, scratching the back of his neck. 'Yes. Yes, you're quite right.'

The Brigadier waited. 'Well?'

'That safe... the newspaper vanishing...' The Doctor looked at him. 'Bernard Forbes *did* die, just as the newspaper reported. But I believe our friend Krashen changed history in some way so that he didn't.'

The Brigadier raised an eyebrow. 'Change history? And why would he want to do that?'

'Money, I imagine. From the amount in his safe and the treasures in his house, my guess is this isn't the first time he's prevented someone's death in return for payment.'

The Brigadier regarded him sceptically. 'Isn't that a bit far-fetched, Doctor? I mean, who is this Krashen, exactly?'

'The girl who kidnapped Jo was wearing combat clothes. And she has a time machine like the one used by Anat and her friends.'

'Do you mean they're also guerrillas from wherever-it-was? But the conference is over!'

'I don't think this pair mean to assassinate Sir Reginald Styles. I think they've simply travelled back to this time to escape the rule of the Daleks. Yes, to escape, and to enjoy the affluence of the twentieth century.'

'And I take it they've decided against earning an honest living...'

'Right,' agreed the Doctor. 'Krashen's using his only asset – a time machine, and a malfunctioning one too, if the readings I took are correct.'

'So that's why he raided your laboratory?'

The Doctor looked thoughtful. 'If Krashen was in contact with the rebels he could well have heard of me, yes... and that raid alone implies he's becoming desperate.'

The Brigadier was still trying to get to grips with the intricacies of

Krashen's operations. 'Let me see if I've got this straight. When Bernard Forbes originally died, his wife paid Krashen to prevent his accident... But if Bernard Forbes didn't die, then she didn't meet Krashen, which means she never gave him the money...' He scratched his head as his mind boggled. 'The whole thing's absurd.'

'That's right, Brigadier. That's exactly what a temporal paradox is. Nevertheless, the money existed at least long enough for him to spend it.'

'But how could it?'

'Well, judging by the energy in that safe, he was keeping the money in stasis – out of time altogether if you like. But you can't cheat time, you can only delay the inevitable. I just wonder how long Krashen's house will remain in its present glorified state.'

'And how long Bernard Forbes will stay alive?'

'Indeed.' The Doctor looked downcast. 'I wish I knew what time is trying to do to him. Anyway, that's not the biggest problem right now.'

'What do you mean?'

'Well, don't you see? We resolved the paradox involving the guerrillas and Sir Reginald Styles. We saved the peace conference, World War Three didn't break out... which means the Daleks didn't invade in the twenty-second century.'

The Brigadier stared at him. 'So what's Krashen doing in this time at all?'

The Doctor sighed heavily. 'Exactly. He's a paradox within a paradox, and with Bernard Forbes, he's created yet another. Who knows how many times he's done this. And if he keeps on... The paradoxes could spiral out of control.' He jumped into Bessie.

'And?'

'I don't know. I've never encountered a loop of anomalies like this. I need to talk to Krashen and send him back before he does any more damage.'

The Brigadier slid into the passenger seat, his mind reeling. He had been given plenty of answers, but was feeling none the wiser.

Jo and Tuala ran through seemingly endless streets until they reached a small crumbling church on the outskirts of town.

'Our rendezvous,' explained Tuala, panting, as she ushered Jo through the battered doors.

The pair collapsed on the rickety pews, sending clouds of dust into the cold, stale air.

Jo took in her surroundings – it looked like a bomb had exploded. Hymn books, rubble and shards of glass littered the cracked stone floor. Light streamed through the remaining fragments of the stained-glass window behind the ancient pulpit. The sound of church music echoed faintly in the gloom, but there was no way it could be coming from the broken shell of the pipe organ.

'Why here?' asked Jo.

'Ruins such as these are all that exist in our time,' said Tuala. 'Uncle often conducts business here. He says it's important never to forget why we're here.'

'So where is he then?'

'I'm here,' echoed a voice.

Jo squinted. A figure was silhouetted against the window, moving up the steps to the pulpit.

'Uncle!' cried Tuala, moving towards him.

Krashen had reached the pulpit and was doubled over it, as if needing it to stay upright.

'You failed, you stupid child,' he snarled. His voice was dry, rasping.

'I got the components –'

'Then where are they?'

Tuala looked away.

'Not only that, but you led the Doctor to us. He's opened the safe, and now he knows of our activities.' Krashen broke off in a coughing fit, grasping desperately at Tuala to keep himself standing.

'We need his help, Uncle. Anat's reports were right, he *is* a scientist.'

'But how do you know we can trust him?' growled Krashen. 'What if he sends us back? You think I'm ready to give up my life here?'

'Uncle, please listen to me. Our machines are harming us more each time we use them. They must be damaging time too. I'm sure the effect is increasing exponentially. We need the Doctor's knowledge.'

Jo swallowed hard. She'd felt ill since her encounter in the house. Could her journey through time have inflicted some permanent damage on her?

Krashen turned away from Tuala and faced Jo, as if noticing her for the first time. 'Who is this?'

'The Doctor's friend.'

Krashen straightened and slowly descended the pulpit steps, towards Jo. She backed away. All she could see was the refracted light of the stained glass window, and the silhouette of Krashen as he edged nearer. He stopped a few feet from her, observing her silently. 'Do you come from this time?' he asked.

'Yes,' Jo whispered.

Krashen gestured vaguely with his hand. 'Don't you find this beautiful?'

Jo thought he was referring to the derelict church, then realised he meant the music, which she deduced must be coming from a cassette player somewhere.

'It's very nice,' she offered, hoping this was adequate praise.

'Bach,' said Krashen. 'The only composer ever to construct melody and harmony with mathematical precision…' He paused, mesmerised, as the music reached an intricate crescendo. 'I'd never heard anything so pure, so utterly captivating, until I arrived here. Every chord and cadence so perfectly crafted, not a single note misplaced…'

Jo shuffled uneasily. Where was all this leading? She felt tired; if she didn't sit down soon she would collapse. 'What are you going to do to me?' she whispered.

'Nothing.' Krashen moved closer. 'As long as you co-operate.'

The Doctor swung open the door and looked about the hall in surprise. It seemed as though the house had been burgled. Many of the paintings and antiques had disappeared, and the decor – once bright and new – was now old and tattered. The place had a neglected, musty smell to it that the Doctor hadn't noticed before.

'Good evening, Doctor. I thought you might return.'

The Doctor squinted in the dim light of a solitary light bulb. He could just make out a figure halfway up the stairs, wheezing and rasping, holding tightly to the banister.

'Good evening, Mr Krashen,' he said cheerily. 'You're a lucky man – I'd expected your machines to have killed you by now.'

'They are merely faulty.'

'What, *both* of them? Can't you take them back to the shop, or has the guarantee run out?'

'I want *you* to repair them.'

'I suppose Jo's safety comes into this somewhere?'

'Correct. Stabilise our time machines and I will let her live.'

The Doctor's face hardened. 'Without my even paying a fee? That's very gracious of you. I must say you take the responsibility of deciding who lives and dies alarmingly lightly.'

Krashen straightened. 'Why should you disapprove of my activities?' he asked, with seemingly genuine surprise.

'Disapprove of them?' glared the Doctor. 'I find them abhorrent, sir! You're meddling with the chain of cause and effect, without a thought for the consequences... and all for a miserable bag of money!'

Krashen shook his head. 'I use my time machines for good, Doctor. Take Bernard Forbes – why *should* he die? A successful career, a loving, devoted family. Why should they have to come to terms with a senseless death? I acted to restore their lives.'

'But with what right? Krashen, time decreed the date that Bernard Forbes died. It happened that way and you can't change it. Nothing can.'

Krashen wasn't listening. 'You haven't seen the horrors of my time, Doctor. Families torn apart, whole communities decimated. I've witnessed more human misery and anguish than you can comprehend, but here, in this time, I have the power to prevent that, if only for a small number of people...'

'...desperate enough to cough up a large sum of money,' finished the Doctor.

'I saved a small boy who would otherwise have drowned,' continued Krashen. 'I saw him last week walking in the park with his mother.'

The Doctor groaned loudly. 'Oh, please, Krashen, I simply cannot comprehend the sheer scale of your philanthropy. Tell me, have you seen any more of your "chosen few" lately? The state of Mr Forbes, for example?'

'No,' said Krashen uncertainly.

'He's an imbecile, purposeless. He shouldn't be here. Time *knows* he shouldn't be here.'

'You talk of time as if it were a sentient thing.'

'Yes, I do, don't I?' said the Doctor quietly. 'Well, something is making others suffer the consequences of your actions.'

'Consequences?'

'Yes, man, are you blind?' the Doctor said. 'Look around you.' He gestured to the light bulb above. 'Where's your pretty chandelier? Why did the money and newspaper disappear when I took them out of the safe? You must have known that things were starting to go wrong, otherwise you wouldn't have built the thing. And why is Bernard Forbes degenerating before his wife's eyes? Time is rectifying the anomalies, ever faster... How long before it's your turn, Krashen?'

'I won't allow that to happen.' Krashen spoke quietly, his voice faltering.

'Face it man, you don't belong here, you'll never fit in. Leave now, before it's too late.'

Krashen didn't respond. He started down the steps until he was standing directly below the light and slowly, deliberately, removed his hat. The Doctor winced. Krashen's head was a mass of blisters and lacerations. Black pulsing veins stood out from the dry, scab-encrusted scalp, thin patches of matted hair unable to disguise ears like melting wax. In comparison, his face was almost normal, although it was covered with scars and bruises. But his eyes were his most striking feature: glacial-blue pools, piercing and hypnotic.

'How did this happen to you?'

'The Daleks,' answered Krashen simply. 'They did this to me because I stole their time machines and built copies for the resistance fighters. They kept me alive, wanted me to betray my friends, but Tuala rescued me and we escaped here together. She'd known Anat, knew the safe places, knew you. Why should I wish to return to certain death? I love this time. My only wish is to live here in peace.'

The Doctor shook his head. 'You can't, Krashen. I've put events in the future on to the right track – there *was* no Dalek invasion. You shouldn't be here at all.'

Krashen's voice raised in pitch. 'A moment ago you were condemning me for choosing what could happen and what could not.'

'All that suffering, all the misery you endured was as a direct result of the ham-fisted meddling of your people with those ridiculous machines,' stormed the Doctor. 'You don't know what you're doing.'

'And you do?' Krashen challenged.

The Doctor placed his hands on his hips. 'Yes, sir, I most certainly do.'

Krashen indicated the stairs. 'I'm losing patience. Miss Grant is upstairs. I'm sure you'd like to see her.'

The Doctor calmed down, nodded and followed Krashen as he took slow, agonising steps up to the bedroom.

When she saw the Doctor, Jo rushed to him and gave him a hug.

'Here we are again, eh, Jo? Are you all right?'

'I think so,' she said uncertainly. 'Just a bit dizzy.'

The Doctor noticed Tuala. She was lying on the bed, pale and sweating. He looked around the bedroom – something was happening to the walls. The plush wallpaper seemed to be dissolving, powdering away to reveal cracked, yellowing walls.

'This is madness, Krashen. Can't you see your presence here is being rejected? Go now, before you're erased altogether.'

'Enough, Doctor,' snapped Krashen. He held up the two black boxes. 'Stabilise the machines.'

'I can't. It's too late. Even if I did, it would do you no good. Look around you! Time has finally caught up with you.'

Krashen looked round the room, then screwed his eyes tight, falling towards the Doctor on his knees. His speech was slurred. 'It seems you leave... me... no...'

He stabbed a button on one of the boxes and the Doctor felt a familiar tingling sensation throughout his body as lights strobed before his eyes – he was travelling through time. The lights subsided and he saw they were in the same room, now lavishly decorated and full of furniture. He felt dizzy, but when he looked around he saw that the others had been far worse affected by the journey. Krashen was leaning against Tuala and Jo had her eyes closed as if trying to regain her sense of balance.

'Now,' said Krashen wearily, 'do as I say, or your friend dies.'

The Doctor glared at him. 'What do you mean?'

Krashen didn't reply. He collapsed and Tuala fell with him, unable to support his weight. 'Uncle! Uncle!' she screamed.

The Doctor rushed over and knelt down beside Krashen's inert form. 'He's out cold, poor chap,' he said. He examined the time machine that had transported them.

'How far back have we travelled?' asked Jo.

'Ten hours, thirty-five minutes, if this read-out is correct,' said the Doctor.

Tuala looked up, startled. 'That means we've been taken back to last night,' she said.

Jo frowned. 'So?'

'That's when I first brought you into this room. Don't you remember?'

'You mean we could meet our other selves again?'

'Yes – at any moment.'

Tuala stood up, but as she did so she let out a piercing scream. She clutched her head and dropped to the floor once more, twisting in excruciating pain. 'Help me,' she wailed.

The Doctor watched in horror as her form shimmered and glowed, then faded away. A patch of the wall behind her was glowing brightly, as if it were on fire.

'It's followed us,' murmured the Doctor. 'It won't give up until the last paradox has been resolved.'

Jo was confused. 'What's followed us?'

'Time, Jo. It wants us all!'

'Get her back, Doctor!' cried Jo. 'Please try!'

Desperately, the Doctor tried to wire his tracking device into the time machine. 'I'm sorry, Jo, I've lost her.'

'Will that happen to us? Can't we just run away from here?' She indicated the wall, where the glowing patch was growing larger, radiating more fiercely.

'It's too risky. We might meet your other self.'

Jo shivered. 'I know. It happened to me earlier.' She brightened. 'It hurt me but I was all right. It can't be that bad, can it? And anyway, when Tuala and I came into this room last night, there was no sign of me and you. Doesn't that mean you'll get the time machines working properly?'

'No, Jo!' he snapped. 'With this accumulation of paradoxes, the past is no longer immutable. Time will take whatever course is necessary to resolve the final anomalies.'

'What does that mean?'

'I've no idea. The resultant implosion of Blinovitch energy could take us with it – us, this house, even this city.' The Doctor could see Jo was struggling to understand, and his tone softened. 'Come on, Jo. Help me buy some time.'

'How?'

'I want you to barricade the landing, use whatever you can to prevent your earlier self from entering this room. Then jam the door. Understood?'

Jo nodded and sped out of the bedroom door. The Doctor glanced at the glowing wall, incandescent now, then turned his attention to the microcircuitry of the time machine. Several components and linkages had apparently melted away – there was no way that the machine could achieve molecular stabilisation of its subjects. But what had caused this? Was it misuse, an accident... or could time itself have somehow engineered the malfunction in order to eradicate Krashen? The Doctor shuddered at the implications. Repairing the damage was child's play, with time and the correct tools – neither of which he had. He selected the microwelding adjustment on his sonic screwdriver and, glancing up occasionally as Jo built her barricade, worked furiously on the broken linkages. Hands clammy with sweat, he went as quickly as he dared, but as he made the final delicate adjustment, the circuit sparked suddenly and the screwdriver stopped working. The Doctor realised the spark had overloaded the microwelding tip. He'd ordered Jo to buy him a few more seconds of time, and now he'd just thrown them away.

Jo appeared in the doorway, breathless. 'We… they're here already.'

'Jam the door, Jo,' he ordered. 'Then hide yourself under the bed. You must be as far from your other self as possible.'

Jo obeyed without a word. She snatched up a door stop and kicked it under the door. 'It won't… it didn't hold Tuala for long,' she said. She was about to crawl under the bed, when it shimmered and faded away. 'Doctor!' she cried.

The Doctor rummaged in his pocket and took out a safety pin. He unclasped it and held the pin against the circuitry of the time machine, and the screwdriver to the pin. If he could agitate the pin's ionic substructure to a sufficient degree… it would either complete the final connection or short out the entire machine. He paused.

'Hurry, Doctor!'

The Doctor looked at her, activating the screwdriver. 'Even if the device works, we could be left drifting helplessly in the vortex for eternity.'

The handle of the door turned and the door shook as Tuala threw her weight against it.

The wall burned fiercely, the heat beginning to scorch their skin.

'Just do it, Doctor!' Jo shouted. 'Do it!'

The Doctor's fingers began to burn. The pin glowed red hot.

Then the circuit was complete and the room exploded.

'Doctor? Doctor, are you all right?'

A familiar, moustached face swam into focus. 'Brigadier,' the Doctor croaked. 'Did it… Is Jo…?'

'You've both had a lucky escape by the look of things,' said the Brigadier.

'Where… where did you find us?'

'In that old house. Unconscious. No sign of the Merc, the tracker was just lying in the street outside. No sign of that Krashen fellow, either, or the girl.'

'Time must have corrected the paradox,' mused the Doctor, 'and returned him to his rightful place in time. Tuala too, I hope.'

Within minutes, the Doctor was up and dressed. After examining the still-unconscious Jo, he instructed the sickbay staff to keep her under observation. Her body needed time to readjust after the destabilising effects of the time machine.

Wandering back to his lab, he stopped in the filing room to look at the papers. He rifled through the pile and found the same newspaper Krashen had had in his safe. His heart sank as he read the front page. No mention of an accident, or Bernard Forbes's death. The Doctor brooded. Why hadn't time simply allowed the accident to happen after all? Presumably it was choosing a more expedient path.

The Brigadier saw the Doctor leave the building, heading for Bessie's garage, his cloak billowing in the wind. 'Doctor! Good news,' he called after him. 'Miss Grant's coming round.'

But the Doctor didn't hear. He had other things on his mind.

Kate Forbes stared into space, absently drinking her tea. Dimly, she was aware of her mother answering the door and she heard the voice of a man in the hallway.

'Mrs Forbes? I'm so sorry to trouble you again.'

'Oh, it's you. You said you'd come back.'

They entered the sitting room and Kate stared at the man, but for some reason he wouldn't meet her gaze. Her mother had started sobbing and she stood up, embracing her gently. Kate looked at the stranger, but he still wouldn't look her in the eye. 'What are you doing here again?' she said. 'Can't you see how upset she is?'

The man stood for a moment, then raised his head. 'Please. Tell me what happened.'

Her mother turned back to him. 'I was in the kitchen making the tea. I'd left him watching television. When I went back to the sitting room, he'd vanished. The front door was locked...'

She broke down again, and this time the man held her, patting her uncertainly on the back.

'He's not coming back, is he?'

The man didn't speak.

'Is he?'

'No, my dear. I'm afraid he isn't.'

Dead Time

by Andrew Miller

It was cold. Freezing. The darkness was so thick and oppressive, the Doctor found himself wondering whether the walls and roof were actually fashioned from it, from patches of night sky resentful that no stars had ever shone in their confines. He had been standing, rooted to the spot, for what seemed like an eternity. His senses were dulled with both pain and the tedium of his incarceration. In this place the moments, the minutes, the hours seemed so stretched out that the words lost all meaning. He felt his face with numbed fingers, reminded himself of what he was, who he was. And Sam, his companion, his friend... taken from him and held somewhere out there in the blackness. He could picture her growing older as his struggles continued, her blonde hair turning grey, her wiry body wizening, her clear young skin wrinkling in this dark and empty place.

'We know you now, Doctor.' The voice was a mocking whisper, but the loudest whisper he had ever heard, up close in his ears. 'We are going to use you, to take from you what we need. We have been waiting so long and so patiently for somebody like you... one of us.' The sinister voice emitted a low moan of pleasure. 'And we are going to kill you, Doctor. We are going to kill you so slowly, so tenderly, you won't even realise... and when the moment of your death has come, we will gloat over your memory through the aeons ahead, for the freezing chill bred in this darkness will make you a monument to us, will keep your memory fresh and dead and ours. No one else's. Ours for ever.'

The Doctor said nothing, eyes closed and mouth clamped shut. But he knew the whispering spectre was telling the truth. And he could tell for certain that whatever was speaking to him was utterly mad.

Another voice came to him, echoing eerily through the void. A girl's voice. Sam's voice.

'It's like being in a tomb, shut in with only the darkness. It's so, so black in here... Oh, Doctor... it's like nothing else has ever existed – everyone I've ever known, everywhere I've ever been... it's like all that was just some kind of a dream.

'It's only when I use crap clichés like that that I realise there has to have been something else.'

'Sam?' whispered the Doctor. 'Sam! Are you all right?'

But the mirthless laughter in his ear told him that she was still somewhere else, that he had been allowed only to listen in on her thoughts for a few moments. The forces here were trying to distract him while they found some new way of burrowing inside his psychic defences... Reminding him that it was his fault that Sam was helpless in the blackness. He was the one who had brought her here.

Memories... Eyes still tightly shut, though it made no difference to the darkness, he remembered...

The TARDIS was a long way out, tumbling through space and time, when the Doctor realised that, as was so often the case when you were a wanderer in the fourth and fifth dimensions, something was wrong. An insistent beep was coming from somewhere on the wooden hexagonal console that was the heart of the TARDIS's guidance systems.

'What is it, Doctor?' asked Sam.

'Oh, the old girl's just being a little overcautious. We may be in for a bit of a bumpy ride, that's all. She's telling us something odd's happening to the time parameters.'

'What sort of odd?' asked Sam. 'What's wrong *now*?' Things were always going wrong around the Doctor, and by now she had developed a kind of Sam Jones-Richter scale of danger to measure them against.

The Doctor shrugged. 'Ah, well, you know – freak ripple effect, a Lucrece shift, something along those lines.'

'Oh, that's all right, then,' said Sam, rolling her eyes.

Unaware of the sarcasm, the Doctor seemed genuinely pleased to have put his friend at ease. 'There's really nothing to worry about.

It's only if that red light starts flashing at the same time that we –'

'This red light?' said Sam, affecting a casual air.

As the Doctor peered at the display Sam was pointing to, an enormous explosion threw them to the floor of the TARDIS. The protesting scream of overworked engines sounded from somewhere deep in the heart of the ship.

'Yes, that's the one,' confirmed the Doctor ruefully, as tremors shook through the control room. 'Hold on!' he yelled as the TARDIS vibrated and trembled as if afraid of where it was going.

A klaxon sounded and instrumentation sparked and spluttered around them. Abruptly, the control room was plunged into darkness. Something – probably one of the large bronze statues at the periphery of the control room – crashed to the ground, and Sam cried out involuntarily.

The sound echoed eerily around her, then died away into silence. A chill ran through her.

'Listen…' she whispered in the gloom. 'The TARDIS… It's stopped!'

The comforting hum of the control room's incredible technology had been replaced by an oppressive silence.

About 8.5 on the Jones-Richter scale.

She listened as the Doctor's fingers flickered over the controls, the sounds seemingly everywhere at once. In response to his caresses, an eerie yellow luminescence bled into the grey stone of the TARDIS walls. In the dim emergency lighting, the Doctor's face was lined with worry.

'We're in deep space,' he muttered. 'Deepest space. There shouldn't be anything out here. Not for millions of years.'

'How can you be sure?' asked Sam.

The Doctor scowled. 'On my planet, children in nursery know that.'

Sam was stung by his reaction, but saw how troubled he looked and walked over to him, tugging lightly on his coat sleeve. 'So where are we?'

'I don't know,' he replied.

'Perhaps we should ask the nursery children?' she inquired, with mock politeness.

The Doctor looked set to make a caustic reply, but his face softened before the words could come out, relaxing into a smile.

Sam smiled back at him. 'What time are we in?'

The Doctor crossed over to the chronometric display. 'We're... How odd.'

'Deeply peculiar,' affirmed Sam, nodding her head authoritatively. 'What are you talking about?'

The Doctor was scrutinising some ticker tape chattering out from a brass housing. 'The read-out's shifting... It won't settle.' He frowned. 'According to this, we've landed in countless different times all at once, over a span of thousands of years.'

Sam frowned. 'Is it up the spout? How can we be in different times all at the *same* time?'

'How indeed?' brooded the Doctor. 'Perhaps that's why we've lost power. Simultaneous arrival in hundreds of different time zones...'

'Like falling into a shredder...?' whispered Sam.

'Precisely,' murmured the Doctor. 'We're lucky to be alive.'

Sam looked at him as he stared straight ahead, his face shrouded in shadow.

'Is it a trap?'

'Perhaps.' Catching her worried look, he smiled. 'Or a natural occurrence – there's always that possibility. In any case, we're rather stuck here until I can work out if the process is reversible.'

'If. Right. And where exactly *is* here?'

The Doctor shrugged at her as he scrutinised further controls. 'No clear reading of mass... It's certainly not a planet... Seems to be made up of layers and layers of material the TARDIS can't recognise, and yet... I have a feeling...'

'Some kind of cosmic papier-mâché?' ventured Sam, and to her surprise the Doctor grinned broadly.

'Precisely,' he said. 'But how did they come by so much paste in the middle of a void, hmm?'

He activated the scanner, but there was only blackness as the old-fashioned monitor warmed up to show them the exterior view. They waited for some time.

'Scanner's broken,' said Sam.

The Doctor took a deep breath. 'No. That's what's out there.'

*'We're going to rip right through you, Doctor. You're going to die.
You're going to die. We're going back and we're going to kill you
kill you kill you...'*

The Doctor felt the whispering demons pulling at his memories,
twisting them, devouring them, attempting to erase them... He
stayed calm, eyes shut, retreating into himself... It was like trying to
keep control of a huge house full of wild children tearing from
room to room. What a pity, he reflected, that his mind contained so
many places to hide.

Suddenly the Doctor could hear cries of anguish over the mad
jabbering of the whispering voices. They were coming from Sam.

'No... please, let her go! Stop hurting her!'

'We're going to kill, kill, kill you...'

But even as the Doctor was distracted by Sam's distress, he realised
that the voices in his mind were taking the scraps of thought and
memory he was sacrificing to the battle for control and building a
new image – pale... yellow... a bloom of some kind... flowers,
tranquil against a deep indigo sky that was glittering with stars.

He recognised the flowers... recognised them from an age long
distant when, as a young boy on Gallifrey, he had watched funerals
being conducted with pomp and magnificent ceremony. The
flowers, almost invisible at first, so far were they from the eye,
dropped fluttering from the far reaches of the vast cathedral-like
arches of the Panopticon and on to the crowd of mourners far
below. As a child it had been easy to believe that the flowers had
fallen from heaven itself.

They were the Gallifreyan flowers of remembrance.

Somewhere in the dark, Sam remembered...

'You can't go outside alone, Doctor!' she protested. 'You've no idea
what's there!'

'Then I'll find the light switch!'

'And what if you can't breathe? If the controls are giving faulty
read-outs?'

'I can go without air for some time, Sam, you know that. Besides… it's as if – as if I should *know* where we are.' With that, he pulled the large brass lever that opened the doors and left the dimly lit sanctuary of the TARDIS for the comfortless dark outside.

'There's air here,' the Doctor called back, then started as he realised Sam was at his side already.

'You don't think I'm going to let you go off out here by yourself, do you? Probably end up enjoying yourself poking around – you'll forget all about me!' said Sam with what she knew the Doctor would realise was forced cheerfulness.

'Tread carefully,' was his only answer. He lit a match, but although it burned brightly, it lit up nothing of their surroundings. Puffing it out, he produced a torch from the pocket of his frock coat instead. 'Less Gothic,' he apologised, 'but never mind…'

The torch beam shone brightly, but still they could make out nothing but shadows.

'I suppose there's no point going back to the TARDIS, is there?' Sam asked tentatively. 'We could wait there.'

'Wait?' queried the Doctor. 'For what?'

'I don't know… It's like… It feels like something's going to happen here.'

The Doctor stared at her a little strangely. Suddenly embarrassed, Sam started striding confidently off into the darkness.

'Sam!' called the Doctor suddenly, whipping out a hand and grabbing hold of her T-shirt. 'Don't go marching off like that. You might step in something. Here, take this.'

Sam felt smooth fabric being wrapped around her wrist, and realised it was the Doctor's silk cravat, its silver-grey colouring lost in the unrelieved blackness.

Since she was blushing anyway, Sam ventured casually, 'Have we just tied the knot?'

The Doctor simply said, 'This should keep us together.'

They moved off warily. It felt to Sam a little like walking on sponge, the way the dark surface of this place absorbed the noise of their footsteps.

BudK.com

www.

Dark

Emporium

Zemeho
inc.
(website ?
((514) 745-
7677

'What's this?' she said, groping the air in front of her and touching something solid and fibrous. 'A wall?'

'It's some kind of archway,' confirmed the Doctor.

The 'wall' was smooth, but she couldn't decide whether it was hard or soft, warm or cool to the touch; it just… was. That seemed to sum up this place. Somewhere that just was.

The Doctor led the way as they moved cautiously through the narrow tunnel. It twisted round and round, becoming narrower and narrower, when suddenly the Doctor stopped dead and she bumped into him with a cry of alarm.

'Shh!' hissed the Doctor. 'There's something up ahead.'

Sam turned behind her then, as if a voice had whispered her name. She caught a glimpse of something moving, a dull, pale-gold shadow some way off, just for a moment.

Then it was gone.

The more the babbling creatures caused havoc in the Doctor's head, the more the confines of this dark citadel were dimly illuminated; the more concrete and definite the sinister shadow of the giant man clawing at his head became, towering over him. He closed his eyes once again. Was this another attempt to make him lose his concentration, to surrender to whatever force was inside his mind? The Doctor wasn't all that concerned about the damage the creatures could be doing to his synapses; he felt strong enough at present to resist their probing, and was keeping their subtle re-routings of his neural pathways to a minimum. What really bothered him was the ease with which they were moving round his mind… He himself found it a baffling, confusing place to be at times, particularly soon after a regeneration. How had these shadows gained access so effectively?

Running round like children.

Like children in a nursery.

The Doctor remembered talking to Sam back in the TARDIS soon after they'd arrived here…

Sam remembered…

The sharp tug on the cravat wrapped round her wrist bade her follow the Doctor, and although she opened her mouth to tell him what she had seen, she suddenly decided against it. What if she *had* imagined it? The Doctor needed someone he could rely on in his travels through the cosmos, not a stupid schoolgirl who jumped at her own shadow. Play it cool, Sam. Say nothing. It *was* nothing.

She cast a look over her shoulder despite herself but there was nothing but the pitch blackness.

She cursed the TARDIS for having to land them here, then cursed whatever had actually made it do so, then cursed the gold thing she had glimpsed… This seemed exactly like being in a bad dream. There seemed no logic to it, no obvious way to respond. Miserably, she accepted that she was totally out of her depth. So, she reflected a little sadly, as usual all she could do was trust in the Doctor.

But what if the Doctor was out of his depth too?

They rounded the corner of the narrow, twisted passage and the Doctor stopped abruptly. They were on a precipice and, for the first time since they'd left the TARDIS, Sam could feel something akin to a breeze. Pinpricks of painfully bright light sparkled, but it was difficult at first to tell just how far away they were. Then the lights began to appear more frequently, like glow-worms in a vast underground tunnel.

Sam peered into the gloom. She could discern shapes in the darkness now, like shadows stretched and twisted into things they were not. Half-formed, stunted shapes that could have been people littered the giant cavern of darkness as if their creators had grown bored sculpting them and had abandoned them where they stood. A shiver of fear ran through her at the sheer scale of it all.

'What is it, Doctor?' she whispered, relieved at least to be able to make out the tall figure of her friend beside her.

The Doctor was transfixed. 'Those flashes,' he muttered. 'I wonder…'

Some of the points of light had begun to coalesce, forming faint patches of luminous mist. In the light they cast, Sam could see that the shapes had distorted, screwed-up faces that should never have been seen this way, the features pinched and pulled. Fear, pain, confusion: basic terrifying emotions in their rawest state seemed to have been carved into these tortured beings.

Then she noticed. The cloud of light was getting brighter, stronger. Closer.

'Back away, Sam,' hissed the Doctor.

'What –?'

'*Back away!*'

Together, they turned and stumbled blindly into the tunnel. Casting a look over her shoulder, Sam could see the patch of light floating towards them.

'It's following us!'

'Quickly,' said the Doctor. 'Down here.'

Once Sam had realised that whatever material formed this place was too fibrous to cause any real physical harm upon impact it made it easier to run like hell. The two of them jostled against each other in the darkness as they pitched forwards at high speed ever deeper into the nothingness.

'Do you know where you're going?' panted Sam.

'Possibly,' replied the Doctor enigmatically.

Everything was silent as they ran, but after some time Sam realised that their footfalls were sounding louder, that the fabric beneath their feet was changing, growing harder, almost like stone. Gradually, she could hear something else, what felt at first like a low pressure in her ears but soon became a throbbing, insistent hum. With the noise came a faint phosphorescence around them. She stopped running.

'Doctor –'

'Shh, Sam. I know.'

The Doctor too had stopped. Then with a tug on the cravat to pull Sam along, he strolled almost casually forward into what seemed like a vast, gloomy amphitheatre. As they stepped inside, the deep, sonorous noise became louder. It sounded in some way familiar... a noise she had grown used to, distorted and twisted, broken up as if heard through giant, crackling, rattling loudspeakers.

'Well, well,' murmured the Doctor sullenly.

Sam could make out weird indentations in the walls, like half-formed circles. Lumps of the spongy black material that composed this alien place were tilting up from the uncertain flooring: a huge hexagonal protuberance grew from the middle of the huge chamber and a giant statue of what might have been a man, clutching a bizarre black shape that was surely its head, towered menacingly some twenty feet above them.

'Well, Doctor?'

'Don't you see, Sam? Of course, since I reconfigured the console room…'The Doctor untied his cravat from her wrist and draped it back round his neck.'All this was once alive, pulsing with power… the power to travel anywhere in time to any point in the universe.' He smiled sadly.'We've spent all this time running round a derelict in space… all that's left of the ragged hulk of an ancient, dying TARDIS.'

'A TARDIS? Of course…' Sam realised what the noise had reminded her of, although it was a far cry from the clean, comforting hum of the TARDIS she knew. This noise conveyed sickness. Pain. As the Doctor had said… death.

A thought struck her.'So did it come from your planet?'

'Almost definitely.'

'And what about him?' Sam gestured to the huge distorted figure, its head in its hands.'Were there many giants there last time you looked?'

The Doctor ignored Sam's remark and gazed around him.'There's something more than just decay affecting this place. The whole aspect has changed, warped around the original way of things. I can just about recognise the design… enough to know it would have been taken out of service millennia ago –' He stopped abruptly with a sharp intake of breath. When he spoke again, it was in a rushed whisper.'One of the earliest time-space vessels.'

'Is that significant?' queried Sam.

The Doctor looked as if he were about to launch into one of his famous flaps.'What is significant is that we seem to have activated something. Switched it back on.'Along with the pleading low whine of power in the room, the deformed roundels in the walls pulsed with a faint light, as if attempting to emulate the emergency lighting of the Doctor's TARDIS.

'You think we tripped something?'

'I think it knows I'm a Time Lord and is responding to my presence,' said the Doctor, distantly, still looking around in sad wonder at the malformed magnificence of the ancient edifice they stood in.

Sam swallowed hard in the gloom and took a deep breath. 'I've got to tell you, Doctor, it's been bothering me. I saw something earlier – I mean, I think I did –'

'Saw something?' He was looking at her strangely again. 'When?'

'Back in the tunnels before we saw the giant's playroom out there... I know it sounds stupid, but it was... gold-coloured. Sort of like fluid.' She realised the Doctor was looking past her. 'Er, hello? You did ask.'

The Doctor straightened up and motioned her towards him. As she moved, he spun her gently around so they were looking the same way. 'If you see it again, could you ask *it* to ask *that* to kindly go away and stop bothering us?'

The luminous cloud that had pursued them before was suddenly there, hovering in the warped doorway. It was as if the sparks and traces of light within it were attempting to depict some kind of image. Sam thought she could see the ghosts of humanoid figures trapped in torment, struggling to get free of the light that bound them.

It hovered near them.

'Confuse it?' asked Sam, looking up at the Doctor.

He nodded. 'We'll split up,' he said. 'You go round the back of the console, try and get its attention. We've got to lure it away from the door...'

He gave her a gentle push to get her going, and she sprinted over to the far side of the huge black outgrowth. 'Come on then! If you think you're hard enough!' she bawled at it, her words echoing around the dismal chamber.

Suddenly, the light cloud changed its slow but relentless course.

'Doctor!' Sam cried warningly. 'It's after *you*!'

'Run, Sam. Get back to our TARDIS, quickly.'

'I can't just leave you to that –' Sam broke off as a glimmer of light down the dark passage caught her eye. She shivered; for a moment she could see someone standing like a statue in the faint glow.

It was herself, arms outstretched as if trying to push away something terrible.

'Run, Sam!'

But Sam was already moving steadily towards her likeness, through the door and into the dark corridor beyond, as if drawn on irresistibly in some way. The image was fading now into a grey mist. She felt fascinated and horrified at the same time. What the hell was going –

Something moved at Sam's feet, like a trail of dull gold spinning upwards in a spiral. As she jumped instinctively, she still felt a thrill of satisfaction. 'Didn't dream you then – worst luck,' she muttered, as she found herself twisting round to follow it, arms raised to defend herself.

Abruptly, she felt her body freeze. She knew in an instant she had become the image that had transfixed her. Unable even to cry out, she felt the dull gold pour into her eyes and nose and mouth.

The last thing she saw before the blackness swallowed her was the Doctor, standing stock still in front of the looming statue of the giant figure as the cloud of light burst over him.

'We know who you are, Doctor. We know where you come from. Where you can take us.'

'I can't take you anywhere. Landing inside your TARDIS has fractured my own.'

'It is not our TARDIS, and we do not need yours.'

'Well, it really is a terribly long walk to the nearest inhabited stellar system and I don't know where you intend to –'

The Doctor broke off as he felt something biting into the back of his mind as if it were a nice fat, juicy steak. He shuddered, willing the feeling out of his thoughts.

'What is it you really want?' The Doctor voiced the words out loud through gritted teeth.

'Freedom again, Doctor, freedom to move…' hissed the whisper.

'To travel… to our remembrance.'

'If you'd only stop speaking in riddles, perhaps I could help –'

'You *will* help us, Doctor… you will help us as you die, as you die, as you go back and back, further and further, younger and younger, and die… *taking us where we need to go*!'

The Doctor screwed his eyes tight shut once again. He felt the presence there behind them bracing itself for a stronger attack. Then he shut down his cardiovascular system and retreated inside himself. Held in stasis by the light cloud, his body barely moved as all signs of life left it.

'That won't do you any good.'

The Doctor opened his eyes. The voice was familiar. It belonged to the figure sitting in a comfortable chair by an old mahogany table, pouring himself a cup of tea.

'That's my best china you're using!' said the Doctor, a little tetchily, rubbing his forehead.

The figure simply gave him a cheery smile, but the Doctor found himself frowning. There was something infuriatingly familiar about this man in his dark-green velvet frock coat, grey trousers and white wing-collar shirt –

'You're me!' said the Doctor, rather indignantly. 'What are you doing serving me tea inside my head?'

'Well, it is my head too, after all,' this Other-Doctor reminded him. 'I'm not exactly trespassing.' He continued pouring the tea, passing a cup to the Doctor, who accepted it with bad grace. 'Nice try,' said the Other-Doctor, as if measuring him up, 'shutting down your body to consolidate your strength of mind. But it didn't confuse them for long.'

'Didn't?' queried the Doctor. 'What do you mean, "didn't"?'

'I know your head is under siege right now, but do try to use what bits you can, hmm?'

The Doctor looked at himself quizzically. 'You're from my – our future?'

'Precisely!' grinned the Other-Doctor, but his smile soon faded. 'And no, I'm not a trick, or an illusion. This ancient TARDIS's telepathic circuits have corroded to the point of dissolution. I was able to use vestigial spillage from them to send an aspect of myself back to myself – well, to you.'

'Very clever,' said the Doctor appreciatively. 'Exactly what I'd have done myself, if I was on the verge of death and had to get a warning across to…'

The Other-Doctor nodded, a gentle smile on his face as the Doctor tailed off. 'It's our last chance.'

'What about Sam?' asked the Doctor hopefully.

'Oh, these idiots will release her soon, unharmed. Humans can't aid them in their plans and they think it the most wonderful fun to let her watch me die before…' The Other-Doctor paused. 'Yes, well, never mind all that. They end up getting so chatty they practically bore us to death…' He shook his head. 'They're insane, but massively powerful and well adapted. We've got no more resistance left in just a few hours from now. This was as far back as I could reach me – you, I mean. I know it goes against the laws of time, but if we don't do something soon there may *be* no laws of time left to break.' The Other-Doctor sipped his tea. 'Biscuit?'

The Doctor took a ginger cream from the proffered plate and dunked it. 'What are these creatures?'

'The Forgotten,' whispered the Other-Doctor theatrically. 'That's the name they've given themselves.' He slurped noisily from his saucer. 'It's no wonder they've been forgotten – just one more shameful secret in the dark scrolls of Gallifrey's history: memory-surfers, using the cerebral cortexes of Time Lords for high tide.'

'What?' The Doctor was incredulous, and yet a dim memory rattled in the back of his head. He wondered vaguely whether that was north, east, south or west of where they seemed to be standing now.

'Yes, it's starting to come back now, isn't it? Way, way back, when the Amplified Panatropic Neural Network of Gallifrey was created, when the minds of our dead were converted into so many neural complexes arranged in a matrix pattern to form the repository of all Time Lord knowledge –'

The Doctor cleared his throat. 'Ah, would you mind sparing me the lecture? Talking to yourself is a terrible habit and I imagine we're running out of time to break it.'

The Other-Doctor took another solemn swig of tea and continued. 'A group of Time Lords working on the neural mechanics of the Matrix learned all sorts of secrets in the course of their work. They reasoned that through exploiting an individual's reserves of artron energy it should be theoretically possible to travel through a Time Lord's actual physical past.'

'What?' The Doctor's eyes narrowed as he frowned in disbelief.

'Oh, yes. Each microsecond of experienced life is stored in our minds. Makes sense – it explains why the APC Net is so terribly efficient at pondering the Time Lords' imponderables.'

'Why it's the ultimate contemplator of Gallifreyan navels, you mean. Go on.'

'I'm sure you can imagine the rest. In their arrogance, their boredom, their irresponsible quest for thrills, this bunch of forgotten nitwits underwent a temporary conversion into aggressive electrochemical impulses and got into some poor soul's head. Back... back through the hundreds of years he'd lived, and then upstream to their present. And on their little jaunt they learned another secret.'

The Doctor put down his cup, lightly cursing his own perennial reluctance to get straight to the point when there was a dramatic tale to be told. 'Well?'

The Other-Doctor lowered his voice to a stage whisper. 'The means by which to interact with the victim's own history, gaining physical access to his past!'

The Doctor was amazed. 'Time travel through an individual's timeline?'

'Through a *Time Lord*'s timeline,' reminded the Other-Doctor. 'Some caprice of the genetic imprimatur that enables any of us to travel through time. And by stopping off at any point in the victim's past when they're in close contact with another, older host, by bridging the synaptic gap –'

'They could move ever further back through time...' breathed the Doctor. 'But why?'

The Other-Doctor poured himself another cup. 'Why not? It was a

219

game to them, a diversion, a proving of their own genius. Imagine if their experiments had proved successful – biological TARDISes, grown from Time Lord cells... But there was a side-effect they couldn't have foretold.'

Abruptly, whatever lighting there was in the chamber dimmed, and sinister whisperings started up around them.

'There isn't much time,' warned the Doctor. 'Quickly.'

'They perfected the move from carrier to carrier. But on exiting the body, the life of the initial host simply... unwound. At the point of entry, the meddlers effectively picked a stitch in the physical pattern of their host, left a thread dangling. When they left the body, they tugged on that thread and the host's entire life unravelled. Imagine it – an innocent life being made to die a trillion times over through every point in its history... The records of time being rewritten with each passing second as that person's life was truncated... cut off at the point these electrochemical surfers left the host body.'

'And started again on someone new.'

'Yes.' The whispering was getting louder, the darkness encroaching on them. The two identical Doctors huddled nearer. 'They were trapped in the subjective past, moving from host to host, killing indiscriminately. I'm not surprised old Rassilon abandoned them to their fate. They ended up inside the poor old owner of this ship. He must have had some kind of seizure while on reconnaissance charting this sector of space for the time-space maps, way, way back.'

The Doctor thought of the huge figure clutching its head in the husk of the control room. 'Brain-damaged... comatose...'

'They went mad with him,' confirmed the Other-Doctor, as the two of them were forced into what amounted to little more than a spotlight in the middle of pitch blackness. Of the tea and the table there was now no sign.

The Other-Doctor shook himself by the hand. 'Well... Lovely meeting me, but I really think you'd better stop them now, don't you? They'll travel back down our timestream to a point before we left Gallifrey, to run amok there. Who knows what damage they'll do – they're desperate to be free… to be *remembered*. Celebrated as pioneers.'

'Pioneers? Hah! Reckless bunglers and murderers!'

The whispering grew louder, swelling into mocking laughter. The Other-Doctor faded from sight, his face pale.

'Deranged killers!' Even as he yelled out the words, the Doctor clutched his temples and the blackness closed in around him.

He came to in the gloom of the ancient cartographer's TARDIS, his mind reeling as he felt the mental dams he had erected beginning to crumble under the onslaught of the Forgotten. An image of the flower of remembrance blazed in his head so brightly it threatened to eclipse all coherent thought.

'Doctor! You're all right!' The voice echoed through to his confused thoughts. He focused on it, used it to consolidate his senses in the midst of the assault. It was Sam's voice.

'Hello, Sam,' he mumbled. 'I'm glad you're all right.'

Sam looked at him with a worried frown. 'Just about. Are *you* all right?'

The Time Lord leapt to his feet. 'On the contrary! I'm going to be used as a bridgehead to wreak havoc across all Gallifrey before ceasing to exist, rewriting about a million histories and wiping out a mighty chunk of the entire causal nexus that holds the universe together!' He shuddered, then gaped at his bemused companion through the gloom. 'You know, when you've been about as much as I have, I really hate to imagine what the universe would've been like without me.'

'What are you talking about, Doctor?' asked Sam, fear and worry lining her face. 'What's –'

The Doctor's cry of pain cut her off. 'Have to do something! It's now or never,' he hissed. 'They're through – they're moving back through my timeline!'

Sibilant whispering laughter echoed around the void as the Forgotten exalted at the continuation of their journey. Subatomic particles flashed and jostled and decayed about them as the impulses travelled faster than inspiration through the encoded DNA patterns of the Doctor's physical history.

'Psychic surgery,' whispered a voice in his head. It was his own voice. 'Come on, you can do it. I'll help.'

Flashes of memories came to him, a rough chart of the impulses' progress. They'd easily broached the point in time he'd last regenerated, pushing past bleary operating tables and bullets in San Francisco... through Cheetah people, Daleks, Nimons, Kraals...

The Doctor was bewildered at the speed with which they were moving back, so fast he could barely register what was happening. And still they were moving through his lives... ever further back.

He tried to focus himself, to concentrate. Another regeneration was imminent. 'Now!' came his own voice from far away, but it was already too late. He shuddered as the grey-haired dandified figure was born from the pain and dismay of the little dark-haired clown, tried and convicted by the very people he was fighting now to save. Back through the past of his second incarnation, through Krotons and Ice Warriors, Yeti and Macra – yes, he could feel them more acutely now –

'Feed them through... That's right, back, back... Come on!'

'*Come on*, Doctor,' urged Sam.

The Doctor knew what was coming. He remembered it had happened in the TARDIS as he'd left Antarctica after his first meeting with the Cybermen, his body changing from that of an old man, rejuvenating itself, jewellery slipping from his new fingers, a part of him dying off so another could be born.

It was there he had to act.

'Step inside,' he whispered quietly as the rushing babbling and laughter reached a crescendo.

'Got you!'

The Doctor sat bolt upright, making Sam jump. He held his head as if impersonating the huge figure above them, and for a moment he winced as he felt something leave him. The ghost of a possible future that had given him the help he'd needed to cheat it. He shook his head. It never paid to analyse paradoxes too closely.

'Come on!' he yelled, then realised Sam was already at the doorway of the blackened control room.

'*You* come on,' said Sam, challenging him, but there was no disguising the tears of relief in her eyes.

In a moment he was by her side, then pulling her along behind him, explaining what had been happening to him as he went. He suddenly seemed to know where he was going, despite the darkness.

'You were held by the defence mechanisms of this old crate,' he continued, although by this time Sam was finding it difficult to boggle and run effectively at the same time. 'A kind of temporal stasis field. We Time Lords were a far more paranoid race back then. Wouldn't get any nasty tricks like that on the TARDISes I grew up with.'

'This place is really that old?' marvelled Sam breathlessly.

'Really. The Forgotten externalised their madness on to the rest of the ship through the telepathic circuits. But now they've made the jump to me, this whole timestream will be becoming unstable. The owner died millions of years ago and this TARDIS never came here.' He skidded to a halt, suddenly reflective and sombre. 'I'm glad that all these aeons of insanity and darkness will be wiped clean.'

Something seemed to be happening. It was getting lighter, and the dull humming of the decaying ship was starting to rise in pitch.

'Not long now,' said the Doctor, looking worriedly at Sam.

'Let's not get wiped clean with it, eh?' she answered, and the pair set off again.

At last they reached the reassuring blue police box exterior of the Doctor's TARDIS.

'And these... Forgotten things,' asked Sam, her mind racing to catch up. 'They're still in your head now?'

'Trapped in a sealed segment of my brain, the tiny part of my mind that dies when I regenerate. It's like shedding a skin – or for the Forgotten, it's like being caught inside a cut that's healed over.'

'Can you contain them there? I mean, for ever?'

'I hope so,' said the Doctor, pausing in the TARDIS doorway. 'I only hope they'll be able to keep themselves entertained.' He grinned.

'I'm planning to be around for quite a little while yet, you know!'

The shades of darkness outside were blurring, shifting. 'This reality is dissolving. Come on, Sam – time we were gone.'

'So the TARDIS will be freed, yeah?' said Sam as she was ushered inside. 'I mean – it'll never have been here!'

'Precisely,' said the Doctor with a grin.

'So will we remember any of it, then?' asked Sam.

The Doctor's eyes were haunted as the TARDIS began to vibrate in sympathy with its surroundings.

'Perhaps some things are *best* forgotten,' was his only answer.

And at that instant, the dark carbuncle in space was no more, leaving the Doctor and Sam free to continue their journeys.

Romans Cutaway

by David A. McIntee

It wasn't the blood, or the dented metal, that struck Ian Chesterton most, but the sudden silence. Where, in a film, one might have expected screams and the screech of tyres, there had in reality been only a strange, hollow smack. Then silence had fallen, giving Ian the impression that everyone was staring at him. He wasn't aware of his just-purchased newspaper dropping from his hand, or of his feet hitting the pavement as he ran to the corner of the street.

The silence was ominous, like the pause taken by a doctor before imparting bad news. That, more than anything else, told him things couldn't be good. People in the street parted around him. He seemed to be moving in slow motion now, but he was still drawing nearer the dented Ford Anglia. If there was anyone in it, he couldn't see them.

He wasn't really seeing much of anything, apart from the bundled figure sprawled on the pavement next to the bus stop. The blood that pooled around her head was almost as black as her hair. Ian tried to stop where he was. He didn't want to get any nearer, to see that pale face. Yet somehow he found himself kneeling next to her anyway, arms tight around her shoulders. He hadn't even got to her in time to say goodbye.

'Barbara…' But it shouldn't be Barbara, should it? Wasn't this the crash mentioned in the newspaper he had just dropped? The girl in that was Suzy, not Barbara. And then something tore at him, wrenching him away from her.

There were insects buzzing around him. Ian stirred. He felt sure that he was lying in a V-shaped ditch. Except it was hard, too hard… It wasn't a ditch. It was the point where the floor met the wall. And now he realised that what he had taken to be insects in flight was actually the familiar hum of the TARDIS's drives at rest. Relief washed over him. 'Just a nightmare,' he muttered.

Recent events jostled for attention in his mind. He supposed he shouldn't be too surprised that he'd had such a dream – the TARDIS had taken quite a tumble, and both he and Barbara had been thrown against the wall. It was only natural that his subconscious should try to warn him that she might be hurt and need his help.

He rose unsteadily, bracing himself against the wall. The floor was tilted at a steep angle, and the central console loomed overhead. Ian turned, looking for Barbara. She was groaning a few feet away. He moved towards her, trying not to lose his footing. 'Barbara?' She didn't answer, and for a horrible moment he feared his nightmare had been a premonition. But then she opened her eyes.

'Ian?' she replied, blinking. She tried to stand but lost her balance on the sloping floor. Ian helped her to steady herself. 'Are you all right?'

She nodded slowly. 'Yes, I think I remember now… the Ship had landed, then it started to tilt –'

'The Doctor tried to take off again, but –'

Barbara gasped. 'The Doctor!'

The concern in her voice made Ian turn anxiously. The Doctor was propped in a delicately balanced chair a few feet away, while a bruised Vicki held a handkerchief to his forehead. His long silver hair was tangled, but otherwise he seemed fine. Ian sometimes thought that for all his apparent frailty, their mysterious pilot had the constitution of an ox. He was far more than just an old man.

Vicki looked up as the two twentieth-century schoolteachers approached. 'You've come round!' she said happily.

'More or less,' Ian agreed. 'How's the Doctor?'

'The Doctor is perfectly healthy, thank you very much,' replied the old man irritably. 'As I told the child here, I merely need to get my breath back.'

'Definitely his normal self,' Barbara said drily.

'And just whose self do you expect me to be? Hmm? Now, are you two all right?'

'A few bumps and bruises, but nothing broken,' Ian said.

'Good. Good.' The Doctor's eyes sparkled brightly. 'Then the first thing we have to do is find out where we are.'

Ian frowned. 'Are you sure, Doctor? I mean, wouldn't it be safer to take off again first?'

'Without knowing where we are?' the Doctor scoffed. 'We might be missing marvels, Chesterton! Besides, did you never stop to suppose this might be Earth in your time, hmm? If it is, you might not get the chance to return again.' He dabbed at his face with a handkerchief. 'No, the TARDIS is... I think the TARDIS is quite stable enough now. Besides,' he said, indicating the console hanging overhead, 'that panel tells us about the local environment, and it is quite readable from here.'

Ian knew the battle was lost. The Doctor balanced himself in a position to read the dials on the panel. 'Atmosphere... Gravity... You know, dear boy, I do believe that it *is* Earth out there. The readings match exactly.'

Ian and Barbara exchanged a glance. Neither dared raise their hopes only to have them dashed on whatever 'marvels' lay waiting outside. The TARDIS had brought them to Earth before, in far-flung parts, but never in their own time. He looked up at the dials himself, but couldn't quite follow them. 'But do you know exactly where on Earth, Doctor? Or when?'

'I'm afraid not, Chesterton. We shall simply have to go out and look.' The Doctor bent to pick up his cane, and reached over to press the door switch. 'Now, stand back, just in case. There is a possibility that some rocks may have fallen on us and blocked the entrance.'

Ian sheltered Barbara and Vicki as the three of them backed away. The doors opened with a tinny hum. Dust and pebbles rolled in as a shaft of morning sunlight illuminated the interior. It was, Ian thought, quite reassuring. But the real struggle would be in actually getting out...

'At least it isn't raining,' Barbara said, lightening the mood.

The Doctor chuckled slightly, clapping her on the shoulder. 'Lucky for us, eh? See, it isn't all doom and gloom.' He beckoned Ian over. 'Come on, Chesterfield,' he said briskly, cupping his hands together in a stirrup. 'Up you go.'

Ian hesitated.

'Well, you're not afraid of heights, are you?'

'No, I –'

The Doctor's eyes glinted, as if reading Ian's mind. 'So what exactly is the difficulty?' He puffed out his chest. 'Think the old boy's not up to taking your weight? Hmm?'

'Well, no, but –' Ian could see the Doctor wasn't fooled for a moment.

'Perhaps you'd feel more comfortable if Barbara or Vicki were to help you?'

Ian grimaced. 'All right, Doctor. You win.'

'But of course, my boy, of course!'

The TARDIS was lying tilted at the foot of a narrow ravine, with a few frail-looking trees clinging to the rocky walls. For a while, Ian was simply pleased to have made it out of the TARDIS. Then he realised his problems were only starting. How was he going to get the others out?

Barbara knew that if anyone could find a way to help them out, it was Ian. She might not have much faith in the TARDIS's ability to get them where they wanted to go, but Ian had never failed her yet. But no, she reminded herself, that was a very selfish way to look at things. It was truer to say that he had never failed *them* yet – the Doctor, Susan, Vicki *or* herself.

Ian's head and shoulders reappeared, framed in the open doorway.

'Well, Chesterton?'

'It all looks pretty peaceful from up here, Doctor. And I think you're right – we're on Earth. Unless wild strawberries grow anywhere else in the cosmos.'

'Well done, my boy, well done.'

'But how do the rest of us get out?' Vicki asked. 'Or do we stay here while Ian feeds us strawberries?'

'I'm not sure... There's nothing much here.' Ian didn't sound particularly disappointed or frustrated, he was just stating a fact. 'Just lots of countryside... Hang on a minute, though, I think I do have an idea.' He disappeared for a few seconds, then returned. 'All right, stay back out of the way.'

Barbara ushered Vicki and the Doctor back into the corner. There was a tremendous rustling and crashing from outside, and then, after a few minutes, a tall but slim tree trunk crashed down past the console. Ian had managed to guide it under the panels, so it didn't hit any switches. Branches jutted out everywhere, providing excellent hand- and footholds.

'There you go,' Ian called down. 'It should be strong enough to take your weight.'

Within fifteen minutes they were all standing together outside in front of the toppled TARDIS.

'Chesterman,' the Doctor blustered. 'Did you think about what you were doing there? Hmm? If that… tree had touched any of the controls, it could have started the Ship's drives, or broken something and stranded us here…'

Ian had learned long ago that the Doctor's idea of gratitude was somewhat limited, to say the least. 'I was being careful, Doctor. Believe me, I didn't want the Ship to go without me either.'

'No, well, I suppose you didn't at that… Still, you should have at least warned me of what you were planning…'

The real fire had already gone from the Doctor's voice, so Ian decided to accept that with good grace. 'All right, Doctor, I'm sorry. Next time I'll warn you.'

'Next time indeed,' the Doctor echoed huffily. He put his knuckles to his mouth thoughtfully. 'I must take some sort of precaution against this happening again…'

The TARDIS was propped up by a large rock in the middle of a clump of bushes. Ian pointed up, to where a chunk had been gouged out of a ledge some yards above. 'The Ship must have landed right up there, and the edge crumbled,' he said.

Barbara shivered in spite of herself. 'It's just as well it wasn't much higher. We could have been killed.'

'Yes… You'd think the Doctor would have some sort of gadget in the Ship to keep the inside steady even if the outside gets knocked around a bit.'

'I know what you mean. I feel like I've been over Niagara Falls in a barrel.'

Ian suppressed a smile at the image of Coal Hill's most dreaded history teacher white-water rafting in a barrel. 'The Doctor certainly has a knack for picking out inconvenient landing sites, doesn't he?'

'It's not really his fault, Ian. It's the Ship that picks where to land.'

'Oh…' He could feel a whimsical mood coming on. 'Perhaps we should make it offerings to find less hostile destinations. Vicki could lay out platters of tropical fruits and wine to appease the spirit of the TARDIS.'

Barbara laughed. 'I can't see the Doctor in a grass skirt and flower garlands, though, can you?'

'I bet if we asked him, he'd say he's tried it.' They laughed together, and that always felt good to Ian. 'I suppose we ought to try to straighten the Ship out.'

Barbara's smile remained even though her laughter faded with the thought of the job at hand. 'We'll need some kind of leverage.'

'One of these trees the Ship broke on its fall might do the trick. It'll be pliable enough.'

'Eh? What?' the Doctor asked, returning with Vicki in tow.

'I was just saying that I think we might be able to right the Ship, Doctor. Between the two of us, one of these trees should be enough to lever it up.'

'I see, I see… Very well, Chesterton, it's possible, certainly. A capital idea, my boy. Now, while you are doing that, Vicki and I will go to see if we can find help.'

'Right,' Ian said with a nod. The Doctor didn't look strong enough to help move the Ship, and, wherever they were in whatever time, an old man and a girl would be less threatening strangers than two dishevelled adults, who could easily be taken for robbers.

'Very well. That looks like a farm road at the top of this rise. We'll walk along for an hour or so, and if we don't see any houses or villages, we'll come back.'

'Good enough, Doctor.'

It was single-storey and open-plan, with wings at each end of a larger building and a bubbling fountain in front. Slim pillars lined the walls and delicately painted statues were dotted around in shaded positions. The roof was covered in terracotta tiles, the colour of a summer sunset. Beyond, rows of vegetables seemed to be flourishing in the sunny conditions.

'There you are, child,' the Doctor said, sounding proud of himself. 'Somewhere peaceful and restful, just like I said it would be.'

Vicki's schooling in ancient Earth history hadn't gone that much further back than the Victorian era, but she still felt a twinge of recognition at the sight of the building ahead. 'It looks like some kind of Roman villa.'

'But of course!' the Doctor agreed. 'That's exactly what it is. We must have landed in Roman times. And in Italy too, judging by the flora. We're probably less than a week's walk away from Rome itself.'

'I've really travelled in time!' said Vicki excitedly. 'But poor Ian and Barbara. They'll be so disappointed not to be home.'

'Disappointed?' the Doctor harrumphed, blustering. 'My dear, how many of their kind get to visit their own history like this, hmm? They should be delighted, delighted, yes...'

He led her in through the pillars to the main room. Couches and bowls of fruit were dotted about, and the walls and floor were decorated with colourful frescoes and mosaics.

Vicki suddenly stopped, noticing the dark spots on the smooth floor. A few feet beyond, there was a similar smudge at about chest height on one of the delicate pillars that supported the silken curtains. 'Doctor,' she squeaked, 'look.'

The Doctor peered sharply at the stains.

'It *is* blood, isn't it?' she said.

Ian heaved on the slim tree trunk once again with all his strength, but still it did no good. The afternoon sun was getting the better of him, so he wiped the sweat from his brow and went to sit beside Barbara. Even though he had taken off his jacket, a collar and tie were hardly the right attire for this sort of work. 'Let's hope the Doctor and Vicki have had more luck than us!' he sighed.

Barbara agreed. Her hair was ruffled, but she still looked quite cool and composed. 'They should be back, soon.'

'If they haven't found help, we'll just have to slide back down into the Ship and risk taking off for somewhere else.'

'Yes, I –' Barbara broke off. 'Did you hear something?'

Ian listened carefully. There was a grumbling and a faint scratching coming from some nearby rocks.

The Doctor straightened up from his examination of the stain. 'Yes, my child, it certainly would seem to be blood.' They both looked about, wondering where the villa's inhabitants were, then the Doctor approached the curtain warily. 'It seems to lead this way.'

'Oh, Doctor, do be careful,' Vicki urged.

'I don't think there's anything here to fear,' he said reassuringly. 'But remember I have this, just in case,' he added, brandishing his cane.

He tugged the curtain aside and stepped through. Vicki followed, but stopped with a gasp when she saw the source of the blood.

A middle-aged man, stocky and weather-beaten, dressed in simple clothes, was propped up on a couch, semi-conscious. He had obviously tried to bandage the savage wounds that crossed his torso, but the bandages had outlasted their usefulness. Even from here, Vicki almost gagged at the stench.

The Doctor lowered his cane and examined the wounded man. 'These are claw marks,' he murmured. 'Some sort of large animal…'

'Lion,' came the weak reply. 'Who are you?'

'I am called the Doctor. My niece and I are travellers,' the Doctor said hurriedly. 'We stopped at your villa to ask for water, but when we saw the blood, we came to help.'

'I am Lucius. I watch over this villa.' The effort of speaking made the man wince. 'You say you are a master of the physic?' He half smiled. 'Too late. My sense of smell has not deserted me. Nor yours, child, I see.'

'What happened?' the Doctor asked with that gentle cheer he could switch on at will.

'I heard movement early the day before yesterday. At first I thought perhaps robbers… but it was a lion. It must have escaped from the arena… I had a spear, I spiked him, but still he cut me down…' The man coughed and his eyes glazed over momentarily. 'Water… please…'

The Doctor pointed back through the curtains. 'I saw some goblets in there, child,' he said softly. 'Beside the little spring.'

Vicki nodded and went back into the main room. There were indeed various golden goblets scattered around. She picked up the nearest and filled it with spring water.

When she returned, Lucius took it with some difficulty, but relaxed a little after a few sips. 'Thank you.' He grabbed the Doctor's shoulder. 'My friend, I know I will not see this night fall. I also know I have no right to ask this of you, but I must do so anyway.'

'Please do.'

'My master is campaigning in Gaul for some time yet. Please... Look after the villa. Make sure that the vegetables in the garden are watered, and that no robbers ransack the place. I will understand if you refuse, but it is my duty to take care of his home – to the last.' His voice was filled with the hope that they'd understand.

Vicki was surprised that he would ask such a thing so soon after meeting them. 'But why would you trust us with such an important task? You don't know *we're* not robbers.'

Lucius forced a smile and indicated the goblet she held. 'If you were robbers, you would have taken the gold without letting me know you were here, not helped me.' He looked at the Doctor. 'And you... There is something in your gaze that is –' And then he was gone.

Vicki shuddered and turned away. 'Never seen anyone die before,' she muttered.

'It's a sad business, my child, a sad business...' The Doctor closed Lucius's eyes gently, then his own widened.

Vicki started to ask him what was wrong but then suddenly realised. 'But if that lion is still in the area... We have to warn Ian and Barbara!'

The Doctor shook his head. 'One of us would have to stay here, to keep our promise. And it would be most unsafe for the other to go out alone.'

'But we can't just let Ian and Barbara stay out there in danger!' Vicki looked at him wide-eyed. Surely he couldn't be that selfish?

'Of course not, child!' the Doctor snapped. 'I said "we" cannot go. I will go myself. You stay here. Do as he said, look after the villa.'

'But what will you do if you run into this lion?'

The Doctor waved his cane angrily, but his words were mild. 'Take shelter and leave it alone until it goes.'

Vicki frowned. A ravenous lion was hardly likely to appreciate discretion. 'Until it goes? But it would eat you up!'

The Doctor gave an irritable sigh, but his expression suddenly softened and he patted her on the shoulder. 'Oh, don't you believe that, my dear. Lions are very misunderstood creatures, you know. It's the females who hunt and attack. Male lions are actually rather lazy. They'd much rather sneak around and steal the food away from another animal than chase it down themselves.'

'But Lucius… it attacked him.'

The Doctor nodded. 'Yes… but he had a spear, remember. I imagine that he thought giving it a little prod –' the Doctor demonstrated with his cane – 'would drive it off before it could attack him. But all that did was provoke the animal to defend itself.' The Doctor smiled happily at his deduction. 'Yes, yes… I'm sure I shall be perfectly safe – and so will Ian and Barbara, if I can persuade them not to try to "defend themselves" as poor Lucius here did, hmm?'

'There it is again!' whispered Barbara, looking at Ian intently.

Ian nodded slowly. 'Sounds like some sort of animal…'

Then, without warning, an enormous lion leapt up on the rocks. The fierceness of its roar and the fact that its paws were caked in dried blood made Ian doubt it was here to ask them for help in plucking out a thorn.

He glanced at Barbara, who was rooted to the spot. He was a science teacher, not a biology one… What the hell would a lion do next? Should he and Barbara move away, or would that provoke it? It was still a cat of sorts though, and in his experience cats were less likely to attack animals that remained motionless.

'That's right, Barbara. Nice and still.'

Despite his own advice, it took a lot of will-power not to bolt up the ridge. Then, to his mounting horror, the lion padded slowly around to Barbara.

The dream. Her head, covered in blood. Never even getting to say goodbye.

The lion was looking at Barbara, who was standing stock still, her eyes tightly shut now, barely daring to breathe. Ian still knew intellectually that moving was likely to be a bad idea, but what else *could* he do? Slowly, painfully slowly, he picked up a large rock and hefted it, testing its weight.

The lion growled, and Barbara whimpered softly.

Ian wasn't going to let the lion get any closer. With a skill honed annually in the pupils versus teachers cricket match, he aimed and threw. As rock cracked off skull, the beast turned to face its attacker.

Barbara fell back and scrambled away as the lion's drooling jaws passed over her. Ian snatched up his jacket and hurled it across the lion's head before it could pounce. The lion rolled over, tearing the jacket free with its front paws, as Ian took a long leap for the TARDIS. He saw with relief that Barbara had taken shelter now under some fallen rocks, but he had no idea how he was supposed to save himself. The TARDIS was locked; where else could he go? How far would the lion climb after him?

The slavering creature lunged forward, slashing at Ian's thighs but succeeding only in clawing the air. Ian rolled, hurling another small rock at the lion's face.

The lion jumped up on to the TARDIS and Ian took a running leap at the ledge in the rock above. If he could just get up as far as the point where the TARDIS had first landed before the lion could reach him…

The lion sprang for a tree in Ian's path. The tree momentarily blocked Ian's way, but then its pliability caused it to swing back, throwing the lion to the ground below. Ian took advantage of the moment, scrambling upwards to the ledge. There was a large boulder there, together with plenty of broken branches. He slipped, felt his palms stinging as they hit the rock, felt the blood pounding through his veins. The lion roared more loudly than ever. That's right, he thought. Keep with me, forget all about Barbara, keep with me. He winced as he cracked his knee against the rock face, but he was nearly there, nearly there…

At last he reached the ledge. 'Hey, Lenny!' he yelled. The lion looked up and roared again, more furious than before. It settled back on its haunches for a moment, then sprang towards him, claws scrabbling on rock.

Ian moved round behind the boulder. 'A little closer... come on, boy...' And the boulder proved to be far more co-operative than the TARDIS. A sharp pressure on a good branch set the huge rock toppling right through the gap in the broken ledge.

There was a hideous wet crunch, as the falling boulder met the climbing lion's forehead, then silence. Ian looked over the edge. The lion's paws were twitching feebly. Bull's-eye. From the mess below, these must be death throes.

'Barbara! Chesterton! Are you two all right?' It was the Doctor, calling from the roadside further along the ridge. Barbara was climbing out from behind her pile of rocks, hugging herself in distress. Ian felt suddenly shaky and fell back against the ledge. He'd just slaughtered a wild animal. He'd had no choice, he told himself, to save his own life, to save Barbara's... Somehow, this act of destruction seemed more real than the killing of something evil like the Daleks, or the Slyther. And the look on Barbara's face... Was she angry with him? Would it change how she saw him?

He wanted to call down to the Doctor that he was fine, but no words would come.

It wasn't the blood, or the dented metal, that struck Ian Chesterton most, but the sudden silence. Where, in a film, one might have expected screams and the screech of tyres, there had in reality been only a strange, hollow smack. Then silence had fallen, giving Ian the impression that everyone was staring at him. He wasn't aware of his just-purchased newspaper dropping from his hand, or of his feet hitting the pavement as he ran to the corner of the street.

The silence was ominous, like the pause taken by a doctor before imparting bad news. That, more than anything else, told him things couldn't be good. People in the street parted around him. He seemed to be moving in slow motion now, but he was still drawing nearer the dented Ford Anglia. If there was anyone in it, he couldn't see them...

* * *

Ian woke with a gasp, the scent of blood in his nostrils and the sound of a car horn still ringing in his ears. 'Barbara…' For a moment he was disoriented, unsure whether he was still in the street of his nightmare or the fallen TARDIS… But the gentle sound of crickets outside quickly reminded him, and he opened his eyes on to the moonlit interior of the villa.

Why had he had the same dream again? There had been no tumble to spark it off this time. He rose, shivering. He was deluding himself if he believed that the dream was merely a reaction to disaster. It went deeper than that. It was about how he felt. How he had felt in the dream and how he had felt back there at the ravine, when that lion had threatened Barbara. When the real version of that newspaper from his dream had landed on his doormat, he had felt the world collapse around him because he had loved Suzy. Her face staring out from under the headline about a car crash had nearly – well… it hadn't killed him, but he'd almost rather it had.

So why feel the same about a threat to Barbara?

'Are you all right, Ian?' Barbara asked from her room.

'Yes… Just a nightmare. Go back to sleep.'

'That'll be easy enough…' She closed her eyes again and lay back on the couch. 'It's very peaceful here.'

Ian couldn't disagree there. 'Well, the Doctor's got everything sorted out. It seems we can occupy this villa for a few weeks, as sort of unofficial caretakers.'

'Poor old Lucius,' Barbara murmured.

'Poor old lion,' ventured Ian, holding his breath for her reply.

'You did what you had to,' said Barbara, her voice still drowsy with sleep. 'Don't think about it now. We can stay here for a while. Nice Mediterranean holiday…'

'That's what I thought.' In spite of himself, he stepped into the room.

'Mm-hmm.'

Ian sat gently on the edge of the couch, so as not to disturb her. 'I suppose the Doctor has actually done what he wanted this time, found a restful place for us all.'

'Mm-hmm.'

'The rest will do you good. I was pretty worried after the crash.' He hesitated; he hadn't actually meant 'crash', but… Well, it was as good a word as any.

'Mm-hmm.'

'It's probably a good thing you're dozing off. I doubt you'd react too well to my being overly concerned for you when you're perfectly capable of looking after yourself.'

'Mm-hmm.'

'Makes it very difficult to say what I think sometimes.'

'Mm-hmm.'

'Can't even say, "I love…"'

As he said the words, he realised suddenly how obvious it was – that *that* was what his nightmare had been telling him. He wondered if he would have had the nerve to say that to her face when she was awake. She was obviously asleep now. He didn't want to wake her, so he settled for kissing her lightly on the cheek, and returning to his own room.

Barbara smiled without opening her eyes. She wondered when she would have the courage to admit to the same feeling for him.

Return of the Spiders

by Gareth Roberts

The Fordyces were entertaining guests.

This was unusual. On the Riverdale Estate in High Wycombe, not a great deal of entertaining took place. Most people in the various culs-de-sac and crescents preferred to hide in their townhouses watching television of a night, so it was with some surprise that they received invitations to a buffet supper at No. 9 Honeysuckle Close. None of those who had been invited knew the Fordyces beyond the occasional wave or exchanged pleasantry about the weather or parking. But it was, they supposed, nice to be asked; and besides, there was always, even in this reserved and well-fed enclave, a sneaky desire to see inside someone else's house.

So it was that Jean Morris and her husband, Frank, entered the smart, dust-free hallway of the Fordyces' home one Saturday evening in early September.

Mrs Fordyce – Jean Morris couldn't recall the woman's first name, if she had ever known it – stepped forward and said, 'Hello, let me take your coats.'

Jean and Frank handed them over, but Jean was puzzled. It was a perfectly ordinary phrase, but was there an icy coldness in the delivery?

'Come into our parlour,' said Mrs Fordyce, waving them into the front room.

'She seems a cold fish,' Jean whispered to her husband.

'The whole house is very draughty,' he replied. 'They must have skimped on their loft insulation.'

In the living room they found a scene of utter normality. A handful of couples stood talking quietly around a table upon which a buffet was presumably laid out beneath a checkered tablecloth.

Mr Fordyce, a tall and rather gaunt fellow, came forward. 'Ah, you must be the Morrises,' he said. 'We were wondering where you'd got to.'

Jean bristled. 'The invite said half-seven for eight.'

'Indeed, indeed. Well, now you're here you'd better have a drink.' He handed them two glasses filled to the brim with red wine. 'You'll enjoy this, I'm sure.'

Jean took a sip and thanked him. When he had moved away she whispered to her husband, 'What a creepy pair. Made for each other, I'd say.'

'Yes, they've both got that peculiar way of holding themselves,' said Frank. 'Round-shouldered. As if they'd been carrying something heavy on their backs.'

Before they could converse further, Mrs Fordyce entered and said brightly, 'Well, hello, everyone. We're all here, so I suppose it's time to tuck in.' As she spoke she closed the door that led out to the hall and turned the key in its lock. At the same time Mr Fordyce took up position in front of the only other exit, to the kitchen.

There was a general murmur of confusion from their guests. 'What are they up to?' asked Frank.

'Oh dear,' said Jean. 'I hope it's not going to be one of those occasions where everyone throws their car keys on to the coffee table.'

The Fordyces closed in on their guests. 'Yes,' they said as one, 'time for our feast to begin.' Their voices took on a strange unearthly quality and their eyes began to glow a hypnotic blue. 'We have waited so long in the wastes of the spatio-temporal vortex.'

Patrick Morris frowned. 'Now, look here, you two,' he said. 'It's another month to Hallowe'en, and you're giving me the willies, so knock it off.'

Mrs Fordyce snarled. 'Pathetic humans. You were fools to come to our buffet!'

Jean was getting angry. 'I don't think it's very clever when grown people start acting the goat like this.' She gestured to the table. 'Now, let's behave like adults and get on with the buffet.'

She leapt back as the tablecloth twitched. The corner was pushed up and a slender hairy leg poked out. 'Cease your prattling,' said the owner of the leg. '*You* are the buffet. And it is time for us to feast.'

Jean screamed as the tablecloth was thrown off to reveal two gigantic hairy spiders the size of cats. She cowered with the other humans as the spiders scuttled towards them, their hungry jaws snapping.

A couple of nights later something possibly even more unusual occurred on the Riverdale Estate. There was a fearsome sound of grinding machinery and a blue police box faded up from transparency. Two very odd-looking people, a man and a young woman, and an even odder-looking dog emerged from inside.

Romana, the odd-looking woman, was wondering where the Randomiser, a device fitted to the TARDIS controls by the Doctor, the odd-looking man, had brought them this time.

'High Wycombe,' the Doctor pronounced gravely.

Romana sniffed. 'High Wycombe.'

K9, their odd-looking robotic dog, piped up, 'High Wycombe. Planet Earth. Level four suburban conurbation, founded *circa* Terran year 1760 –'

The Doctor cut him short. 'Spare us the lecture, K9.' He stuck his hands deep in the pockets of his long frock coat and strode towards the houses, looking rather downcast. He let out a sigh and gestured to the ranks of identical houses. 'Just look at those.'

Romana shrugged. 'Simple human dwelling units.' She was surprised. The Doctor normally had an almost tiring enthusiasm for every far-flung shore the TARDIS washed up on. 'I thought Earth was your favourite planet,' she said.

'Oh, it is, it is,' said the Doctor. 'And humans are quite my favourite species. But I've never been at all keen on suburbs, wherever in the universe they are.' He pointed a thumb back at the TARDIS. 'I think perhaps we should pull the handle on that old fruit machine again.'

Romana disagreed. 'You don't know what's going on behind the net curtains, Doctor.'

He scoffed. 'That's what people always say. The true tragedy of suburbia, Romana, is that *nothing* is going on behind the net curtains.' He started to walk back to the TARDIS. 'Come on, Romana. And you, K9.'

But Romana stood her ground. 'I'm sure we could find some sort of drama or intrigue if we only stopped and looked.'

'Pointless,' said the Doctor. 'Come on.'

'I bet you we could,' said Romana. She knew the Doctor could never resist a challenge.

The Doctor swung about. 'Bet?' He narrowed his eyes, intrigued. 'How much?'

Romana considered. 'Oh, I don't know... Shall we say five Gallifreyan pounds?' She put out her hand.

The Doctor shook it firmly. 'Done. You'll regret this, Romana.' He smiled. 'I'll be able to get a new pair of socks, instead of relying on K9 to darn the old ones all the time.' He waved to the front doors directly opposite. 'You'd better get going. Go on, ring on a few bells. I'm telling you now, you won't find anything. High Wycombe is the last place on Earth, or should I say in the universe, where anything unusual is *ever* going to happen.'

Suddenly there was a hideous, unearthly gurgling noise. It took Romana a moment to locate its source. She realised it was coming from the grille-covered drainage system that ran along the gutter at their feet. 'What's that?'

'Shoddy plumbing,' said the Doctor authoritatively, although he did look a little perturbed at the ferocity of the thrashing, gurgling noise.

Romana knelt and peered through the nearest grating into subterranean darkness. As the awful noise faded away, she thought she glimpsed, just for a split second, some sort of movement – a spindly, hairy shape scuttling away as if it feared discovery. She shuddered. 'There's something moving down there.'

'A rat, I should think,' said the Doctor.

Romana beckoned to K9. 'What do your sensors make of it, K9?'

K9 trundled forward and extended his eye-probe towards the drain covering. His ear sensors whirred and clicked like miniature radar dishes. 'Animal life detected, Mistress,' he reported.

'There you are, what did I say?' said the Doctor.

K9 went on. 'Exact nature of animal conflicts with my – er...' Suddenly, K9's red eyescreen began to flash bright blue. He backed away from the drain as if stung and began to babble. 'Sensors detect animal life inimical to functioning.'

Romana hurried over. 'What is it, K9? What animal life?'

'Take no notice of him,' said the Doctor. 'He's just having a funny five minutes.'

Romana was concerned to see that K9 actually seemed to be shaking with fright. 'What's the matter, K9?'

'Functioning endangered.' K9's head drooped and all his lights went out. 'Withdrawing personality matrix interface...' His voice slurred.

The Doctor knelt to examine him. 'Come on, K9, don't be a mimsy hen.' He blew in K9's ears. 'Dead to the world. Typical. It'll be fluff in his circuits again.'

Romana shivered. 'Whatever that thing down there was it frightened him half to death.'

'Don't be silly,' said the Doctor, standing up. 'I'll tell you one thing for sure, Romana, the most dangerous animal you'll find in High Wycombe is a hedgehog.'

Their conversation was interrupted again, but this time by a very different – and much more prosaic – noise. A motorbike was making its way along the crescent of houses and seated upon it was a helmeted figure who wore a red and white striped apron. Behind him, strapped to the seat, was a tower of about twenty square cardboard boxes. The bike drew to a spluttering halt outside a particular house, and the driver clambered off, removing his helmet to reveal the acned face of a boy in his late teens.

'A native,' said the Doctor. 'Why don't you ask him about marauding animal life? Perhaps you'll listen to him.'

Romana approached the boy. He regarded her very strangely, almost as if he was frightened. Romana had noticed that she tended to occasion this response in human males, so she smiled to put him at his ease, but this only seemed to make him shakier. 'Hello,' she said. 'Have you noticed any unusual animal life in this area?'

The boy frowned. 'Eh? Sorry?'

The Doctor came up behind Romana. 'Forgive my assistant, she's not familiar with the ways of your planet.'

'Er, right,' said the boy.

'What we want to know is whether you've noticed anything odd in these parts of late?'

'I don't think so,' said the boy.

'Hah! There you are,' said the Doctor, putting out his hand to Romana. 'Five pounds, please. I'll accept a cheque.'

'Wait a moment,' said Romana. She addressed the boy. 'What do you mean, you don't think so?'

The boy shrugged. 'Well, I've not seen anything myself, but they say there *are* some strange goings-on round here.'

'What kind of goings-on?'

'Well, a couple of weeks ago – I read it in the free paper – everyone on this estate woke up in the middle of the night, at exactly the same moment. They all said they'd had a nightmare, but none of 'em could remember what it was about.'

'Mass hysteria,' said the Doctor. 'It proves nothing.'

'But then,' the boy continued, 'people said they'd heard strange noises.'

Romana's ears pricked up. 'Do you mean a sort of thrashing and gurgling? Coming out of the drains?'

'That's right. And ever since, nobody at my place has wanted to take orders from round 'ere.' He indicated the nearest door. 'And 'specially not from them.'

The Doctor leaned forward. Romana realised that, despite himself, he was becoming interested. 'What exactly do you deliver?'

The boy gestured to the boxes on the back of his bike. 'Pizzas.'

Romana whispered to the Doctor, 'What are pizzas?'

'They're a sort of glorified Welsh rarebit.'

'What's Welsh rarebit?'

'It's a sort of glorified cheese on toast.' The Doctor peered at the boxes. 'And whoever they are, they like it.'

'That's just it, sir,' said the boy. 'Every night for two weeks, they've phoned through with the same order. For the special meat-deal meal, four times over.'

'What's a meat-deal meal?' asked Romana.

'A whopper-sized eighteen-inch meat-deal pizza – that's with ham, pepperoni, bacon and beef – with chicken wings, coleslaw and complimentary bottle of diet cola,' explained the boy. 'Four times over, every night.' He looked around and shuddered. 'But that's not the weirdest part. When you come back each night, they've done this.' He led them to a dustbin at the side of the front door and flung the lid up.

'Good grief!' exclaimed Romana. For what lay inside the bin was a quite alarming sight. The remnants of cardboard boxes that had been viciously torn apart were covered in a sticky green substance. Scattered among the mess were chicken bones and some plastic containers.

'They always leave the coleslaw,' said the boy.

The Doctor took an extendible slender metal probe from one of his capacious pockets and used it to lift up a piece of cardboard. He pointed out a set of marks. 'Teeth,' he said. 'And not human teeth either.' He probed the green matter. 'This has the viscosity of drool, but a creature that produces this much is quite uncommon on this planet.'

'Five pounds to me, I think,' said Romana.

The Doctor let the cardboard fall and shut the dustbin lid. He turned to the delivery boy. 'I tell you what. We'll do this delivery for you. You get home and put your feet up.' He started to unpack the pizza boxes and pass them to Romana.

'I've got to get the money,' said the boy.

The Doctor waved a hand airily and produced a drawstring bag. 'Take this. Spend it wisely. Now off you go.' He shook the boy's hand. 'And thank you very much for coming along with all that useful information.'

The boy opened the bag and his eyes boggled. 'Is this *gold*?'

'Yes,' said the Doctor. 'Now run along and leave this to the experts.'

The boy climbed back on to his bike and zoomed away. The Doctor smiled after his retreating form, then turned to the front door and coughed. 'Now, we'd better take things very carefully, Romana.'

'Are you sure this is wise?' she asked.

The Doctor rang the doorbell, loudly, three times.

Somewhere, not very far away, a fearsome alien intelligence was roused from its slumber. It was time to be fed, it knew – but something else had woken it. An intimation, a dread foreboding... Its large, hairy body shuffled uneasily. It sensed an enemy.

Romana steeled herself as the door opened. But instead of the carnivorous alien monster she had expected, she saw a very ordinary-looking man in his early forties with greying temples and a kindly expression. 'Hello,' he said.

'Hello,' said the Doctor, adopting a local accent. He thrust the boxes forward. 'Four meat-deal meals, guv'nor. Plenty to get through there. You 'avin' a party?'

The man's expression changed instantly to one of suspicion, mixed, Romana noted, almost with fear. 'No,' he said stiffly. It was almost as if he was receiving the words he spoke from an ear-piece. 'Not tonight. We are not having a party.'

''Ere, guv'nor,' asked the Doctor. 'You look a bit peaky. You all right?'

'Yes,' the man replied stiffly. 'I am perfectly all right.' He took the pizza boxes from the Doctor in a rigid, marionette-like way and handed him a fifty-pound note. 'Perfectly all right. Here is your payment. Keep the change.' He slammed the door in their faces.

'Did you notice the delay in his replies?' asked Romana. 'Do you think he could have had some kind of mental implant?'

The Doctor considered her suggestion. 'It's possible. Or perhaps he's under some form of hypnotic control.' He drew himself up to his full height. 'I think there's something very fishy going on here, Romana.'

'Or meaty. So what are we going to do about it?'

He pointed over his shoulder. 'First off, you go round the back into the garden and watch what happens.'

'Watch what happens when?' asked Romana.

The Doctor rummaged in his pocket and produced his sonic screwdriver. 'I'm going in through the downstairs toilet window.'

Romana frowned. 'Are you sure that's wise?'

The Doctor shrugged. 'Well, I could try the kitchen, I suppose.'

'I didn't mean that,' said Romana. 'Shouldn't we try to work out what we're up against before we confront it?'

'That'd take all the fun out of things,' said the Doctor. 'I like surprises. Now off you pop.'

Romana sighed. 'Heaven knows what I'm supposed to do if

anything goes wrong.'

'You're a bright girl, you'll think of something,' said the Doctor. He started to fiddle with the settings on his screwdriver.

Romana realised she wasn't going to get anywhere, so she set off along the paved path that led round the corner of the house and to the back garden.

The evil intelligence stirred. It saw through the eyes of the male host as he gave payment for the nutrients. The delivery human was not the same as usual. It wore strange adornments and its large eyes stared penetratingly.

The evil intelligence communicated with its minions in its clear, cold, cruel voice. 'This human is not of the usual kind.'

A telepathic reply came back, clear as a bell. 'I sensed this also, O Queen,' it said. 'Could this be the enemy we detected?'

'We must wait and watch,' said the Queen. 'Be vigilant. The Great Web must be protected.'

The Doctor slipped through the toilet window and landed softly on the carpeted floor. He closed the window, pocketed the sonic screwdriver and looked around. At first everything appeared to be in its place. Then he noticed something very strange. The bath next to the toilet was filled with a shifting wispy substance. Curious, the Doctor poked with a finger and discovered it was tougher than he'd expected. 'And definitely not native to this planet,' he told himself. He pressed harder and touched something soft and cold as stone. Carefully he broke apart the spongy coating – and recoiled in alarm when he saw a human face looking up at him. He felt for life signs and was pleased to detect a very faint pulse in the neck. He leaned close to the supine figure, brushed aside some more of the wispy coating from her face, and whispered, 'Are you all right, my dear?'

The figure's teeth chattered. 'Help me…'

'Yes, yes, I'll have you out of there in a jiffy. But first, tell me, who did this to you?'

The woman's eyes clouded with fear. '*They* did…'

'Who's they?' asked the Doctor.

'The Fordyces,' the woman went on.

'The Fordyces?' said the Doctor. 'Very odd name for an alien race.'

The woman went on, 'I hadn't seen hide nor hair of them for a couple of weeks. Then, out of the blue, last week she sent invites for a buffet,' she said. 'Said she wanted to introduce me to some new friends.' She started to quake in fear. 'Then *they* appeared…'

'Yes, yes, but who are they, mm?'

The poor woman was now moaning in terror and the Doctor realised he wasn't going to get any sense out of her. Effortlessly putting her into a light hypnotic trance, he replaced the wispy strands over her face and took a peek through the door into the hall. The hall was in darkness, but light spilled out from the living room opposite. Taking care to keep as quiet as possible, the Doctor broke from cover and crept across.

What he saw in the living room filled him with foreboding. The man who had been at the front door was standing with a woman of about the same age, presumably his wife, in the centre of the room. They were clutching each other and looked terrified. Before them on a rug were the pizza boxes.

The woman – Mrs Fordyce, the Doctor guessed – spoke. 'Please,' she said, wringing her hands. 'Haven't we done enough? You said you were going to go, to leave us alone.'

She seemed to be pleading with thin air, but then a voice replied. The Doctor seemed to hear it more with his mind than with his ears. It was thick with malign intent and had a gurgling, rasping quality. 'You are Two-Legs,' it said smugly. 'Two-Legs must not question the actions of their masters.'

The Doctor racked his brains. He was certain he had heard that voice, or something like it, before. But his memory was crammed with the adventures of the past seven hundred plus years, and it was often difficult for him to recall details of the strange alien species he had encountered. He had always meant to sit down with K9 one day and compile a book of monsters and mechanical creatures as an *aide-mémoire*.

The woman sank to her knees. 'But please. You promised.'

'Be silent. Now it is time for the feast. You will remain still as we eat.' There was a pause and then the voice said, 'Turn your backs.'

Mr Fordyce whispered to his wife, 'We'd better do as it says.'

The two terrified humans turned around, so that their backs were facing the pizza boxes. The evil voice spoke again. 'Two-Legs will remain still,' it warned, 'or we will feast again on living meat.'

A ghostly blue glow began to form at the base of the two humans' backs and two indistinct shapes began to appear there.

The Doctor was more convinced than ever that he had met this particular menace before. He mumbled to himself, 'Well it's not the Daleks – I'd know them straight off. The Cybermen wouldn't have the imagination for something like this, and it's far too subtle for the Zygons…'

The blue glow grew stronger, and the shapes within took on scuttling, hairy form. 'Let us prepare for the feast,' they said.

'Got it!' said the Doctor. 'The giant spiders of Metebelis 3!' He recalled their last encounter. 'I thought I'd polished them off. Come to think of it, they very nearly polished *me* off. This is going to be more difficult than I imagined.' He peeked around the door again and gulped as the two giant spiders sprang from the backs of their helpless hosts and, with frightening speed, launched themselves at the pizzas. They cooed and smacked their jaws as they tore through the boxes and wolfed down great mouthfuls of the spongy meaty cheesy substance within.

The Doctor withdrew to consider his options.

Romana was in the back garden, as ordered, and had seen the materialisation of the spiders through a chink in the living-room curtains. She stared, rapt with terror, as the evil arachnids feasted.

'Creatures like that shouldn't exist in the Earth's ecosphere,' she mused aloud.

Something nudged the back of her leg and she jumped. For a fleeting second she feared she might have to fend off an attack from one of the voracious spiders, but it was only K9, who looked in better spirits than before.

'Mistress,' he said.

'K9, you nearly made me jump out of my skin!'

He whirred and clicked, confused. 'Negative, Mistress. Your physical envelope is secure.'

'Are you all right now?' Romana asked her metal pet.

'Affirmative. I have reprogrammed my fear circuits.' He nodded to the window. 'Suggest you divert your attentions to the gigantized arachnids inside this dwelling.'

'What do you know about them, K9?' asked Romana.

'My data banks indicate that these creatures originate on the planet Metebelis 3 in the Acteon Group,' he replied. 'Their bodies and brains were mutated by prolonged exposure to particles of fluon radiation.'

Romana gulped. 'Fluon? I thought the Time Lords had destroyed all sources of that stuff. It's incredibly dangerous in the hands of lesser races.'

'So it is,' said a voice at her shoulder.

Romana leapt up again. 'I wish people would stop doing that!' she told the Doctor.

He patted her on the shoulder. 'Hello, Little Miss Muffet. You shouldn't be so jumpy.'

Romana sighed. 'Is it any wonder, the life we lead?'

The Doctor ignored her. 'Yes, fluon crystals have enormous power. There was a large pocket of them in the mountains of Metebelis, and over a couple of centuries the spiders that landed there aboard an Earth colony ship grew to enormous size under their influence.'

'You seem to know an awful lot about them,' mused Romana.

The Doctor rubbed his chin. 'Well, I know an awful lot about an awful lot of things. I thought these particular giant spiders were gone for good, but somehow they've opened up a bridgehead through space and time, here, to High Wycombe.'

'What do they want?' asked Romana.

'Well, their ambition has always been to rule the universe,' the Doctor said.

'Why doesn't that surprise me?' asked Romana.

'But High Wycombe is a very strange place to start.' The Doctor paused, deep in thought, and then clicked his fingers. 'Of course!'

'What?' asked Romana.

'It's obvious. I should have thought of it sooner!'

Romana sighed. 'What?'

'Leylines,' said the Doctor. 'The lines of telekinetic energy that run through the very structure of the universe.'

'Yes, I know what they are, thank you,' said Romana haughtily.

The Doctor gestured to the house. 'And a vital point on one such leyline must pass right across this estate. If I had my divining rod on me I bet you it'd go straight up.'

'So,' said Romana, 'the spiders travelled along the leylines and hopped off here?'

The Doctor nodded. 'In a manner of speaking. Of course, they can't actually hop, not with eight legs, but generally they're very nimble creatures.' He turned back to look up at the house and rubbed his chin thoughtfully. 'I reckon they must be exhausted after the journey, and they're getting their strength up in preparation to emerge and try to take over the universe again.'

'Hence the pizzas,' said Romana.

'I'm afraid it's worse than that,' said the Doctor gravely. 'They've got at least one live human all wrapped up in there.'

Romana was appalled. She felt a wave of coldness pass through her body. 'That's disgusting.'

'Quite.' The Doctor tutted. 'I'm afraid it looks very much like we're going to have to do something to stop them, Romana.' He knelt down and patted K9 on the ears. 'Listen, dog. We're going to go in there and confront the enemy in its lair. You stay out here on guard, all right?'

'Affirmative, Master,' said K9.

'But,' the Doctor continued, loosening his scarf a little around his neck, 'if we're not out of there in fifteen minutes, K9, I want you to turn that little nose of yours on and bring the whole building down, spiders and all. Got it?'

K9's eyescreen flashed in concern. 'Master,' he protested, 'my function is to protect and assist you –'

The Doctor cut him off. 'No buts. Now…' He pointed to the drainpipe that ran up the side of the house. 'Come along, Romana – we've got work to do.'

* * *

The two spiders had completed their feast and were smacking their jaws contentedly on the Fordyces' carpet. The terrified humans cowered before them.

'Most pleasant,' said the first spider. 'The meat and grease is good for us, and our energy levels have nearly returned to optimum.'

Mrs Fordyce stepped forward. 'Then – you will soon leave us, as you promised?'

The spiders seemed to catch each other's beady eyes and giggled. 'Oh, yes,' said the second spider. 'We Eight-Legs never go back on a promise. Soon, we shall leave this house for ever, never to return.'

Mr Fordyce spoke up. 'And you'll let all of our friends go?'

The spiders giggled again. 'Yes, they will soon be released from the webs. And neither of you will have anything to worry about. Ever again, ha ha ha.'

Mr and Mrs Fordyce didn't like the sound of the spiders' words and wicked cackle at all. But before they could remark on the spiders' puzzling sense of humour, both the alien monsters twitched suddenly and went deathly still. Another spidery voice, even more horrible and sibilant, spoke. It seemed to come from thin air.

'Underlings,' it said, in the commanding tones of one not used to being questioned. 'Cease your gibbering. This is the dawning of the New Age of the Eight-Legs. It is not a time for frivolity.'

The spiders cowered and sagged. 'We are sorry, O Queen.'

The evil voice spoke again. 'Now hear me. I am almost ready to release the eggs. Hatching will begin soon after.'

The spiders cooed. 'Good news, O Queen.'

'Indeed,' said the voice. 'But know that I have detected a deadly enemy in our midst, one who wishes to destroy us.'

The spiders hissed. 'Who is this enemy?'

'I cannot be sure. But you must seek him out and destroy him, do you hear me?'

The spiders inclined their vile bodies to their unseen mistress. 'We will seek him out and destroy him.'

The Fordyces clung to each other desperately and watched as the spiders scuttled out of the front room. Mrs Fordyce's teeth chattered. 'Did that thing say hatching will begin soon after?'

* * *

The Doctor and Romana were now on the first floor of the house, having climbed through an open window into the Fordyces' bedroom. The Doctor pressed the light switch but nothing happened. He lit a match and cast light on a horrific scene – the double bed was occupied by two human shapes entirely wrapped in sticky web.

'You know what I think, Romana?' the Doctor whispered. 'These spiders are pretty much like their titchy cousins in many ways. I think there could be a leader somewhere. A guiding influence.'

'I see. And if we put pay to him we'll be out of the woods?'

The Doctor nodded. 'Although I think it's probably a her. The grandmother of them all.' He padded as quietly as he could across the carpeted room and gently opened a door in one corner. A wave of heat shimmered over his face. 'Ah. The airing cupboard.' He lit a second match and gave a low whistle. Romana craned over his shoulder to see.

The small airing cupboard contained a number of neatly folded items of clothing, a boiler and a tangle of pipes. This was normal enough. But everything was coated in sticky strands of web – and most terrifying of all, a huge, thin, hairy jointed limb curled from a hole in the ceiling and around the pipes.

'I think that must be her leg,' said the Doctor.

Romana looked down and saw that the leg came to rest inside a large glass tank on the floor. There was a murky brown liquid inside. 'What's that?'

'It's taken another opportunity to feed,' said the Doctor. 'It's absorbing the liquid alcohol from that canister.' He sniffed. 'Barley wine, I'd say. The man of the house must be a keen home-brewer.' He smiled suddenly. 'My auntie was a keen home-brewer.'

Romana shook him. 'Never mind about her. The Queen Spider must be upstairs, in the attic.'

'Indeed.' The Doctor tapped her on the shoulder. 'Right. Plan of action. I'll slip up and deal with her. You stay here. If anything goes wrong…' He trailed off.

'If anything goes wrong?' prompted Romana.

'Just do your best and don't worry.' He was gone before Romana could object. She looked at her watch. There were now only ten minutes left before the expiry of the Doctor's deadline to K9. She was confident of the Doctor's ability to improvise, but she knew also that he had an unfortunate tendency to make mistakes. Were ten minutes long enough to defeat such a menace?

She was just looking at her watch again when she felt a gentle pressure on her shoulder. 'Doctor,' she sighed, 'I do wish you'd stop doing that. You'll give me the fright of my lives one of these days –'

Her words become a scream as she saw that perched on her shoulder was one of the spiders. She thrashed about wildly in an attempt to dislodge it, but the canny creature had entangled its legs in her long blonde hair. She felt a weight land on her back, as if a blow had been struck, as the second spider jumped up. And then it started to invade her mind.

'Who are you?' it demanded.

Romana was powerless to resist.

The Doctor had found a ladder to the loft in place on the landing and ascended it carefully. He estimated he had only a matter of minutes to defeat the spiders, and was still trying to think up a way of doing so when he popped his head over the hatch and into the dark, musty recesses of the attic.

The Queen Spider dominated the scene, its huge furry body slumped malignantly in the centre and its eight horrible legs stretched out in all directions. The Doctor knew instinctively that there was no reasoning with such an evil being.

He peered closely at it, and was pleased to see that its row of eyes looked dormant and unseeing. He listened intently. There was a steady rising and falling tone on the air. 'Good grief,' he whispered. 'It's snoring. Must still be whacked out and need to conserve its energy. This puts a new light on things.' The Doctor considered his next move. Suddenly he had a brainwave.

Treading with the utmost care and caution, he stepped over the Queen Spider's nearest leg, lifted it ever so gently and slowly, and then did the same to the next. When he had both legs in hand he carefully tied them together, checking all the time to see that the

Queen lay undisturbed. He examined his handiwork with pleasure. 'And they said I was a rotten knotter,' he said. 'I should have this business tied up in no time. With the Queen Spider put out of action the others should be easy to pick off.'

He had just started work on the third leg when there was a fearsome clattering on the metal steps of the ladder. Immediately the Queen Spider began to stir. 'Who dares to disturb my rest?'

The Doctor watched as Romana appeared at the top of the stairs. He tried frantically to shush her. 'What do you think you're doing?'

Romana spoke in a strange, cold, icy voice. 'O Queen, it is us, your underlings. We have taken possession of this, your enemy, and brought her to you.'

'Oh no,' sighed the Doctor. 'She's been got at. These girls can't look after themselves for five minutes. I wonder why I ever leave them alone.' He slunk into a dark corner where he hoped he would go unobserved.

'Bring her closer,' said the Queen.

Romana stepped right up to the Queen's body. At her feet scuttled the two spiders. The Queen's row of glittering eyes bored into her very brain. 'Yes,' it said. 'Yes… interesting… very interesting… This creature is a Time Lord.'

The other spiders gave a sharp intake of breath. 'The one who nearly destroyed us before was a Time Lord!' they cried. 'Could this be the same one? Can she be the Doctor?'

'Pah,' the Doctor muttered under his breath.

'No,' said the Queen. 'But this one also has much knowledge. We will drain her mind of its secrets… Learn the power to travel freely through space and time… Discover the weaknesses of a thousand million different species across the universe… The Eight-Legs will be unstoppable!' The Queen paused and licked her lips. 'And then we shall feast on her body. How fitting that a Time Lord should be the *hors d'oeuvre* on our menu of galactic domination!' She rattled her huge legs in excitement – and shrieked as she realised that two of them had been tied together. 'What is this? Who has dared to perpetrate this – this outrage on the Queen of the Almighty Eight-Legs?'

The Doctor, who had been feeling rather left out of things in his corner, stepped forward. 'Ahem. I'm afraid that was me. I'm dreadfully sorry, you know, because everyone *should* have their ambitions, but I really can't allow you to do the things you've just said you're going to do.'

'What? Whaaat?' The Queen rose up as far as she could. 'And who are you to address me in this way?'

'Oh, just a humble traveller,' said the Doctor.

The Queen's piercing gaze transfixed him. 'No – you are the Doctor! I recognize you, although you have completely changed your appearance and personality!'

'Thanks,' said the Doctor. 'It's always nice to have made an impression.'

'You destroyed our colony on Metebelis 3!' shrieked the Queen. 'You are the deadliest enemy of the Eight-Legs!'

'You old flatterer,' said the Doctor. 'Any very talented, intelligent and amusing person who happened to have been passing by could have done it.'

'You will pay for your crimes!' the Queen ranted. She turned to her underlings. 'Prepare them. We shall feast on their living bodies as we suck the knowledge from their minds.'

The first of the spiders leapt through the air and knocked the Doctor to the ground. He struggled to stand, but its strong legs had him pinioned. Drool started to fall from its snapping jaws. He twisted his head and saw, on the other side of the attic, that Romana was in an identical predicament. 'Hang on, Romana!' he cried.

'Doctor,' she called, now released from her trance. 'They're going to kill us!'

'Try not to panic,' he called. 'Lie back and think of Gallifrey!' But as the spider's snapping jaws came over closer, the Doctor found it very difficult to follow his own advice.

Meanwhile, outside in the garden, K9's internal clock had ticked down fifteen minutes. He waited just a moment more – the Doctor had a habit of emerging just in the nick of time – but nothing happened. So he wheeled himself a short distance back for safety, cocked his head, and let forth a beam of red-hot laser energy at the roof of No. 9 Honeysuckle Close. There was a blast of white fire and then flames started to pour from the exposed section.

The patio door slid open suddenly and the Fordyces, looking bedraggled and confused, emerged. K9 turned his attentions to them. 'Halt. Are you friend or foe?'

Mrs Fordyce gave a little yell. 'What is it, Patrick?' she asked her husband.

K9 decided they were little threat and directed another laser blast at the house, this time on the lower floor. A window shattered and smoke billowed out.

The scene in the attic was one of utter chaos and confusion. Smoke had blurred Romana's vision, and she was coughing violently. Thankfully the spider's grip on her had been loosened and she was able to knock its fat, furry bulk away.

She heard the voice of the Queen Spider. 'What is happening? What is happening?'

Romana sensed the Doctor's reassuring presence at her side. 'That'll be K9,' he said. 'We'd better get out of here, and take those humans with us.'

He led her to the ladder and lowered her down. Romana turned for a last look at the Queen, who was struggling to move. 'No... stop them...' the creature cried. 'Destroy them...'

There was another huge blast of K9's ray and the whole roof was sliced off.

Out in the garden, K9 considered the sight of the Queen Spider. It appeared to be an incredibly tenacious creature, and he doubted whether even his firepower would be enough to cope with it.

It was with great relief that he saw the Doctor and Romana, joined by an odd assortment of humans who looked half-dazed and were covered in strands of cobweb, running from the house.

'I have followed your instructions, Master,' K9 said.

'I'd noticed,' said the Doctor.

Romana tugged the Doctor's sleeve and pointed. 'Look!'

The two underling spiders were scuttling for their lives from the burning house. Quick as a flash, the Doctor threw himself spectacularly through the air and managed to come crashing down on them with his full weight.

Romana raced over. 'Well done, Doctor!'

The Doctor pulled himself up and dusted himself down. 'I can't take all the credit. J. P. R. Williams taught me that tackle.' He wagged a finger at the spiders, who were getting unsteadily to their feet. 'They'll have sore heads for a week now.'

Suddenly the voice of the Queen boomed out over them all. 'Doctor, you are a fool to think that such a puny attack could destroy me!'

The Doctor looked up. The Queen sat on the exposed roof, but had somehow managed to put out the fire.

The Doctor called up, 'How did you do that?'

The Queen cackled, 'Simple. I blew it out,' emphasising the point by opening its mouth wide and blowing hard, knocking them all over like ninepins.

The Doctor got to his feet. 'You're finished. You're just an old queen who doesn't know when it's time to give up.'

'On the contrary, Doctor,' said the Queen, 'my plans are about to begin. Soon, the eggs beneath me will hatch. The Eight-Legs will swarm over this pathetic speck of a planet and consume all the humans!' The spider lifted its legs to reveal clusters of slimy eggs.

The Doctor whispered to Romana, 'She's got us there. If she manages to hatch those eggs we'll be done for.'

There was a sudden noise of a ringing alarm bell. From out of the darkness surrounding the estate there emerged a gleaming red fire engine. Within seconds, a team of firefighters dressed in oilskins and yellow helmets poured out into the garden.

'Blimey,' said their leader, 'what's happening here?'

The Doctor gaped at him. 'Is that a hosepipe in your hand?'

'Yes,' said the fireman.

'In that case,' said the Doctor, snatching it from him, 'I'm very pleased to see you.' He called over his shoulder, 'Switch on!'

The firefighters in the fire engine took this to be an order from their leader, and moments later a fountain of water gushed from the pipe. The Doctor angled it expertly up, right at the Queen Spider's eyes. It shrieked and curled up its legs. 'Come on, everybody!' he called.

Romana took her cue and grabbed another hosepipe. Soon the firefighters had joined in, and the Queen was being doused from many different directions. Ruined eggs went slewing off from under the spider's bloated body in the deluge of water, and its grip on the roof was weakening. A couple of legs slid off.

'She won't be able to blow this out!' cried the Doctor.

He was right. After a couple of minutes, the drenched Queen Spider, shrieking in its death throes, had toppled from the roof of No. 9 Honeysuckle Close and was splattered all around the garden.

Time had passed. The Doctor had sent the firefighters and the Fordyces' party guests on their bewildered way, although he had lingered briefly to take a cup of tea with the unhappy couple themselves.

And now, he, Romana and K9 were preparing to leave. At Romana's feet was a large box.

'Are you sure this is a good idea?' she asked.

The Doctor nodded. 'Everyone deserves a second chance.' He knelt down and put his mouth to the grille on the front of the box. 'You won't try anything like this again, will you?'

The first spider said meekly, 'We were the victims of a false doctrine.'

The second piped up, 'Now that the Queen is gone we wish to live only modest lives.'

The Doctor nodded, satisfied, and stood up. 'There you are, Romana. We'll take them with us and drop them off on Arachnos. There's a planet full of giant spiders there, and they're all very pleasant chaps. There are giant flies too, so they won't go hungry again.'

Romana took a last look around the Riverdale Estate. 'There's still the small matter of my five pounds.'

The Doctor pretended to be baffled. 'What five pounds?'

'Five pounds to me if anything unusual was happening here,' she reminded him.

'Oh, that.'

'And I think being attacked by giant spiders qualifies.'

The Doctor considered. 'That's not unusual. Romana, things like that are *always* happening to us.'

He ushered her and K9 into the TARDIS, and a little later the blue police box faded away... on its way to new adventures.

Hot Ice

by Christopher Bulis

It was one o'clock in the morning when Len Skeggs slipped through the back gate of No. 47 Risemore Way and stole silently up the garden. The night was cool, still and moonless, with a haze of mist in the air. The distant orange glow of streetlights silhouetted the rows of houses all around him, but the strip of common ground on to which their gardens backed was pooled in shadow.

No. 47 had attracted Len's professional interest for several reasons. It was a large detached house in a good area, but looked a little shabby. There was no sign of any alarm system, and the sole occupant was a hunched old man who hardly ever ventured out. In Len's experience, people living in such circumstances often preferred to keep their cash and valuables at home rather than in the bank.

Len reached the small brick patio on to which French windows opened from the back lounge. Through the glass he could see the key glinting in the door lock. This was going to be too easy. He attached a suction cup from his tool bag to the pane beside the lock, then he drew a circle about it with a glass cutter.

The hardened blade of the cutter simply slid across the glass without making a scratch.

He scowled and tried again, pressing harder. Once more the tool slid aside as though moving on a film of oil. He simply could not get the cutter to bite. Obviously this was some new type of security glass he had not come across before.

Cursing silently, Len picked out a jemmy. It would be noisier, but he was not a man to give up easily. He thrust its claw end into the gap around the doorframe and heaved.

There was no snap of splintering wood and the door remained absolutely rigid and immobile. With a grunt of anger, Len heaved again with all his strength. There was a sharp metallic twang and he sat down heavily. The tip of the jemmy had broken off.

Even as he gaped at the door incredulously, he became aware of an eerie sound. It seemed to reverberate through the very ground under him, faint and breathless; a whirring and groaning that rose and fell as it grew steadily stronger.

Snatching up his bag, Len darted away from the patio into the shadow of a garden shed.

The Doctor stepped out of the TARDIS doorway, playing a torch beam about the cool, dark and silent chamber in which they had materialised. Peri cautiously followed him.

'It feels like some kind of cellar,' she said.

'Probably because it is,' the Doctor agreed, placing his panama hat on his head, his youthful face bright and alert. 'Be it ever so humble, however, this is the place.'

'But you don't think this coherent neutrino pulse thing you detected is dangerous?' Peri asked, trying to sound nonchalant. 'Nothing to do with an invasion of googly-eyed monsters or something?'

'Most unlikely. The source seems relatively low-powered and isn't steady enough for a beacon. It just doesn't belong in this time and place.' He smiled mischievously. 'Besides, whoever heard of aliens starting an invasion in Surbiton? A common north-west of Woking perhaps, but never Surbiton.'

Peri recognised the allusion. 'Do you have to bring up H. G. Wells? Those blood-sucking Martian octopuses of his always did give me the creeps.'

'I can assure you, Peri, from personal experience, that there are absolutely no blood-sucking octopuses on Mars.'

'That's a relief.'

'Just seven-foot-tall humanoid warrior lizards. Ah, here we are…'

There was the click of a switch and fluorescent tubes flickered into life, filling the room with cool light.

Peri blinked and looked about her. The cellar was some twenty feet square, brick-lined, with stone flags on the floor. In the corner an iron-balustraded flight of steps led up to a wooden door, standing slightly ajar. Running the entire length of one wall was a wooden workbench, fitted with power points and scattered with hand-tools and items of salvaged electronic equipment. Resting on a small stand in the middle of the bench was a fluted tube of red metal, about six feet long, ringed at one end with a cluster of dull black spheres, each of which trailed a bundle of multicoloured wires. The Doctor stepped over and examined the device with deep interest.

'Yes, this is the source of the neutrino pulse all right,' he pronounced.

'No kidding,' Peri said. 'If I asked what it was for, would I understand the answer?'

'Well, it's part of a star-drive module. It functions rather like a spark plug in an internal combustion engine, giving the initial kick to initiate the lepton-flux implosion –'

'OK – I get the picture,' said Peri. 'So we guess an alien's broken down on Earth and he's trying to fix his engine with bits and pieces he's found here, right?'

'That is the most likely explanation.'

'So where is he?' She looked about her nervously. 'Or do I mean, where is *it*? And is he, or it, friendly?'

Just then they heard the groaning. It was very faint and came from the direction of the half-open cellar door. After a few seconds it degenerated into a fit of feeble coughing.

'That doesn't sound too good,' Peri said.

'No,' agreed the Doctor, making for the steps.

The cellar door opened out from under the house's main staircase on to a wide bare hall, with the front door at one end and three other doors, all closed, leading off it. Except for a single dim bulb burning at the very top of the stairwell two floors above, all was in darkness.

'Hello,' the Doctor called out loudly. 'Is anybody there?'

There came another moan, louder than the one they'd heard before, followed by what might have been a string of muffled, indecipherable words.

'Upstairs,' said the Doctor, leading the way.

All the doors opening off the first landing were closed and no lights showed underneath them. The distressed voice still came from above, getting steadily louder as they ascended. A single door opened off the second landing. Coughs and groans and muttering could be heard behind it.

'Hello,' the Doctor said. 'Are you all right?'

The sounds continued undiminished. With a small shrug, the Doctor tried the door. It opened smoothly.

The long attic room with half-sloping walls was unlit except for the glow of city lights filtering in through a single dormer window. The Doctor switched on his torch again and swung it about. In the far corner was a iron-framed single bed. On it was a body-shaped mound covered with a blanket, from which came more groans, interspersed with slurred, rasping words.

They stepped quickly over the bed, the Doctor saying reassuringly, 'It's all right. We're here to help you.' Handing Peri the torch, he pulled back the blanket.

Underneath was a portable stereo cassette player resting between two pillows laid lengthwise. Even as they stared at the machine in surprise, another fit of recorded coughing issued from the speakers.

The landing door slammed shut behind them, followed by the sound of heavy bolts sliding into place.

The Doctor ran to the door and twisted the handle, at the same time throwing his shoulder against it, but the door remained firmly shut. He gave a resigned sigh and thrust his hands into his pockets.

Peri fought to keep her voice steady. 'Looks like we've walked into a trap, huh?'

'I'm afraid so. What about the window?'

They examined the dormer. The latches had been removed and the frame had been screwed securely into place.

'Even if we could get out, it would be a dangerous drop,' the Doctor admitted. 'And I don't think we could improvise a long enough rope from that blanket. Somebody seems to have thought of everything.'

'Can't we signal with the torch?' Peri suggested.

'I don't think many people will be looking out for SOSs at this time of the morning.'

Peri stared out into the misty darkness, trying to stay calm. Just what the hell wanted to keep them here?

* * *

Len crouched beside the garden shed thinking hard. He'd rationalised away the odd sound that had disturbed him as some old central heating boiler starting up. Now he was reasoning further that security doors that tough had to be protecting something valuable. If only he could find a way through them.

Just then a flicker of movement at the bottom of the garden caused him to shrink further back into the shadows. Two figures were making their way silently towards the house. As they passed within a few yards of him, he realised that they were wearing dark full-length robes with hoods pulled over their heads, bearing an uncanny resemblance to monks in cassocks. They paused before the French windows. After a minute there was a brief flash of light. The door opened and they passed inside.

Len knew he should go now that there were others in the house, but the lure of the wide-open door, and the thought that this unlikely duo were hardly stiff opposition, held him back. He waited a couple of minutes to see if the 'monks' would emerge again, then cat-footed over to the door – only to stop short in amazement. A perfect half-circle about the frame had been neatly cut away. The 'monks' had broken in. They were in the same line of business as he was!

Len now knew for certain he was on to something big; maybe the job of a lifetime. He smiled, grimly; he'd poke about himself, find out just what this pair were after, then take it off their hands. Pulling on his balaclava mask, and reassured by the weight of the jemmy in his hand, he stepped inside.

Up in the attic room, Peri held the torch while the Doctor methodically ran his hands around the doorframe, looking for any hidden catch or weak point.

'I really must get round to building another sonic screwdriver,' he muttered. 'It's just the thing for this sort of situation.'

'Give it up, Doctor,' she said. 'Why don't we check the walls again?'

Just then there was the sound of bolts being withdrawn from outside. The Doctor raised his eyebrows in surprise and cautiously tried the handle. The door opened easily.

'How did you do that?' Peri said, impressed.

'I didn't. Somebody wanted to keep us here for a while and now they want us to leave.' The Doctor looked about him, a grim expression on his face. 'Well, we're not going to play your game any more,' he said clearly. 'We're staying here until you show yourself and explain what's going on.'

There was a sudden hissing sound. A plume of white vapour poured out of a vent in the skirting board beside the bed and billowed across the room. The Doctor swept Peri out through the door with him and slammed it shut behind them.

'Perhaps a strategic withdrawal is indicated,' he said, as the vapour began to seep under the door.

They hurried downstairs to the ground floor and turned towards the cellar. As they went through the hall, they failed to notice that the lounge door, which had been closed when they'd passed earlier, was now open a crack. In the crack an eye glinted.

Len had spent some minutes in the lounge rifling through a bureau and checking hopefully for wall safes behind pictures. But the room had proved disappointing; sparsely furnished with dusty furniture. He had decided to explore the rest of the house and actually had his hand on the door handle when he heard rapid footsteps on the stairs.

He didn't know what to make of the joker in the weird clothes – was that really celery on his coat? – or his companion, except that she was a very tasty piece indeed. Had they been the ones in the robes and hoods, he wondered? And why were they in such a hurry to go down to the cellar? He listened intently for a couple of minutes and thought he could just make out the faintest murmur of voices from below, but that was all. Cautiously he started to ease the door open, only to hear a faint click and swish from the hall. Once more he peered through the crack between door and jamb.

The hunched figure of the occupier of No. 47 appeared from the direction of the kitchen and moved silently across the hall to the open cellar door. In his hand, Len noticed, he carried a short stick. He stood there for a minute as though listening for any sound from below. Then, obviously satisfied, he also descended into the cellar.

* * *

The Doctor and Peri stopped short as they reached the bottom of the cellar steps, as they realised things were not as they had left them. A heavy cable now ran from the half-open door of the TARDIS over to the workbench, where it was wired into the mechanism from the alien star drive.

'Somebody sure is playing games with us,' Peri said, as the Doctor led the way into the TARDIS, stepping over the snaking cable.

A panel at the base of the main console had been opened, exposing a junction box into which the cable had been plugged. But it was not this that caught their attention.

Resting on top of the console was a flat black box about eighteen inches wide. On it was mounted a transparent dome containing within it the largest gemstone Peri had ever seen. It was the size of a small fist and its faces glittered with blue-green fire under the lights.

'Wow! Will you look at that!' she exclaimed, gazing at the jewel in fascination. 'It must be your birthday, Doctor. Somebody's left you a present.'

'An unwanted gift,' the Doctor said tersely, 'which I think we would do well to –'

'Stay where you are, blasphemers!' said a flat voice behind them.

They turned round. Two black-robed figures stood by the doorway, their faces concealed within the shadows of their hoods. Each had one arm extended towards them, and from their voluminous sleeves projected what looked like magician's wands. For featureless rods they appeared unaccountably menacing.

The two figures glided forward, and Peri realised with a start that though their trailing robes did not quite touch the ground, there was no sign of feet or legs under them. As they came closer she felt unnatural warmth radiating from their bodies, causing beads of perspiration to form on her brow. The figure on the left extended another rod, silver and bulbous-tipped, from his other sleeve and pointed it at the gem and its container. Immediately the tip pulsated with green light.

'Our quest is ended,' he said, quiet triumph sounding in the flat tones. 'The tracer has led us to the Eye of Gaar – and to those who stole it!'

'The Eye of Gaar?' echoed Peri, incredulously.

'Careful, Peri,' the Doctor said airily. 'It really doesn't do to mock the nomenclature of alien icons.' He turned back to the priests. 'So. You're Ventrosians, I take it.'

'We are priests of the Temple of Gaar on Ventros Prime, and we have been entrusted with the task of recovering the Eye.'

'Well, how do you do? I'm the Doctor and this is my friend Peri –'

'Silence! We have already scanned you. We also recognise this vessel, Time Lord. Did you use it to aid your Ventrosian accomplice in the theft of the Eye?'

'But we didn't steal it!' Peri protested. 'We've been framed.'

'Keep your native servant quiet,' the priest warned the Doctor.

'Who are you calling a servant!' Peri said indignantly.

'I'm afraid Ventrosians aren't the most subtle of beings, Peri,' the Doctor explained, an edge beneath his light words. 'Always had something of a superiority complex. That was why, millennia ago, we refused to share our technology with them – and they've resented us for it ever since. But I didn't think they would be so foolish as to believe we would covet one of their holy relics!'

'Then why is your craft connected to a drive unit from the thief's vessel?' the priest asked.

'As my friend tried to tell you, someone wants you to believe that we're the guilty parties. We've been used, can't you see that?'

'We see only thieves and conspirators who have been caught with the Eye in their possession. For this crime there can be but one punishment.'

'Why can't you listen to reason?' the Doctor pleaded.

'We sense the protective fields within your craft, Time Lord, but our personal auras can negate them,' the priest continued remorselessly. 'The sentence will be carried out immediately. When your accomplice returns, he will suffer the same fate.'

The Doctor frowned. 'For the last time, we don't have an accomp–'

The priests raised their wands a little higher.

'No!' the Doctor shouted.

Even as Peri threw herself sideways, a flicker of blue fire lashed out and transfixed her.

It was as though she had received an electric shock. Her muscles spasmed, then went numb. She stumbled and fell, slumped helplessly against the wall of the console room, with the Doctor, similarly incapacitated, collapsing at her side. The priests loomed over them like black ghosts.

'There is no escape. Now you will die – slowly and painfully, so that you will have time to reflect upon the enormity of your crime. May Gaar have mercy upon you.'

The wands glowed red, and it felt to Peri that her skin was on fire. She tried to scream, but even that release was denied her.

Len peered down into the cellar from the shadows at the top of the steps. Greed and curiosity were finely balanced within him now. He had to know what was going on almost as much as he wanted to find something of value.

What was the old man doing standing in front of the half-open door of old-fashioned police call box, his whole attention apparently focused upon it? What was the box doing here anyway? And where were the man and the woman he'd seen coming down? They couldn't be hiding in the box itself, could they? Why would they, anyway? Even so, there was an odd sort of light coming from it, and he imagined he could make out the murmur of voices.

Then the old man stepped forward.

Peri was hardly aware of a fifth figure entering the console room through the agony that was racking her body. All she knew was that the room was suddenly lit up by two quick bursts of intense light, accompanied by a searing crackling sound, and then that the terrible pain vanished as though turned off by a switch.

Smoke was billowing in the air, together with fluttering scraps of burning fabric. Glowing ashes and twisted metal lay where the priests had stood, while their power wands and tracer device rolled loosely across the floor.

Unable to speak or turn her head, it was all Peri could do to blink her eyes until they focused on the stout, slightly hunchbacked figure of an old man, dressed in crumpled trousers and a baggy jumper. The benign expression on his wrinkled face was so reassuring that she would have cried out in relief, if she had been able to move her lips.

Then she saw he was carrying a power wand identical to those of the priests.

'At last I am rid of them!' he said, as though half to himself. His features did not reflect the triumphant nature of his words, which were, if anything, in even flatter tones than those of the creatures he had killed. His dark eyes flickered across Peri and the Doctor as they lay helplessly against the wall. 'The paralysis will soon wear off, but by then I will have gone.'

He walked over to the console and carefully gathered up the box holding the Eye of Gaar. Peri felt a wash of heat as he moved. He looked at the Doctor.

'You would not understand why I had to steal the Eye. Suffice to say I felt it necessary,' he continued. 'But I could not escape my pursuers. Eventually I was forced to land on this inhospitable planet. Fortunately I soon detected the energy signature of your TARDIS's frequent visits here, and used my own star drive to lure you – and the priests – to me. You were most convincing targets for their wrath.'

The Doctor concentrated, screwed up his eyes, forcing out words. 'A... diversion...'

The old man nodded. 'The interior of this vessel, you see, was the only place they would not be able to sense my approach until it was too late.'

Out of the corner of her eye, Peri caught a flicker of movement. A black masked head had looked in through the door, then withdrew. She tried to speak, but all that came out was a groan.

'Now it is over and I am free to leave,' the old man went on. 'I will take the priests' vessel. No one from Ventros Prime will ever find me again. Thank you, Time Lord, for your unwitting assistance.'

He turned away and walked out of the TARDIS.

Len did not care how the trick with the inside of the police box was done, or what had happened to the man and woman slumped against the wall. He had eyes only for the most fabulous gem he had ever seen. He was right: this really was the chance of a lifetime.

And so, as the old man stepped out through the narrow door, Len hit him across the back of the neck with his jemmy.

He knew there was something wrong even as the blow struck. The old man's body radiated impossible heat, and it was not flesh and bone that crumpled under the blow as he fell to the floor, dropping the gem case to claw at his hunched shoulders. To Len's horror a flap of white-haired skin was hanging loose from the back of the man's head, revealing a shell of torn foil and spongy fibres underneath.

Then, even as Len froze in sickened disbelief, the old man ceased his writhing and rose back upright – except that his legs were now dangling limply, and were clearly not supporting him.

Len snatched up the gem case and dashed for the stairs. Halfway up, a hole exploded in the wall behind him, peppering him with fragments of brick and mortar. He glanced fearfully over his shoulder. The old man was pointing some kind of weapon at him with his shaking hands, and sparks were playing about its tip. And he moved forward as though carried on invisible wires, his legs trailing behind him, toe-caps dragging across the ground. In a voice that was rapidly losing all semblance of humanity, the old man cried, 'Thief! Return that crystal or die!'

Len dived through the cellar door, and the old man glided unsteadily up the steps after him, thin tendrils of steam seeping out of his clothes.

They had heard the commotion in the cellar from inside the TARDIS, then the sounds of pursuit fading into the distance. After a few minutes, Peri felt the tingling of life returning to her limbs. With an obvious effort, the Doctor sat up beside her. With his support, she struggled to her feet.

She licked her lips and managed to say, 'Pretty ironic… I think our thief got mugged.'

The Doctor picked up the priests' tracer device and tried the control switch. The tip remained dark. 'Power cell burnt out by secondary discharge,' he muttered. He retrieved his torch and they walked stiffly out into the cellar. He sniffed, frowning. 'Can you smell that?'

There was a sickly odour of decay hanging in the air.

'Yeah, it stinks. What does it mean?'

'It means that at least one thief is going to die tonight if we don't prevent it. Come on.'

They followed the foul scent through the lounge, its French windows now blasted apart and smoking, across the patio and down the garden. Out on the common the trail faded into the misty night air.

They found the alien after several minutes of searching by torchlight. He was lying amid the tussocky grass, a crumpled form wreathed in steam and twitching feebly. There was no sign of the man in the balaclava.

The stench grew worse as they drew nearer, and Peri covered her mouth, retching. The Doctor, apparently now oblivious to the smell, knelt beside the creature. A voice grated from somewhere within the body, but the lips on the macabre face no longer moved; the benign expression was now frozen, mask-like, on the face.

'Lost… him. Motivator unit… failed.'

'We must get you back to the house,' the Doctor said.

'Too late, Time Lord… At least the priests did not get the Eye…'

Then he sagged and was still. Vapour began to pour more rapidly from his clothes.

'Stand back,' the Doctor warned.

The human disguise split and fell away, the clothes disintegrating to reveal the rods and joints of mechanical limbs and layers of insulation underneath. Within all this Peri glimpsed a slender worm-like creature that seemed to be melting before her eyes. It was supported by a lattice of metal bands and tubes that connected to a complex backpack which was cracked down one side. With a furious rush of steam, the thing bubbled and flashed into flame.

'He chose to chase after his precious Eye instead of waiting to repair his life-support unit,' the Doctor said sadly, as they stood back from the blaze. 'He must have built an environment chamber for himself somewhere in the house.'

'What happened?' Peri demanded. 'It looked as though he was melting away. But he was hot, like the priests. I felt it.'

'You felt the heat from his cooling unit, like the coils at the back of a refrigerator. The Ventrosians live on a frigid world and have an appropriately volatile body chemistry to compensate. Exposed to Earth temperatures, he simply burnt up.'

Even as they stared at the dying embers, Peri became aware of a reddish glow beginning to show through the mist about fifty yards away. In seconds it had become a perfect sphere of growing intensity, flashing through orange and then yellow.

'Down!' the Doctor shouted.

There was a dull boom as the sphere disintegrated into a shower of flaming fragments and a fiery cloud that boiled skyward.

Peri lifted her face from the grass. 'And what was that?'

'The priests' ship, I should think,' said the Doctor. 'It must have had a timed self-destruct mechanism, activated when it lost track of its owner's life signs.'

'Those guys were playing for keeps,' she observed.

'Yes. And they've all come out losers,' he said bleakly, before scrambling to his feet and pulling Peri up with him. 'Now, back to the house before people come out to see what's happening. I must repair the tracer. There's still one thief to track down.'

'The guy? No one's after this Eye of Gaar thing now, are they? What's the rush?'

'Because he doesn't realise what he's stolen,' said the Doctor, grimly.

The phone in the house was working normally – Peri wondered what had happened to the original owner of this place, and shuddered. She dialled a number the Doctor gave her and passed on the request for a 'clean-up squad' to an organisation she'd never heard of called UNIT.

'That's right,' she concluded. 'He said to tell you to call a Brigadier Lethbridge-Stewart if you wanted to check this is on the level… No, my name's not Smith, it's Brown… Look, just come round here and pick up the pieces, guys. Good night.'

She hung up and went back to the TARDIS. The Doctor had just finished inserting a fresh power cell into the tracer. He switched it on and immediately the tip began to flash green.

'Right,' said the Doctor, 'if I can just fix a range and bearing –'

The light flickered and died. The Doctor worked the switch but to no effect.

'Flat battery again?' Peri asked.

The Doctor sighed heavily and for a moment he seemed old and tired, his youthful energy drained. 'No, Peri. The gem-case circuitry has been damaged. I'm afraid it may be too late.'

In the back of a lock-up garage a little over a mile away, Len Skeggs swung another frantic blow with his sledgehammer at the gem case, which he had clamped into a large bench vice. The gemstone he could conceal easily enough, but its bulky container was a liability. He wanted nothing lying around that might connect him with the crime – or whatever that thing was that chased him out of the house. He would have to break the gem up to sell it on, of course, but even the fragments of something that size would set him up for life.

The double-walled protective dome suddenly cracked and popped out of its securing collar, spilling the gem on to the concrete floor. Len dropped his hammer and eagerly snatched up the precious object before it could roll away.

A second later he cried out in pain and surprise. The gem was sticking to his hands, burning his skin with intense cold. As he struggled to tear it free it began to boil away into gas that stung his eyes and seared his lungs. Choking and blinded, gasping for clean air, Len collapsed to the floor and then lay still.

Still clamped in the vice, the gem's environmental-support unit sparked as its power cells shorted out, sending out a trail of smoke before hungry flames began to lick up towards the cluttered shelves over the workbench.

Peri could hear the distant sirens of emergency vehicles as she took one final look around the cellar, while the Doctor finished making sure the alien star-drive component that had lured them here was completely useless.

'And all for a chunk of ammonia and methane ice,' she said.

'Value is often a purely arbitrary concept,' the Doctor said sombrely, tossing aside the cable that had been connected to the TARDIS console. 'Many famous Earth jewels have a history of theft and death behind them, and it would seem that alien gems are no exception.' He sighed. 'Come on. Let's go somewhere more cheerful. Leave the tidying up to the professionals.'

She followed him inside the TARDIS, where the air was clean and fresh. She breathed deeply, but the stink of the alien thief's decaying body seemed to linger on in her lungs, mingling with dark thoughts of obsession, greed, and the dead.

uPVC

by Paul Farnsworth

I

Jamie was invariably uneasy whenever the console room was left unattended. It had become something of a ritual for both Zoe and him to tease the Doctor over his apparent inability to control the temperamental time machine, and yet Jamie always felt much safer when the mysterious little man was in attendance – dancing around the mushroom-shaped console, checking dials, adjusting controls, muttering to himself as he brooded over the instruments.

This time the Doctor had set the co-ordinates quickly before disappearing into the labyrinthine depths of the TARDIS, assuring Jamie that his machine was perfectly capable of looking after itself. Jamie knew from experience that this was rarely ever the case. Something usually went wrong, so he took it upon himself to look in occasionally, just to ensure that no major catastrophes were taking place. In all likelihood, Jamie wouldn't recognise a major catastrophe if it gave him a new kilt for Christmas, let alone be in a position to set the problem straight, but as long as he was actually here he figured that that was enough.

He paced around the console, fixing it with a stern gaze as if daring it to misbehave. The little coloured lights were all winking, apparently normally, and there was the familiar, persistent hum from the central column. As far as Jamie was concerned, everything was as it should be. Then he heard a curious sound.

BANG-BANG-BANG!

Startled, Jamie looked up from the console. The sound seemed to be coming from all around him, vibrating through the walls. At first he assumed it to be some mechanical fault, but when the noise repeated itself it became clear that it came from an exterior source.

BANG-BANG-BANG!

His attention was drawn to the outer doors. It was as if there was

277

someone out there, knocking on the outside of the TARDIS. Surely that wasn't possible, Jamie thought. The Doctor had said that it was impossible for anyone to be outside the TARDIS while it was moving. Well, impossible or not, he had definitely heard the sound, plainly and clearly – twice. Keeping his eyes firmly fixed on the door he moved to the back of the room. 'Doctor!' he called over his shoulder, into the depths of the time machine. 'Doctor, come here quickly!'

The noise came again, only this time Jamie thought he could hear a fragile voice accompanying it. He crept closer to the door, bent down and pressed his ear pressed to it.

'Hello?' he murmured. 'Hello, is there anyone out there…?'

'Jamie, what on earth do you think you're doing?'

The young Scot stood up straight, finding Zoe standing behind him.

'There's someone out there,' he said.

'Outside the TARDIS?' Zoe looked at him sternly. 'Is this some kind of prank, Jamie?' she warned him. 'Because if it is –'

'Och, it's no' a joke, I tell ye,' Jamie insisted. 'I heard someone out there.'

Zoe shrugged and cast a baffled look at the door. 'Well,' she said, 'whatever it is, it seems to have stopped now. It's probably nothing.'

As Zoe was speaking the Doctor arrived. 'Hmm?' he said absently. 'What's probably nothing?' He had his head down and was fumbling with a bundle of odds and ends: a screwdriver, a pencil, a small plastic tube, all tangled up together with a roll of sticky black electrical tape. The more the Doctor tried to separate them, the more the tape became entwined around his own fingers.

'Jamie thinks he heard someone outside,' Zoe explained.

'Outside where?' the Doctor said. 'Outside the TARDIS? No, no, that's quite impossible.' The Doctor had managed to peel the tape from his fingers and had twisted it up into a sticky ball – which was now stuck to his other hand. 'Well,' he said, preoccupied with trying to himself shake free from the gluey mess. 'What sort of noise, Jamie?'

'It was as if someone was knocking on the doors!' Jamie insisted.

Zoe came forward and helped the Doctor peel the tape from his fingers. 'Oh, oh, thank you, Zoe,' he said with a grateful smile as she deftly disposed of it for him.

'Doctor, could there be something wrong with the TARDIS?' she asked.

'You mean, could the noise be the result of some mechanical fault?' the Doctor pondered as he deposited his collection of odds and ends on to the console. 'Well, I suppose it's a –'

BANG-BANG-BANG!

'Ah!' Jamie cried triumphantly. '*Now* do you believe me?'

The Doctor stood back from the console, folded his hands over his chest and looked around the room in alarm. 'Good grief,' he said. 'Now that's not right. That's not right at all.'

'What is it?' Zoe asked.

'I really don't know, Zoe,' replied the puzzled Doctor.

'There's someone outside,' Jamie insisted. 'Will ye no' listen to me?'

BANG-BANG-BANG!

This time the sound was followed by a tiny muffled voice.

'Hello, is there anyone there?'

'Great jumping jellybeans!' exclaimed the Doctor as he cast his startled gaze at the outer door. 'I think I owe you an apology, Jamie.' He walked over to the outer doors and pressed himself against them, listening. 'Hello?' he said after a pause. 'Is there anyone there?'

'Hello?' the voice called back. 'Can anyone hear me?'

The Doctor turned away from the door, shaking his head violently. 'No, no,' he said firmly. 'This is quite impossible.' He flashed Zoe a conspiratorial glance. 'Shall we just ignore it? Then perhaps it will go away.'

He started to walk off, but Zoe stopped him.

'Doctor! You can't just forget about it.'

'I most certainly can, Zoe,' the Doctor said defensively. 'If I put my mind to it.'

'But it might be someone who needs our help!' Zoe argued.

'But nobody can exist out there in the vortex!' the Doctor protested.

The sound came again. 'Is there anyone there?' they heard the voice call faintly.

'Aye, well perhaps someone ought to tell him that,' Jamie said.

The Doctor watched the door uneasily. 'You don't understand,' he said, and his voice was almost childlike. 'Out there, in the vortex, there are… things. Phantoms,' the Doctor said. His tone became dark, melodramatic, but his expression made it clear that he was serious. 'Strange creatures that live in the void and prey on unwary travellers.'

'Oh dear,' Zoe said anxiously. 'I never realised…'

'Well, how can we tell?' Jamie asked. 'How do we know whether whoever's out there is one of these "phantoms" or is someone who really does needs our help?'

The Doctor looked at him, then suddenly came to a decision. 'Yes, Jamie,' he said. 'You're quite right. Now stand back, you two, I'm going to open the doors.'

Jamie stared at him. 'What? Do ye not remember what happened when Salamander tried to do that?'

'It's risky, Jamie, but if I land first we could lose whoever's holding on outside for ever.' He clapped his hands together. 'Now come on, find something to hold on to. No, not Zoe, Jamie, something more substantial!'

The Doctor moved to the console and stood waiting with his hand on the door control. Once his companions were gripping the console firmly, he gave the control a sharp twist and the doors began to open.

Jamie and Zoe screwed up their eyes as they looked into the swirling patterns of light beyond the open door. They felt the tug of the vortex, like a wind whipping around their clothes, dragging them, almost *tempting* them out. They saw shapes forming and re-forming, waves travelling like ripples through fog. Then a shadow stepped over the threshold and into the TARDIS, resolving into a tall man with an elegantly shaped moustache. Stranger still, he was wearing a long beige coat and held an umbrella above his head. A strange orange glow formed smokily behind him, although Zoe couldn't see if that was the Doctor's doing or the stranger's. The din died down, the wind stopped abruptly and only the usual hum of the TARDIS could be heard.

The stranger smiled. 'Good afternoon,' he said as he collapsed his umbrella and shook it – needlessly, since it was obviously as dry as a bone. 'The name's Rigby,' he announced, reaching inside his coat and producing a small, white rectangle of card. Zoe took it from him and read it aloud.

'Bill Rigby, ThermoPort Windows Ltd.'

'That's right, Miss,' Rigby said. 'Now tell me, have you ever seriously considered installing double glazing?'

'Double glazing?' asked Zoe, still somewhat taken aback by this man's sudden appearance.

'We're not interested!' the Doctor snapped quickly, hovering uncertainly around the other side of the console. He took a step nearer, but seemed wary about getting too close to this strange man.

Rigby looked at him and turned up his disarming smile another notch. 'I see, sir,' he said graciously. 'Well, that's fair enough, I'm sorry to have wasted your time… Although, before you dismiss me out of hand, why not see exactly what we have to offer?' He had the condescending air of a schoolteacher coaxing a small child. 'I have some leaflets here if you'd care to peruse them?'

He hoisted his briefcase on to the console, clicked open the catches and opened the lid.

'Leaflets?' the Doctor repeated suspiciously. 'Leaflets? What leaflets?'

'Doctor, what is he on about?' Jamie asked.

'I don't know, Jamie, I don't know.' The Doctor replied. He edged around the console, hoisting himself up on tiptoe to peer into the visitor's briefcase.

'Ah, here we are!' Rigby said as he pulled out a thick brochure. 'Now as you can see, we have quite a wide range of styles. I don't like to boast, but I think I can say without fear of contradiction that there's something here to suit every taste. Installation is included in the cost and you can choose from a wide range of available materials, including aluminium, wood and uPVC.'

The Doctor cautiously took the brochure from him, turned the page and furrowed his brow at it.

'Ah! The mock-Georgian leaded bay window,' Rigby crooned

approvingly. 'Yes, that's a very popular line. It looks like real wood, doesn't it? In actual fact it's tough, lightweight uPVC – very hard-wearing and so easy to clean!'

'It *is* very nice,' Zoe said. She and Jamie had joined the Doctor and were looking over his shoulder at the brochure. 'I like the decorative sill.'

'Yes, it is rather nice, isn't it?' the Doctor agreed. 'I much prefer it to these other ones over here.' Suddenly his manner changed. 'Hang on a minute, what am I saying? This is no good to me.' He slid the brochure hurriedly back into Rigby's briefcase.

'But sir!' Rigby protested. 'I don't think you've fully considered the benefits of good-quality double glazing. Think how it will reduce heating costs.'

'Not a problem, thank you,' the Doctor said as he gathered up Rigby's case and thrust it at him.

'Doctor, what's the matter?' Zoe asked.

'We don't need windows!' the Doctor snapped. 'Jamie, Zoe – whatever you do, don't sign anything!'

'But sir, these windows will enhance any room,' Rigby was keen to point out.

'That's immaterial!' the Doctor said, almost frantic. 'Can't you understand? What would I want with a window? I mean, I can't have people hacking great holes in the walls of the TARDIS, now can I? Come along, please, it's time you were leaving.'

He bundled Rigby towards the door. The orange glow began to dissipate.

'But I haven't told you about our excellent credit facilities,' Rigby babbled.

'Not today, thank you,' said the Doctor.

'The guarantee!' Rigby said. 'Did I mention the guarantee?'

'Thank you for calling. Bye-bye.' The Doctor gave him a final shove and pushed him through the luminescent shield and back into the void. The doors closed behind him and the Doctor then fell back against them, drew his silk handkerchief from his top pocket and used it to wipe the back of his neck.

'Good heavens,' he said with a relieved smile. 'Those fellows are remarkably persistent, aren't they?'

Zoe was utterly perplexed. 'What was all that about, Doctor?' she asked. 'Was that man one of the "phantoms" that you were talking about?'

'What, him?' said the Doctor, pointing to the closed door. He stuffed his handkerchief untidily back into his pocket. 'No, he was just a double-glazing salesman, Zoe.'

'Aye, well, what is this double-glazing stuff anyway?' Jamie asked. 'In that wee book of his they just looked like ordinary windows to me.'

'It really doesn't matter,' the Doctor insisted. 'After all, he's gone now.'

'Aye,' Jamie said. 'But he's left this.' He reached down to retrieve Rigby's umbrella, which must have fallen to the floor as the Doctor had bundled him out.

'Oh no,' the Doctor said. 'Oh well,' he added, 'he'll just have to make do without it, won't he? Put it in the cupboard.'

The Doctor pointed to the small equipment locker that stood on one side of the console room. Jamie crossed over, bent down to open it then quickly took a pace back. A long, agile leg protruded horizontally from its interior; a polished shoe twisting this way and that, snake-like, as it searched for the floor. Rigby emerged sideways like a limbo dancer, heaved himself upright and plucked the umbrella from Jamie's startled grasp.

'Thank you very much,' the salesman said with a smile. 'I was wondering where I'd left it.'

'I thought we'd already asked you to leave!' the Doctor blustered angrily.

'You did, you did,' Rigby said. 'But then it suddenly occurred to me that you might not fully understand exactly what it is that I'm offering.'

'We understand perfectly, Mr. Rigby,' the Doctor replied bluntly. 'It is you who seems unable to grasp the fact that we simply *don't want any windows*!'

'But sir, I'm not selling windows,' Rigby said. 'I'm selling *dreams*!'

'And, frankly, I'm unimpressed with your overblown sales pitch,' said the Doctor.

'You see, I'm selling the whole package.'

'We're not interested.'

'It's all included: installation…'

'We don't want any.'

'A full lifetime guarantee…'

'They are of no use to us.'

'The view of your choice…'

'I tell you,' the Doctor said, 'you are wasting your –'

'Wait a minute, Doctor,' Zoe interrupted him. She turned to Rigby. '*What* did you just say?'

Rigby looked momentarily surprised. 'Your choice of view?' Rigby ventured.

'View?' snapped the Doctor. 'What's that all about, then? What do you mean by view?'

'Exactly that, sir,' Rigby said. 'You can choose whatever outlook you wish your window to have… Did I not mention this earlier?'

'No,' the Doctor replied. 'No, you did not.'

'When you say view,' Jamie quizzed him, 'you mean, like a picture, yes?'

'No, I mean the actual view itself,' Rigby enthused. 'You can look through your window and see, for instance, the Virgo Mountains on the planet Mitak. You can watch them from sunset to sunrise. Watch the birds wheel between the peaks in summer. See the first snows of winter settle and soften those lofty, jagged crags.'

'Extraordinary,' said the Doctor, visibly softening. 'And are there many different views to choose from?'

'Every view is tailored to each client's individual specification,' Rigby explained, a smile lifting his moustache.

'Och, can ye no' imagine that, Doctor?' Jamie enthused. 'Think about it, you could look out of the window any time you like and see Culloden Moor awash with heather.'

'Or we could look out over my home city!' Zoe said. 'We could watch as people went about their business in the street below. See the hovercars on the highway. Oh, Doctor, wouldn't that be marvellous?'

'Yes, Zoe,' the Doctor said in a rather noncommittal way. 'I suppose it probably would.'

'Yes,' said Rigby, 'think of the luxury of being able to look out of your easy-to-clean, mock-Georgian style uPVC bay window any time of the day or night and see the view of your choice – confident in the knowledge that the frame is guaranteed against corrosion, water damage and certain categories of terrorist assault. But anyway, you've made your position clear. I think I've wasted quite enough of your time as it is. Thank you very much for your hospitality.'

He crouched down and started to climb back into the locker.

'Wait! Wait!' the Doctor cried. He dashed forward to stop him, then stood rubbing his hands together apologetically and looking rather sorry for himself. 'Perhaps I've been a little harsh on you. You know, I really would be terribly grateful if you could tell me more about these windows of yours...'

II

Whenever Ace got really bored she would lose herself in the corridors of the TARDIS; just take off in some random direction to see where she would end up. Rarely did she take the same route twice, and more often than not she managed to discover some previously unexplored area of the Doctor's machine – places that she suspected the Doctor himself had long since forgotten.

For the past twenty minutes she had been investigating a network of poky little passageways, slightly narrower than those in the rest of the ship and with numerous twisting intersections that had Ace thoroughly convinced she had been traipsing around in circles. Then, just when she was beginning to think that she would be lost in this maze for ever, the corridor brought her to a door: tall and white with a single, translucent roundel at the top. A door, in fact, just like any other in the TARDIS, except for the rather incongruous addition of a thick iron plate inexpertly riveted to its surface, overlapping the frame. A thick metal hoop fixed to the wall passed through a slot in the iron plate and was secured by a padlock, keeping the door firmly closed.

Or at least, it would have kept it closed had Ace not been around.

Getting into places where she wasn't meant to be was second nature to her. She viewed a locked door as an open invitation.

She stood up on tiptoe to peer through the treacle-coloured window, but the room beyond was in darkness. She concentrated on the padlock, rattling it impatiently. It was too large to pick, she decided, but it wasn't going to be a problem. She reached inside her jacket, rifled through the folds of the lining and produced a short, stubby jemmy.

'Be prepared,' she muttered. 'That's my motto.'

She wedged the jemmy behind the lock and tried to lever the whole thing away from the door, but its ramshackle appearance was deceptive, and the metal plate barely moved. Annoyed, Ace clamped her teeth together and gave it a short, sharp tug. This time she felt it give slightly. On the third attempt it came away completely and she stumbled backwards as the padlock skittered across the floor and came to a rest at the Doctor's feet.

He bent down and picked it up, then fixed Ace with a grim scowl.

'All right, Professor,' Ace said in embarrassment. 'I didn't see you there.'

'No,' the Doctor replied curtly. 'Evidently.'

'I was just –'

'I could see what you were just doing,' the Doctor pre-empted her. He turned the twisted padlock over in his hands. 'Useful things, locks,' he mused, his voice soft. 'So many uses: keeping things in, keeping people out.' He looked up pointedly at Ace.

'I just wanted to see what was inside,' Ace responded. It wasn't much of an excuse but it was all she could come up with at the time.

'Did it not occur to you to ask?'

'Why, would you have told me?' Ace asked, her mood brightening momentarily.

'No,' the Doctor replied, wiping the smile from her face. 'You know, Ace, you've got a lot to learn about respect – for other people's privacy, for other people's property.'

Ace looked at the door, then at the Doctor. It was rare that she saw him angry. Rarer still that he was ever angry with her. She nervously shifted her weight from one leg to the other. The Doctor was the only person she knew who was able to make her feel guilty.

'It's just...' she began with an uncomfortable shrug. 'Well, I didn't think we had any secrets from one another.'

She waited for the Doctor to offer a reply; to deliver some kind of an explanation, but the Time Lord just stood and looked at her in silence.

Ace couldn't let the matter drop. 'What have you got in there, Professor?' she pressed him. 'There aren't any skeletons in your cupboard, are there?' She tried to lighten the mood. 'I've got it! It's your portrait, right? It keeps getting older and older while you –'

She saw he wasn't smiling and her words tailed off into thin air.

'Nothing,' the Doctor said, quietly. 'There's nothing in there. Nothing that will mean anything to you Ace. Why don't you go back to the console room. We'll be landing soon.'

'Yeah,' Ace said. 'Yeah, OK then, Professor.' She started to go. 'I'm sorry,' she added in a small voice. 'I was way out of line.'

The Doctor shook his head, offered a hand that suggested everything was all right now. 'I'll join you shortly,' he said.

Ace nodded and left him. The Doctor waited until she had gone, then turned his attention to the door. He placed his hand against it and paused, struggling to make a decision. Then he gently pushed it open.

It had been a long time since the Doctor had come here, and the air was stale and musty. The room was about twice as wide as it was long and in keeping with the architecture of the rest of the TARDIS the walls were dappled with the familiar pattern of circular indentations. There was nothing in here – the only feature was a large mock-Georgian bay window in the wall opposite the door, starkly out of place.

The Doctor walked slowly towards it. Beyond the diaphanous ghost of his reflection, the landscape outside was in twilight. The dark silhouettes of overarching branches framed his view as he looked out across the valley to the grassy slopes where he had played as a boy.

He used to visit this room often. He would stand and delight in his reminiscences of home. When autumn came he saw the trees shed their leaves, carpeting the ground in a patchwork of purple and amber and brown, and he could almost smell the smoky air. It was then that he had realised that it was no longer enough to just come here and watch: he wanted to be there, to take a walk up the slope, the dew-soaked grass brushing his feet. He wanted to climb to the top and sit and watch the river hiss and bubble as it snaked along the valley floor. But it was impossible, and he knew it, so he had padlocked the door and hadn't set foot inside since.

Until now. But things were different now, weren't they? He was no longer a fugitive. There was nothing to stop him going back now. He had simply to key in the co-ordinates for Gallifrey; the TARDIS knew its own way home. But what was the point? The window could show the place, but it was showing it to the man – the old, old man – not the child who had belonged there.

The Doctor reached out and touched his fingertips to the glass. It was cold and slightly damp with condensation. He had considered trying to smash it in the past, but he knew that would be pointless. It had a lifetime guarantee.

He was still clutching the broken padlock and he looked down at it thoughtfully. He had more elaborate equipment in his workshop that was capable of sealing this room permanently. It was time he did the job properly, he thought, so he set off to fetch it.

Good Companions

by Peter Anghelides

THIS STORY FIRST APPEARED IN THE COLLECTION *WOMANUSCRIPTS: 21ST CENTURY FEMALE FICTION* (LONDON, 2041).

I thought they were friends when I first saw them – 'good companions', as as my aunt used to say. The crumpled man stood close beside the woman's seat, with one hand placed on the shoulder of her pale-yellow dress. Her dark hair sprayed over the headrest, and the way she looked at me reminded me of William's Exeter first-years, their eyes appraising me throughout the previous day's university service. But today, I could hold this woman's gaze. I could make the kind of brief human contact that had escaped me for so many years. Just how William had taught me, after I'd left Shawlands. After I'd returned to the world.

The crumpled man called her Anna. As the carriage rocked to and fro, he stared out into the rain which drove against the window. I listened more carefully, picked out the sound of his voice from the soft hiss of the rain and the rattle-and-thump of the track. He was giving her detailed, almost pedantic instructions about preparing his house for his return the following day. Eventually he plucked a fob watch from his mustard-yellow knitted waistcoat, gave a little sigh, and moved off down the corridor in my direction.

I looked away, embarrassed that I might be caught spying on them. I studied my rail ticket intently, as though I'd never seen one before. But as he moved past, and although my legs were both beneath the table, he trod on my foot.

'My dear madam, I am too clumsy.' He peered down from his stooped height, examining my bruised instep. 'How can I make amends?'

A decade of apologising for William's gawkiness had drained me of any accusation. I couldn't meet this tall stranger's gaze, my eyes darting around in panic. 'No, no,' I could hear myself mumbling.

'It's… that is…' I found myself strangely, unexpectedly fascinated by the thinning patch of tweed at his cuffs where the material of his jacket was worn through to the lining. Over his arm was a clumsily folded afghan coat, which smelled faintly of patchouli. He wore two thin bracelets around one wrist. Pinned to his grubby lapel was a battered oval brooch, and clutched in its scratched gold was a flawless stone, as smooth and blue as a starling's egg. The golden clasp seemed to be slightly squashed, the filigree of interwoven leaves blurred a little, almost melted.

'Ah, yes,' said the man, unclasping the brooch. 'Of course, I should have offered first.' His pale green eyes held me as he gazed through his ragged ginger fringe.

'Oh no,' I said, embarrassed and confused by his strange offer.

He took my left hand. The gold of the brooch felt warm in my palm when he folded my fingers over it. 'I insist.'

I'd hardly realised the train had stopped at Bidbridge. Within moments, I could see the untidy man running across the rainswept platform, dragging the afghan over his shoulders.

'Is your foot OK?' The dark-haired woman had moved down the carriage to sit opposite me. She peered at the mark on my stockinged foot. 'Sorry about him. His mind is always elsewhere. Some other place, some other time. My name's Anna, by the way.' After thirty years in England, I still struggled with accents – hers was northern, Manchester perhaps, or Yorkshire.

I shook her outstretched hand and introduced myself, worried that my hesitation implied indifference.

'Haybourne?' she said. 'Sounds very English. But your accent suggests… New Zealand?'

'Australia. But I've lived here so long I've gone native.'

'Sorry,' said Anna, with a frown of embarrassment. 'And sorry about your foot, too.'

'No worries,' I said. 'It's fine. I'm sure it was an accident.'

Anna said: 'Usually is, with the doctor.'

I suppose I must have dropped the brooch, because it clattered across the formica table-top. 'The Doctor?' I breathed.

Anna had a slightly panicked look. 'Dr Smith,' she said. 'I should have explained, Mrs Haybourne, I'm...' She passed the brooch back. 'I'm his London housekeeper.'

'Where has he gone?'

She thought for a moment. 'Business, he told me.' There was another awkward pause, after which she said, 'I like your dress. Are you going somewhere special?'

I fastened Dr Smith's brooch to the cool black material. 'I haven't changed since the funeral. My husband,' I added, as though it had just occurred to me.

I saw the embarrassed frown again. 'This muffled sound you hear, Mrs Haybourne, is because I'm talking with my mouth full of foot.'

'Spit out those toes,' I said, trying out my first smile of the day. 'And stop calling me Mrs Haybourne. You sound like that crowd of stiffs I just left back in Exeter. Call me Tegan.'

'Womanuscripts,' *said the Doctor. He studied the white and red lettering on the book's black spine.* 'So, what am I supposed to be looking at?'

'"Good Companions", *by Tegan Haybourne. I found it by accident when I was looking in the library for something else. This would have been useful a few weeks ago.' She threw her chin out accusingly.* 'Did you know it was there, Doctor?'

He propped the book on the central console, where it promptly fell down against a row of brass switch-hooks. A klaxon sounded deep in the TARDIS, and a pair of marquetry shutters closed across the main entrance. He clucked with irritation and flicked the switch-hooks back with a brusque movement.

His companion jumped as the shutters rattled and vanished again. 'Doctor, if you had that book all along...'

'Why, what does it say?'

She realised she didn't know. By the time she'd thought of a suitably cutting reply, the Doctor had loped out of the console room.

Anna found her page, and continued reading.

William had worked in Exeter for more than a decade, but I'd known few of his colleagues. I hadn't even known the vicar at the funeral service. In the staff club afterwards, the only person I'd recognised was the department secretary, and that was only from her phone messages:

'Dr Haybourne sends his apologies, but he will be delayed again this evening.'

'Sorry to disturb your weekend, could Dr Haybourne spare an hour or two for Head of Department?'

'Dr Haybourne fell ill during one of his lectures, and has been taken to the General Hospital by ambulance.'

And yet, although I'd never met Anna before, I could talk to her as though I'd known her my whole life. I could tell her how I feared returning to Cambridge after William's death. How I dreaded the lonely house awaiting me there, the house we had only just bought after William's appointment to the new chair at St Cedd's. The house which now would never be our home.

We also talked about what we liked: the theatre and art galleries. I told her about my painting, my writing class and the stories I'd published; I didn't tell her how my newly discovered creativity had developed from my therapy, from my time in Shawlands. Instead, we talked about our shared dislikes: south coast weather, airport paperbacks, and what had happened to the railways since re-nationalisation.

'I have to go by train,' I said. 'Old biddies like me have no choice, now that any boy racer can fling a ton of metal down the motorway like a rat down a pipe and call it "driving".'

We were standing on King's Cross station, trying to read the main display board to locate my connecting train up to Cambridge. The monsoon rain continued to rattle down on the arched roof high above us.

'How old is Dr Smith?' I asked. 'He can't be much older than you. And you can't be more than... forty?'

'Looks can be deceptive,' Anna said. 'I still can't believe you're – how old did you say, seventy-three?' She pointed to the Departures board. 'Cambridge train's cancelled,' she observed. 'Well, you can't stay here. Come on back to the... house with me.' She had picked up my small case, and was already moving off towards the taxis.

I hurried after her. 'Shouldn't we consult Dr Smith?'

'No need, we've got room to spare,' she grinned. An electric taxi sprayed to a stop at the kerb. 'You'd swear the place couldn't possibly contain so many rooms.'

London seemed busier than ever. Even in the driving rain, more buses loomed, more brash car horns sounded, more angry pedestrians scurried between the traffic than I had remembered. Our surly taxi driver barely grunted throughout the whole journey, so I wasn't too sorry that Anna refused to let me pay the fare.

As the taxi rattled away, we scurried into the shelter of a huge forked elm, which rose slightly crooked from a square of earth, the pavement around it raised and cracked by the tree's roots. The late summer evening's light was fading. I peered past a nearby crumbling archway, and could see a substantial Edwardian town house through the rain. Its windows were dark, and its red brick was coldly illuminated by the sagging, saffron-yellow half-moon. We ran through the arch, and into the shelter of the house.

To my surprise, the hallway was already illuminated by a weighty chandelier. The large square room was bordered by heavy, dark oak furniture. A broad flight of stairs, bordered by banisters with turned wooden spindles, rose to the first floor.

Anna eased me out of my overcoat, hung it on a hatstand and ushered me into a long, cavernous library with shelves twice my height. There were lit candles all around, on tables, on the mantelpiece, on the heavy dark sideboard by the tall windows.

At the end of the room were two carved oak doors. Anna had stopped in front of these. 'Tegan, I have to check some things. Get yourself warm by the fire.' She pushed lightly on one door, and it swung easily ajar with a low creak. She slipped through swiftly, and the door closed behind her.

I approached the oak doors, wondering if I should follow Anna. I tried the handle, but the door remained firmly closed. I hadn't heard her lock it behind her.

I looked into the grate. Orange flames danced in an odd, regular movement above the glowing coals. I wondered who had made the fire before we returned, who had lit the candles. The owner, perhaps? But he had left the train ahead of us, and the hall hatstand had been empty.

The room was in a chaos of scattered papers, forgotten piles of books, and furniture in random positions. At awkward angles by the window were several busts, each of the same person – an old man with a bushy beard and a severe expression, so that he looked like a grumpy Father Christmas. Only the library shelves showed any sign of order, each book butted tidily to the edge. I chose a book at random, and the spine read: Sir Richard Steele, *The Funeral*. When I picked out the next title along, I was disappointed to discover that the library was not organised at all – this second book was Walt Whitman, *Leaves of Grass*. I lifted a pile of loose papers from a nearby chair, dusted the seat cushion, and sat down to leaf through the slim volume.

I could remember first reading Whitman when I was a schoolgirl. My favourite had been 'Out of the Cradle Endlessly Rocking'. What was it my teacher had said about the poem? Something about bird-song. Strange that I could remember some things so clearly, yet other parts of my life were an unread chapter to me. My Aunt Vanessa used to joke that she could remember every gift she received for her twenty-first birthday, but not what she'd had for breakfast that day. Strange that I could remember that about her too, but not when I had last seen her. That must have been when I was twenty-one. Half a century ago.

A clock rang distantly from the next room but, when I checked my watch, I noticed that the chimes were wrong. A pair of finger-cymbals lay on the table and I tapped them together experimentally. Their tinkling sound softly filled the large, still room. I breathed in, half-expecting the dust to catch in my nose, but recognised instead a background smell, the heavy perfume of patchouli.

The Doctor?

No, I was still alone in the room. Why had I thought the untidy man on the train might be him? The Doctor, the man I had invented more than four decades ago. Before I was married. Before Shawlands, of course. Too much of my earlier life read to me like a poor transcription, passages unclear, pages torn or missing. In Smith's library now, I closed my eyes and tried to recall my fictional Doctor. He would have to be my age now, wouldn't he? I imagined his long blond hair turned grey, his young face lined, his blue eyes rheumy and faded.

I started to imagine how the mess around me could simply echo the creative disorder of the Doctor's work, that perhaps he'd need this scattered array of objects around him to feel comfortable doing... doing whatever he did. What was that, I wondered. What *had* it been? Why was I starting to believe that Smith could be my Doctor reincarnated? My fiction made flesh.

I carried the slim Whitman volume back to my table and sat down again. Across the table, I spotted a small pile of mail. One envelope had already been opened, and I discovered that it contained a handbill for a play, illustrated with what looked like a stylised wheelchair. The other correspondence was unopened. I slipped a perished rubber band from around it, and counted seven handwritten envelopes, each with a different value of stamp. Some of the frankings were blurred, but at least two were more than a year old. Another had next year's date misprinted on it. They were all addressed to 'Dr J. Smith'. The oak door creaked open, and I leapt up like a guilty schoolgirl. Anna had returned, and I was still holding the letters. 'I... was reading while waiting, and found these on the table.'

Anna closed the door behind her and came to take the letters from me. 'I'm afraid I haven't been here for several weeks, so the place has rather gone to seed. Are your shoes dry yet?'

I looked at my feet, surprised to find no evidence of the earlier downpour. 'Nice warm fire,' I said aloud. 'Did Dr Smith light it before we returned?'

Anna shook her head, but smiled at me as though she had a secret. 'I never know *when* he'll be here. Recently, I don't think he's known either. Business,' she added.

'He reminds me of some character from long ago. He was a doctor too. What business is Dr Smith in?'

'Risk management.' Anna shuffled across to stand in front of the fire, and arranged the small pile of letters on the mantelpiece. 'I'll show you to your room, Tegan. And then, perhaps we can go out. The weather seems to be lifting at last.'

Since the rain had eased off, we decided to walk. Anna had changed her yellow dress for a cream blouse with a wide collar, and a dark suit. She explained that Dr Smith knew I was interested in the theatre and had suggested we go to a nearby venue to see a play by a visiting company. It was only later that I realised this meant she had spoken to Smith since we had arrived at the house.

We walked through wet side roads, staying on pavements well lit by orange streetlamps or by the yellow moon. Anna walked slowly, to allow my old legs to keep up with her, and we were careful not to get too close to the fluttering of the spray from passing hover vehicles.

'He particularly recommended this production,' Anna explained. 'It's described as "an intimate theatrical venue". I think that means "small".'

'Does Dr Smith work in the theatre?'

'Not that I've noticed,' said Anna. 'Though he claims some involvement in a couple of Shakespearean productions.'

Our destination, I soon discovered, was the Loft Theatre, where a visiting group called 'The Sigrarnon Troupe' were performing one of their own pieces, 'New Tenants'. It was only when I saw the small poster pasted on a nearby lamppost that I recognised the same stylised wheelchair design from the handbill in Dr Smith's library. I wondered why, if he'd received a personal invitation, he hadn't come along this evening.

The Loft Theatre was appropriately named, because it turned out to be a long attic room above a large pub. At the far end was a stage area, curtained off from several straggling rows of plastic chairs. Apart from Anna and me, there were only three people in the audience. The sounds of the pub filtered up through the patched grey linoleum, a low hum of noise and the occasional shout of laughter.

Ten minutes later than advertised, the stage lights came up. Within minutes there were more people on stage than in the audience.

I struggled to understand the play. Its tone was decidedly pessimistic. The dialogue was largely pointless, and the plot mostly irrational. The cast of six whirled and danced about the stage and, as each scene progressed, each character ended up in a wheelchair, chittering away to the others in high-pitched gibberish. Eventually, only the tall lead actor was unaffected, surrounded by the chair-bound figures.

There was a dream-like quality to the performance until, with a dramatic lighting change, the mood changed to nightmare. The circling figures became more mechanical, more robotic, except for their faces, which stayed human, although distorted, leering, awful.

'I think it's Absurd,' I whispered to Anna.

'It's worse than that,' she replied.

'No, I mean Theatre of the Absurd. It reminds me of a play we studied at school. Our teacher said it was once an off-Broadway production.'

'Any good?'

'No, it stank. We told him it was a "gone-off Broadway" show. He gave us all Ds, I think.'

In the corner of the stage, a figure – until then unseen – slowly grew and grew, chirruping away meaninglessly to the wheelchair figures. In a bizarre conclusion, this figure's distended body expanded wildly like a rapidly inflating balloon, shooting the actor's bloated red face up into the rafters. The chair-bound characters closed in on the lead actor as the stage was plunged into darkness.

When the house lights went up, the actors were standing on top of the empty front row of seats, hands linked, bowing solemnly. We applauded in embarrassment.

The three other audience members collected their possessions and swiftly left the room, clattering down the steps at the rear. Anna was helping me to my feet when I heard a voice from the stage area.

'Thanks for coming,' said the lead actor. 'Perhaps we can buy you both a drink?'

* * *

We took a large table at the rear of the downstairs bar, away from a noisy crowd of customers who were partying hard. Anna ordered several bottles of Beaujolais. It was headier than I'd expected.

The lead actor was a strikingly good-looking young man of about thirty. His mates, three men and two women, seemed to be the same age. The low lighting of the pub made it difficult to be sure, but I got the impression they could all be related; all had the same healthy tan and mousy brown hair – even similar body language, from the way they handled their glasses to their unnervingly bold gaze.

At first, Anna had thought it very amusing that the audience were entertaining the cast. After only a few minutes, however, her manner changed. I could sense this more than I could understand it. Maybe it was the way she nervously fingered the collar of her blouse, like she was searching for something that wasn't there. Or maybe it was the way I felt excluded from her conversation with the actors, just like the times when William had talked university politics with his academic colleagues, speaking English but using words that made as little sense to me as the dialogue in the play.

Right in the middle of something the lead actor was saying, Anna blurted out: 'I think we have to be going now.'

'So soon?' said the actor. 'Not quite what you were expecting?'

Anna stood up, tugging on her smart jacket. 'A bit sooner than I thought. Excuse us.'

Two of the women had also got up. 'We thought we'd surprise you,' said the nearest, and I recognised her face – she had played the character who had ballooned up at the end of the show.

'You know we need you,' said the lead actor.

Anna nodded towards the crowded main section of the pub. 'We're going to walk out now, through all these people.'

'We'll meet again,' said the actor. He lifted his head, and inhaled sharply through his nose, as though he were breathing sea air instead of the smoky atmosphere of a London pub. 'We sense your temporal trail. Its odour clings to you.'

The other actors were sniffing too. 'Like the stench of decay,' said one of the women in a soft voice.

Now I had got up too. 'Charmed, I'm sure,' I said.

The actors stared at me. I could feel my face flushing, my heart racing, a cocktail of adrenalin and Beaujolais. I saw now what was so disconcerting about their gaze. When someone talks to you, you can usually see their eyes flicking backwards and forward, looking at each of your eyes in turn; these actors gazed straight at you, their eyes unmoving.

I pulled my coat around my shoulders, shivering despite the warmth of the pub. 'My friend's right, we've got to go. Thanks for a night to forget.'

We pushed past the women, through the boisterous partygoers in the other bar, and out on to the wet pavement. The cold night air stung my cheeks.

Anna went off at a brisk pace, fumbling in her bag as she strode away. When I'd caught up at the first corner, she brought out an old-fashioned key.

'Front door key,' she said. 'You'll need it to get in.'

'What about you?'

'I'll use the back. They're bound to follow me.'

I held her arm. 'Are you worried about that weird guy? He was hitting on you, I guess.'

'More than you can imagine,' Anna said.

'Well, "Not quite what you were expecting" isn't much of a pick-up line.' I gave a little laugh. 'And I didn't fancy mine much.'

She didn't smile back. 'Go on ahead. I'll let them follow me.'

'No! We should stay together. If those creeps are after you, we should get help.'

Anna pushed me forward with a small, urgent motion. 'I don't think so. Go on!' She turned, crossed the street, and walked smartly away.

I admit, I panicked for a moment. My mind whirled through the possibilities: Anna running off and abandoning me in a strange part of London; me wandering lost in unfamiliar streets; the threat of rain and darkness and the unknown.

Then a cloud moved, and I saw the swollen yellow half-moon, and I suddenly knew this road after all, this low brick wall, that next junction. There was the forked elm, leaning drunkenly in the pavement beneath the streetlight.

The lights were on again when I slipped into the hallway. I thought about bolting the door, hesitating in case this meant Smith would be locked out too. My temptation to explore the empty house was balanced by my fear that Anna would spot me if she returned home quickly. I decided to go into the library, anyway. A figure glared at me from the window and I stifled a cry. It was just one of the busts of the bearded man, oddly illuminated by the sputtering candles. At the end of the room, the carved oak doors were closed. I tried the handles, but neither door would open. I couldn't see a lock, or any light from the room beyond.

So I went back to the library table, threading my way between the clutter of furniture and other objects, and sat down. As soon as I did, my whole body eased and relaxed, as though it had only just discovered how tired it felt. The Whitman volume was on the table in front of me. I settled into the comfortable chair and read for a while, but I was soon asleep.

I was in a cold room, its expanse of dusty concrete floor littered with metal fragments and bullet casings scattered between the support pillars. Two figures stood by a tall opening in the far wall, a loading bay doorway leading out to the street. The figures had their backs to me, awkwardly angled, still as statues, staring out over Docklands. One wore a beige coat, his long blond hair touching the collar. The other wore a dark suit, and had short-cut grey hair. The two were talking, but I couldn't make out their words.

The figure with the beige coat placed his hand on the shoulder of his companion with the dark suit, a parting gesture, a sign of solidarity. Then he stepped towards the loading bay, and out into the night. Far away, Big Ben was starting to chime the hour: one, two, three…

The dark suit turned round, and I saw it was William. He drew me to him, held me close, whispered to me. 'I'm tired,' he said.

'Don't go,' I said. 'I miss you. I miss you so much. Why is it the good people who have to die?'

'A lot of good people die every day.' He straightened, as though preparing to go.

'Don't leave,' I said, my heart racing suddenly. 'Not like this.'

'I must, I'm sorry.'

I held him so that I could see his pale blue eyes one more time. They were rheumy and faded. 'Brave heart,' he said.

Before he walked away, he smiled his unique smile.

Beyond the warehouse, Big Ben chimed thirteen.

A clock was chiming somewhere in the house beyond the open door. Anna was peering at me where I sat, slumped in my chair. 'Are you OK, Tegan?'

'I guess,' I said. 'Are you...?'

She was fiddling with something on the collar of her blouse, adjusting it. 'I'm OK now,' she said. 'But *you* look whacked. Come on, you'll be more comfortable in your own room.'

I agreed, and was making my way to the stairs when I realised what Anna had been doing with her collar. She had been pinning a distinctive gold brooch to it, a gold brooch with a single opalescent blue stone in the centre. It looked new, as though she had just polished it.

'Hey! That's mine,' I said.

Anna ushered me towards the stairs. 'No, it belongs to me. It was... a gift from the Doctor.'

I shook her off gently. 'No way, it's mine. He gave it to me. On the train. He gave it to me.' The more I said it, the more I felt my face flushing. Perhaps it was because I was tired, or maybe it was the wine, but I felt my temper flaring.

'Up you go,' said Anna quietly, insistently.

I reached out for the brooch. 'D'you mind?'

'No!' shouted Anna, stepping back. 'I have to have it.'

'Keep the damn thing,' I retorted. 'If you'd wanted it earlier, you could've just asked.' I hitched up my skirt, and hobbled up the stairs as fast as I could manage, angry words choking in my throat.

I slammed my bedroom door, and sat trembling for several minutes on the edge of my bed. I went over things in my mind, hardly able to believe the change in Anna. She'd sounded like a kid refusing to share one of its toys.

My breathing got steadier after my dash up the staircase, though I could feel a headache beginning. I washed my face and hands in the sink. While the dirty water swirled down the plughole, I slipped on my night-dress, leaving the neck buttons unfastened as usual.

I stood before the mirror in the vanity unit and studied my troubled reflection. My hair was long and tangled, so I combed it through, left side and then right side, just as my mum had taught me. Back then my hair had been curled and strong, and red as a sunrise. At sixty, I'd allowed the colour to grow out, so now it was grey as a winter's day, as grey as my mum's had been when I was a child. There were strange tears on my cheeks now, the first time I had cried since before the funeral.

While searching for a tissue in my pile of clothing, I saw something shining on my folded black dress. It was the brooch that Smith had given me. Anna hadn't stolen it; hers was different, newer, not as scuffed as mine. Perhaps they'd once been a pair.

I knew at once that I had to go and apologise. I unpinned the brooch and walked out of the room.

The moon was visible through a high casement window and threw odd shadows across the upper landing. I could hear noises at the front door, a clattering sound like someone was coming in, though I couldn't see whether it was just Anna locking up. If Smith was returning, I decided, I'd save my apology for the next day. I stole across the polished floorboards of the landing in my bare feet, gliding, silent, avoiding the moonbeams, blending myself with the shadows. The clattering sound downstairs became a crash, and the front door burst open.

It was the Sigrarnon lead actor, filling the door frame. He swooped into the hallway. Anna had rushed to see what was happening, but now fell back again into the library, trying to slam that door in his face. Then the other actors swarmed in behind their leader, and Anna could no longer hold them back.

My pulse thumped in my head as I crept barefoot down the staircase. Through the wooden banisters, I could see the actors pushing aside furniture, overturning objects and spilling candlewax as they pursued Anna. I risked a look through the angle of the library door.

Five of the actors had surrounded Anna, chanting at her in a mysterious tongue. The sixth Sigrarnon, a woman, stood in the corner of the room, near to the locked oak doors.

And then their bodies started to change. Their movements became more mechanical, almost robotic, and their limbs seemed to harden in the room's dim light. Their faces were transforming too, becoming twisted parodies of humanity, the features smeared, distorted, horrible.

The sixth Sigrarnon had raised her face to the ceiling, her neck pushed back almost at a right angle to her chest. At first, it seemed as though she was moving closer, but then I saw that she was growing larger, filling the corner of the room like an expanding balloon. Her twisted face was beatific, like an unholy medium channelling the other world, her voice crying out in a throbbing, exalting shriek.

I choked back my own wail of fear and horror. The other actors had taken up the repulsive chorus, their stiff limbs reaching out towards Anna. But she stood, her eyes closed, her face serene, clutching a small golden object between her outstretched fingers.

It was the brooch, its blue stone shining with an ethereal light. An impossible sound issued from it and the air around her began to shimmer, distort.

'Anna!' I called to her, powerless.

All the Sigrarnons turned to face me. Even the huge bloated creature in the corner snapped its gaze towards me, and my whole body froze like ice. They barely broke the tone of their howling chant, but I felt it directed now against me. I struggled to bring my arms up to my throbbing head and was almost blinded by something.

It was my own brooch, glowing like a light bulb in my hand, except that there was no heat, no burning sensation. I stepped into the library. My brooch flickered along with Anna's, emitting a low, booming vibration quite incongruous with its size. Anna's brooch sounded back. A thousand warbling echoes filled the tall room and the Sigrarnon chant faltered.

Anna had opened her eyes now and her whole face was alive with a huge smile.

There was a monstrous sucking sound from the corner of the room. The huge Sigrarnon obscenity had folded in on itself, the head tumbling into its distended stomach mass. The air around the other Sigrarnons seemed to swim, like a heat haze on a summer road. Then the Sigrarnons all gave a shrieking wail of despair and swirled into nothing like dirty water down a plughole.

With a resounding crack, the brooch in my hand shattered into a thousand pieces. The lights went out, my headache boomed and boomed in my skull, and I fainted dead away.

Anna read out a few paragraphs to the Doctor. He seemed to be half-listening. 'So, where were you hiding, then?' she asked him.

'The Sigrarnons create short cuts in the cycles of time. I couldn't let them meet me – that's what they wanted, what they needed. And I couldn't let you tell Tegan what was really happening, she would have messed things up dreadfully.'

'So you knew. You must have read this book.'

'No, it couldn't exist until we returned to the TARDIS.'

Anna shook her head. 'That's a paradox.'

He seized her arm, and the bracelets around his wrist tinkled gently. 'The Sigrarnons trade in paradox. To them it's just an act, a performance – why do you think they rehearsed their attack right in front of you in the theatre? They thought it was amusing, that's why. What havoc they could wreak if they ever had access to a Time Lord, or Time Lord technology.' He gestured at the shelving above them. 'Why, they'd even try to use this virtual library as a weapon, if they could.'

'This what?'

The Doctor tapped meaningfully on the open pages with his forefinger.

I woke to the sound of Anna calling through my bedroom door. 'I've started making breakfast, Tegan. Will you come down?'

I stared about the room, with that odd, disorienting feeling that you get when you wake up in a strange bed. Fierce morning sun burned through the brightly patterned curtains, dispersing the gloom of the previous evening. I sat up and reached for my watch: 08:15.

'I'll be there in twenty minutes.' My voice sounded thick.

'OK. We'll be in the kitchen.'

My clothes were in a tidy pile on a bedside chair, my case still on the stand by the window. I went to the basin in the corner and it slowly filled to the chugging sound of hot-water pipes. When I wiped the steam from the mirror, I saw no sign of the troubled face from yesterday. My night-dress was fastened right up to my neck. I couldn't remember doing up the buttons.

But I remembered the dream. I remembered the strange transformation of the actors, their obscure shapes, the echoes, the sounds and sights of my old woman's imagination. It was as vivid as the curtains in my room now, but in the stark light of morning I could believe it had all been an illusion.

In the kitchen, Anna was serving the breakfast, mounds of hot porridge ladled from a stout copper saucepan into large white china bowls. A cafetière of thick black coffee stood in the centre of the scrubbed pine table. On the far side sat Smith, brandishing a buttery knife and a clutch of mail in one hand, and an opened letter in the other. They were the envelopes I had seen in the library yesterday.

'Good morning,' said Anna, placing a steaming bowl before me. 'How was your night? You were fast asleep when I finally got back. I took the long route back, to lose our actor friends.'

'Good morning,' added Smith, without looking up. He set down the letter and brushed crumbs from his knitted waistcoat with the free hand. 'You seem well rested. Pleasant dreams, I trust?'

With this prompt, I decided to tell them the whole of my odd nightmare about the Sigrarnon troupe. I explained that I was a bit embarrassed to mention the argument over the brooch.

Anna laughed, and said she didn't have a brooch like that. 'Besides, how could I be offended by an argument in your dreams? Perhaps it was caused by worrying about your journey back to Cambridge? Or those oddballs with their weird play.'

'Or that Beaujolais at the theatre,' I smiled.

Anna leaned back in her chair and began to secure her long dark hair with a tortoiseshell hairslide. I took a moment to study the kitchen, which was filled with a wild array of antique cooking implements. On a peg behind the kitchen door, Dr Smith's afghan coat hung alongside an almost-shapeless brown felt hat.

I looked at Smith again, considering whether he could be the Doctor. Smith's wild ginger hair looked like he had just slept on it and, after getting up, failed to find his comb. He'd picked up the letter again and was reading the reverse of the page, which was written in a series of strange symbols, possibly Greek.

'What are you a doctor of?' I asked abruptly.

He looked up, apparently amused. 'Are you asking academically, or philosophically? Dear, oh dear, yes, that's it. I'm a Doctor of Philology.'

Anna poured a noisy cup of coffee. 'I've not heard it called that before.'

I finished my porridge and said something about having to catch my train. I went upstairs and packed my case. When I came back down to say goodbye, I found Smith standing in the doorway to the library. He presented his palm towards me and I could see he was holding my brooch.

'You must have dropped this when you returned yesterday evening,' he said.

I thanked him and took it from him. The distinctive scratch across its clasp seemed brighter, less tarnished, more recent. I pinned the brooch back on to my coat.

Smith led me into the library, where he stood silhouetted against a tall window. On the murky glass, I could see shadows of leaves from the trees outside. His red hair licked about his head like flames.

'Perhaps,' came his voice from somewhere in the dark shape, 'you'd like to take a few books to read on your journey.'

I laughed and gestured at the tall bookshelves stretching all around us. 'There are so many to choose from.'

Smith stepped forward so that I could see his smiling face. 'I'm sure you'll find something to your taste, something relevant.' He rubbed his hands together in anticipation. 'Ah, you can't beat walking round a *real* library. On-line computer searches just aren't the same, are they? When you walk around the shelves for yourself, you may not find the book you originally wanted. But you'll find a different one. Maybe it's better. And you'd never have gone looking for it to begin with. You know, librarians have a phrase for that.'

'What, for finding the wrong book?'

'No, for discovering the perfect book that you were *not* looking for. Such books are found close to the one you first wanted, so they call them "good companions".'

I thought about his disorganised library. 'Sounds like an accident.'

'Well, a happy accident, at any rate. Serendipitous. One of my companions taught me about that, many years ago.'

I took the Walt Whitman from the table where I had left it the previous day. 'I've already found what I'd like,' I said politely, '*Leaves of Grass.* It's got this really great poem in it, called "Out of the Cradle Endlessly Rocking".'

'Must be the third edition,' said Smith, taking the book from me and considering it. 'I remember that poem from when I first met Whitman… through his writing, I mean. It's about a man who recalls a boyhood experience, when a mockingbird lost its mate in a storm at sea.'

I remembered now what our teacher had said to us about the poem. 'The memory of the bird's song teaches the man the meaning of death and thus the true vocation of a poet.'

'Which is to celebrate death as merely part of the cycle of birth, life, death and rebirth.' Smith smiled as he held out the book. 'We can't change the past, even if we'd like to. Our past actions determine our future. Our lives yet to come.'

'Once upon a time,' I said, 'I didn't believe in life after death. Since William died, I'm not sure what I want to believe.'

'Perhaps you'd like something a little lighter for your journey.' Smith had reached down a fatter volume from the nearest dusty shelf. Its spine said it was *The Good Companions.* 'What a coincidence, eh? It's a novel by J. B. Priestley. An amusing story about a wandering music-hall troupe. Anna tells me that you enjoy the theatre.'

I thought that his eyes twinkled with wicked amusement.

She found him lolling on a chaise-longue. The library shelves behind him curved away down the wall and vanished into the darkness hundreds of metres away. 'Are you always so generous with your books, Doctor?'

'This isn't a lending library. You don't get a ticket telling you when you have to return your book. You can't reserve a title. The TARDIS is constantly updating the catalogue, reconfiguring the sections. She knows what you've been doing recently, and determines what you'll want to read in the future. It might be a related title, or a suitable subject, or…'

'Quite the school librarian,' said Anna, unconvinced.

'Exactly!' he beamed back at her. 'The library gives you what you want before you know you want it, and all within easy reach. A virtual library, based on the principles of karma and good ergonomics.'

Anna snorted in disbelief. 'My parents wouldn't let me read karmic books.' She looked at him thoughtfully. 'Tegan knew you, didn't she?'

'Is that what she says in the story?'

I followed Smith to the front door, aware once again of the disarray in the house, the haphazard assortment of curiosities on every available surface. I knew I must have longed for some kind of familiarity since William's death, some reliable point from the past to focus on while I was alone. It was obvious now that Smith was not that point. He clearly could not be my Doctor.

Smith carried my case to the front gate through the tangled shrubbery of the garden and loaded it into the taxi beside me. We parted without another word, though he shook my hand solemnly, holding it just too long, almost as though we might never meet again.

I looked through the rear window as we drew away. Smith was standing by the archway, his battered felt hat crammed on to his head and his hands thrust into his pockets. He watched my taxi until we had vanished around the bend.

'Tegan was just one of countless lives I have touched, her planet

just one of many worlds I have… changed. Sometimes I feel that Fate is punishing me in my current incarnation for the consequences of those earlier actions.'

'*Fate?*' grinned Anna. '*Like, you've met him?*'

The Doctor didn't smile back. '*Fate is a constant companion on our journey through the cycles of time, Anna. The wheel has turned so many times for me. I need to know that my next incarnation will be happier, more virtuous, and not a step on the path to evil.*'

'*Eeeevil,*' teased Anna. '*You don't want to bump into him on a dark night.*'

'*I bumped into Tegan on the train, quite by chance,*' said the Doctor softly. '*Shortly before I first met you, Anna.*'

'*But that was years ago.*'

'*Not for Tegan.*'

Anna reopened the book.

Traffic delayed even my short journey to the station. I missed my train and had to wait ninety minutes for the next one. I started to read the Priestley novel as we pulled out of King's Cross, but soon found my mind wandering. Through the filthy glass of the train window, the urban landscape turned into damp green countryside and the rhythm of the track lulled me into a fitful sleep. I dreamed of William.

I could smell a distinctive, heavy fragrance and woke with a jolt. The man opposite looked up apologetically. 'Oh dear, I didn't mean to disturb you, madam.'

It was Smith.

'I recognised your aftershave,' I said.

'Patchouli oil,' he enthused. 'I've just discovered it. A dab on the wrists, a little behind the ears, works wonders. Would like to try some, Miss…?'

'Mrs,' I said, trying to recall if I'd mentioned this to him before. 'Mrs Tegan Haybourne. But you can still call me Tegan, Dr Smith.'

His eyes widened fractionally. 'Of course, Tegan.' He took off his hat and placed it on the table. 'Good to see you.'

The hat seemed to be a newer version of the battered brown felt number he had worn earlier. Wrapped around this one was a saffron-yellow scarf with an ethnic pattern. I noticed that he wore a less crumpled tweed suit too, and there was no afghan coat.

A long silence followed, interrupted only by the sound of the train and a sneeze from the next carriage. I felt that Smith was studying me.

Eventually, I said: 'If I hadn't missed my train, we wouldn't have met again.'

'Again,' said Smith pensively. 'Yes. Quite a coincidence.'

'After we met on Tuesday,' I said, 'Anna and I got to talking, and I thought you could be someone else.'

'Anna,' said Smith. He would not hold my gaze, preferring instead to stare out of the train window.

'Yes, between you and me, Anna's not much of a housekeeper. Is she often away? Your place looked like it needed a thorough spring clean.' He was looking at me blankly now. 'Oh dear, I hope I'm not being rude.'

'No, no,' said Smith, smiling suddenly. 'Who did you think I was?'

'Someone I thought I knew, once. He never really existed. "My impossible adventures with the Doctor", they called them when I was at Shawlands. My vivid daydream imagination. My quack called him my Dream Doctor.' Smith hadn't reacted to this confession. 'This was all around the time my aunt went missing. That's where it had started to go wrong. Or so the quack said.'

'The quack? This was the man you thought I was?'

'No, my quack in Shawlands. Not my Dream Doctor. Besides, that was all a long time ago. He'd have to be very old by now.'

Smith was looking out of the window again, watching the hedgerows flashing by. 'I suppose he would be, this Doctor…?'

'Dunno,' I said. 'But you reminded me of him. Perhaps that's why I had another weird dream last night. About the Sigrarnon troupe.'

He did react to this, leaning forward, his green eyes suddenly staring into mine. 'Tell me about the Sigrarnon troupe. It sounds fascinating.'

So I did – everything from the time I first met him on the train until the moment my taxi pulled away from his Edwardian house. I showed him the brooch, still attached to my overcoat, which was heaped on the seat beside me. He listened politely throughout my story, not interrupting, never taking his eyes off mine.

'This must all sound like the ramblings of a crazy old lady,' I admitted. 'When you get to my age…' I laughed as I caught myself saying the words. 'That's a phrase I used to hate when my Auntie Vanessa used it. And I told myself I would never say it myself when I was her age. I don't suppose you can ever control your future as much as you believe.'

'Be careful what you wish for,' said Smith.

'I suppose. William once told me that some people believe their present actions determine their future destinies in this world, in heaven, or in hell. I hope that's true for him.'

'William?'

'You remember, in the library? I mentioned my husband…'

'Ah, yes,' said Smith, 'it would be interesting to meet him.'

He could see he'd said the wrong thing and looked away at once, as though embarrassed.

The jolt of the carriage coming to a halt woke me from a dreamless sleep. The train had pulled into Cambridge station. The seat opposite was empty again, and where Smith's hat had been on the table my overcoat now lay, neatly arranged. When I lifted the coat, I noticed that the brooch was missing. I searched the seat and beneath the table, and couldn't see it anywhere. But I did find Smith's piece of saffron-coloured silk, which he must have taken from around his hat, folded carefully, and placed on the seat beside me. Which meant he'd probably removed the brooch. I thought about this strange discourtesy: if he'd wanted the piece of jewellery, why had he returned it to me earlier that same day? I picked up the silk bandana, and studied the stars and whorls in its ethnic pattern.

Anna marched into the console room to confront him. 'So she did know you?'

'Long ago,' he said, turning away. 'In a previous life. She must have suffered dreadfully when she travelled with me. She finally

chose to leave, of course. But then it seems she had a breakdown.'
His lowered his eyes. 'I thought she would be safe in the care of her
own people. But they merely… put her into care.'

'Shawlands?'

'In the early twenty-first century, it's a well-known convalescent
home.'

'Did you know?'

'I should have. I should certainly have known that they wouldn't
believe her stories about our travels, especially those awkward
examples that the embarrassed Earth authorities could actually
verify. So they had to convince her that they were just that – just
stories. They did that in Shawlands. And to my shame, I did
nothing.' The Doctor's voice was low, pensive. 'That was all several
lifetimes ago. Then, when I met her for the first time on that train,
Tegan told me how she'd banished the Sigrarnons, and saved your
life, without really knowing what she was describing. So I took the
resonating frequency generator – the brooch – from her, and
concocted a suitable plan.'

'Why didn't you tell Tegan what was happening? Why not tell her
who you were?'

'Have you finished the story?' His eyes were unreadable. 'Finish
the story.'

A few weeks later, I returned to London from Cambridge. Our
lawyer was one of William's university friends, a man called
Brewster whom I'd never met. But I needed to sign papers relating
to William's estate, and although Mr Brewster offered to handle it all
by correspondence, I told him that I preferred to deal with them in
person. To be honest, I wanted to visit Smith and Anna again, to ask
him about the brooch. I planned to use the excuse that I was
returning the scarf he'd left on the train.

The weather was cold but clear. My taxi driver, a cheerful
youngster with a pink complexion, soon found the street of
Edwardian buildings. But although he drove the length of the street
twice, I couldn't identify Smith's red-brick house. I decided to
explore on foot, and paid my driver with a generous tip.

I walked along the street, imagining the place in darkness, trying to remember the route Anna and I had retraced from the theatre that night. In the end, I realised that I kept coming back to the barren scrap of wasteland at one end of the street. A forked elm stood crookedly in the cracked flagstones.

I stood on the pavement for several minutes, studying the clumped grass and piles of discarded rubbish, until a police hover vehicle hissed to a halt nearby.

'Can I help you, madam?'

I smiled my crazy-old-lady smile. 'I'm sorry, officer. I was hoping to see a house I once visited here. I think I must be mistaken.' I took a scrap of envelope from my coat pocket, on which I'd scribbled the address.

'I think you *are* mistaken, madam,' said the policeman kindly, and he handed back my envelope. 'There's been no house here for years.'

THE END

Anna wanted to throw the book at him. She contented herself by flinging it towards the library shelf. 'No wonder you were in such a hurry to leave. You'd read the story. You knew all along.'

'No,' said the Doctor sadly. He retrieved the fallen book.

Anna felt her face flush. 'You set me up. Even before you met me, you sneaky deceitful bugger, you set me up. And Tegan, too. You lied to us both.'

Oh Anna! How can you think I could simply overturn her life yet again? Start her on a path that could only lead her back to Shawlands? And lead me to...' The Doctor turned a little impatient circle in front of her, snatching at his wild red hair in frustration. 'All I could do was ensure that Tegan would receive the brooch originally, and thus protect her. And protect you too. Tegan saved your life, you know. A fine pickle you got yourself into!' He gave her a sulky look, then reached past her and pushed the book back on the shelf. He wiped the dust off a peeling white label, on

313

which was written in copperplate writing:'Humanian Era'.

'You made her a brooch, too?'

'Same brooch, different times,' muttered the Doctor.'When you activated the frequency generator in yours, it created a harmonic resonance in its later self – the brooch that Tegan had. Which banished the Sigrarnons back to their own dimension.'

'Another paradox.And you took a bit of a chance while you were at it.'

He looked stung by the accusation.'I would never put you at risk, Anna.We're good companions too, aren't we?'

Anna watched him walk off stiffly, climb the staircase and vanish from sight. She turned away, back to the library bookshelf, faintly embarrassed and ashamed.'Yeah, right.'

Womanuscripts *was still just visible. She lifted out the book to its left, glanced at it, and frowned. She angled the book in the guttering candlelight to read its title properly: Carlo Goldoni,* The Liar.

Missing
Two: Message in a Bottle

by Robert Perry and Mike Tucker

It was difficult to tell how long the bottle had been drifting. The clear glass surface had been scoured clean by the solar winds. Light from the distant binary system glinted off the myriad tiny slivers of ice that tumbled alongside it like tiny crystal moons, records of an endless cycle of freezing and thawing. A long strand of red hair, caught in the stopper, trailed elegantly against the stars.

The paper inside was frozen and brittle, the neat handwriting in blue biro nearly faded to illegibility. The promise had been made on another frozen world. 'It will reach you – in time,' she had said. But Time had other ideas, and the bottle had drifted, from system to system, from star to star, the message inside unread.

The author has long since forgotten the words on the single page. The futile act had passed into memory, a relic of another life. Had it been written in a moment of whimsy, an inconsequential postcard from the edge, or was it something more desperate, a cry for help from a traveller stranded and alone, millions of light years from home?

Occasionally, on still cool nights, she stares at the sky, watching the pinpricks of light, wondering if the bottle is still up there. It is, but its journey is nearly over now. It has been caught up in the stream of matter drawn inexorably across the void to the swirl of stellar debris that outlines a black hole. It will take centuries to get there, but its fate is sealed. There is no escape. Its journey will end with the crushing nothingness of the singularity, passing over the event horizon into oblivion, its message undelivered.

As the bottle begins to tumble gently a shape is reflected in its surface. Just for a second, if you had been watching, a large blue box, the light on its roof glinting like the distant suns, would have been visible in the glass, but only for a second. Just as quickly it would have faded, travelling on, unaware of the letter from a friend. Unaware of the message in a bottle.

Femme Fatale

by Paul Magrs

Before lunch, in Chelsea. It's 1968 again. The sun is bright on white buildings. He thinks about taking a walk down the King's Road. He's immaculate. He shoots his cuffs, swings his brolly round. He parries, thrusts, pretends he's fencing. The Doctor is ready for action. He tips his bowler hat rakishly. Like I said, immaculate.

He wonders if he might pop across to Paris this weekend. This is well before the Eurostar or any of that nonsense. But he can be there in a flash.

Maybe Mrs Jones will condescend to come with him.

Not that he's seen anything of Mrs Jones since that nasty affair with the brutish clones in that rundown mansion in Tunbridge Wells.

He deserves a weekend away, at least. And so does Mrs Jones. If he gives her a ring now, she can start packing.

He crosses his fingers. Don't let Mother phone. No silly business for a week or so. He rolls his eyes, remembering how much Alistair hates to be called Mother.

And of course the phone rings.

'Yes? Hello?'

Business as usual. 'Some pop artist chap has been shot and nearly killed. You know the one. Weedy little feller.'

'Hardly my department, Alistair.'

'We suspect foul play, Doctor. Of a particular sort.'

'I see. Shall I ring Mrs Jones?'

'It would save me a job.'

Alistair's such a lazy old devil. The Doctor straightens a couple of paintings around his flat, deep in thought, before turning to the phone and dialling her number.

Lunch in a diner round the corner. Back at the Factory nobody ate anything other than candy. I could never neglect myself like that.

They took a load of pills and carried on sitting around, watching the light show, watching everyone who came in and bitching. I wanted fries and I wanted a quarter-pounder and a milkshake. I came and sat in a booth and took a breather. Quite honestly, I was trying to catch up with myself. I was shocked and excited by the Doctor's sudden arrival, but I was also mortally offended that he hadn't spared me the slightest of glances or gathered me up in a warm reunion hug. I was suspicious.

This was the way I was thinking when Valerie turned up. She looked her usual filthy self. Her hair was matted and fluffed up in places and she wore that stupid hat. She was dressing in the dowdiest clothes again. For a while she'd been dressing better, when her drag queen pal helped her to glamorize herself for her meetings with her new publisher. But things had turned sour for Valerie again and she'd let herself go. Poor girl. She was so confused.

'Hey,' she said, sliding into my booth. 'What's up?'

She had an armful of those hand-printed manifestos again. I met Valerie on the street about two years before, when I'd first come to the city. She sold me a ratty copy of her opus for a dollar. She was amazed when I bought it and read it and it made me laugh. It was a manifesto for doing away with all the men in the world and the women taking over. She had some scheme to replace men with clones, without personalities. Just enough of them left to fulfil various procreative functions for those women who wished to dabble in such things. Next time I saw her, I told her it was a fantastic idea. We got a little drunk in the room she'd taken in the Chelsea Hotel and talked into the early hours and I'd talked too much, and told her about the planets I'd been to where women really were the rulers and men were banished. She thought I was stoned. Sometimes, though, she liked hearing about my trips to other planets, yet I could see she was taking it all with a pinch of salt. This was the life I was in now – when someone as mad as Valerie looked at me sceptically, whatever I said.

'You got it all wrong, Iris.'

They were having lunch in Paris in 1934. Iris looked slightly different again. Tighter around the eyes and mouth, as if she'd recently had surgery. Sam wondered how long it had been since they had met.

'Did I, Sam, dear?'

'The way you wrote it. About the Warhol shooting.'

Iris fiddled with her salad. 'I'm sure the Doctor would say that. I'm sure he would object to any number of things I say in my book.'

'You'd be right. But, for now, the most important thing is what you say about Warhol. That we tried to save him. That's the most damaging part, according to the Doctor.'

'Because you were both interfering in the messy fabric of time?'

'Something like that.'

'You know I don't give two hoots about stuff like that.'

'I know.' Sam rallied. 'But you were wrong. It wasn't like that. We weren't trying to save him. He had to be shot. I knew that. I know better than trying to change things for the better. We all do.'

'Well, forgive me for being so presumptuous.' Iris was eyeing the waiter, who hovered beside their table. 'What exactly were you up to?'

I was sitting with the usual afternoon crowd. The usual hangers-on. A rabble of druggies and stars and drag queens. We were just kind of chatting away, waiting to shoot the afternoon movie. Someone said they were bringing a horse into the Factory. It was going to be a cowboy movie and that sounded cool to us. Someone else said there was a party on that night and some famous people were coming. We'd recognise them when they came in. We nodded and decided we'd wait and see.

You spoke up then. You came round to face us all on the couch.

'Hello, everyone. There was no one at the door, so we just walked in.'

The star on my left – a tall skinny fella in black jeans and Ray-Bans, I forget his name – shrugged.

'We were looking for Andy.'

Caroline, the girl on the scatter cushion on the floor, said, 'He's in a meeting. He's painting. He's shooting a movie.'

'All at once?' Sam asked.

'He's a busy guy.'

'Yes, of course he is,' you said, and plunged your hands into your oh-so-capacious pockets.

As I pressed the button that would take us to the upstairs office, she stared at me. I feigned all innocence as she said to you, 'Doctor, I think that's…'

You shushed her. 'Not now, Sam. I'm thinking. And lifts always make me nauseous.'

'But…'

You went green about the gills then. Ridiculous, Doctor, to get so funny about lifts when you spend your time haring about like you do. Anyway, the lift stopped and there we were on the office floor.

Plate-glass windows, a whole wall of them. Desks with heaps of papers and magazines. Chic-looking ladies and pretty boys handling the phones, many of them actors just paid to look busy. Sprays of lilies in glass bowls.

'I can't promise he'll actually see you,' I warned.

You waved me away. 'That's all right. Thanks for your help.'

I watched you stalk determinedly towards the studio. Sam was at your heels, giving me only the quickest of backward glances.

She rings the doorbell of his Chelsea flat. She's always very proper.

When he opens the door she's leaning casually against the frame. He raises an eyebrow. She's in a black catsuit again. Work clothes.

'I was hoping to get off this weekend, Doctor.' She marches in.

'My thought exactly, Mrs Jones. Something's cropped up.'

'Mm.' She flings herself down on his velvet couch. From her handbag she produces a paperback book. 'I've found something you might be interested in.'

'I don't get much time for reading these days,' he sighs. 'More's the pity.'

But he takes the book. *Wildthyme*.

'It's just been published by the Olympia Press in Paris. It purports to be a collaborative time travel novel by three authors separated by hundreds of years. The Marquis de Sade, Gustave Flaubert and Gertrude Stein.'

'The Olympia Press? Really, Mrs Jones, I'm surprised you read risqué books.'

She shrugs carelessly. 'This one claims to be all about you. And me.'

He opens the book. 'I can skim it on the way.'

'On the way where?'

'New York. Then Paris.'

'Well. The days are just packed, aren't they?'

'Oh,' I said. 'I got sick of hanging round that place. They were just making another movie. Some kind of cowboy thing. They had a real horse.'

'That's cruel to animals,' Valerie said. 'They'll probably kill it and that'll be, like, art.'

'I hope not,' I said frostily, my accent slipping. 'How's your book coming along?'

Valerie's face darkened. 'I'm not writing it. I've given up, Iris. That contract he made me sign ripped me off. I wasn't getting anything out of it.'

'But you said he was a great publisher! He did *Ulysses, Lolita, Tropic of Cancer*…'

'All of it sexist crap,' said Valerie, rather primly. 'And he's a scummy French bastard.'

'So you're not writing any more?'

'Nah. Well, yes. But not that novel. I'm still pushing my play. I still want Andy to film it.'

'I don't think he uses a script, Valerie. I think he just turns the camera on and lets things happen.'

'Well, he should use a script. And he should use mine.'

I shrugged. 'I'm writing a book, you know,' I said.

That night at Mr Chan's you and Sam were at the special table in the corner. You were sitting with the usual crowd. When I came in, I suppose I was surprised you'd got yourself into the in-crowd so fast. But I shouldn't have been. You always seem to get yourself in there.

'Gee,' Andy said, when I came up. I was in black PVC and dark glasses.

I was wearing the tallest hat in the restaurant. 'You look fantastic tonight.'

The whole twenty-strong table turned to look at me. I had a cigarette on the end of a silver holder. I'd spent about an hour ransacking the wardrobe on the top deck of my bus for this outfit. I wanted it to be just right.

'Hey,' Andy said, 'why doesn't everyone move up for her? Can we make some space? There should be some space here.'

I sat directly opposite you, and smiled, and flashed my gorgeous gem-like eyes over my glasses.

If you really want to know the truth, this is it. This is the story of how I almost got him shot. The man I love! Almost shot! It was 1968. We were in New York. I'd been there a year or two already, hanging around the fringe art scene, getting into art movies, getting seen round and about, getting to know people. It was a heavy scene. It was a great scene. I kept off the pills, didn't inject a thing. I was drinking like a fish, but that's just me.

And besides, I was in a different body then. This was Iris Mark Six and, in the process of adopting this heavenly new bod, a whole new life to use and abuse had opened up for me. I has masses of honey-gold hair, jade cat-like eyes to die for and the slinkiest body imaginable. I wore bikinis and spangly catsuits to show it to best advantage. Well, the assorted freaks I was hanging around with thought I was fantastic. Especially when I dropped into the Factory.

For the first time in ages, I felt like I was settling down somewhere. After my regeneration – a rather hasty, nail-biting affair on the hectic and magical world of Hyspero – I thought I deserved a little time in one place to get myself together. I thought I'd have another bash at the 1960s; in a different city this time. The last time around I'd been in Paris and hadn't seen much action. For my new self, I settled upon New York and this time I would definitely make the in-crowd.

The Doctor took us off to an Italian place for lunch. While he was in the Gents, Sam looked at me and her eyes flashed. 'Did you see? He almost did it! He almost changed things! When it came down to it, he still tried to jump in and change history!'

'Oh, Sam,' I shook my head. 'You don't know how much that will have shaken him up.'

'There's all sorts of things we could change...' Sam said.

The Doctor came back. 'Their carbonara is excellent, apparently.' Then he turned to Sam. 'You want to know why we change things on other planets, overturn regimes, thwart invasions and so on, and when it comes to Earth we have to be terribly careful not to change anything?'

She nodded. 'That's right.'

'Well,' he said, 'the truth is, Sam, that...' He looked up then, over his menu, to check that I would back him up. 'Iris?'

But I had already gone.

'See?' Andy was saying lazily. 'He recognises you. You must be famous already, honey, and you haven't been in a movie yet.' Andy turned to talk to some of the others beside him then. I was left with the Doctor and Sam staring at me. I rolled down my Audrey Hepburn gloves and peeled them off, one finger at a time.

'I know it was you!' Sam yelled, jumping up and grabbing me in a hug. That blew my cool straight away. The Doctor didn't look so pleased.

'What do you think you're doing here?'

'Just hanging around, having fun. Seeing art.'

He scowled at me.

They drove to the airport in Mrs Jones's vintage roadster, Bessie. Mother had been as good as his word and arranged the private jet. It was thrumming ready for them on the airstrip, where the wind whipped violently and various Ministry men were waiting.

'Benton,' he said 'Good to see you.'

Benton was silent.

As they boarded and readied for take-off, the Doctor asked Mrs Jones, 'Who would want to write a book about us?'

'Who'd be able to?' she asked, with a sigh. She nodded to the steward for champagne. 'We *are* meant to be top secret.'

'Yes, very.'

'Ah, well. We'll know soon enough.'

They were quiet until they were up in the air. The Doctor, Mrs Jones noted, was completely absorbed by the book in his hands. 'Apparently,' he said, smiling, 'we travel the universe in a space and time vessel which is huge on the inside and disguised as a sort of police box.'

She tutted. 'If only.'

'Quite.'

'I don't think we need worry about this. It *is* rather fruity, though.'

'This woman, Iris,' Mrs Jones mused. 'She claims to exist. She apparently travels in a double-decker bus.'

'I'll have Mother check the files. We may have run up against her before.'

He reached for the phone.

Sam was talking to Andy. She was thick with him. It looked like hero-worship on both sides. I heard him say something about liking the way she dressed like a boy, in her denim jacket and her T-shirt. Her T-shirt had one of the Marilyn faces on it and he kept asking her where she got that from. Sam told him Camden Town and he was none the wiser. 'I didn't think I'd licensed any merchandise,' he said. 'Did I license any merchandise?' He was ghostly white, even under the pink-shaded lamps of Mr Chan's. He had his dark glasses on too, as well as his usual leather coat and his white, synthetic, slightly lopsided wig. Suddenly he looked at me.

'Gee, I don't think I'm being a very good host here,' he said. 'Mrs Jones, Doctor, you haven't been introduced to my star here.'

'We met earlier,' I said. 'In the Factory.'

'Oh, sure,' Andy said. 'You already know them, Iris.'

The Doctor was swallowing a lychee, which he promptly coughed up into a napkin. 'Iris?' he asked, looking at me darkly through his tangle of hair. I beamed at him.

Sam lowered her voice. 'The Valerie who shot him that day. She was the wrong one.'

'Oh, yes?'

'The real Valerie was here in Paris the whole time. Selling her book. The Valerie in jail in the States is a fake. A clone.'

'And who's been cloning mad women?'

'You tell me.'

I'd parked my bus in an alley at the back of the Factory. There was so much weird stuff going down in this part of town that no one noticed the completely erroneous presence of a bright red double-decker bus apparently bound for Putney Common. My wonderful semi-transdimensional home-from-home. No one here knew that I lived aboard it. No one apart from Valerie, who was waiting for me, looking her usual unkempt self, when I staggered back down the alleyway tipsily at three in the morning.

She was sitting beside the bus and she was in a hell of a mood.

You came into the Factory and stared around. You pulled a face at the smell of drugs in the air. Oh, you're so upstanding. In came Sam, trailing after you as always. Her hair trimmed again, looking sharp. That morning she was in a black leather one-piece. Her style had changed somewhat. And you were in a classic Savile Row pinstripe. What happened to the velvet number, Doctor? You shot your cuffs and coughed. Everyone turned to look at you.

I spoke up. 'Maybe we could go and see. Andy can talk while he paints. He likes doing that. He says he gets lonely painting.' I got up and wriggled my silver dress straight. I was in fantastic stack-heeled boots. They were actually from 1973, which was naughty really – but what the hell; we were meant to be before our time. 'Who did you say you were?'

You grinned at me. So affable. I couldn't believe you still hadn't recognised me. All right, so the only time you'd seen my new incarnation was on a video I'd sent you to assure you I was alive and well, but the least you could have done was remembered my new face, perfect and heart-shaped as it was. But nothing. Not a glimmer of recognition. You said, 'Thank you very much indeed. I am known to those in the know as the Doctor and this is Mrs Jones.'

I led you through the dusty, labyrinthine halls of the Factory. Our voices echoed as we went. There were a few others scattered about, moving canvases, installations, setting up cameras, lights and those funny reflecting umbrellas. Someone was clumsily manhandling a whole stack of painted Brillo boxes. 'You two here for a screen test?' I asked, motioning them to follow me to the lift.

'Ahm, not exactly,' you said.

'You should,' I said. 'You've got definite potential to be a star.'

'For about fifteen minutes.' You laughed.

'For about a thousand years,' I said. The lift doors opened. 'And your little friend looks quite foxy too.'

As we got into the lift and the doors slid to, Mrs Jones gave me one of her stares.

'Oh, God,' said Mrs Jones. 'How I hate New York.'

They were struggling through the crowds. 'I find it all rather exhilarating,' said the Doctor.

'Roll on Paris.'

'Ah, well. There's no comparison.'

The next morning the groupies and the hangers-on in the Factory were all talking about the movie they'd made yesterday. 'I think it's his best. He's really transcended the low mimetic this time.'

'Gee,' I said.

The lift doors opened and Sam came out. She hurried over to me. 'Can I have a word?'

'What's up?'

'I've left the Doctor with Andy. He's showing him the silk-screen process. That'll keep them busy.'

'You look all worked up, Sam.' Sam did too, glancing about sideways as if something awful were about to happen.

'Yeah, well,' she said. 'I think the Doctor's going to be furious with me.'

This was delicious. 'Why, what have you done?'

Sam looked at me and said in a low voice, 'Iris, it's the third of June, 1968.'

'So?'

'Don't you know?'

I didn't. I really didn't.

'This is the real reason I made him bring me back. I thought if we could get here, to this exact date, and get in the right place, then we could prevent it happening.'

'What?' I wanted to shake her. She was worse at explaining things than the Doctor was.

Behind us, the freaks on the sofa were catcalling someone just coming in.

'Hey, here she comes now. Miss Lonelyhearts! How're you doing?'

A very aggressive female voice swore. We heard her rapid footfalls across the floor of the Factory.

'You can't go up there! Andy will be angry if you disturb him!'

There was another shout as someone got in the lift and the doors shut.

Sam was saying, 'My parents told me about him. He got shot and it nearly killed him and that spoiled his life afterwards. They told me how great he was and…'

I wasn't paying attention. 'I think that was Valerie passing through just then.'

Sam went white. 'Who?'

'Valerie, this girl I know, she told me she was going to barge in and make Andy talk to her.'

Sam sprinted off to the lift.

He worked late in the office that night. He liked the hard, satisfying clunking of the old typewriter. Girodias had given him an office at the top of the building, a room crammed with yellowed scripts and crates of new copies of books waiting to be sent out. The Doctor had Iris's book open in front of him. He was doing her proofreading for her.

He hated the idea of suppressing books. He hated the idea of censorship. What he told himself was that he was only rewriting it. Changing it slightly. He was only writing over the top of Iris's version, in just the way she had. Still, as he worked through the night and rewrote the book word for word, he was gradually erasing her testimony.

Around dawn, when he was starting to feel tired, a thought struck him. He could get someone else in on this. Someone only too happy to do the work.

He packed his satchel hurriedly and rushed out of the office, down the spiralling, dusty staircase, into the barely lit street. There, underneath the lamplight, the TARDIS was waiting.

He dashed into the calm, dusty chamber and worked busily at the console, totting up figures, making arrangements. Then he ripped Iris's book into three.

When the lift doors opened it was on to a very calm scene.

It was almost as if nothing was wrong. Andy was in his usual black outfit and his sneakers. Not a hair on his silver wig was awry. He stood by the desk with two of his assistants. The Doctor stood a little way across the wide room and he looked aghast. He seemed to be realising exactly what was going on.

All the men were facing the same direction. They were facing Valerie, who was fishing about in a paper bag and producing a neat, stubby .38.

One of the assistants told her not to do it.

She levelled the gun.

Mrs Jones started to run towards her.

I shouted, 'Sam, you can't…'

And then the Doctor pelted forward.

Valerie fired at him. Missed.

He knocked her flat.

She fired again, the gun going off in her hand. She shot Andy once, twice, in the chest, so that the bullets passed through his lungs and out of his back.

I was frozen to the spot. I wasn't sure if I was more horrified by the shooting, or that the Doctor had tried to prevent it.

Mrs Jones high-kicked the gun out of Valerie's hand. As the assistants went to help Andy, Valerie picked herself up and was about to jump at Mrs Jones. The Doctor pushed himself between them. The room was full of shouting. By then I'd dashed across and I whirled Valerie around. 'Just go, Valerie. Just go.'

She left by the same lift. Shaking and talking to herself.

The Doctor stared at me, appalled.

Ten minutes later, the ambulance arrived.

It was in all the papers.

I'd parked my bus in an alley at the back of the Factory. There was so much weird stuff going down in this part of town that no one noticed the completely erroneous presence of a bright red double-decker bus apparently bound for Putney Common. My wonderful semi-transdimensional home-from-home. No one here knew that I lived aboard it. No one apart from Valerie, who was waiting for me, looking her usual unkempt self, when I staggered back down the alleyway tipsily at three in the morning.

She was sitting beside the bus and she was in a hell of a mood.

'Have you seen Andy?'

I nodded.

'They told me he was out of the country. They wouldn't let me anywhere near him. I've been cast out.'

'I'm sure that's not true.' But I knew it was. I'd heard some of the in-crowd talking. Valerie was definitely *persona non grata* these days. She was too stroppy, too uncool when she came round.

'He's still got my script. He won't send it back. He says he lost my only copy and now he won't return my calls.'

'Gee, Valerie…'

'God, now you're talking like him, Iris! Can't you see he's like a vampire? He takes over everyone!'

'Well, why don't you barge your way in there? Why don't you go marching in and confront him? Have it out with him. Tell him you want your work back. He's a good fella really…'

She set her jaw. 'Maybe that's what I'll do.'

She stalked away, brushing past me, and hurried down the alleyway.

They visited him at home. He was sitting up in bed. He was drawing cats for Mrs Jones. He was using his old technique of drawing in ink and then blotting it on to a clean sheet so he got a lovely dotted-line effect. 'Gee, I haven't drawn anything by hand in the longest time.'

He signed the cat drawing and gave it to Mrs Jones. 'This is for you. For coming to see me. Not one of those groupies and junkies at the Factory has been up.'

Mrs Jones clutched her drawing and beamed.

'I used to have about twenty cats, when I lived with my mother,' Andy said.

'So did I,' said the Doctor.

'Iris?' Andy asked Iris. 'Is there any news on Valerie?'

'They picked her up in the park. She walked up to a cop and said she'd murdered you.'

'She was so confused,' he said. 'Sometimes I think these people only hang around me when they can't face being in their own lives.'

The Doctor said, 'Mrs Jones and I should be going now. We have appointments in Paris we really ought to keep.'

'I need to sleep. I'll see you later.'

With that, he seemed to fall asleep.

'Have you seen Andy?'

I nodded.

'They told me he was out of the country. They wouldn't let me anywhere near him. I've been cast out.'

'I'm sure that's not true.' But I knew it was. I'd heard some of the in-crowd talking. Valerie was definitely *persona non grata* these days. She was too stroppy, too uncool when she came round.

'He's still got my script. He won't send it back. He says he lost my only copy and now he won't return my calls.'

'Gee, Valerie…'

'God, now you're talking like him, Iris! Can't you see he's like a vampire? He takes over everyone!'

'Well, why don't you get out of the country? Take that ticket Girodias offered you. Go to Paris and finish your book. Get away from all of this, Valerie.'

She set her jaw. 'Maybe that's what I'll do.'

She stalked away, brushing past me, and hurried down the alleyway.

In between the various courses – and there were lots of them, as Andy talked and did business and listened to everyone – I went to the Ladies, which was spacious and pink and decorated floor to ceiling in ostrich feathers. By the time I came out of my cubicle, Sam was sitting by the wash basins, waiting for me.

'Hey,' I said.

'You've got an American accent,' she said.

'It's put on,' I said. 'I like to blend in.'

'You look wonderful, Iris. I never properly believed in regeneration, until…'

'Until you saw it happen to me.'

'I was glad you got away safely.'

'You all left me!' I cried. 'They had me in a kind of tomb!'

'We waited for you to recover. We were there the whole time, Iris.'

'You were?'

'And you only regenerated because the Doctor risked his neck going to fetch the honey from the bees that made it and…'

'He saved my life?' This was news to me.

'Of course!'

'I'll have to thank him.' I did a quick calculation. 'I've let two years slip by without thanking him.'

'But it's only about four months since we were all together on Hyspero…'

'Relatively speaking, it's actually about eight thousand years, but it all gets too dizzying if you think about it too much.'

Candy, one of the drag queens from Andy's gang, came tottering out of her cubicle then. She looked us up and down. 'You guys are too much,' she said, and turned on her three-inch heels.

'We must sound mental.' Sam laughed.

'Listen,' I said, 'why are you here?'

'I want to find out,' she said, 'if it's possible to change things for the better.'

I pursed my lips and shook my head. 'Impossible. You'd cause a dreadful mess. I know I look like I interfere, but you can't really. And I can't believe the Doctor would let you.'

'He wouldn't. I've never said anything like that to him.'

'He'd be appalled. All we can be, Sam, really, is tourists. All we can do is watch. Just… sort of… turn on the camera and see what happens.'

'I suppose so.'

'So how did you get him to bring you here? There aren't any invasions to thwart or monsters on the loose.'

She looked serious. 'I badgered him. I wanted to see this time. I wanted to see the Factory first hand. We never meet famous people usually.'

'And he said yes?'

'He owed me one.' Sam smiled wryly. 'More than one. I always wanted to meet Andy. My parents used to talk about him.'

'He's a laugh,' I said. 'I realised I had to come here when I was reading this book about art and saw myself in one of the group shots at the Factory. I was standing at the back, looking *très chic*. So I had to come back.'

We walked back through the restaurant, towards our table.

'Is that how time travel works?' Sam asked me.

We took our places.

'It works any way you want it to, honey,' I said.

'Listen to them!' Candy sighed. 'I heard these two gossiping about time travel in the Ladies Room!'

'Gee,' said Andy.

The Doctor was still scowling.

I got into the lift with her. She really didn't seem like the girl I remembered. Far too sure of herself. Much too sophisticated. And where did all that leather come from? I thought she was an ardent vegetarian. Gloomily, I thought about clothes. They were everywhere, of course.

'The third of June, 1968, Iris,' she gabbled. The lift seemed to be taking hours to reach the top. 'It's the date that Andy gets shot! I can't believe you don't know the story!'

'I'd forgotten!'

'And I wanted to change it!'

'But I told you, you can't!'

She kicked the wall. 'I've gone and messed it up. I've left the Doctor up there with him…'

My hearts leapt up at that. The Doctor was in the firing line. And I'd just about talked Valerie into going up there.

Fancy coming after me, you stupid man. I didn't ask you to follow me. I wasn't looking for you. One day I was sitting on the old couch in the Factory with some of the others and we were just hanging out, and in you walked. I thought I was seeing things. In you breezed, blithely as you always do. You were in your green velvet coat and your grey cravat. You still had your brown swept-back hair. You still had that air of boyish arrogance and charm. God, I was pleased you were still in that body. Last time I saw you in it, I was old as the hills. I still wanted to see you on equal terms, with me looking fantastic too. And here you were. You have this habit of turning up even when I don't expect it.

For a little while they kept an apartment in Paris. Nothing too big, nothing too fussy. Mrs Jones and the Doctor and, later on, Fitz went back to it over a period of months at the end of the 1960s. Mrs Jones got herself involved in various student uprisings. She came back one day to tell them that she'd been throwing bricks into the barricades alongside none other than Michel Foucault. The Doctor gave her a hard stare.

He, meanwhile, had been calling into the offices of a certain Maurice Girodias, a publisher.

One evening Mrs Jones returned home to the flat to find the Doctor reading a proof manuscript, sipping from a tall frosted glass of Chardonnay.

He looked up as she walked in. 'She's gone and done it.'

'You knew she would.'

He sighed and tossed the manuscript on the table. 'She'll cause a great deal of bother.'

'She always does.'

'And this!' he cried, clutching a brand-new hardback, fresh from Girodias's Olympia Press. 'This isn't supposed to exist either.'

Mrs Jones took the book from him. '*The Scum Manifesto*, by Valerie Solanis.'

The Doctor put his head in his hands. 'Valerie's meant to be in jail for shooting Warhol. She never came to Paris. She certainly didn't publish her manifesto here.'

'So that was definitely a clone we saw shoot him?'

'It seems that way.' He flung his feet up on the table and poured some more wine.

'Doesn't Maurice Girodias mind you taking all these books from the office?'

He shrugged carelessly. 'I've made myself indispensable. I can type faster than anyone he's ever seen. And I just happened to find an exceedingly rare text by De Sade knocking about. He's publishing it in January. *The Education of Jean-Claude*.'

'You're as bad as Iris.'

'Don't say that'

Carelessly Mrs Jones had a flick through the proof copy of Iris's book. It was called *Wildthyme: Confessions of a Time Lady*. She pulled a face. 'This is filthy,' she said.

'Spiced up for the European market. I warned her about this. When I found all her journals in the bus on Hyspero. It was one long plagiarised version of my life. Now she's turned it into pornography.' He looked disgusted. 'I don't think you ought to read it, Mrs Jones.'

It was the following week that Mother came to stay. He rang ahead, just to make sure they weren't too busy to meet him.

'He's being sarcastic, of course,' said the Doctor.

'Of course,' sighed Mrs Jones.

They met Alistair for lunch.

Alistair sat at a table on the pavement. A pot of tea and three cups were laid out ready for them.

'Alistair,' said the Doctor warmly.

Mother didn't stand to greet them. 'Shall I pour?'

Mrs Jones sat beside him and said coaxingly, 'Have you come to check up on our progress?'

There were no preliminaries. 'I'm taking you both off the case,' said Alistair, crisply.

The Doctor's jaw dropped. 'Well! You've never done that before.'

'It's the book, Doctor.' Mother seemed to relent somewhat, but only for a moment. 'We can't afford to have exposés like that flying about the place.'

'It was all lies,' said Mrs Jones.

'Enough of it was true to cause problems. It really isn't on, you know.'

'Yes,' said the Doctor, 'I see.' He sipped his tea.

They celebrated their sacking by driving to Normandy. The car they hired wasn't a patch on Mrs Jones's roadster, but it sufficed.

'Smell the air, Mrs Jones,' the Doctor cried.

'Lovely,' she said, and he knew she was as gutted as he was.

The countryside stretched lushly before them, until the hitcher turned up. He stood arms akimbo in the middle of the road, a white-haired man in shades and leather jacket.

The Doctor slammed on the brakes.

'That was a rather good stop,' said Mrs Jones.

The hitcher came over to the Doctor's window.

'Gee,' he said. 'Fancy seeing you guys out here.'

There was a sudden, urgent hissing then as a noxious green gas filtered sharply from the dashboard.

'Oh,' said Mrs Jones. 'We should have seen this coming.'

Mother was waiting for a bus.

A particular bus. A bright red London bus, and he was waiting for it in Paris.

When it came he climbed aboard and peered around at the cramped but homely interior with interest. He took the drink that Iris offered him and sank into her sofa.

She was in lime-green silk. A dressing gown.

'Iris,' he said. 'I might have a little job for you.'

* * *

'And where are we now, Doctor?'

As he woke he could already tell that Mrs Jones was peeved. Not content to be alive, to be in possession of all her faculties, she was actually annoyed at not recognising their whereabouts. When the Doctor sat up, clutching his head and his hat, he had to admit that he didn't know either.

Someone had deposited them on a village green. They were boxed in by buildings in a variety of colours and styles.

'It looks like a proper dog's dinner of a place,' said Mrs Jones.

Above, the sky was the clearest blue. It was as if they had been left in a place where the weather was always perfect.

The Doctor picked himself up and dusted down his black blazer. 'I fear, Mrs Jones, that we'll be here for a while.'

About the Authors

PETER ANGHELIDES writes for fun, not for a living.
Well, that's the kind of guy he is: no take, but lots of giving.
His writer wife Anne Summerfield's a constant inspiration.
(Their young sons, Sam and Adam, were a joint collaboration.)
He's written for the Beeb before – *The Listener*, *Kursaal*,
An audio, some TV script appraisals… er… that's all.
However, since this short biography's been posted off, he
Has proved, if nothing else, he can't write poetry for toffee.

IAN ATKINS: 29; tall and slim, likes chocolate, music and genre-TV. Has written TV comedy, music journalism, prize-winning short-stories, TV series treatments and edited/written *Doctor Who* fan fiction. Genuine SOH, looking for a long-term relationship with an agent. No time-wasters please.

CHRISTOPHER BULIS admits to being old enough to have watched *Doctor Who* live from the very first episode. Since then he has acquired a degree in architecture and also worked in the fields of art and design before turning to writing. Unaccountably, he has failed to pursue careers in the SAS, gold prospecting or white- water rafting, which traditionally make these biographies much more interesting to read. Unlike a rather more famous fantasy author, he has never kept carnivorous plants.

PAUL FARNSWORTH, 29, comes from Derby where he is a retail bandit on the frontier of the domestic video game trade – or, as some would have it, a shop assistant. In his spare time he pretends to enjoy writing. So far, his work has been routinely rejected by some of the best magazines in the country, and *Private Eye*. The only publication ever to have accepted one of his submissions folded shortly afterwards, an achievement which Paul still believes to be his crowning glory.

SIMON FORWARD was born in Penzance in 1967. From the age of three he was probably dreaming about writing for *Doctor Who*. For a while he was a computer programmer, but between reading, films, role-playing and writing, much of his life has been based in fantasy. Recently, while completing two novels, reality caught up in the shape of his fiancée, Debbie, two children, two cats and, in the near future, two weddings. Still a dreamer, he's no longer an insomniac.

PAUL LEONARD has written more *Doctor Who* stuff than is entirely proper, and sometimes counts TARDISes in order to go to sleep. He lives in Bristol with his word processor and several plants, some of which are trying to turn into triffids. He's hoping one day to write a 'real' novel, but until then will content himself with dreams.

JASON LOBORIK is half-Hungarian and decided to take a break from editing a *Teletubbies* magazine to write his story. He's big on keep-fit, organic foods and… well, actually he's just *big*. However, he protests that, contrary to popular opinion, he does not resemble Tinky Winky in the slightest.

STEVE LYONS lives in Salford, and still doesn't regret leaving his job at a large, well-known bank to become a full-time writer. His published work includes the best-selling *Red Dwarf*

Programme Guide, plenty of magazine articles and several short stories featuring the Marvel superheroes. He has written seven *Doctor Who* novels, and is a regular contributor to the official *Doctor Who Magazine*. When he isn't working, he reads *Spider-Man* comics and watches *Prisoner: Cell Block H*.

DAVID A. McINTEE was born at a very young age and hasn't died yet. In between reading *Batman* comics, watching Bond films and playing *Doom* or *TIE Fighter*, he occasionally cobbles a book together. He has written, among other things, nine *Doctor Who* novels, with a tenth to come. He collects weapon props from SF shows/movies, and his favourite movie is *The Blues Brothers*. David's primary role models in youth were Tom Baker's Doctor Who, Kerr Avon and Graeme Garden, so members of the public should be wary of approaching him.

PAUL MAGRS was born in the north-east in 1969. He has published four novels, *Marked for Life*, *Does it Show?*, *Could it be Magic?* and *The Scarlet Empress*, and a collection of stories, *Playing Out*. His next novels are *Fancy Man*, published by Faber and Faber, and a second *Doctor Who* novel, *The Blue Angel*. He lectures in English literature and creative writing at the University of East Anglia.

ANDREW MILLER is, interestingly, a miller, from a long line of milling Millers based in the south of England. He was born in 1967 and was soon nicknamed 'Windy Miller' after the popular character from *Camberwick Green* (and for no other reason). After years of putting his nose to the grindstone (quite appropriately), he has finally had a short story published. He is married with a child who shares his love of yachting and watersports.

Although the two stories in this collection break with tradition and feature characters other than the Seventh Doctor and Ace, ROBERT PERRY and MIKE TUCKER are currently in the throes of writing their third story for that particular teaming – *Storm Harvest* – to be published by BBC Worldwide next June. In their other lives, Robert is working as a storyliner on *Emmerdale* and Mike is still with the BBC Effects Unit (just). Whilst Robert can be found racing between London and Leeds on a regular basis, Mike has been spotted in a number of West End restaurants in the company of Tara Samms.

GARETH ROBERTS has written several original *Doctor Who* novels and lots of derivative ones. His favourite Doctor Who is Tom Baker, his favourite assistant is Romana, his favourite monsters are the Sontarans. His other favourite old TV programmes are *Blake's 7*, *Emu's Broadcasting Company* and *Man About The House*. He lives in north London and Leeds and is currently the story editor of Yorkshire TV's *Emmerdale*. He wishes someone would put *Doctor Who* back on television on dark Saturday evenings.

GARY RUSSELL has been an actor, *Doctor Who Magazine* editor and is currently a producer of audio drama. In between all this he has somehow managed to write seven *Doctor Who* novels, a *Doctor Who* CD-ROM, some original fiction novels and a handful of factual books about comedy television programmes. He has a good grasp of the English language, but claims to have a blindspot over the word 'deadline'.

TARA SAMMS has endured stalkers, talkative dog walkers and odd, obsessional letters since she last wrote for *Doctor Who*, and is desperate to set the ball rolling again with her latest story. She is twenty-seven, enjoys being both behind and in front of the artist's easel, and has been spotted in a number of West End restaurants in the company of Mike Tucker.

DAVE STONE. Half man, half ocelot and half award-winning mathematician, he is a deeply serious person of complete and serious seriousness, and is not, incidentally, the same man as the comparatively well-known evangelist from Kentucky – and he's getting a bit tired of having to point out, to the people who think that he is, that he is in fact a bisexual Marxist atheist living in London.

BBC DOCTOR WHO BOOKS

THE EIGHT DOCTORS *by Terrance Dicks* ISBN 0 563 40563 5
VAMPIRE SCIENCE *by Jonathan Blum and Kate Orman* ISBN 0 563 40566 X
THE BODYSNATCHERS *by Mark Morris* ISBN 0 563 40568 6
GENOCIDE *by Paul Leonard* ISBN 0 563 40572 4
WAR OF THE DALEKS *by John Peel* ISBN 0 563 40573 2
ALIEN BODIES *by Lawrence Miles* ISBN 0 563 40577 5
KURSAAL *by Peter Anghelides* ISBN 0 563 40578 3
OPTION LOCK *by Justin Richards* ISBN 0 563 40583 X
LONGEST DAY *by Michael Collier* ISBN 0 563 40581 3
LEGACY OF THE DALEKS *by John Peel* ISBN 0 563 40574 0
DREAMSTONE MOON *by Paul Leonard* ISBN 0 563 40585 6
SEEING I *by Jonathan Blum and Kate Orman* ISBN 0 563 40586 4
PLACEBO EFFECT *by Gary Russell* ISBN 0 563 40587 2
VANDERDEKEN'S CHILDREN *by Christopher Bulis* ISBN 0 563 40590 2
THE SCARLET EMPRESS *by Paul Magrs* ISBN 0 563 40595 3
THE JANUS CONJUNCTION *by Trevor Baxendale* ISBN 0 563 40599 6
BELTEMPEST *by Jim Mortimore* ISBN 0 563 40593 7
THE FACE EATER *by Simon Messingham* ISBN 0 563 55569 6
THE TAINT *by Michael Collier* ISBN 0 563 55568 8
DEMONTAGE *by Justin Richards* ISBN 0 563 55572 6

THE DEVIL GOBLINS FROM NEPTUNE *by Keith Topping and Martin Day*
ISBN 0 563 40564 3
THE MURDER GAME *by Steve Lyons* ISBN 0 563 40565 1
THE ULTIMATE TREASURE *by Christopher Bulis* ISBN 0 563 40571 6
BUSINESS UNUSUAL *by Gary Russell* ISBN 0 563 40575 9
ILLEGAL ALIEN *by Mike Tucker and Robert Perry* ISBN 0 563 40570 8
THE ROUNDHEADS *by Mark Gatiss* ISBN 0 563 40576 7
THE FACE OF THE ENEMY *by David A. McIntee* ISBN 0 563 40580 5
EYE OF HEAVEN *by Jim Mortimore* ISBN 0 563 40567 8
THE WITCH HUNTERS *by Steve Lyons* ISBN 0 563 40579 1
THE HOLLOW MEN *by Keith Topping and Martin Day* ISBN 0 563 40582 1
CATASTROPHEA *by Terrance Dicks* ISBN 0 563 40584 8
MISSION IMPRACTICAL *by David A. McIntee* ISBN 0 563 40592 9
ZETA MAJOR *by Simon Messingham* ISBN 0 563 40597 X
DREAMS OF EMPIRE *by Justin Richards* ISBN 0 563 40598 8
LAST MAN RUNNING *by Chris Boucher* ISBN 0 563 40594 5
MATRIX *by Mike Tucker and Robert Perry* ISBN 0 563 40596 1
THE INFINITY DOCTORS *by Lance Parkin* ISBN 0 563 40591 0
SALVATION *by Steve Lyons* ISBN 0 563 55566 1
THE WAGES OF SIN *by David A. McIntee* ISBN 0 563 55567 X
DEEP BLUE *by Mark Morris* ISBN 0 563 55571 8

SHORT TRIPS *ed. Stephen Cole* ISBN 0 563 40560 0

THE NOVEL OF THE FILM *by Gary Russell* ISBN 0 563 38000 4

THE BOOK OF LISTS *by Justin Richards and Andrew Martin* ISBN 0 563 40569 4
A BOOK OF MONSTERS *by David J. Howe* ISBN 0 563 40562 7
THE TELEVISION COMPANION *by David J. Howe and Stephen James Walker*
ISBN 0 563 40588 0
FROM A TO Z *by Gary Gillatt* ISBN 0 563 40589 9